Born in Paris in 1947, Christian Jacq first visited Egypt when he was seventeen, went on to study Egyptology and archaeology at the Sorbonne, and is now one of the world's leading Egyptologists. He is the author of the internationally bestselling RAMSES series, THE STONE OF LIGHT series and the stand-alone novel, THE BLACK PHARAOH. Christian Jacq lives in Switzerland.

Also by Christian Jacq

The Ramses Series
Volume 1: The Son of the Light
Volume 2: The Temple of a Million Years
Volume 3: The Battle of Kadesh
Volume 4: The Lady of Abu Simbel
Volume 5: Under the Western Acacia

The Stone of Light Series
Volume 1: Nefer the Silent
Volume 2: The Wise Woman
Volume 3: Paneb the Ardent
Volume 4: The Place of Truth

The Queen of Freedom Trilogy
Volume 1: The Empire of Darkness
Volume 2: The War of the Crowns
Volume 3: The Flaming Sword

The Black Pharaoh
The Tutankhamun Affair
For the Love of Philae
Champollion the Egyptian
Master Hiram & King Solomon
The Living Wisdom of Ancient Egypt

The Tutankhamun Affair

Christian Jacq

Translated by Geraldine Le Roy

POCKET
BOOKS

LONDON · SYDNEY · NEW YORK · TOKYO · TORONTO

First published in Great Britain by Pocket Books, 2003
An imprint of Simon & Schuster UK Ltd
A Viacom Company

3 5 7 9 10 8 6 4 2

Simon & Schuster UK Ltd
Africa House
64–78 Kingsway
London WC2B 6AH
www.simonsays.co.uk

Simon & Schuster Australia
Sydney

A CIP catalogue record for this book is available from
the British Library

ISBN 0-671-02855-3

Typeset by SX Composing DTP, Rayleigh, Essex
Printed and bound in Great Britain by
Cox & Wyman Ltd, Reading, Berkshire

To you, Viking, my everyday companion who left for the beautiful paths of the west on 3 November, the day on which were written the first pages of this book; to you who were good, faithful and available and whose role it is to open the routes of the other world where, as the Anubis of Tutankhamun, you will be our guide.

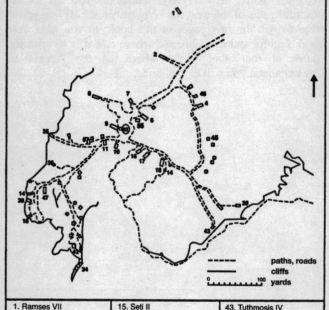

VALLEY OF THE KINGS

Location of main tombs
(from Erik Hornung, *The Vallley of the Kings*, New York, 1990)

paths, roads
cliffs
0 ————— 100
yards

1. Ramses VII	15. Seti II	43. Tuthmosis IV
2. Ramses IV	16. Ramses I	45. Userhet
4. Ramses XI	17. Seti 1	46. Yuya and Tuya
6. Ramses IX	18. Ramses X	47. Siptah
7. Ramses II	20. Hatshepsut	55. Smenkhara
8. Meneptah	34. Tuthmosis III	57. Horemheb
9. Ramses VI	35. Amenhotep	
10. Amemesses	36. Maiherperi	**62. TUTANKHAMUN**
11. Ramses III	38. Tuthmosis I	
14. Setnakht and Twosret	42. Tuthmosis II	

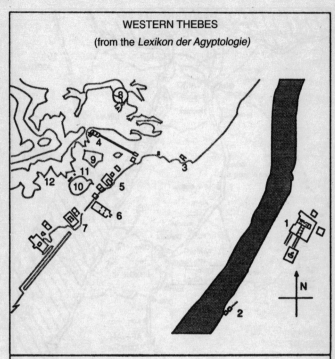

WESTERN THEBES

(from the *Lexikon der Agyptologie*)

1. Temples of Karnak
2. Temple of Luxor
3. Temple of Seti I
4. Temple of Deir el Bahari
5. Temple of Ramses II (Ramesseum)
6. Temple of Amenhotep III, of which only remain The Colossi of Memnon
7. Medinet-Habu (temple of Ramses III)
8. Valley of the Kings
9. Sheikh abd el-Gurnah (tombs of the nobles)
10. Gurmet Marai (tombs of the nobles)
11. Deir el-Medineh
12. Valley of the Queens

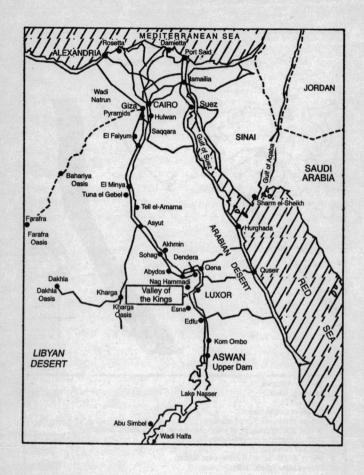

1

George Edward Stanhope Molyneux Herbert, Viscount Porchester, nicknamed 'Porchey' by his few close friends and seen by envious people as the future Earl of Carnarvon, punched the Greek sailor who was refusing to obey his orders. As the sole master on board his yacht *Aphrodite*, Porchey was not going to tolerate insubordination, even though a violent storm was spreading panic among the crew.

The Greek got back to his feet, dazed. 'I still say your cook is a goner, sir . . .'

'Here, take the helm. An appendicitis attack is no death sentence. You should know, my friend, that Aphrodite is the sea goddess; I shall entrust the ship and the crew to her during the operation.

Ignoring the incredulous man, Porchey walked down to his cabin, where he had settled the sick man. He liked this Brazilian cook, recruited on his last journey around the world.

The man was wriggling with pain.

On the deck, most of the sailors were kneeling and praying. Porchey hated this type of display, such a lack of self-control. When he had learnt how to sail in the Mediterranean, in front of the villa his father owned in Porto Fino on the Italian Riviera, the young Viscount Porchester had never called on the Almighty for help. He would either navigate or drown on his own, without disturbing a celestial assembly, busy with more important tasks than lending assistance to a sailor in distress.

He gave the cook half a bottle of excellent whisky to drink. Then he sat in front of the piano and played *Inventions in Two Voices* by Johan Sebastian Bach. The mixture of alcohol and peaceful music would make the patient serene again. If he did not survive, he would at least leave with final sensations of great quality.

Before her death, Porchey's mother had required that, in accordance with the education he had received at Highclere Castle, he never saw nor heard anything common or base. As he got ready to open the belly of the Brazilian who probably had one or two crimes on his conscience, the Viscount apologized to the spirit of his parent.

The sick man asked him, with feverish eyes: 'Have . . . have you . . . ever operated on anyone before?'

'A good dozen times, my friend, and without the least failure. Relax and everything will be all right.'

As a great reader who, besides the English of Cambridge's Trinity College, could also speak German, French, Greek and Latin and handle a few of the rare dialects of the Mediterranean basin, Porchey had effectively absorbed surgery manuals and rehearsed an appendectomy. It was the greatest fear of sailors leaving for long journeys, and he had equipped himself with an instrument case worthy of a professional surgeon.

'Close your eyes and think of a good meal or a beautiful woman.'

A ribald smile crossed the cook's lips. Porchey took advantage of this moment of weakness and knocked him out with a mallet. Several brawls in dubious bars in Cape Verde and the West Indies had taught him how to perfect this technique of anaesthesia.

He operated with a steady hand. At the same time he was thinking of a time when his own life was in danger from a measles epidemic. His treatment had been to be splashed with cold water to make his temperature drop. When he came to think of it, that was typical of the way he had always been treated at Eton. From his first moments, he had hated pretentious teachers who seemed full to bursting with useless knowledge. He had worked in his own way at his own pace, indifferent to marks and punishment. He had therefore often been described as lazy, even though he developed an amazing power of concentration and completely independent thinking. A collector of stamps, China cups, French etchings and snakes in glass jars, he was deeply bored when he read the classics, be it the repetitive Demosthenes, the killjoy Seneca or the inflated Cicero. The scandalized headmaster had complained to his father about his insufferable attitude. He said that a member of the landed aristocracy had a duty to preserve the very values and tradition Porchey was wilfully trampling underfoot. Yet at Trinity College he had found one fascinating occupation: the renovation, totally at his own expense, of the panelling there.

A great opportunity which opened to the young nobleman, who was also an accomplished sportsman, was to sail around the world to discover for himself South Africa, Australia and Japan, hopping from one continent to the next in search of an ideal that was always escaping him. Other than that, when life seemed too dull he immersed himself in history books. Antiquity attracted him because its impressive character was so different from the petit bourgeois mentality into which Europe was sinking.

He was fascinated by Egypt. Had it not bypassed man by integrating him into a different, huge scale, with temples in proportion to the universe itself? Yet he had avoided the land of the pharaohs. It was as if a respectful fear had prevented him from moving into that unknown territory.

The Viscount considered his work with satisfaction. 'Not bad . . . not bad at all. I can't swear that he will survive, but the handbook was right. There is nothing like following the instructions of a good textbook.'

Dinner time was approaching. The Viscount changed into a white jacket and grey flannel trousers. He did not forget his captain's cap and walked back on to the deck where the crew was still praying in the storm.

'God is bountiful,' said the aristocrat. 'The *Aphrodite* has been through this little squall, without anybody falling into the sea.'

Several sailors rushed towards him.

'Quiet, gentlemen! Our cook has now been delivered of his cumbersome appendix. He will probably not be fit to prepare any meals, so we will have to manage with pot luck until our next stop. This incident should not prevent you from going back to your posts.'

The Carnarvon heir cut a fine figure at the helm of the yacht. His high, wide brow crowned with reddish hair, the natural distinction of his nose, his perfectly trimmed moustache, and his clear-cut chin made him look like a conqueror on his way to the infinite. Only Porchey knew that the image was misleading. He would readily have squandered part of his inheritance to give meaning to his life. Intelligence, culture, wealth and the ability to do whatever pleased him . . . none of these things could take away his feeling of being empty and useless.

The Greek shouted. 'The cook is alive! I saw him open his eyes!'

The Viscount shrugged his shoulders. 'My good fellow. Didn't I promise to save him?'

2

The man had been looking at young Howard Carter for half an hour. Thin and elegant, he had a severe face and an inquisitive gaze.

Taking advantage of a fine day, Howard had put up his easel in a field where a mare was suckling her foal. Norfolk was enjoying an exceptionally beautiful end to summer, thus offering a hundred subjects for painting. At the age of seventeen, the young man was following his father's steps. He intended to become an animal painter like him. Instead of sending his son to school in town, his father had taught him how to read, write, draw and paint. Horses and dogs had been his main subjects. Although endowed with eight brothers and sisters, Howard felt like an only child, and the only one who could continue the artistic tradition. He fully expected not only to perpetuate the lineage but also to make his living by his art. Thus he worked with perseverance and strove to improve each detail.

Although he had been born in London's Kensington on 9 May 1874, Howard Carter had spent his childhood in Swaffham, a small village whose green quietness he liked. The previous evening a sort of miracle had occurred. For the first time he had been almost content with one of his paintings. He had really caught the frolicking motion of the horse, and the brightness of the eyes which made the drawing seem alive. He knew the legs lacked slenderness and the head

5

should be reworked, but his hand was becoming more sure and he was beginning to know his trade.

The man picked an autumn crocus, slipped it into his buttonhole and walked a few steps towards the teenager, who stood up and, despite a well-trained politeness, looked at him without lowering his gaze. The man continued to stride slowly across the grass, ignoring the green stains on his beautiful aristocratic suit and stopped in front of the watercolour, which he examined, his neck stretched out like that of a bird of prey.

'Interesting,' he concluded. 'Your name is Howard Carter, isn't it?'

The boy hated rich people's manners. They were so ridiculously over-polite when they addressed each other! Yet their tone was full of contempt when they gave orders to those they felt to be inferior to them.

'I don't know you. You're not from the village.'

'As there is nobody to introduce us except this fine mare currently busy with other tasks, allow me to make the introduction myself. I am Percy E. Newberry and we have a mutual friend. Would you please be so kind as to draw a duck for me?'

He offered a piece of paper.

'But . . . why?'

'Our mutual friend, Lady Amherst, who lives in the nearby castle, told me that you are an outstanding painter. She bought three canvases of yours. Your mare is rather well painted, but a duck is another story . . .'

Furious, Howard took the piece of paper. In less than five minutes, he had sketched a most beautiful mallard.

'Lady Amherst was right. Would you agree to draw and colour cats, dogs, geese and a number of other animals for me?'

The artist's distrust remained.

'Are you a collector?'

'I am Professor of Egyptology at the University of Cairo, in Egypt.'

'That's a long way from here, isn't it?'

'A very long way. London is much closer.'

'Why London?'

'Because our beautiful capital boasts the British Museum. I would like to take you there.'

The most famous museum in the world . . . His father had often told him about it. One of his paintings might be exhibited there one day!

'I have no money for transport, nor accommodation . . .'

'It's all settled. Would you agree to leave your family and your village for at least . . . three months?'

Swallows were playing in the sky, while a green woodpecker was pecking at the bark of an oak tree on the edge of the forest. How could he leave Norfolk, his parents and his childhood? In his excitement, he knocked over his easel.

'When are we leaving?'

Several months of unremitting work followed. Howard leaned relentlessly over his table to reproduce hieroglyphs depicting not only animals, but also human beings, objects, buildings, geometric designs and many other features of the language which the Egyptians had considered as sacred. Like a scribe of ancient times, Howard Carter was learning how to draw the signs before he could understand them. The mere act of tracing these words of power transformed his hand and his way of thinking. He scrupulously followed the models Professor Newberry gave him, and gradually he came to draw the way ancient people had drawn.

Alone in a study, shut away in a small bedroom, he did not make friends with anyone. The British Museum and its starchy gentlemen made him feel shy. He preferred the company of hieroglyphs.

A veil of icy rain spread over London. Professor Newberry had summoned Howard and his drawings were spread on his desk. 'I am totally satisfied with your work. Would you like to become the youngest member of the Egypt Exploration Fund?'

'What duties does the distinction carry with it?'

Percy E. Newberry smiled. 'Honestly, Howard, you are the fiercest and most independent character the Creator has ever placed on my path.'

'Are these flaws?'

'Fate will decide. As for the private scientific foundation which would be pleased to welcome you, it is devoted to the study of the arts of ancient Egypt and to a better understanding of its civilization.'

Although Howard Carter had made up his mind not to show the slightest emotion, a wave of enthusiasm seized him.

'That's . . . that's wonderful! I can now stay here and continue to draw hieroglyphs!'

'I fear that is not what will happen.'

Newberry suddenly appeared like a demon from hell to torture him. There was an inkstand within reach, but the professor anticipated him.

'Don't make any rash gesture, Howard. This is a critical situation.'

'Have I done anything wrong? Why do you want to dismiss me?'

'You jump to conclusions without knowing anything. This thoughtlessness might cause you a lot of trouble.'

'Keep your advice, for later. First tell me the truth!'

With his hands crossed behind his back, Percy E. Newberry turned towards the window and looked at the rain. 'The duck in the hieroglyphs is a poisonous animal, Howard. Once you've been bitten, it's for life.'

'I will draw thousands of ducks if you want me to.'

'Do you also agree to sacrifice everything to draw these feathered creatures?'

The warning did not frighten him. 'When you have the good fortune to meet real friends, you do what you can to keep them.'

Professor Newberry turned again towards the teenager. 'So,

Mr Carter, you're now an archaeologist. There is only one
more detail to settle.'

'What is that?'

'Your suitcases. We are leaving for Egypt tomorrow.'

3

Howard Carter did not see anything of Alexandria; Professor Newberry was in a hurry to take the train to Cairo. As soon as he set foot on Egyptian soil, the young man felt relieved of seventeen years of England and of a family which receded into the mists of oblivion. On his own, but suddenly drunk with the millennia of an immortal civilization, he began to live.

Carrying the professor's precious suitcases, which were full of scientific material, he did not have the leisure to taste the colours and perfumes of the Orient. But he did not conceal his surprise at the railway, the telegraphic lines, the postal service and the bustling railway station.

'Well, Howard, Egypt is moving into the modern world. Unfortunately it has just adopted Arabic as the official language for the administration and allowed the publication of a newspaper championing independence. That's pure folly! Without us, the country would be doomed to ruin and misery. The damn newspaper has been named *al-Ahram*, 'the Pyramid'! What a profanation . . . Fortunately extremists have no future. They will end up in jail, mark my word!'

Leaving the professor to his condemnation, Carter contemplated the landscapes of the Delta, made of a mixture of water and earth. Villages built on hillocks were slumbering in the sun. Flocks of white birds were flying over green expanses of reeds. Heavily loaded camels walked at a majestic pace on the crest of dams overlooking wheat fields. His nose was pressed to the train window. His amazement increased with each strange sight he encountered.

'Aren't you forgetting to sketch?'

Shamefully he drew out his sketch pad and began to draw.

'Work, Howard! Only work matters. You are now a scientist, even though you don't know anything. Content yourself with taking notes and analysing. If you let yourself be charmed by the magic of this country, you will lose your soul.'

With its ten races, hundred languages, myriad colours of turbans, dense crowd of Egyptians, Syrians, Armenians, Persians, Turks, Bedouins, Jews and Europeans, women in black veils, donkeys loaded with alfalfa or earthenware, roofs of dilapidated houses strewn with litter, smells of excrement mingling with the perfume of spices, muddy floors, shops in walls, smoke from open-air ovens where meat and bread were baked and predatory kites stealing food in the baskets peasant women were carrying on their heads, Cairo, the mother of the world, appeared to him like a crazy, grandiose and inhuman dream.

They stayed at a hotel in the centre of the city which seemed exactly like a London establishment. The professor ordered soup and porridge for supper. Exhausted and delighted, Howard fell asleep listening to the constant voices of the city.

At five in the morning, Newberry woke him up without further ado.

'Get up Howard! We have an appointment.'

'So early?'

'The civil servant we must charm works from six to eleven on Mondays. If we miss him today, we'll waste a week.'

The first cafés were opening. In the almost deserted streets people seemed to feel the cold. The brisk air was sweeping up the clouds, uncovering a pale sun whose first rays rested on the numerous minarets. The changing of the guard was just being performed in front of the great mosque of Mehmet Ali.

Percy E. Newberry entered a sordid street cluttered with

crates, the remnants of fowls and heaps of rubbish. Half-crumbling dwellings leaned out so far that their *mucharabieh* touched each other, thus enabling housewives to confide to each other without going out of their homes. They strode through the poor district, passing men who sold oranges and sugar cane. Behind a sycamore was concealed the entrance to a rundown palace guarded by two elderly men. They greeted the professor, who only nodded to them and hastened to a once-sumptuous marble staircase.

A Nubian clad in a long red robe escorted them to the door of an office, where a fellow countryman of his, as brawny as him, was keeping watch.

'I am Professor Newberry. Tell His Excellency that I am here.'

A small tyrant with a moustache and a twitching face, His Excellency agreed to receive them. His den was cluttered with stacks of files and administrative reports, among which he sat like a pasha. Because of the cramped nature of the room, it was impossible to fit in chairs. Therefore they remained standing in front of the civil servant.

'Delighted to see you again, Professor. What can I do for you?'

'Your Excellency holds the key to my safety.'

'May Allah protect you. Who is this young man?'

'Howard Carter, my new assistant.'

'Welcome to Egypt.'

Howard bowed clumsily. It was beyond his power to utter the words 'Your Excellency'. Why did a scholar like Newberry waste time with this sententious fellow?

'And how is your family, Your Excellency?'

'Wonderful, Professor. I can see that your health is blooming.'

'Not as much as yours.'

'You're flattering me. Do you intend to go back to Middle Egypt?'

'If that pleases Your Excellency.'

12

'It would please me, Professor, it would please me indeed! The permits are on top of this pile on the left. I would be so happy to sign them and give them to you, but . . .'

Percy E. Newberry grew pale. 'Is there any trouble in the area?'

'No, no . . . the local population is quiet.'

'Are the roads unsafe?'

'There have been no incidents.'

'Would you please explain to me, Your Excellency.'

'Administrative fees . . . The prices have been increasing a lot over the last few months. Alas the money you paid in advance no longer matches the present costs.'

The professor seemed relieved. 'Would His Excellency consent to tell me the amount of the increase?'

'It is twice the amount you paid.'

Percy E. Newberry took a bunch of sterling notes out of the pocket of his jacket and gave it to His Excellency, who offered profuse thanks, opened a safe in the wall and carefully put the nest egg in. Once the door was closed again, he condescended to deliver the permits.

The Nubian brought Turkish coffee. Numerous platitudes were exchanged over the drink.

When the meeting was over, Howard gave vent to his anger. 'This is corruption!'

'This is a ceremonial, Howard.'

'Never shall I give way to such blackmail.'

'In Europe, corruption hides behind the masks of politics and justice. Here it is an institution. Everything has a price, provided you know the right one. Otherwise you will look a fool and you will lose face – that is to say, everything.'

A laugh shook the professor. 'Considering the treasure you are going to discover, I did not pay much.'

4

'Did you say a treasure?' asked Porchey sceptically.

The Brazilian cook repeated his statement in a mixture of Portuguese and English that was very unpleasant to the ear. 'A huge treasure!'

'Jewels?'

'Rings, necklaces, diamonds, emeralds . . . they were hidden by pirates.'

The future Earl of Carnarvon looked at the map.

'On which island?'

'Lanzarote.'

'That is not on my route.'

'Don't let this opportunity pass, my Lord.'

Lanzarote . . . the name of this Canary Island rang a strange bell. He concentrated on his student days and then it dawned on him that this was where a ruined Scottish squire of his acquaintance with a passion for astrology, exotic women and white wine had retired, at the other end of the world, 600 miles south of Europe and 70 miles off the African coast, where ancient people located the fields of paradise, where the blessed were enjoying eternal sun, and also where those who loved marvels situated Atlantis!

'Fortune Islands' was what mariners called the Canaries. Lanzarote was said to be an island of purple, a huge field of lava spewed out over the uneven slopes of its volcanoes.

The *Aphrodite* drew alongside Arrecife with great

difficulty. The manoeuvre was made all the more perilous by
pouring rain, a violent wind, dangerous currents and a narrow
channel. Porchey held the helm firmly and, not for the first
time, avoided a wreck. The Brazilian cook had taken refuge in
a litany in which the Virgin Mary was invoked along with a
voodoo demon.

Desolate and hostile, Lanzarote did not look to a well-
educated Englishman like paradise. Once the anchor had been
dropped, Porchey took a local boat to a poor harbour, where a
pirates' brig was rotting. A fortified tower looked over the
emptiness of a deserted sea, with its rusted guns ready to fire
useless balls at the ghosts of corsairs.

'Where is your treasure?'

'In the capital,' answered the cook.

Porchey paid a small fortune to rent a cart driven by a *mago*,
a local peasant with a wide-brimmed straw hat, as talkative as
a piece of lava.

The islanders had not yet developed so far as to have roads.
Vehicles were drawn by donkeys and camels, which managed
to get along together. They progressed at a leisurely pace on a
stony track through a landscape too devastated for even a tree
to grow.

The aristocrat noticed that the cook was becoming
increasingly nervous.

'You are ungrateful. I conducted a successful operation on
you and yet you want to have me shot.'

'Me! But why . . .?'

'I'm afraid you might be more interested in my purse than
in my unpublished paper on Etruscan vases.'

'My Lord, you do me an injustice . . .'

'Let's summarize the present situation: your friends are
waiting for me at the turn of some cactus with the strong
intention of taking my life and my guineas.'

The Brazilian's complexion turned green.

'A gentleman would make you talk before disposing of
you.'

'But you are a gentleman, my Lord, aren't you?'

'Sometimes I like to mix with the riffraff.'

The cook jumped off the cart and ran away. The *mago* did not slow his pace, indifferent to the quarrels of strangers. As there was no way in which Porchey could prepare meals himself, he would have to engage a kitchen boy in the hope that he could hide his incompetence by using spices.

The capital was a poverty-stricken town with low white houses, seized by a thousand-year-old slumber. It was unlikely to be a place where Porchey would find the necessary passion to put an end to his boredom.

With wooden balconies, the governor's dwelling stood on the main square, where old peasants were dozing beneath their hats. A man dressed in white was talking to some peasants boasting about the quality of their wines. In spite of the stoutness and the beard, Porchey recognized a fellow student.

'Glad to see you again, Abbott.'

'Porchey! So you survived college!'

'More or less.'

'Are you coming to settle here? The girls are a bit fierce, but the white wine is excellent! Vine stocks that grow in lava . . . the taste is unmistakable! Try this.'

The liquid was bright yellow.

'Not too bad,' said Porchey appreciatively. 'You couldn't compare it with a great Burgundy, but it could improve a desperate situation.'

'You're still as exacting as ever . . . Of course, I'll put you up!'

The evening passed enjoyably. Abbott offered grilled beef and rice pudding.

'I'm not unhappy here. Nothing happens, and I'm slowly dropping off my perch!'

'You're lucky, Abbott.'

'I know myself. I'm a good-for-nothing and I cultivate the feature. You are different . . . Wait a minute, do you remember that I had your chart drawn?'

Abbott came back with a square diagram containing symbols representing the planets.

'Sun and Mercury in Cancer, Jupiter in Aquarius . . . the past and the future, tradition and invention. You will surprise us all yet, Porchey.'

'Listen to you!'

Slightly affected by the white Malvasia, the future Earl of Carnarvon was longing for sleep. When his bed moved, his first thought was that he had drunk too much of the delicious wine. When the walls of his bedroom trembled, he first questioned the architect's skill, then he went out on to the balcony.

The full moon was shedding a silver light. In the distance, a wisp of smoke was rising from a volcano.

Abbott appeared on a balcony on his left. 'It's an eruption,' he announced happily.

The earth continued to quake. A red glow burst out of the mountain. Lava would soon spill out down the slope.

'Splendid,' said Abbott. 'Is there anything more exciting than living by the gates of hell?'

'Yes, going through them.'

5

In Beni Hassan, Howard Carter experienced his first real Egyptian night. In this forgotten site in Middle Egypt there still flourished the soul of Middle Kingdom noblemen whose clifftop tombs overlooked the Nile. Below were little gardens along the river and a Muslim cemetery. On patches of grass on the islands egrets were playing. The air was transparent. He was copying a hieroglyphic inscription when the sunset took him almost by surprise. Sitting on an escarpment, he gazed at the glowing disc sinking quickly below the horizon. Gold, purple and mauve fought for supremacy before giving way to the pure light of the stars.

A peace from another world came over him. The mist, the drizzle, the road shiny with rain, the smog and the sad processions of serious men in a hurry to earn a living that would at the same time shorten their lives had made way for this special light and that divine river. Time had come to a halt. He had found his homeland. His destiny now belonged to him.

'Howard, let's remember how Pescennius Niger rebuked his soldiers: "You have Nile water and you ask for wine!" However, despite the brave Roman warrior's views on the matter, I suggest that we taste this excellent vintage.'

'Thank you, Professor!'

Newberry looked anxiously at his collaborator. 'You look strange. Are you by any chance suffering an ailment?'

'Whoever has drunk Nile water, will drink more of it, so goes the saying. I ask for nothing more.'

Without waiting for approval the professor filled the glasses. The day of rest at the archaeological dig at Beni Hassan gave them an opportunity to improve on the everyday routine. Living conditions were harsh, but sleeping on the site made it possible to start work at sunrise and to draw with no other concern than the pursuit of perfection.

The apparently simple Egyptian outline testified to an extraordinary mastery, but Howard Carter would not surrender without having exhausted all his resources.

'You work too much, Howard.'

'Professor, doesn't work matter more than anything?'

'Don't take me for a fool; when your working day is over, you start another one. It is not enough for you to draw and paint, you also spend your nights reading.'

'I am fascinated by the history of ancient Egypt. Is that a crime? If I remember, you are the one who had me bitten by the hieroglyphic duck.'

'What could bring you back to your senses?'

Howard opened one side of the tent in which they were eating. 'You know I think this landscape we love so much cares more for us than we do for it. It takes me up and feeds me with each minute that goes by. It enables me to see death as a fruit of eternity. These tombs are alive, Professor. I revere the smiling dead depicted on the walls. Their eyes will never close.'

'Beware, Howard. You are becoming an old Egyptian. It would be an infamy to abandon your nationality.'

Someone was climbing up the path. Stones were moving under his feet. Afraid, Newberry went out of the tent.

'How dare he!' he murmured. 'How dare he . . .'

The man was climbing steadily. His face hidden by a thick white beard, he might have been fifty or a hundred. Lean, almost emaciated, his skin tanned, he walked as if in home territory.

'Happy to see me again, Percy?'

The professor answered icily. 'Who wouldn't be charmed to welcome Sir William Flinders Petrie, the greatest Egyptologist of all?'

'You're not mistaken for once. I suppose this young man with the fierce face is Howard Carter?'

Percy looked strangely at him, almost as if he knew what would happen. 'He's my assistant.'

'Not any more. From now on, he enters my service.'

Howard clenched his fists. 'I'm not for sale. You may be Petrie, but I am a free man and Professor Newberry is my boss.'

Sir William sat on a block of stone, facing the Nile and the soft countryside of Beni Hassan. 'Freedom is a modern illusion, my young man. There is only one reality in this world; it divides into rulers and those who obey them. Today I belong to the first category and you belong to the second. I intend to teach you your trade. You won't have to hang around here any more.'

'And if I refuse?'

'You won't be the first one to do that. But it's me, Petrie who gives the orders round here. If you refuse, our friend Newberry will be forced to go back to England with some beautiful drawings and you as a free gift.'

The professor was furious, but he did not dare protest.

'That is obnoxious blackmail.'

'A huge amount of work is waiting for me and I need enthusiastic and skilful collaborators, even if they are bad tempered. There's no time to think it over. I'm going back to my ship immediately. So, either you follow me or you give up Egypt.'

Petrie walked down the slope with the nimbleness of a goat. He would soon be out of sight.

Newberry laid his hand on the young man's shoulder. 'You have no choice, Howard. Follow him.'

'But, you . . .'

'Petrie is the best. Thanks to him you will become a real archaeologist.'

An Englishman does not cry. To hide his tears, Howard Carter rushed down the slope with his portfolio and his box of watercolours, at a speed which risked breaking his neck.

6

Shortly before sunset, the sky turned sepia. Huge ochre clouds filled the horizon and formed a menacing dome.

'We must get to the boat and make everything fast,' ordered Petrie.

The wind was quicker than the archaeologists, however. Blowing as though the end of the world had come, it brought a rain of sand, which penetrated every crack. Even though they were sheltered from it, their eyes burned. Sir William made Howard cover his head with a blanket and stay down. The cabin of the old skiff could not be shut tight and sand settled on the beds, the furniture and every piece of crockery. After ten hours of fury, the *khamsin*[1] calmed down, leaving a whitish layer on the houses of the village near which they had landed.

The following day, the desert wind produced spirals which veiled the sun and prevented them from going out.

'How long will this last?'

'Three days, three weeks or three months, Howard. Let's take advantage of this time to check your knowledge.'

Sir William questioned him on his Egyptology, pointing out his deficiencies. 'So much ignorance is almost a joke, my young man.'

'I hadn't had the good fortune of going to university.'

'I don't care. Your good fortune is to be here. As you don't

---

[1] A strong wind blowing once a year.

know anything, you haven't been able to learn the wrong things.'

Petrie proceeded to teach Carter grammatical rules, made him translate simple sentences and memorize lists of words. Then he showed him his own excavation reports.

'Egyptologists are like butterflies or moles, Howard. Either they fly from one site to the next without seeing anything or they are so narrow-minded that they spend ten years on a piece of broken earthenware. I, on the other hand, try to give order to the jumble left over the centuries.'

Carter suddenly felt an immense respect for Sir William, his close attention to the monuments and his desire to share his knowledge. They would never get on, but their common love of Egypt fostered a dialogue that lasted to the spring day when the master introduced his disciple to Tell el-Amarna.

The city of the sun had been built in this barren plain between the Nile and the cliff. It was the short-lived capital of the heretical Akhenaton, whom Petrie did not like because he considered him decadent.

The desolate vastness pained Howard's heart. Suddenly he saw the huge open-air temple, the white palace with frescoes on the banisters, the freshwater ponds, and the aviary full of exotic birds. He saw the King and his great wife Nefertiti on their silver chariot, acclaimed by their subjects. He saw the ambassadors of Asia and Nubia come to pay tribute to the royal pair.

'It's useless to dream, Howard. Reality on its own gives us too much work.'

Obedient and silent, he measured the outlines of houses that had been razed to the foundations. As he was applying Sir William's rigorous techniques, he could not stop thinking about the cursed Pharaoh whose work had been destroyed with so much determination. In spite of the battle for survival between acacias and sycamores, in spite of the irrigation canals, the desert was winning. It granted the Nile a fertile stretch of land but regained territory as soon as men became lazy.

'You are progressing, Howard,' said Petrie. 'But beware of the luminous death called the desert. The Arabs are afraid of it. They believe it to be inhabited by monsters, evil geniuses and uncontrollable forces. You should listen to them.'

Petrie was asleep. Howard left alone for the desert, heading west. He had to talk to this wild area, to uncover its secret. The heat would soon be unbearable but he was not afraid. There, in the infinity of sand, at the bottom of a dry wadi, the ghost of Akhenaton was waiting for him.

The sun reached its zenith. Carter had walked for four hours when he made out an encampment. A Bedouin with a rifle made him enter the chief's tent.

'Who are you?'

'I'm Howard Carter. I work on the site of el Amarna.'

'With Petrie?'

'True.'

The chief spoke excellent English.

'Petrie . . . he's an excellent scientist who will never understand anything about Egypt. For him, everything is just figures, measurements, calculations, surveys . . . You're still young. What are you looking for?'

'The tomb of Akhenaton.'

'Take your shoes off. My servants will wash your feet. Then we will share dates and roast lamb and drink goat's milk.'

He was being granted a huge favour. Six children paid tribute to their father and stood silently by his side, waiting till he had taken the first mouthful before they ate. Some sixty years old, the chief adopted the posture of a scribe.

'Don't rush straight at an obstacle, Howard Carter. Take a winding path, learn to bide your time. Grow stronger with the tenacity of the righteous, follow the winding paths with patience and you will reach your goal.'

'How do you know my goal?'

'It isn't Akhenaton whose tomb lies nearby.'

'Will you take me there anyway?'

'There is no point. Looters have ransacked it. Look for the son of his spirit, the one who succeeded him and whose trace has been lost to mankind. That is your destiny, Howard Carter: you must discover a treasure, the most fabulous of all treasures. But for that you will have to face many dangers.'

The chief raised his eyes towards a future he was the only one to perceive.

'Please say more,' begged Carter.

'Go back to the ruined city and start looking, persistently and without haste. Try to lift the veil and remember: if a day goes by without you learning anything that brings you closer to God, may the day be cursed. Those who look for this wisdom are more beloved by God than the greatest heroes of the holy war.'

Nervously, Carter went through the handbooks of Egyptian history Petrie had given him. Sir William surprised him in the middle of the night.

'So you're back . . . where have you been hiding?'

'Who is the son of Akhenaton?'

'He only had daughters.'

'And his successor? These books are so unclear!'

'The whole period is not very well known. I would bet on a totally obscure kinglet called Tutankhamun.'

'Has his tomb been discovered?'

'Not yet.'

'Could it be near that of Akhenaton?'

'It is more likely to be in the Valley of the Kings. Strong clues seem to suggest that at the end of the heresy, Tutankhamun went back to Thebes. Even his name, which means "living symbol of Amon" proves that he had come back to revering the almighty Amon. Why are you interested in these old theological quarrels?'

'I want to discover the tomb of Tutankhamun.'

'Who put that idea into your head?'

'A Bedouin chief revealed my fate to me in the desert.'

'Ah! The crazy old man who pretends to know the location of Akhenaton's tomb . . . He thinks he is a seer. Don't worry: none of his predictions ever come true. Forget about his prophecy and set yourself more serious goals. All the tombs in the Valley of the Kings were plundered many centuries ago. The place has no interest whatsoever for an archaeologist.'

Noticing his distress, Petrie tried to cheer him up. 'I would like to entrust you with a delicate mission, Howard. My Swiss colleague Naville will soon be working in Deir el Bahri. He will need a watercolourist to reproduce the paintings and bas-reliefs of the temple of Queen Hatshepsut.'

Carter agreed without showing any enthusiasm, although he felt like shouting with joy. Wasn't Deir el Bahari on the west bank, very close to the Valley of the Kings?

7

When Porchey turned back, he could see his footprints in the virgin sand of Orient Bay. A haunt of pirates and smugglers, the island of St Martin had large, lonely beaches overflown by pelicans. The future Earl of Carnarvon cared little about the green and limpid waters, whether there was a strong wind or a warm sun. He had not chosen this stop where the Greater and the Lesser Antilles met to swim, but to add an item to his collection of personalities: a meeting with the last of the Arawaks, the Indians who first inhabited the island.

Discovered by Christopher Columbus in 1493, St Martin had fallen into oblivion before the French occupied it in 1629. They had been followed by the Dutch in 1631 and in 1633 by the Spanish, against whom Peter Stuyvesant had fought in vain. The island had passed from one nation to another, according to how wars and battles went. The British had played their role before ceding the better part of the island to the Dutch and the poorer one to the French.

Porchey remembered the route explained to him by a West Indian exiled in the Canary Islands. He left the beach, heading towards Mount Vernon and passed a ruined house which had been eaten by termites. Cyclones and bloody struggles had regularly destroyed the walls of the forts and of the most beautiful dwellings. It was just as if peace was impossible in this apparent paradise.

The aristocrat had read with interest the tale of Brother

Ramon Pane, a preaching brother of the Order of St Hieronymus, and a travelling companion of Columbus. He had explained how the Arawaks took *cohoba*, a hallucinogenic drug, to make contact with gods and demons, which they then carved in stone or wood. The sculptures became dangerous beings, which their creators had to present with cassava every day for fear of being cursed or falling ill. The last Arawak pretended that he had seen the great god and enshrined him in a form that revealed his true nature. A touch of excitement had taken hold of Porchey. To a reasonably sceptical Briton the prospect of contemplating what some thought was the Creator was worth a detour.

At the time of the Arawaks, there had been no crime on the island. The inhabitants lived naked and fished. But the arrival of Caribs from the jungles of the Amazon had put an end to this quiet period. Violent and cruel, they had exterminated the Arawaks, on whose flesh they had fed. Porchey considered this to be shocking behaviour, displaying a great lack of elegance on the part of the Caribs. Later transformed into the adjective Caribbean, the name originally meant cannibals. When you have the good fortune to discover happy people, is it necessary to eat them?

Everybody thought that the Arawaks had been annihilated, and the survival of one of them was a miracle. A miracle – that was really the only phenomenon for which Porchey had ever felt an interest. After having sought them all around the world, would he find one at last?

He took a very narrow path along the foot of Mount Vernon into a small forest, out of which rose coconut trees. At the prescribed place, near a dead tree hemmed in by thick creepers, he saw a hut with a roof of palm leaves. An old black woman was sitting in front of the door, cooking rice in an earthenware pot. Her shack was hidden by hibiscus, castor berry trees and alamendas[2]. Nearby sweet

---

[2] Exotic trees with very bright foliage.

potatoes and cabbages were growing on a patch of land.

As there was nobody to introduce them, Porchey was compelled to introduce himself. The enumeration of all his titles, however, seemed superfluous.

'I'm Mammy,' said the old woman.

'Are you the last of the Arawaks?'

'I've been brought up with pea soup and nobody has ever insulted me.'

'That is not my intention. Do you have a sculpture by any chance?'

Mammy smiled. 'So, you have been taken in too! The legend attracts two or three visitors a year . . . Who could enshrine God in an idol?'

'The Arawaks tried to do that.'

'They are dead . . . I would like to eat in peace.'

Porchey recognized the justice of her request. He left Mammy and headed towards Marigot, the French capital. With the help of a donkey and his owner, he reached it before night.

The place did not look like any capital he had ever seen. The main street – which was the only street – was lined with painted wooden houses whose solidity left much to be desired. At the end of the road was the ocean, with the town hall on the left and the school and the police station on the right. A dignitary had built a gallery on the first floor of his house.

Porchey made exhaustive enquiries. He consulted archives and questioned authorities, but his quest for the last of the Arawaks resulted in a failure. He had been the victim of a deception.

The following day, he watched a dance where girls threw oats on the floor so as to be able to glide while they were dancing. Although charmed for a moment, he quickly became bored. He left the gathering and sat near the water. The trade winds were blowing strongly, bending the coconut trees.

'Are you waiting for someone?' asked a laughing girl with a hibiscus flower in her hair.

'Maybe.'

'What's his name?'

'I don't know.'

'Is it a friend?'

'A friend . . . yes that is the right word. A friend I could trust, a real man who would sacrifice himself for an ideal.'

The girl ran away.

As he looked at her, Porchey wondered whether the nameless friend would come from the sky, the ocean or the earth, whether he was born in a neighbouring country or a distant one, and whether he would know at a glance when he met the person who would put an end to his roaming.

8

With an infernal noise, the train left Cairo at eight in the evening. Travellers were yelling, laughing, shouting at each other and running from one compartment to the next. Packed between an obese dignitary leaning on his stick and a stout woman, veiled and dressed in black, Carter remembered Petrie's cold farewell. Sir William assumed that he had taught him the basics of applied archaeology. With sound historical knowledge and an ability to decipher some hieroglyphic texts, he thought that the young man could now begin a brilliant career, in which Deir el Bahari would be a crucial stage.

Carter felt like an orphan. After having lost Newberry, he now felt abandoned by Petrie. Would fate doom him to solitude? Yet at the end of the new journey would be Thebes! Thebes and the Valley of the Kings, which he intended to question until it revealed its secrets.

A family was having dinner. They spread cucumbers, salad leaves and hard-boiled eggs on the seats and emptied earthenware water jugs without ever stopping talking in loud and strong voices. When he had drunk his fill, the father took off his oriental slippers, and settled himself against a bag to go to sleep, despite the squawking. When three low-ranking civil servants decided to join them in the compartment, talking importantly in clouds of cigarette smoke, Carter was forced to flee. The tobacco nearly choked him. Fortunately, he was able to reach an open carriage.

Alone in the starry night, he experienced the most beautiful railway journey of his life. Because of the slow speed of the train, the wind was mild. Breathing was a delight. He enjoyed each mile as a celestial present. Minutes passed slowly, as if they were hours.

Suddenly a red glow coloured the east. In a pool of flames, the young sun battled triumphantly against the darkness. Gold filtered through the green of the palm trees. Crops undulated under the morning breeze and the Nile shook off its torpor. Luxor station appeared, dusty and sundrenched. The train stopped under a metal bridge. Gesticulating passengers in a hurry sprang out of the coaches. Caught in the turmoil, Carter followed the human stream. Pedestrians, pedlars, donkeys and barouches mingled in a moving chaos. Getting used to the hubbub, he found himself in a cloud of sand rising from the stones, and he experienced an ineffable sense of eternity from the temples and the tombs. Free from the crowd, he stopped in front of an open-air kitchen, where he ate hot broad beans and rice. This substantial meal would provide him with the necessary energy for the day.

He should probably have introduced himself to the servant brandishing a notice with his name on the quay who was to take him to Naville. But he had no wish to talk to anyone. He first had to get in touch with the land, the sky and the light, at the same time tender and violent. His gaze was transfixed by the Theban mountain on the west bank. At this time of the day, it was pink and blue.

On the pier, he hailed a man with a felucca. Once the price of the crossing had been settled by a discussion in which Carter used his basic knowledge of Arabic, the boat pushed out into the Nile. It passed a ferry loaded with peasants and animals, slid into the current and reached the opposite bank too quickly. The short trip was a moment of extreme happiness. The sound of the wind breathing on the white sail was for him a purifying ritual, the message of an invisible master of the millennia.

The west bank was given over to a market, where wheat, barley, broad beans, pistachios, chickens in cages and material was being sold. Curious onlookers were crowding around a seer tracing strange signs in the sand. Several donkey owners assailed him to offer their services. He chose an animal with a roguish look and a beautiful mane.

'Where do you want to go?' asked its owner.

'To the Valley of the Kings.'

'It's a long way. It will be expensive.'

'I know exactly how far it is and how much it costs to get there. If you want to be my friend, don't try to take advantage of me.'

After a tense dialogue with his commercial conscience, the man agreed to Carter's terms. They left for the valley of wonders at a slow pace, through a smiling countryside where wheat, alfalfa, clover, lupins and cotton were growing. They came across various types of oxen and dromedaries.

The guide stopped before the Colossi of Memnon, two very dilapidated royal statues.

'This is a great mystery,' he mumbled. 'Formidable geniuses. Sometimes, they sing.'

'They have been silent ever since the Romans repaired them.'

'Not necessarily. We may no longer know how to listen properly.'

Carter remembered the lesson. With Petrie, he had studied the wisdom of the Old Kingdom, in which an old scribe said that listening is the key to intelligence. Didn't the Egyptians call ears 'the living ones'?

Taking up their path again, they passed the village of Gurnah. Dirty children were playing half-naked in front of adobe houses. Some of them smiled at him, while others fled. Beneath the friendly faces of the *fellahin*, he could feel secrets that were better left hidden in the darkness of cellars or the recesses of mountains. By contrast his work consisted in digging, excavating and unearthing. They left the temple of

33

Seti I, abandoned to herds of goats and overgrown by weeds, to follow the road to the tombs. The cultivated fields abruptly disappeared. The desert started immediately, with no transition whatsoever. The sand, the heat and the aridity deterred all living presence, human, animal or vegetable. Here the mineral ruled supreme, celebrating its grandiose wedding with the sun. Nothing Carter had ever seen before could compare with this universe, dominated by the west summit pyramid. He knew in a flash of intuition that he would spend the most beautiful years of his life there.

The light burned his eyes. The donkey slowed its pace between limestone walls. He was entering an apocalyptic land where the raw matter used to create the world seemed to have concentrated. Step by step, he penetrated deeper into the hot gorge. On both sides he could see furrowed slopes left over by heavy rains. Each one of these stones was loaded with memories. Hadn't they been witness to funerary processions which had taken the same route in the past?

He climbed off the donkey. The poor beast had carried him for too long. He continued on foot into the valley, a fault in time and space where an ultimately mysterious power had preserved the glory of the kings.

Desert of all deserts, absolute solitude, infinite silence . . . How could he describe this place of truth, where all human activity seemed incongruous? He felt the souls of dead kings watching over their last homes.

It was said that not a single burial place had escaped robbers. Unable to believe it, he went from one vault to the next. Alas, they had all been plundered and emptied of their furniture and treasures.

Turned into monks' cells with the triumph of Christianity, the tombs had been neglected by the new Muslim invaders. Later on they had become the homes of jackals and bats, now replaced by surprised or hurried tourists.

Becoming used to the spell of the valley, he visited the monuments, with their magnificent relief and paintings, plunged into the ground, came back to light, climbed up slopes and walked on paths, filling his eyes with this vision of the other world carved by man in the rock.

As the rays of the setting sun shrouded him, his fatigue vanished. The western mountain became light, the huge blocks lost weight, and the last gold of the day became one with the silver lights of the earth. He climbed to a crest overlooking the Valley, sat on a flat stone and thought of the words Forbin had uttered on the spot:

Everything around me said that only because of his soul is man something: a king in his thinking, vulnerable in his bodily envelope. Only the hope of another life and the knowledge of his celestial origin allows him to triumph in the constant struggle against the misery of his present life . . . Hieroglyphs figure in all the history of human knowledge: the priests of Egypt hid them to shield them from the turmoil of earthly life. It seemed that I was guided by the light of a wonderful lamp and about to be initiated into some great mystery.

9

The figure stood out in a ray of moonlight, tall and well built. His head was covered by a turban and he was dressed in a *galabieh*. A gun hung at his belt.

'You're not allowed to spend the night here,' he said in English.

'My name is Howard Carter. I'm an archaeologist.'

'I'm Ahmed Girigar. I belong to the security services.'

'I'm not a thief.'

'You are the one who should be protected, Mr Carter. Are you unaware of the danger?'

'Apart from stupidity and malevolence, I don't see any danger.'

Ahmed Girigar sat down by his side. *'B'ism'-illah-ma'sha'llah*. May God divert evil,' he said gravely. 'Those are certainly fearsome enemies, but you should also look out for gangs of pillagers in the hills of Gurnah. They demand a ransom from the peasants and rob strangers.'

'I don't feel like a stranger. This valley is mine.'

'Have you got a concession?'

Concession . . . that magical word meaning that he would be allowed to dig here wherever he would feel like digging.

'I'm only Naville's assistant.'

'The Swiss man who works in Deir el Bahari?'

He was astonished. 'You seem to know the archaeologist caste very well.'

'My father was a *reis*, a sort of chief. I'm following his steps and, like him, I want to lead teams of workers searching for treasures. I am awaiting the man who will love this valley enough to devote his life to it. The valley will talk to him, if he finds out how to tame it.'

'I read Benzoni's works.'

Ahmed Girigar smiled. 'A strange excavator . . . He was a giant moved by furious passion! He only dreamed of sensational feats and forced the doors of tombs with a heavy hammer. He did not even mind using dynamite.'

'After Champollion he explored the valley thoroughly. I know his conclusion by heart: "It is my opinion that no tomb remains to be discovered after my work."'

Carter played the devil's advocate, expecting to hear words of hope. Ahmed Girigar did not disappoint him. 'That was the hasty opinion of a man in a hurry.'

'But a pioneer like him would not chase shadows.'

'Of course . . . but he lacked patience. The valley has been hurt and humiliated. Now it hides and keeps silent. Only a scrupulous man, determined to the point of stubbornness, will be able to lift the veil of time and sand spread on its mystery. Nobody ever listens to us because we are *fellahin*, poor and without education. But we walk these paths every day and we listen to the stones. Now, Mr Carter, you have to leave, otherwise I shall be obliged to report you for your unauthorized visit.'

'We'll see each other again.'

'If Allah wishes it.'

Ahmed Girigar watched the young Englishman leave. He bowed and, as he stood up again, he moved his outstretched hand to his mouth and his forehead. He was saluting an important character who did not know yet the greatness of his vocation.

The temple of Deir el Bahari, 'the wonder of wonders', was built back on to a cliff overwhelmed by sun. In front of the edifice with its terraces, the hot desert had replaced the orchards, the ponds of pure water and the groves of incense trees Queen Hatshepsut had brought back from the marvellous land of Punt. Carter walked towards the portico of Anubis, the god who guided the dead on the beautiful paths of the other world. This was where his new chief was working.

Edouard Naville's welcome was less than warm. Stiff in his colonial suit, he addressed him coldly. 'Did you miss the train?'

'No, sir.'

'Ah . . . Did my servant not hold the notice high enough with your name on it?'

'No, sir.'

'Then why didn't you introduce yourself to him?'

'There was an emergency. May I start work?'

Naville showed him the bas-reliefs. 'They're incomparable masterpieces carved by an artist whose hand was so light that time will soon erase them . . . We must publish them so as to preserve them in the memory of humankind. Everything will have to be drawn and painted, Carter. This is a Herculean task.'

'Or an Egyptian task, don't you think?'

He smiled and the ice broke.

'Watercolour will be the best medium. You will also reproduce the texts.'

'On condition that we decipher them together. I want to learn.'

They shook hands. For a Briton and a Swiss, such a display of cordiality was almost indecent.

Night was falling over Luxor. Clarinets accompanied melancholy songs. The last ferry was landing. The small lights of the cafés were coming on. Seated at the terrace of the Winter Palace, Carter was drinking a beer with Naville.

'Would you mind explaining the "emergency" which delayed your arrival?'

The Swiss archaeologist seemed to be a man of honour. He was less severe than Newberry and less majestic than Petrie, and his attitude was not dogmatic. Carter trusted him.

'I needed to start taking notes on the Valley of the Kings. I've already filled two big notebooks. I record each discovery, be it a tomb, a mummy or a simple vase. I'm a long way from my goal, but I want to know everything about the excavations.'

'To what purpose? Belzoni has already explored it from top to bottom! I deplore his methods: breaking open an old door with a ram or shooting at rivals are not scientific techniques. Yet, at a time when people did not hesitate to kill each other to steal a scarab, somehow he did some good work.'

'I admire him, as you do. Like me, he was of humble origin and he sacrificed everything to his passion. But he charged straight ahead without taking care of the minute details which might reveal the existence of other tombs.'

'I must disappoint you, Howard. Belzoni's opinion has been confirmed by such meticulous and level-headed scholars as the German Lepsius. He only found disappointing remnants and the exploration of the valley was dropped for good.'

'That is nonsense! Do you agree that all the pharaohs of the Eighteenth and Nineteenth Dynasties are buried there?'

'That is probably so.'

'Quite a few are still missing, don't you agree?'

'The argument presents problems. Which rulers are you thinking of?'

'I'm thinking of a good dozen of them . . . and particularly of Tutankhamun.'

Disappointment showed on Naville's face. 'That unimportant kinglet? His rule was so short and dull . . . To my mind he was buried elsewhere or burned like Akhenaton. This minor monarch was too close to the heresy.'

'Wasn't he crowned in Karnak, like the greatest kings?'

The question embarrassed the Swiss. 'It's possible . . .'

'He reigned almost ten years,' Carter added enthusiastically.

'And we don't know anything about him. He has remained the most secret pharaoh in history. No object related to him has ever been seen on the antiquities market.'

'I sense your hasty conclusion: his tomb was never violated.'

A flame-like light flickered in Carter's eyes.

'Young people are crazy. That is one of their charms . . . But you have to follow a serious career, Howard. First think of your reputation. You are neither a scholar with a good family background, nor an aristocrat who is rich enough to obtain a concession in the Valley of the Kings. So forget about it.'

10

After several years of travel, Viscount Porchester was exchanging memories with a former jockey, who had twice been third at the Epsom Derby. The meeting was taking place in the inner room of a sordid tavern in Constantinople, out of reach of inquisitive eavesdroppers. Highly strung, the jockey constantly turned round.

'Who told you about this place?'

'A Genoese pirate. He assured me that you would be the right man.'

'Maybe . . . Are you an aristocrat?'

'As much as one can be, my good man. That is the way things are and nobody can do anything about it.'

'Then I shall make you pay a very high price.'

'I'm used to that. In exchange, I demand perfect service.'

Dressed in a yacht captain's uniform, Porchey was drinking Turkish coffee. The former jockey was taking care of his nerves with rose spirit. 'When do you want to meet Abdul the Cursed?'

'As soon as possible.'

'He's in town this week, but his schedule is busy. Why do you want to see him?'

'Just to see him.'

'What do you mean?'

'Isn't he the most famous bandit in the Bosporus, a thief of genius and a first class strategist?'

'This is all true, but—'

'Well, my dear chap, you should know that I collect interviews with out of the ordinary individuals in most diverse areas. After so many trips, I believe that I know our old planet better. South Africa amused me for a few days, Japan for a week, France for an evening and the United States for a month. I'm now getting weary of geography. I'm looking for the company of those who are most distant from my own circumstances, like you for instance. You do not know how self-important and boring aristocrats are. As for the great of this world, in whose company my late mother wanted me to move, they are only liars. As you are.'

'Me? Why . . .?'

'Because you do not know Abdul the Cursed and you try to take money from me in a way that I would see as dishonest.'

'That is wrong! I act on his behalf.'

'Then tell him that I shall meet him tomorrow at midnight, at the south corner of the old harbour, so as to complete my portrait gallery.' The heir of the Carnarvons stood up, avoided taking leave of his companion and left the tavern whistling an old Welsh song.

At the expected hour and place, Porchey saw a small boat, with two men rowing rhythmically and silently. He thought of his father, who was waiting for his return in Highclere Castle. The old lord criticized his son for his constant coming and going, his excessive love of travels and his dreadful habit of appearing and disappearing without notice. Porchey was willing to admit that his behaviour was not that of a future earl, responsible for one of Britain's most respectable estates. But how could he satisfy in any other way the impatience to live and the supreme boredom that was eating his soul away? He had hoped to satisfy his hunger by devouring space. But he had only succeeded in increasing his world-weariness. Oceans and seas had not managed to fill his dull and useless existence. Maybe only a human being could appease his torments by opening an unexpected way. Would the Messiah be Abdul the Cursed?

The two sailors were sinister-looking. Unshaven, with beards, greasy hair and dirty clothes, they told him to come down into their very derelict skiff. A sane man would have hesitated, but Porchey took the risk.

Fetid smells rose from the dull blue-green water. Their hands clenched on the paddles, the two Turks made haste.

'Where are we going?'

'Where we are going,' answered the elder in bad English.

'So I shall see Abdul the Cursed.'

The man sniggered.

'That would surprise me.'

'Why?'

'Because Abdul is a long way from here. He has at last been caught. It's now his turn to be the prey of vultures.'

'There is no denying that this new information changes the situation. The best solution is to go back to the harbour.'

The boat stopped. 'That is out of the question.'

'You're wrong, my friend.'

'We're certainly not your friends.'

'In a way, that pleases me.'

'You're a rich man . . .'

'That's true.'

'You carry a large amount of money with you.'

'It should be enough to buy your beautiful boat.'

'Alas, my prince, we have other intentions.'

'Just viscount will do.'

'Is the money in the bag at your feet?'

'Right.'

'Give it to us.'

'What will happen if I refuse?'

'You'll drown.'

'That is a bad fate for an experienced sailor . . . And if I accept?'

'You'll swim to the quay and you'll get away with a bath.'

'You forget, my dear fellow, that a good captain doesn't know how to swim and that he stays on board until the last moment.'

The thief became angry. 'Open that bag.'

'Robbing an honest traveller is a nasty occupation. If I were you, I would give up.'

'Do as I tell you.'

The Viscount took a magnificent silver gun out of the bag and pointed it at his attackers.

'I'd better warn you that I'm one of the United Kingdom's six best shots. With more practice I would have been the best.'

The two Turks immediately dived into the cloudy water.

'What a pity!' said the aristocrat. 'I missed another opportunity to improve my shooting.'

11

Every day Carter thought of the Valley of the Kings, to which he was both so close and so distant. But Deir el Bahari did not leave him much respite. It was impossible to give free rein to his imagination: each watercolour had to reproduce faithfully what was offered to the artist's eye, whether a boat on the Nile or a column of hieroglyphs. He did not paint for his own pleasure, but in order to pass on to future generations the splendour of a temple where Hathor reigned with a magical smile. Recreating the smile of the goddess on paper evoked such intense emotion that his hand trembled.

Unable to carry on with his task, he asked Naville for permission to leave the site for a few hours.

Where could he relax if not in the temple of Luxor whose columns, the slenderest in Egypt, elevated the soul to the heavens. So he took the peasants' ferry, in which there was, as usual, a joyful hubbub. Nobody could explain how so many men, animals and goods could be packed in such a limited space. Women took advantage of the trip to gather and gossip. Did these good Muslim women know that Christian Egypt had launched the fashion for black dresses in the first centuries of our era to mourn Christ's death?

When everyone was settled, and no one could move an inch, the ferry set off. It progressed at a moderate speed for, according to the scriptures, haste comes from the devil.

They were in the middle of the river when he saw her.

About twenty years old, wearing a long red dress, a necklace of lapis lazuli around her neck, a gold armband around her right wrist, she had a fine face, long black hair, eyes the green of water. Black make-up lined her eyelids. Henna coloured her fingernails and she had sandals on her bare feet. She was separated from him by a peasant with a fat belly eager to reach the quay to sell a load of onions and broad beans.

'My name is Howard Carter,' he said in a voice he hoped sounded self-assured. 'Forgive me for addressing you in such a casual way, but you look like the goddess Hathor I have just been painting at Deir el Bahari. It . . . it is deeply moving to meet a living goddess.'

She looked annoyed, but she answered. 'You should never praise a woman excessively, Mr Carter. You might attract the evil eye and offend her husband.'

'Are you married?'

'Not yet. Are you an archaeologist?'

'I'm preparing a publication on the temple of Deir el Bahari.'

'It is a magnificent temple. I often tell my pupils about it.'

'Are you a teacher?'

'I'm a voluntary schoolteacher in my village. Sometimes I am a nurse or even, occasionally, a guide for tourists.'

'Hence your good English.'

'Can you speak Arabic?'

He tried a few polite phrases, beginning with the essential 'In the name of God the compassionate and the merciful' by which all talk should start. Her smile delighted him.

'That's not bad . . . You should be able to progress.'

'Would you accept me as a pupil?'

The ferry slowed down, and the crowd began to move. Everybody was getting ready to disembark with an impatience uncharacteristic of the Orient. Desperate at the prospect of losing her, he used his elbows to make sure he was among the first ashore. As soon as he saw her again, he joined her.

'May I escort you?'

'I'm going back home.'

'Could we hail a barouche? You could introduce me to the countryside and to your village. Egyptian hospitality is so famous that you cannot refuse.'

Caught in his trap, she agreed to climb into a clean barouche. He had chosen a healthy and well-cared-for horse which galloped easily. They left the small town quickly and entered the network of fields and irrigation canals which had remained unchanged for millennia. She remained silent during the trip.

As they entered the village, she ordered the driver to stop.

'My name is Raifa. Would you like some tea, Mr Carter, or do you want to go back to town?'

'The decision is yours.'

He followed her. They walked between the areas for the crops and the public oven where women were baking bread while others were drawing water from the nearest well. Hostile stray dogs looked at the. Hidden in a palm grove, Raifa's village consisted of low adobe houses, with neither electricity nor running water. The roofs were covered with plaited palm leaves. Bricks of dried cow dung were used as the basic combustible matter. They went through narrow dusty streets which formed a real maze. Below the mosque, whose minaret rose over the compact mass of houses, kneeling men chanted to their beads.

Raifa lived in the prettiest house, near the mayor's. On the blue door were a horseshoe and a hand of Fatima to ward off evil spirits. Some twenty children surrounded them. Raifa calmed everybody and opened the door of her realm.

In the first room, which had a hard-packed surface, a donkey was sleeping. An old toothless woman with a torn black dress was kneading flour. Frightened by the sight of a

Western man, she pulled the material over her head so that
only the slit of her eyes could be seen. Raifa ordered her to
prepare tea and invited him to enter a second, rather large
room with a tiled floor. There were multicoloured cushions
and seats along the walls.

'Sit down, Mr Carter.'

'Do you live on your own?'

'I live with my brother Gamal. He is a landlord and a tax
collector.'

'Your voice grew graver when you said his name.'

'I like him very much, but . . . he is sometimes violent. He
has to be harsh and to thrash bad payers. He is very attached
to tradition and he won't be very happy about your presence
here. In the village I'm considered to be too free a woman.
Fortunately the mayor, whom I cured of an illness, gives me
his support. There are so many unhappy and ill people . . . It's
a woman's duty to relieve their misery.'

The old servant brought tea and honey cakes. A well-set
young man suddenly appeared. He had a very brown skin and
black bushy eyebrows which met to give him a frightening
aspect. He was holding a whip in his right hand.

'Get out of here. You have no right to be alone with my
sister.'

'It would have been an insult not to respond to her
invitation. My name is Carter and I take my leave. Please
allow me to pass.'

Indifferent to Gamal's fury, Carter put down his glass of
mint tea, stood up and left the room. On the threshold, a tame
cobre blocked his way.

'Don't be afraid,' said Raifa. 'He lives here and he is
begging for milk.'

She turned to her brother. 'Our snake only introduces
himself to sincere friends. You should be reassured, Gamal.'

When Carter left the village, veiled women uttered strings
of '*yuyus*', with their tongues undulating against their palates,
an expression of their joy.

A few days later, his steps took him to the Ramesseum, the temple of Ramses II. The edifice had been severely damaged. In the large open yard in front of the columned room lay the biggest colossus ever carved. Intact and standing, it had weighed over 1,000 tons, but fanaticism and stupidity had succeeded in knocking it over and almost destroying it. Its face, however, lit by the glowing sunset, continued to express a serene power.

A herd of black and white goats was grazing on the site. Carter dodged in and out of scattered blocks and tamarisk bushes, careful to avoid pricking weeds, and sat down under an acacia which was blooming in the ruins.

Ever since his meeting with Raifa, he had thrown away a dozen unsuccessful watercolours. Unable to forget the young woman, confused, he did not know anyone he could confide in. He was obsessed by the thought of seeing her again. Of course if her brother lodged a complaint about him, Naville would be compelled to dismiss him – he hated conflicts and he was only thinking of publishing his work on 'his' temple. None the less he decided to take the risk.

The warden of the site came up with a stick in his hand. 'Be careful. Snakes are fairly common here.'

Ageless, with wrinkled face and slow gestures, he sat on a block covered with hieroglyphs and looked towards the sunset.

'Are you looking for the tomb of an unknown king?'

'Who told you?'

'The wind blows bountifully and I have a very fine ear.'

'Have you ever heard of objects bearing the name of Tutankhamun?'

'Neither salesmen nor thieves have any. Is there anything more normal? Didn't the great Ramses destroy his temple and plunder his tomb so as to erase all trace of this evil time?'

These words filled him with dismay. The *gaffir*'s advice mattered more than that of the Egyptologists.

'Follow your way, Mr Carter, without paying attention to

Christian Jacq

others. Don't pillage or become hard-hearted. If you were not an Englishman, I would give you a talisman to protect you against enemies who, in darkness, prepare to harm you. But Englishmen do not believe in God.'

12

'God bless you, son. Those two bandits could have murdered you.'

'It is wise to believe in Him from time to time,' acknowledged Porchey.

'Where have you come from this time?'

'From Constantinople.'

'Did you meet any important people?'

'I was supposed to talk with Abdul the Cursed, but the appointment was delayed.'

The old earl raised his eyes heavenward. 'Porchey, Porchey! When will you stop running around the world?'

'When the world starts making sense. You should have a rest, father. I can tell that you are tired.'

Porchey called the butler, who rekindled the fire in the grate of the large sitting room. Then he poured a glass of whisky for his father and made sure that he was comfortably settled in a high-back leather armchair.

'I've been very worried about your future ever since your mother's death. What are you looking for, my son?'

'I don't know.'

'Didn't all your travels bring an answer?'

'They brought anecdotes, but nothing essential. Anybody can sail the oceans and cross continents. Everything I believed to be an adventure turned out to be just one more banality. Have you received any new history books?'

'Deadly boring handbooks from the British Museum. I piled them up on your desk.'

'You are the best of fathers.'

'Would you like a game of chess?'

'With pleasure, after you've had your rest.'

Between two showers, Porchey took a walk in the huge park of Highclere. The castle was austere. Massive rectangular crenellated towers gave it the look of a medieval fortress, enclosed on its past and traditions. He liked its grandiose character. He was even more appreciative of the charms of the lawns, perfectly kept by a legion of gardeners. A large staff of devoted and loyal servants looked after the integrity of the estate. It was an honour to serve the Carnarvons and preserve one of the most beautiful landed properties in Britain for future generations.

Porchey relaxed by walking for hours on the estate with his retrievers. He meditated under the cedars of Lebanon, walked along the lake overlooked by a white marble belvedere, ventured among hawthorn bushes in search of game, climbed up hills covered with oaks and beeches. Highclere was sheltered from the turmoil of the time. Nobody among his fellow aristocrats could understand why the future Earl of Carnarvon did not just enjoy a peaceful existence in this paradise.

He came back at dark. He gave orders that his dogs be fed and took refuge in the library, one of the largest and best stocked in the country. Everything on ancient history was gathered here. Casting an amused glance at two strange treasures, the desk and the armchair used by Napoleon during his enforced stay in Elba, the Viscount hesitated to sit there. Out of respect for the enemy, he made do with a more ordinary seat and looked at a study of oriental ceramics.

His father opened the door. 'Did you forget me?'

'Forgive me.'

'I would rather see you studying finance and investments.'

'How could I equal you in that field?'

'Sometime soon, I won't be here any more.'

'Nonsense! You are built like an oak.'

'I'm getting old, Porchey. Do bear that in mind, old chap!'

The game of chess took place in front of the large fireplace. The towers of the castle were shrouded in thick fog. The old earl had ordered a bottle of Dom Pérignon and toast, with caviar that was a present from a Russian minister. His son was trying to counter the well-known Sicilian opening.

'You're getting better.'

'I've had time to read the best treatises during my travels.'

'We should have a serious discussion.'

'Whenever you feel like it.'

With some concern, Porchey saw that his father was growing weaker. In the past he would have used his bishops more aggressively.

'How long will you stay in Highclere?'

'That is the kind of question I can't answer. It depends on the humidity of the atmosphere, on my mood, on an idea which I have at the moment . . .'

'Could you tell me a bit more? Have you a definite plan?'

'On reflection, yes I do.'

'What is it?'

'I don't really want to tell anyone.'

'I insist, Porchey.'

'Well . . . this may surprise you, but I do not know Italy very well, especially the south. Naples is a rather attractive town.'

'Naples! A haunt of thieves and murderers.'

'Precisely . . . I would like to meet the head of the Mafia.'

'Porchey! Are you aware that—'

'Absolutely, father. I'm in no danger, as this is only for my collection of portraits. I am not thinking of doing business.'

The old man put his son's king in check.

'I give up trying to understand you. I only beg one favour: get to know how to run the estate. As an old man, that would give me the greatest pleasure.'

'I make a solemn promise: Highclere will remain the

property of the Carnarvons and the most beautiful estate in the country.'

'Thank God for that, my son.'

As soon as his father was asleep, Porchey consulted the administrative and financial documents he had left on his desk. One night was enough for him to assimilate the main points and realize that the family fortune was managed with the utmost competence. Therefore, he headed for Naples on the very next day.

13

The flaking façade of the house in Gurnah hid a patio with a limestone floor, a well in the centre, and wooden benches and chests covered with fabrics around the walls. Seated in an armchair with a low back, dressed in a dazzling white *galabieh*, his host looked at Carter with a mixture of curiosity and cruelty. Half his brow was hidden by a turban. His thin lips contrasted with his thick chin. Howard could sense a man used to giving orders that were never questioned.

Naville had advised him against this visit to the chief of the Abd el Rassul clan, the powerful Theban mafia which had been plundering tombs and demanding ransoms from incautious travellers for decades, and did not hesitate to get rid of their most troublesome adversaries. But information from the Swiss archaeologist himself was at the root of Carter's foray, as it was he who had told him in detail what had happened in Deir el Bahari in 1881: forty royal mummies had been found in a cave in the cliff! The original 'archaeologists' had been members of the Abd el Rassul family. They had entered the cache a few years before, determined to sell their finds gradually for maximum profit. Charms and jewels had appeared on the antiquities market, first in a small number, then in such a large quantity that they had attracted the attention of the police.

Under close questioning by the French scholar Maspero, a member of the clan had confessed. Once saved, the royal mummies had left for Cairo by boat to the applause of the *fellahin* gathered on the banks.

A worrying doubt had crossed the mind of the young researcher. That was why he was facing the most fearsome bandit in Egypt. 'Forty royal mummies of the Eighteenth and Nineteenth dynasties . . . Was that the treasure?'

Abd el Rassul nodded affirmatively.

'You remained silent for six years.'

'We had to take an oath, Mr Carter, and we were encouraged to keep silent. Mustafa Agha Ayat, the agent for Britain, Russia and Belgium, had guaranteed his protection. Alas, he was a liar and a usurper! Because of him, we lost a lot of money. When the mummies left the cache, I felt like attacking the procession . . . but there were too many policemen and some of them knew how to shoot. *Malech*!'

Malech might be translated as: 'This is how things are. It had to be like it was and there is nothing you can do about it.' The word served as a talisman to dispose of intricate problems without really dealing with them.

'I must ask you another question.'

Abd el Rassul frowned. 'Are you a policeman?'

'I'm an archaeologist.'

'That is what I have been told, and I don't like that very much either. Who sent you?'

'Nobody.'

'A European is always someone's employee.'

'My boss is Edouard Naville.'

'I'm not afraid of that one. He avoids digging into the sand. What about you?'

'I draw and I paint.'

The thief seemed reassured.

'When you found those mummies, didn't you intend to sell them?'

'Mummies are now less valued than in the past. Our preference has been for gold ever since the origin of the Abd el Rassul dynasty, seven hundred years ago.'

'You discovered forty mummies in 1875, there were forty when Maspero arrived on the site of the cache in 1881. That is too good to be true. None of them had disappeared in the meantime . . .?'

'None.'

His vexed air, suggesting that he should have been a better thief, told Carter that he was telling the truth. Suddenly his gaze became fierce.

'Be careful, Mr Carter, and don't change your occupation. Don't play treasure hunter. Such foolishness would bring you serious trouble.'

The threat did not impress Carter, who was prey to a marvellous hope: Tutankhamun's mummy might be sleeping in his still undesecrated tomb.

Winding paths skirted round stretches of clover and dark fields of broad beans. *Sakiehs*, hydraulically operated wheels, creaked rhythmically. Wreaths of jasmine filtered the sunlight. Donkeys sought the shade under the palm trees. Raifa and Howard Carter were sheltering from the blazing rays of the sun in a sycamore grove and contemplating the golden green of the countryside.

Gamal had been summoned to Qena by his superior, and the young woman had taken advantage of her brother's absence to go across the Nile to meet Carter in Dier el Bahari. As Naville had left for Cairo to deal with some administrative matters, Howard was free to take a walk with her.

She told him about the poverty of her fellow countrymen, epidemics that carried off the weakest children, endemic bilharzia of which so many peasants died. She rebelled against the way young boys spent their days. After being taught the holy book at the Koranic school, they had to lead oxen in the fields, all this with frugal meals of bread and cheese and too little sleep. Raifa dreamed of whitewashed schools and happy children. Carter advised her against expecting too much from England. She was horrified to hear

57

that ten-year-old children died of exhaustion in coal mines.

He acknowledged his increasingly intense liking for the slow pace of life in this unchanging world, where light ruled supreme. He had learned to lay aside his brushes to look at kingfishers snatching their prey, herds of hump-backed oxen with bent horns on dusty paths and women walking with jugs on their heads. Brown night birds and large-winged owls which could be seen by daylight became familiar to him.

Raifa made him converse in Arabic and she corrected his mistakes. At the end of the day, she took him for tea to a farm where one of her friends did watercolours. Imposing in his long white dress, a rod in one hand, their host fetched them at the edge of the desert with his two dogs. He took them to his adobe house, near which he had arranged his studio between hurdles of reeds. Always full, the teapot stayed on the kitchen stove in the open air. His wife prepared honey cakes, which were coveted by the dogs. The painter introduced Carter to his numerous friends: they were peasants, donkey owners, wardens of tombs, pedlars, civil servants and even policemen. Very soon he was integrated into Gurnah society on the west bank of Thebes. Close to the ordinary people, he shared their joys and sorrows.

The horizon became orange and violet. The Nile turned silver. A flight of wild ducks accompanied the feluccas going back home. It was his first sunset with her.

The sacred mountain was adorned with the pink and blue folds of the fabric which would shroud it till dawn. Palm leaves fluttered in a light breeze. According to the custom, those who guarded the fields began their watch from their vantage points. On the bank of the river, they saw the stars appear. Carter identified the Great Bear, the circumpolar stars and the pole star.

'You speak good Arabic, Howard. You can now manage without me.'

'It's impossible. I miss too many nuances.'

'Gamal is coming back tonight.'

He did not dare ask her to stay longer. His words seemed superfluous. He kissed her hands. She turned red and fled.

As a boat took her back to the bank of the living, he stayed on that of the dead. The warmth was so pleasant that he would sleep outside, by the temple of Deir el Bahari, so as to start work at sunrise. In the deserted hill, full of caves, he found a plundered tomb and used it as a bedroom.

Far away from the world, he dreamed of happiness.

14

The telegram reached Porchey in Naples on the morning after his disappointing meeting with the head of the mafia. '*Return to Highclere as soon as possible. Your father is dying.*' It was signed by the steward.

The Italian holiday was forgotten . . . Without wasting a moment, he crossed Europe. The rain was beating down on the castle when he arrived. In his fur-lined raincoat, he entered the large neo-Gothic hall where all the servants had gathered.

The steward came towards him. 'Your Grace . . . how can I tell you . . .'

'When did it happen?'

'Your father died last night in his sleep. He had received the last rites and reread his testament. On behalf of all the staff, I offer you our most sincere sympathy and I assure you of our unfailing loyalty to your lineage.'

'Where is he?'

'In his bedroom.'

Porchey spent the night at his father's bedside. Death had been necessary to bring his roaming to an end and to compel him to settle at Highclere, which would now be the object of his care. An orphan, deprived of advice he had not listened to except for reassurance, he wept. He did not cry for himself, nor for the lost opportunities of learning more from a man of experience, but for those all too rare moments when father and son understand that they descend from the same stock and are made of the same wood.

Part of Porchey had just died too.

There followed the funeral, the burial, mourning suits, and appropriate gestures, and the sad procession of relatives and friends . . . the fifth Earl of Carnarvon yielded to the demands of the ceremonial with dignity. Despite his youth, the aristocracy immediately judged him able to fulfil his duties.

At twenty-three, George Herbert became a very wealthy man, at the head of a 36,000 acre estate.

More distressed than he appeared, he spent a month in isolation. He walked with his dogs, rode his horses, hunted and carefully read his father's financial and administrative files. They enlightened him about the outstanding role played by the old lord in the politics of his country. He was therefore not surprised to receive a request to meet an emissary from the Prime Minister.

The emissary was an austere man of some forty years. His dark pin-striped suit, greying whiskers and cold, inexpressive face gave him the appearance of the respectability essential to a faultless career. 'Under such unhappy circumstances, Lord Carnarvon, you should know that the Government and I appreciate your gesture. We would have understood your refusal.'

'You would have returned a dozen times to the attack. I think you'd better tell me what's on your mind.'

The emissary was shocked by the expression. But his innate sense of diplomacy let it pass. 'Your father belonged to the Disraeli cabinet, where he became famous as an upright politician. As a scrupulous man, he never departed by a hair's breadth from his duty.'

'Let's admit that this is most unusual, and, moreover, true. I'm very happy that Britain recognizes the merits of one of its most loyal sons.'

'Alas, this great servant of the State is no more. But the State goes on.'

'I don't doubt it.'

'I am pleased we understand each other, Lord Carnarvon. So much maturity fills me with admiration.'

'Me too. I probably owe it to my travels.'

The emissary cleared his throat elegantly. 'That is precisely one of the reasons for my visit. Considering your new position and the responsibilities you will hold, sooner or later, it would be better—'

'That I confine myself to a sedentary life? Don't bank on it.'

'Nobody asks you to do that.'

The aristocrat was intrigued. The conversation began to take an interesting turn.

'Your father was one of the pillars of society. As an upholder of order and morality, he encouraged the government's policies and took part in directing the affairs of the country in a most resolute way. I hope that you won't betray his memory and that you will pursue his work.'

'If the Government doesn't betray my confidence, why would the Carnarvon lineage reverse its direction?'

The emissary refrained from sighing with relief. 'You are very different from your father, Lord Carnarvon. He only liked his estate, the English countryside and London. You, on the other hand, display a strong taste for the exotic. Our enquiries reveal that you have been around the world several times and have met . . . diverse personalities.'

'Have I been shadowed?'

'Watched, from time to time, the way every promising young man is.'

'What did you conclude?'

'That you are brave, lucid and capable of getting out of the riskiest situations.'

'Too many compliments point to disaster.'

'As we suppose that you are planning to go back to distant countries, would you agree to be useful to Britain?'

'That's rather an odd question.'

'You can choose a destination that suits you; we have no

intention of forcing one on you. But the authorities would be pleased to know your views on the countries you visit. These precious pieces of information help them to preserve peace. Observations which people like you pass on are essential.'

'On this last point I would agree with you. But may I have the liberty to decide what I pass on?'

The emissary gave a little cough. 'Of course, Lord Carnarvon, of course . . . But how could we doubt your patriotism?'

'Your tact is perfect. Shall I now ask my servants to see you to the door?'

'It is for the good of the Empire.'

'Measure for measure, said Shakespeare.'

15

A terrible doubt had taken hold of Carter: could Tutankhamun's mummy be among those discovered by the Abd el Rassul clan, unidentified? Relentlessly he questioned Naville. The royal cache was just a modest tomb with a low ceiling. Hastily hidden, the mummies had been carelessly wrapped. Some of them had been moved several times. The efforts at preservation had certainly been successful, for the most illustrious pharaohs had escaped destruction. But the description of the 'archaeological' discovery made him shudder. Within two days civil servants from the Antiquities Service had emptied the vault, without making a list and without noting down the positions of the precious remains, and hurriedly transferred them on to a boat! Tags might have been lost during this incredibly inept move, some identities might have been mixed up.

Naville understood that Carter's obstinacy would prevail, so he allowed him to spend a week in Cairo and gave him a letter of introduction.

Those who called the Museum of Cairo 'the cave of Ali Baba' were right. Treasures unearthed from the Egyptian soil had accumulated there: sarcophagi, statues, funerary figurines, steles and many other objects which would all have been worth a careful study. As he walked through the dusty galleries, Carter discovered work of art after work of art. How many years would be necessary to show them to advantage and give them a setting appropriate to their beauty? Mariette would certainly have been happy to have so much space instead of his cramped museum in Bulaq. But 4,000 years of history deserved better.

In spite of his excitement, Carter managed to hold his tongue when he introduced himself to the only person on duty that morning. The man received him amiably after he had perused the letter from his boss.

'So you want to examine the mummies from the cache of Deir el Bahari . . . Nothing is easier. The room is open to the public.'

'I would like to be on my own.'

'Ah . . . I could allow you to stay after closing time. Let's say . . . an hour?'

'It's too short.'

'May I know the reason for your interest?'

'I am afraid there might have been some confusion.'

The civil servant threw up his arms. 'You're not the first one to say that! The circumstances of the discovery were a bit . . . troubled. Numerous scholars have been preoccupied by this and have proceeded to a careful examination of the mummies. You can now be assured that they were all identified with the greatest certainty.'

'Was . . . Tutankhamun among the mummies?'

'I do not know this pharaoh.'

'Do you have any documents on archaeological digs in the Valley of the Kings?'

'We have archaeologists' notebooks and diaries from the eighteenth century . . . Over fifty archaeologists worked there. It's a fact that the valley no longer has any secrets.'

'I don't share your opinion.'

'You are wrong. You forget that Gurnah's professional robbers have been in competition with archaeologists and scholars. No treasure could have escaped them. But, if you want to consult our archives . . .'

'That is indeed my wish.'

Carter climbed the monumental staircase and respectfully entered the room where the eternal bodies of the New Kingdom kings rested. The empty silent room seemed hostile to all profane presence. He would have liked to cover up the fleshless corpses with bandages, put them back into their sarcophagi and remove them from the morbid curiosity of a sceptical or frightened public.

Two faces retained an extraordinary power: that of Seti I, the builder of the temple of Abydos, and that of Ramses II. They had undergone a transfiguration that was visible in their remains. Anyone who looked at them knew that Egypt existed beyond time.

The examination of the royal mummies corroborated the words of the civil servant: the mummy of Tutankhamun had not been discovered. Since there was neither a tomb nor a mummy, was Tutankhamun just a mirage?

He went through the museum archives and carefully noted the archaeological work without finding the slightest clue to the King or to the location of his last dwelling. There were not even any rumours or false tales. It was as if he had never existed. On the one hand, the silence disturbed him. On the other it reinforced his hopes.

Colleagues visiting Cairo were astonished to see him working day and night. One of them invited him to dinner, but he refused. Water, bread and some fruit were enough for him. His real food was the documentation that nobody had ever examined carefully.

On the morning of his last day in Cairo, his efforts were rewarded. An anonymous archaeologist had devoted a hand-written study to the seal of the royal necropolis, depicting the jackal Anubis above nine kneeling and fettered figures. This was how Egypt symbolized the triumph of knowledge over evil forces. Bound hand and foot, unable to do anything, they gave thanks to the god opening the gates of the other world and leading the initiated to the light. That was why the seal had been affixed on the entrances of tombs in the Valley of the Kings and nowhere else. Would he have the good fortune to touch it with his own hands some day?

With this image engraved in his memory, he continued his reading and wondered about a curious phenomenon: the entrances to some tombs, with majestic portals, had remained clearly visible, but in other instances the vaults had been blocked and hidden behind rubble, as if someone had wanted to make them unreachable. If the tomb of Tutankhamun existed, it would be one of the latter. It would probably be necessary to remove tons of sand in order to clear it.

An appendix was attached to the text: the beginning of a papyrus described Seti's assault on his brother Osiris before dealing with a sinister topic, a series of curses against those who robbed royal tombs.

He translated the hieroglyphs over and over again. Afraid of being mistaken, he consulted two curators and a German scientific attaché undergoing some training at the Museum. The three of them confirmed his interpretation. Thanks to the registration number of the papyrus, it might be possible to get another fragment with the rest of the text.

Carter should have gone back to Thebes to resume his work, but his excitement was too great. He obtained permission to continue his enquiry in the museum storerooms, where outstanding works slumbered, some of which would now stay for ever in darkness and oblivion.

After many fruitless attempts, the gods of Egypt favoured him again. He was able to hold in his hands the second half of the papyrus, with the same registration number, to which an *a* had been added. The separation of the two fragments seemed strange, but actually this type of incident was fairly frequent. Why did he care about such modest remnants?

The text was not difficult to decipher:

I was the only one to watch over the building of the tomb of His Majesty, sheltered from all eyes and ears. Nobody saw. Nobody knew. I was scrupulously careful to make the most perfect work. It surpasses those of my ancestors and will be talked of long after I have gone.

His excitement reached a climax. Was it an official document describing the building of Tutankhamun's tomb, now impregnable through an accumulation of blockages preserving its secrets over centuries? He only had a few more signs to decipher: the names of the king and his project manager.

Shivering, his forehead covered with sweat, he closed his eyes and attempted to control his breathing. The emotion was unworthy of a scholar. Suddenly furious, he faced the truth.

The disappointment was heartrending. The project manager was Ineny and the Pharaoh was Tuthmosis I, the first king who had chosen the Valley of the Kings to shelter his last dwelling from plunderers. The ruler had thus initiated a tradition which had then been respected by his followers of the Eighteenth, Nineteenth and Twentieth Dynasties. Thanks to Tuthmosis, the wild west bank had become universally famous.

But Tutankhamun remained out of reach.

16

'The British are monsters!' declared Raifa, her eyes full of anger.

Howard Carter took her hands softly. 'Not all of them.'

'All of them!'

'Me too?'

'You, you're only half British now! I'm talking to your Egyptian half.'

Sitting in front of the canal, they watched the buffaloes taking their bath and shaking off the water. Naked children were swimming and playing beside them. They were trying to climb on their backs and dive from there.

Abbas Hilmi had just succeeded his father Tewfiq, the Khedive, as head of state. As a mediocre economist, the Khedive had put Egypt into debt to such an extent that it was now under the control of foreign powers, and particularly of Britain. The latter had easily displaced France, which had always been ready to talk and unable to act. Favourably disposed towards the nationalists, Abbas Hilmi had espoused the way to emancipation. The Consul-General of Britain had hurried to crush these vague impulses, to the great displeasure of Raifa and of the Egyptians, who were convinced that their land had to become free from the foreign yoke.

'Egypt needs us, Raifa. You know that.'

'I refuse to understand and I forbid you to support that view.'

Christian Jacq

Indignation suited her well. Howard certainly did not want to talk about politics. He was always delighted to look at her, no matter whether she was gentle or hot-tempered. One month after his return to Deir el Bahari, Naville had threatened to dismiss him if he ever deserted the excavations again. But, taking advantage of her brother having to levy taxes right in the heart of the country, Raifa had left her village. They would be able to see each other for a week in the morning and in the evening, in the shade of some palm trees, hidden in a sycamore grove or in a reed cabin on the edge of a field. They would have had so many things to tell each other if Khedive Tewfiq had not had the misfortune to die.

'The British should be chased away. The invaders are responsible for the misery of my people.'

'Egypt was ruined by the Turks,' Carter reminded her with annoyance.

'Europe modified our way of life. Never should we have accepted the building of the Suez Canal.'

'Britain opposed it.'

'Because it was afraid of losing control over the route to India! It did not care about the people's distress . . . only its economic interests matter.'

'You're exaggerating, Raifa. Egypt initiated an agricultural revolution when it opened to Europe. It does not depend on just flood for its survival, now that it makes use of constant irrigation.

'Is it progress to make the *fellahin* work constantly . . . to turn them even more into slaves? Because of this famous irrigation, the parasite transmitting bilharzia has proliferated in the canals where peasants bathe, wash their laundry and do their dishes. In the past the water was pure. Now it brings death! The worm attacks the liver and the spleen and exhausts the organism. Blood replaces urine and agony ensues! Why should we love those who have infected us with this poison?'

'Why do you love me?'

She was frightened by the abruptness of his question. He

70

immediately regretted having asked it. She was already standing up, escaping and disappearing for ever. Newberry, Petrie and Naville had already warned him about his impulsiveness, without producing the slightest improvement.

But Raifa did not take her hands back.

'Forgive me.'

'For what, Howard?'

'I shouldn't have attacked you like that.'

'It is not like you to show regret and remorse. Are you being insincere?'

He almost became angry again, but her smile disarmed him.

'Nobody has ever puzzled me in this way.'

'Nobody has ever fallen in love with you.'

Their fingers intertwined. He did not know what to say or do. How could he declare his love to a young Arab woman? What should he do? With an English lady, his instinct might have told him how to behave. But here, on the bank of the Nile, under the autumn sun, a hundred paces from a pair of oxen enjoying their bath, his archaeologist's knowledge was not much help.

'I would like to paint your portrait.'

'That is forbidden by the Koran. I should be veiled. Keep me in your heart, but do not retain an image of my features.'

'It would be like having another you.'

'I refuse. You would create an evil genius.'

They spent the whole afternoon walking through the deserted countryside. Raifa mentioned her father, a peasant who had died at a very young age. Howard described the landscape in Norfolk.

As the sun declined, they stopped near a *shaduf*, an irrigation wheel. Raifa threw the contents of a water jug over her dusty feet and noticed that the henna had partly faded. Vexed and afraid of becoming prey to wandering spirits, she took him to a group of houses where she called an old woman who had the precious paste. The oval leaves of henna, a bush similar to privet, produced clusters of flowers like lilac. They were crushed and transformed into powder before being turned into cosmetics and magical protection. Sitting with her legs tucked up under her, Raifa dyed her toenails. As Carter watched her, he felt that he was stealing glimpses of her intimacy.

Her expression suddenly froze.

Frightened, she stood up and flattened herself against the wall of the adobe house. In a roar of hooves and a cloud of dust, Gamal stopped his horse between her and Carter. At his belt hung the *kourbash*, a whip made of hippopotamus leather.

'I forbade you to see my sister again!'

'Raifa is a free woman.'

'British dog! Do you believe that you can soil her?'

The horse reared up. Carter did not move an inch. 'I respect your sister. We enjoy talking together.'

He seized the whip and cracked it several times. 'After the punishment I am going to inflict on you, you won't feel like talking any more.'

'Only a coward flogs an unarmed man. Fight with your fists, if you have the courage.'

Gamal threw down the *kourbash* and jumped to the ground.

Taller and broader than Carter, he did not know that a young Englishman brought up in the country can sometimes box as soon as he can walk. Howard had learnt the rules to his own cost and he had practised a large series of legal and illegal blows. Gamal's only tool for attack was contempt. That was his mistake. It was a confrontation which did not last very long: two blows, one on the chin, and the other one on the plexus left him groggy, with a knee on the ground.

Carter stretched his hand out. 'This quarrel is stupid. Let's become friends.'

Gamal spat. 'May the Prophet's hatred befall you!'

Doubled up with pain, he managed to climb on his mount and rode off.

Raifa burst into tears.

17

Carnarvon read again the article on the Sudan in *The Times*. Most informed observers were predicting serious trouble and recalling the extraordinary feats of Kitchener, the only soldier who had been able to restore a lasting peace. The Earl could not explain why the sound of boots disturbed him more than usual. Although he denied it, he was becoming prey to premonitory visions. 'Sudan' and 'blood' now rang like insoluble terms.

Such thoughts were incongruous by the beginning of the beautiful summer of 1895. Within a few hours the 29-year-old aristocrat would celebrate his birthday and take as a wife the young and frail Miss Almina Wombwell who looked like a Greuze[3] model. This was to be a memorable 26 June. A magnificent ceremony would be held at St Margaret's, in Westminster, followed by a most conventional banquet at Lansdowne House. Tender and touching in her pink gauze dress studded with emeralds and diamonds, Almina appeared like an expiatory offering to a now quiet traveller.

Those around Carnarvon whispered that he had reached the age of reason. Others achieved it with less good fortune. He had a title, he was wealthy and educated. She was intelligent, gentle and beautiful. They formed an ideal couple certain of success and two or three children who would be an honour to their parents.

---

[3] French eighteenth-century painter.

The Earl both enjoyed his present situation and hated it. Unlike many other men, he felt no fear of the future and he should have enjoyed perfect bliss. But his taste for wide spaces had not left him. Almina felt no attraction whatsoever for travel. Highclere Castle was a universe that could fill a whole life. She wanted to have a son and a daughter, to give them a traditional education in quiet surroundings, and to take the best care she could of an outstanding husband.

Although she had not said it, Carnarvon was convinced that his betrothed intended to transform him and rid him of the feeling of emptiness and uselessness which often plunged him into the fires of hell. Becoming a father would be a significant step in the process.

He regretted the time when, as Porchey, he could act according to his fancy, spending two months at sea in search of a storm, talking to bandits in a dubious bar at the end of the world and getting lost in the unknown. Although he felt that Porchey's roaming had had an intrinsic justification it should now give way to George Herbert, the fifth Earl of Carnarvon.

The valet presented him with a dinner jacket.

'My Lord, you should consider the time. It would be a pity if your Lordship was late.'

'For whom would it be a pity?'

The valet bowed and left.

'A pity,' repeated Carnarvon, thoughtfully. 'And what if I were not fit for marriage?'

Moments of tenderness with Almina sprang into his memory. He was genuinely in love with her and he did not marry under constraint. Yet he wanted to flee, jump on the deck of the first boat and say farewell to England.

The spirit of his father talked to him. Such an escape, so typical of Porchey, was not worthy of a Carnarvon. Did not his distress feed on his selfishness and on his exclusive attachment to his own self, his own joys and sorrows? A wife and children would rescue him from the emptiness into which he was sinking.

Compelled to be concerned with the destiny of other people and the prosperity of his estate, Lord Carnarvon would do the right thing.

But this was not a very attractive perspective. He would rather have married Almina on the high seas, on the slope of a volcano or at the bottom of a lost valley in the New World with naked Indians as witnesses.

Surround on all sides, the Earl made a gallant last stand. He ignored the dinner jacket, put on a blue serge jacket and a straw hat.

Flabbergasted, the valet mumbled a few indistinct words on the threshold of the room.

'Well, my friend, have you lost your tongue? Please be frank if anything shocks you.'

'My Lord, your . . . your hat is sideways.'

Carnarvon looked at himself in a mirror. 'True. Remind me to give you a rise. Without your perceptive remark, I would have scandalized people.'

The household had been waiting impatiently for the happy event. As soon as the first pains had started, the obstetrician and midwives had rallied to Highclere. Lord Carnarvon's wife dutifully gave birth to a male heir.

In the library, the Earl was reading a book by André Chevrillon entitled *Terres mortes*. Back from Egypt, the author was writing about the Valley of the Kings: 'Other Pharaohs are still sleeping in the mountain, in vaults never ever disturbed by man since the day their doors were closed. They sleep, under the watchful eye of the gods.' This was a clever literary effect, but an archaeological absurdity. It had been known for a long time that the sinister place had released all its mummies and treasures either to robbers or to Egyptologists. Like many French people, Chevrillon had far too romantic a soul.

The obstetrician's steps resonated in the corridor.

Carnarvon interrupted his reading.

'Congratulations, sir. You have an heir.'

'He'll be called Henry. He will live to a very advanced age and he will be the sixth Earl of Carnarvon.'

'May God make it so!'

As soon as he had kissed Almina and his son, Carnarvon left for London. He was expected at the Foreign Office, at his bank and in two other offices in the City. But he ignored these distressingly banal appointments to spend a few hours in the company of a team of mechanics in a warehouse in the northern suburbs. They could hardly hear each other for the noise of engines. But the annoyance did not disturb the Earl who was discovering his latest passion: automobiles.

18

While Kitchener, after his triumph over Caliph Abdullah in Omdurman[4], was reconquering the Sudan and compelling the French commander Marchand, to abandon the country to Britain, Carter was considering the plans of the tombs in the Valley of the Kings. What did they have in common? An entrance door, a corridor disappearing into the ground, an antechamber, the sarcophagus room and sometimes a well to collect rainwater so as to symbolize the primeval ocean and Osiris's tomb. On the walls, relief and paintings depicted the various stages of the pharaoh's resurrection and the transformations of his soul.

Alas the sizes of the vaults were extremely variable, ranging from a few square yards to over a hundred! Under such circumstances, it was impossible to imagine the size of Tutankhamun's. Moreover he was certain that the Pharaoh's immortality was based on two elements, a temple and a tomb, but Tutankhamun's temple had disappeared . . . if it had ever existed.

Friday was a rest day in Egypt, but not for Howard Carter. Relieved from his work in Deir el Bahari for a few hours, in his determination to collect everything that had been written or said, he used this brief time of leisure to complete his files on the valley. Spring was flourishing. Orange trees, honeysuckle

[4] A town in Sudan.

and jasmine bushes were blooming as well as fields of alfalfa and broad beans. As the heat increased, the shadows decreased and dust spread everywhere. Slightly weary, he left his papers to walk along the Nile.

He had not seen Raifa for five months. Any attempt to talk to her would have put her in danger. He could not stop thinking of her and he fought with all his energy the impulse to take her from her brother.

Suddenly she was there by his side. He did not recognize her immediately for she was wearing a bright blue gown and her hair was caught in a white veil which covered her forehead. Her gait betrayed her, before she had time to utter a word.

'Raifa . . . why are you taking such risks?'

'My brother has been promoted and appointed to Aswan. Today is the first day of spring, Howard, and the festival of *Cham en-nessim*, the fragrance of the breeze. There is no milder time for our reunion, if you can agree to forget your work.'

'Such a serious proposal requires some thought.'

Her smile enchanted his soul. 'I brought you a turban and a *galabieh*.'

'Such a fashion doesn't look very British to me.'

'It will be extremely convenient for merging into the crowd and remaining unnoticed. And . . . I want to know whether a certain Howard Carter is willing to change his looks so as to prove his affection.'

Fortunately there was no mirror around, so he was not able to see his get-up.

Cham en-nessim made the people exuberant. Those who lived in the towns invaded the countryside, entire families set out on the roads and had lunch along the Nile. Boys and girls proudly wore bright new outfits and dresses. They entered open houses and, in exchange for coloured hard-boiled eggs, were given pigeons, salt fish or oranges. Hawkers selling jasmine had a field day. There was a whiff of betrothal in the air.

Raifa was enchanting. She almost made him forget the Valley of the Kings. Lost in a festive crowd, as happy as a child, Howard Carter departed from the usual suspiciousness and followed the most charming of all guides. She reminded him that, in the distant past, the country had been a place of festivals and celebrations, in which everybody enjoyed life.

As city dwellers headed back to town, Raifa did not release him. She led him to her own village, where a few Chinese lanterns glowed in the falling night. The children were sleeping, exhausted. They entered the silent house.

'Wait for me here,' she said, leaving him in a pretty room with green and white walls. Carter suddenly felt a lump in his throat. She had introduced him into her private apartments. This was a serious breach of local morals. How could he escape from the trap? Unable to discover a way out, he waited.

She surprised him again. Without her veil, with bare feet, wearing a skirt that stopped over her ankles and a golden bolero that left her stomach uncovered, she was holding a *darabouka*, a drum in the shape of a vase with leather on the bottom, in her right hand. Fragrant with jasmine, mistress of a desire that was all the more ardent for being contained, she displayed her youth and beauty and offered him a belly dance, a refined art from the Silk Road. With infinitely slow movements, initially almost imperceptible, she drew circles around an invisible axis. Lean and supple, her body played subtle variations. Her ankles set the rhythm, while her breasts heaved and her hips quivered.

She did not take her eyes off him for a moment. He did not know where to look. The vision set him on fire, but he was not able to confess his passion. Raifa unfastened her bolero, let the piece of fabric fall on the floor and came to him with a lascivious gait. She dropped the drum, took his hand and drew him to her.

He should have pushed her away and convinced her that they were mad. He should not have accepted a short-lived affair . . . but Raifa was bewitching, her skin fragrant and his

79

desire ardent. His hands slipped the skirt over her hips. He became tense and awkward. She helped him with an undulation. She continued to dance naked and drew him into a swirl of kisses and embraces. Tangled in her long black hair, drunk with the water of her eyes, he offered her a love like the Nile in flood, assailing its banks.

19

On the morning of 9 March 1898, Howard Carter was torn from Raifa's arms by a rumour which had grown in village after village and was now on everyone's lips. The public writer excitedly told anyone who would listen that a French archaeologist named Victor Loret had just discovered an untouched tomb with the sarcophagus of an unknown king in the Valley of the Kings.

Through the open window, veiled by a curtain, Carter did not miss a word. Smiling in half-sleep, his young mistress had other fantasies.

'Where are you going, Howard? It's only dawn.'

'The sun is already high, Raifa. We have been asleep a long time.'

'Have we really been asleep?'

He kissed her tenderly.

'Can I go and see the mummy?'

Away from her, his joviality disappeared. The news had shattered him. When on 12 February, the same Loret had found the empty sarcophagus of Tuthmosis III, the Egyptian Napoleon, Carter had been seized by what he feared might be a premonition. After all, the Frenchman was allowed to excavate in the valley! In addition, fortune seemed to be on his side . . . could he have laid his hands on Tutankhamun's tomb?

When Carter arrived at the site, where a dozen or so *gaffirs* kept watch, Loret had left for Luxor. The Englishman wanted to ask him about the precise nature of the marvels he had been pulling out of darkness. In his absence he had to convince the fierce doorkeepers to let him go into the cave of treasures.

As one of them knew Carter, the task was fairly easy and he quickly got permission. Going through a gap in the sealed door, which was an indisputable sign of the entrance of a royal vault, he progressed by the light of a torch. Without the faint glimmer, he would have fallen into a large and deep well. He had to go back to the surface and ask for a ladder. Throwing it sideways over the gaping hole, he made a makeshift bridge which enabled him to get past the obstacle. Impatient, he proceeded hurriedly to the sarcophagus room.

The sarcophagus was in place. He approached it respectfully, for fear of meeting the pharaoh he had been obsessed with ever since his arrival in the land of gods.

Inside the coffin was a king with a bunch of flowers on his head and a wreath of foliage at his feet. It was the first time an archaeologist had discovered an Egyptian monarch in precisely the place where, thanks to ancient rituals, he now lived for ever.

And the discoverer was not himself.

With his eyes closed, and taking a series of rapid breaths, he concentrated. It was useless to delay any longer the moment when he would have to decipher the inscriptions and know the name of the pharaoh. He had never before shrunk from reality. If his dream was dashed, he wanted at least to pay tribute to Tutankhamun.

He moved the torch near to the hieroglyphs and made out the cartouches containing the fatal word. He read 'Amon' . . . but not 'Tutankhamun'! The mummy and the sarcophagus belonged to Amenhotep II, a ruler made famous by his feats in archery and rowing.

Serene, and as happy as a child who has won a game, he sat for a long time on the dusty floor of the sepulchre. What he had experienced as a missed opportunity was now turning into a new inspiration. Loret had proved that vaults remained intact in the depths of the valley. Among them, Carter knew, figured that of Tutankhamun.

His torch lit up the entrance of a chamber. Inside were nine royal mummies. Again he was seized by anguish. Was his king one of the inhabitants of the new cache? Each of the venerable relics revealed a name, but Tutankhamun was not among them.

Carter's work in Deir el Bahari was making good progress and he spent his leisure time relentlessly examining the site of Deir el Medineh, close to the valley. In the little village had lived the craftsmen who, in the utmost secrecy, built and decorated royal tombs. Their community enjoyed a particular legal system and depended directly on Pharaoh's prime minister, the Vizier.

What remained of Deir el Medineh? A temple, the foundations of houses, the layout of streets and the tombs of stone cutters, painters and draughtsmen. Thousands of pieces of broken limestone used by apprentices as draughts had been extracted from a huge pit.

Going through the village's main square, near the well where the women came to fetch water, Carter thought of life here 3,500 years before. Craftsmen left this haven of peace, surrounded by solitude and barren expanses where hyenas roamed, to follow a path along a crest to the Valley of the Kings. Quarrymen, stone cutters, painters, sculptors and draughtsmen liked to take a rest in rudimentary cabins halfway there before coming home to 'the place of truth', according to the Egyptian name of Deir el Medineh.

High vertical cliffs, rocks and a natural amphitheatre gave the place an austere look. The builders' enthusiasm was still floating in the mild air. Far away from his fellow men, Carter felt close to these people, whose soul survived through the perfection of their works. One of them had dug the tomb of Tutankhamun. Carter hoped he might also have engraved some text or left some clue that might put him on the right track. That was why he had been examining each wall and stone for several months.

As he was leaving the tomb of Sennedjem, harvesting with his wife in the paradise of the other world on the decorated wall, he collided with a small, stout man with no hair and a moustache, plump hands and a hard look behind his round spectacles, dressed in the distinctive clothes of a European dignitary.

'Are you Howard Carter?'

'I have not had the honour of being introduced to you.'

'I am Gaston Maspero, the Manager of the new Antiquities Service.'

Carter dropped his pencil and his sketchbook. So this was the leading light of Egyptology, who had discovered the Texts of the Pyramids, excavated in Abydos, Saqqara, Karnak and Edfu, the investigator who had brought to light the cache of Deir el Bahari, the author of *Histoire ancienne des peuples de l'Orient classique*, a professor at the Collège de France in Paris at the age of twenty-seven, in short the erudite man before whom all scholars of the world bowed.

But he was not totally what he seemed to be. Maspero had left Egypt to build his career, after having been for a long time in charge of a permanent mission in Cairo. As for Carter, he would never leave.

'So, you are back . . . For how long?'

'The advantage of being fifty-three, Mr Carter, and of having spent forty years as an Egyptologist is my experience of men and of the field. I now possess powers which were refused to me in the past and I won't be taken in by anyone.'

'Congratulations on your appointment, sir.'

His hands crossed behind his back, firmly planted on his feet, Carter probably looked like a student ready to hear his punishment.

Maspero took off his glasses and wiped them with a fine handkerchief. 'However the present situation is not easy: Kitchener and Britain have taken control of the Sudan while

Mustafa Kamil and the National Party demand the departure of the British from Egypt.'

'That is just short-lived provocation.'

'Egypt now numbers seven million inhabitants against three million in 1820; families produce more and more children so as to send them to work in the cotton fields. Tomorrow they will be patriots and demand independence.'

'Are you angry with Britain?'

'On the contrary! To be frank, the British Consul-General, Lord Cromer, gave his strong support to my appointment.'

'That means that Loret—'

'Although French, my predecessor was a mediocre archaeologist. Of course he was restless and he made discoveries worthy of some interest.'

'Hasn't he just uncovered the tomb of Tuthmosis I, the most ancient in the valley?'

Maspero dismissed the statement. 'Loret digs in a hurry. He does not take any photographs and scribbles illegible notes. More serious, Carter, the "Loret tombs" are open to the four winds. People come . . . far too many. Some objects are said to have disappeared in illicit transactions. English and German archaeologists actually used the term smuggling and criticized Loret to the authorities. This is why I was appointed. Now that my moral, financial and material conditions have been accepted, I will take things in hand again, even though my fellow countryman is certainly wrongly accused.'

'"Things" . . . Do you mean all the sites?'

'All the sites, divided up into five administrative districts which will be managed with the utmost care by five general inspectors assisted by local inspectors and an increased number of wardens. Learned societies, institutes and wealthy individuals will obtain permission to excavate if I think it's a good thing, in agreement with an international consultative commission.'

'Consultative . . .'

'You are well aware of the nuances: the only power that

matters, the executive power, is mine. It was time to bring back order to the chaos. How old are you Carter?'

'Twenty-six.'

'How long have you been living in Egypt?'

'Almost nine years.'

'Do you speak Arabic?'

'I speak several dialects.'

At last satisfied with the cleanliness of his glasses, Maspero put them on again.

'So rumours about you were right. People also say that the Theban area has no secrets for you.'

'This time, the rumour is excessive. I would like it to be true.'

'Modest, too . . . you will get over it. Mr Carter, I am appointing you General Inspector for Upper Egypt and Nubia in charge of monuments. Your administrative headquarters will be in Luxor. Of course I will require regular reports.'

Gaston Maspero made a show of going, stopped and turned back. 'Ah, I forgot . . . a man of your importance should dress much better. You have an unfortunate disposition to adopt the local fashion. Correct your attire immediately, for you are taking up your post today.'

20

Lord Carnarvon was the happiest man in the world. At the age of thirty-four, he was a wealthy aristocrat, celebrated and cherished, who would soon father a second child. A skilful manager, he could watch his bank balance increase regularly and he had no worries whatsoever about his everyday life. He declared to whoever wanted to listen that life was a sport where the skilful gained because they could appraise a masterpiece as much as the gait of a racehorse. He was as excited by the discovery of an ancient bronze in an antiques den as by hunting.

As a member of the Jockey Club, Carnarvon spent long days taking care of one of England's best-kept stables, and he had won many races. But he was getting weary of the accumulation of successes. His conscience was beginning to reassert itself to the extent that he was only happy externally. He could still find new passions, but as soon as one palled or lost its substance, he felt bored.

Automobiles, speed, with the rush of air against his cheeks and the miles being eaten up by the wheels, long straight roads where he could accelerate, curves where he could exercise his driving skill . . . such were his latest passions. He had bought the first racing cars in France, before Britain had any interest in them. During his first drive, he had even had to have a pedestrian walking ahead with a red flag. In the opening year of the twentieth century, progress was rapid, compelling

Christian Jacq

Highclere's owner to change cars frequently. In love with risk without ever being besotted, the Earl had secured the services of a professional chauffeur, Edward Trotman, with whom he shared the driving. When he felt tired, Carnarvon avoided taking the wheel. That morning, in Germany on the road to Schwalbach where he was to meet his wife, the aristocrat felt fine. Seated near him, his chauffeur was suffering from a head cold.

'The open air will cure you, Edward. No germ can resist it.'

'I hope so, sir. My eyes are weeping. I didn't feel fit to drive. And you went to bed quite late.'

'The reception was deadly boring. A Viennese professor exposed the theories of someone called Freud, the author of a recent book on the interpretation of dreams. Not only is it inept, but it is also dangerous. If a number of stupid or credulous academics propagate these theories, they will spread a kind of plague which it will be difficult for the world to get rid of. This Freud is the worst of nightmares.'

'Be careful, sir. The road is a succession of bends.'

'You are right, Edward. I am suspicious of bends. They have been the cause of all recorded accidents. Do you know what a Turkish multimillionaire suggested to me? That I should buy cotton fields in Egypt! It is said that landowners make a fortune by creating huge estates at the expense of small peasants driven to the brink of misery or compelled to leave their patches of land to crowd into Cairo. Our times are becoming insane and we live in a witch's cauldron. Eventually it will all explode in our face.'

Edward Trotman sneezed. His cold clogged his mind to the point of distracting him from all thought. Carnarvon concentrated on his driving. Fog and showers had made the roadway slippery. He could not help thinking of his recent conversation with a new emissary of the British government. He was no longer being asked to be a voluntary information agent, but to become an official oriental specialist and to begin a political career which would take him far. The Foreign

88

Office needed personalities like his. This might turn into a new
passion, when automobiles became no more than a fad.

Carnarvon drove over a humpbacked bridge too quickly.
Edward Trotman was lifted off his seat and clutched hold of
the Earl's arm to recover his balance.

'Please forgive me, sir.'

'I am the one who should apologize, Edward. I shall now
slow down.'

The succession of bends forced him to be cautious.
Eventually, a long straight line enabled him to release the
energy of the engine.

'This vehicle is crawling along. It should—'

Carnarvon did not finish his sentence. Two ox-driven carts
left a track and crossed the road, indifferent to the automobile
rushing towards them. As he did not have the distance to brake
in time, the Earl turned the wheel, left the road and climbed the
embankment. One of the tyres burst. Trotman had the good
fortune to be ejected, but the vehicle fell into a muddy ditch on
top of Carnarvon.

Trotman was saved by a thick coat, which softened the fall.
Careless of possible injuries, he flew to his employer's rescue.
Terror-stricken, he saw that Carnarvon's head had sunk in the
mud. He did not have the strength to move the car on his own
and to save him from a slimy death.

He ran out shouting. The peasants who were responsible for
the accident remained motionless in the middle of the road.

'Come here quickly! I need your help.'

Two of them fled.

'You will be prosecuted if you leave!'

The Germans did not understand the Englishman's words,
but his threatening tone convinced them to follow him.

Carnarvon's face was unrecognizable. Seizing the pail one
of the peasants was carrying, Trotman poured water on his
nose and lips. Then, leading the operation, he ordered the
Germans to push the car. They jibbed. Trotman became angry,
grabbed one by the collar and forced him to help. Another man

89

came to their aid while a third one, at last aware of the seriousness of the situation, left to fetch assistance.

The vehicle was heavy. At first it did not move, but under the direction of the wild Englishman, the peasants used all their strength. At last the metal body budged.

'In God's name push, you cretins!'

Carnarvon was now released. But he was no longer breathing. Carrying him under his arms, Trotman removed him from his covering.

'Talk to me, sir . . . I beg you to talk to me!'

The chauffeur laid his master on the embankment. 'Water, again . . . *Wasser, bitte*!'

Trotman through the content of the bucket over Carnarvon's head. The cold liquid produced a reaction: The Earl's lids opened, his lips quivered and he regained consciousness.

'You are alive, alive!'

His gaze seemed lost. In a very weak voice, Carnarvon managed to ask a question which stunned his chauffeur. 'Did I kill anyone?'

Trotman did not have time to answer. The Earl had fallen into a coma.

21

Dressed in a three-piece, pin-striped suit, with a spotted bow tie, a white pocket handkerchief, a wide-brimmed hat with a black ribbon, a cigarette-holder and white canvas shoes, Howard Carter looked like a genuine antiquities inspector in line with both the best British tradition and Gaston Maspero's demands.

In this attire, he had no trouble in imposing his authority on the various excavation sites of which he was in charge.

The promotion gave him great satisfaction. He travelled from Edfu to Kom Ombo, from Abu Simbel to Luxor and from El Kab to Hermonthis. How could he not marvel at the myriad temples, bas-reliefs and statues that had to be preserved? How could he not want to lift tons of sand to bring to light new monuments? However his thoughts always brought him back to the Valley of the Kings, now under his control. Alas, he was not able to devote much of his time to it. Maspero did not have any interest in a site he now considered as exhausted, so he would not have agreed. Drawing his argument from Loret's finds, however, Carter did manage to arouse some interest in his chief, who agreed on a routine visit to the location.

'The tomb of Queen Hatshepsut. Isn't it fascinating?'

'It is interesting indeed, but it is now just an empty vault without objects or treasures . . . She was an old, faded and unattractive seductress.'

'I am convinced that there are still hidden wonders here.'

'This is just dreams, Carter. The valley is no more than a desolate area now.'

'I would like to run a big excavation campaign.'

'The Antiquities Service is poor,' objected Maspero. 'My budget is small, and the money has been provided for the upkeep of famous monuments.'

'I am sure—'

'That is enough. If you want to dig, first become rich. Then recruit a hundred workers and spend several thousand pounds. Are you able to do that?'

Furious, Carter bit his lips. 'My only wealth is the salary you pay me.'

'Well, then take care to keep it and forget this sinister place. The valley is dead, Carter. Don't become buried there.'

Early morning in Luxor smelled of coffee and jasmine. The pink mountain of the west bank and the world of the gods mingled with humans in a luminous silence. As the sun rose higher, Carter stood by a small mosque surrounded by rose bushes and hibiscus. An old man was reading the Koran inside. Birds were drinking in a trough near the entrance decorated with marble and mosaics.

Dressed in the European fashion, Raifa stopped a yard away from her lover.

'You look very impressive, sir. I would prefer you in more modest attire, but I shall get used to it. Why did you ask me to come here?'

'I do not have much choice.'

'Are you sacrificing me to your new duties?'

'Raifa . . .'

It was impossible to take her in his arms to hug her in the middle of the street. 'Do you have to torture me like that?'

'Don't you deserve it? My brother lives in Qena. You have become an important person. We are both free, and yet we don't see each other any more. If your work becomes your mistress, Howard, I shall replace it. I love you and I want to marry you.'

The demand did not surprise him. He had both feared it and hoped for it.

'You are Egyptian and I am English . . .'

'There is a solution: convert to Islam. Look at this mosque. It is all peace and serenity.'

'That is true, but . . .'

'You will only have five duties to fulfil: professing your faith in a single God, daily prayers, charity, fasting and the pilgrimage to Mecca. Will you accept, Howard?' A wild hope shone in her eyes.

'I need to think it over.'

'I understand, Howard. God is Great. I praise his perfection. He will know how to enlighten you.'

'I hope so.'

Gaston Maspero banged his fist on the table. 'This is a scandal, Carter. I want to know the truth.'

'Aren't you satisfied with my reports, sir?'

'They are precise, concise and in constant progress. At this pace you will soon be the best of my inspectors.'

'I shall deserve your trust.'

'On condition that you put an end to your escapades!'

'My existence is dedicated to work.'

'I wish it were, Carter! You are a young man, full of ardour . . . It would be a mistake to live on your own. Luxor is full of charming European ladies whom you might meet.'

'My work—'

Maspero's face turned crimson. 'It does not prevent you from going out with someone called Raifa!'

As red as his employer, Carter did not flinch at the attack. 'Who betrayed me?'

'Everybody knows, Carter! You are both a laughing stock and a shame in the small European world of Luxor . . . so much so that your disastrous escapade leads you into degeneracy.'

'What are you alluding to?'

'Don't act dumb! Your "fiancée" has been spreading the news that you have decided to convert to Islam.'

Standing upright, with a steady gaze, Carter faced up to him. 'That is the price I have to pay for marriage.'

'There will be no marriage. Your conversation would be utterly stupid. Muslims won't accept you and Europeans will reject you. The woman will have to leave you and you will have lost your job. Worse, you will lose your vocation! Listen to me, Howard: religions spoil men. I was expelled from the École Normale Supérieure because I took a stand in favour of free thinking and free examination. Although I was reinstated I have never stopped fighting to rid science of the yoke of beliefs which stifle it. Don't fall because of the follies of youth!'

'Raifa wants to make our union official. She initiated me into the land, its tongue and customs. I owe my success largely to her.'

'Incorrigible romanticism! A person's success depends only on his own talent and ability to use circumstances to the best. I begin to know you well, my son. If you succeed, nobody will be grateful to you. Because of your stubborn character and your unfortunate taste for rectitude, people will envy you and be jealous of you.'

'*Mektoub*.'

This Muslim fatalism did not amuse Maspero. 'The affair is over.'

'I don't believe so, sir. I could not bear the dishonour of betraying a woman's love.'

Behind the rimmed spectacles, Maspero's gaze became icy. 'The first quality of a scholar is to adjust to reality. You ignore a major fact: Raifa's brother has just come back to Luxor. His sister has sent me a letter in which she begs me to intervene and to stop you pestering her. Otherwise her brother will lodge a complaint against you.'

'I want to see the document.'

Maspero handed it over to him.

'It is obvious that the text was written under duress!'

'I don't care. It puts an end to this indecent affair. Now, Inspector Carter, go back to your excavations. The monuments need you. They will last much longer than the Egyptian woman.'

22

'I want to know the truth,' demanded the Earl of Carnarvon.

The surgeon hesitated. 'You are out of danger, my Lord. Isn't that the only thing that matters?'

'No. I don't think I have lost my head and I recommend you to keep yours.'

Carnarvon remembered the moment when, in the inn near the scene of the accident, he had opened his eyes again in the presence of his wife, his chauffeur and several physicians. His sight was blurred at first and a few minutes later a black veil obscured it altogether.

'Am I blind for ever?'

'No, I don't believe so, my Lord.'

'What about my injuries?'

'Your legs have been burnt, your jaws are broken, your rib cage has been smashed and you suffer from various bruises.'

'How serious is all this?'

'They are all fairly serious.'

'When shall I be able to walk?'

'In three or four months, but . . . with a stick.'

'And run?'

'You will have to give that up.'

Carnarvon would not be able to drive again. Nor would he sail the oceans in search of some unattainable freedom.

'I feel a terrible pain in my arms.'

'They are dislocated. But you will recover complete use of them. But . . .'

'Go on.'

'Several operations will be necessary. You will require courage and patience, sir.'

Highclere park was verdant under the pale spring sun. Carnarvon was trying to play golf and to increase the length of his round, day by day. Having recovered his sight, he felt more able to fight adversity. Irritated by his lack of energy, he returned to the castle.

On the threshold, Almina was waiting for him.

'Don't give up, darling. You have to live. For me, for your son and for your new-born daughter.'

'I am weary.'

'The rehabilitation will take a long time. Your doctor—'

'A liar, like all doctors. My rehabilitation will never end. I shall suffer to the end of my days.'

Almina looked at her husband with tenderness and kissed his hands.

'You are probably right. But it does not change anything for me.'

'Is it possible to love a cripple?'

'You are not a cripple.'

'Even your love cannot change reality. I walk with difficulty. The slightest effort tires me. My past has been a sequence of absurdities and I have no future. Isn't that the sad truth?'

'It is not true. The experience you have gathered is irreplaceable. Your family loves you and your first photographs reveal a real talent.'

Carnarvon cheered up. 'Are they really good?'

'Go and look for yourself.'

As fast as he could, Carnarvon went to the darkroom which had been set up in one wing of the castle. Photography, his latest passion, required a meticulousness he believed himself incapable of. After initially mediocre attempts, he hesitated to continue. The last series seemed good, however. Their sharpness, centring and composition immortalized Highclere park.

'So we will take photographs,' he murmured.

Letters began pouring in from around the world. Official bodies and amateur societies congratulated him on his pictures and his reputation spread throughout the United Kingdom. Carnarvon was going to be a famous and talented photographer.

'Your appointment, my Lord.'

Carnarvon hesitated. He should not have agreed to the visit. Seated in Napoleon's armchair, he received his visitor in the library. The man in the black suit greeted him.

'Does London still remember an injured aristocrat?'

'You are recovering pretty well, sir. Your misfortunes are now in the past. Most of the members of the Government await your entry into politics.'

Carnarvon stood up and recited some fifty lines of *Macbeth*. His guest remained impassive.

'I like Shakespeare, but—'

'Did you listen carefully?'

'I hope so.'

'In that case, you noticed.'

'I don't understand you.'

Carnarvon turned his back on the Government's emissary. 'Your discretion does you honour, but it is useless. The aftereffects of my jaw injury have left me with a speech defect which only those close to me can stand. Can you imagine me making a speech and arousing only laughter? It would not be long before humourists would poke fun at me and my career would be nipped in the bud.'

'You are wrong, sir. The defect only exists in your imagination.'

'You should not flatter a disabled man.'

'You are not disabled. Your courage has won everybody's admiration. A man of your calibre will become a first-class ruler.'

'I can accept adversity, but not ridicule.'

'Let me reveal the plan my friends and I have devised for your election.'

'It's useless. I do not want to do it.'

'This is mad. You are not going to bury yourself here and—'

'My destiny does not belong to Her Majesty's Government. Our meeting is at an end.'

He had been useless and he had become even more so. Carnarvon kept turning over the thought which his children's affection, his wife's love, his servants' devotion could not chase away. Suffering from dreadful headaches, he only found rest in his estate, under the cedars of Lebanon. It was so painful to concentrate that he often had to interrupt his reading or his photography. At meals he maintained an endless silence, as absent to himself as he was to the conversation.

At the age of thirty-four, the brilliant Earl of Carnarvon was a finished man. The more help he received, the more self-contempt he felt. His dependence on the devotion of those close to him or even on a simple stick agonized him. Had suicide not been an awful lack of taste, he would have resigned himself to it.

His dogs were his best therapists. Always faithful, attentive to his slightest gesture, they only wanted his presence and long walks with him. He learned to endure his suffering and not to regret his lost health. Life became less gloomy and his despair less intense. How could he deny that his horizon had narrowed? Yet the adventurer felt that another door would open and another way would appear. It was up to him to prepare himself for that.

23

Carter's office in Gurnah was neither large nor luxurious, but it marked an extraordinary success and the possibility to set up a research project which would need several years to complete, one which included his beloved valley. Sitting at the far end of a rectangular room where two fans stood imposingly, he received few people, for he preferred the company of erudite books to that of insufferable beggars. His three subordinates, born in the next village, had been instructed to keep intruders away. This is why the seats along the two long walls remained empty most of the time.

How easy it was to dig in the valley with a map and a pencil! Carter planned to penetrate it in ten different places and to have several hundred people working there. Their joyful songs would herald the discovery. But he lacked the thousands of pounds without which no excavation could start.

'Two of your fellow countrymen would like to see you, sir.'

'What are their names?'

'They refuse to give them, but claim to be in possession of highly interesting information.'

Curiosity drove him to agree to the meeting. The two Englishmen were middle-aged men, with seamed faces and coarse features. He would have sworn that they were brothers.

'We live in Luxor,' declared one of them, 'and we are intrigued by the valley. This is why we ask you for permission to dig.'

'You mentioned information . . .'

'We need the permission first.'

'Are you archaeologists?'

The second man stepped forward. 'We worked with Loret. That should be enough.'

'Are you intending to set up a traffic in antiquities?'

'That is not illegal.'

'It is now. As the inspector in charge of the area, I disapprove of such practices and I shall have those who indulge in them punished.'

The two men looked questioningly at each other and stepped back.

'Don't leave so quickly, gentlemen. What about your information?'

'We were wrong, we—'

'Either you talk now or you will be charged.'

The threat stopped them.

'I shall help you, gentlemen. If you want an excavation permit, that means that you already know where to start digging. I suppose that Loret found the entrance to a tomb. When he heard of his dismissal, he chose to fill it up.'

Neither of the two men protested. Carter was right.

'Here is a map of the valley. Now show me the place and disappear.'

A number of workers had gathered by the entrance of the valley, as if moved by some presentiment. Whenever anything happened, a centuries-old instinct mobilized them.

'Bid the chief warden to come,' demanded Carter.

Striding through the lines, the *reis* stepped forward.

'Ahmed Girigar! You've been promoted.'

'So have you, Mr Carter. I am glad to be able to work with you.'

'And I with you.'

'When do we start?'

'Immediately. I need experienced men.'

Ahmed Girigar selected the best men. He gave his orders calmly and he was obeyed immediately. They headed towards the cliff. Carter went first, in a hurry to reach the unknown tomb.

Work was quick and easy. There were a few big blocks, some rubble, some sand . . . and a cavity! It opened on to a fairly large staircase, in excellent condition. No inscription mentioned the name of the owner. As soon as Carter entered the high, straight corridor, followed by Ahmed Girigar, he knew that the tomb had been violated. The oval-shaped burial chamber was a remarkable work, although the sarcophagus remained uncompleted and free of writing.

He kneeled and picked up a rosette. 'Look Ahmed. It comes from a gold pendant inlaid with precious stones. The goddesses I painted in Deir el Bahari wore similar ones.'

Like so many others, the tomb had probably contained fabulous treasures, but only some meagre relics remained with the name of one of Thebes mayors, Sennofer, and his wife. Carter allotted the number 42 to their last dwelling.

The two scholars were savouring grilled pigeon in a restaurant in Luxor. One was French and the other English. For both of them Egyptology in this place was only a stage in careers which would lead them to positions as professors in Paris and London, far away from a country they did not like.

'Have you read the latest volume of the *Annals of the Antiquities Service*?' asked the Frenchman.

'Even though he is my fellow countryman, this Carter begins to irritate me.'

'You're not the only one to feel that. He antagonizes the whole scientific community. What misplaced effort to publish something about the tomb 42, which does not contain any treasure at all!'

'If we let him, he will write reports on violated vaults and the slightest holes in the valley. He ridicules his predecessors and puts his colleagues in an awkward position. Maps, lists, sketches! As if we did not have other preoccupations . . . Carter wants to overload us with unnecessary work. He is ambitious, vindictive and extreme, probably because of his poor background.'

'We'll prevent him from doing harm, *cher collègue*.'

'I am glad to conclude this *entente cordiale*: Carter will either yield or break.'

Carter was aware that he was disturbing a bunch of lazy and incompetent people for whom Egypt and Egyptology were just a somewhat posh hobby. He believed that those who searched for the truth about the past should devote as much care to the observation of the present and the preparation of the future.

One month after the discovery of tomb 42, Ahmed Girigar asked for a meeting away from inquisitive eavesdroppers. Carter closed his office and joined him in a small, barren valley, where a torrent ran when there was a storm.

'Four people who worked for Loret have confessed to attempted theft.'

'In which tomb?'

'In an unknown tomb, which the Frenchman filled in again, as with tomb 42. The four men were trying to enter it, when an *affrit* disturbed them. This is a very aggressive spirit which grabs people's necks and prevents them from breathing.'

'Did they tell you where?'

'I'm taking you there.'

The *reis* led Carter to the small ravine sheltering the tomb of Ramses XI. He showed him a hollow in the sand where broken pieces of stone had accumulated.

'Summon some workers, and let us dig.'

Fifteen feet under the rubble, they uncovered a well. There was an intact door at the bottom!

Ahmed Girigar saw Howard Carter's enthusiasm. 'Don't rejoice too soon. Loret has already been here.'

Worried, Carter slid inside. On the ceiling he could see

adobe wasps' nests, typical of Theban tombs violated a long time ago.

Two wooden coffins, covered with white resin, and a third white one containing a mummy belonged to singers of the temple of Karnak. Between the bandages, mimosa, lotus and persea leaves had been inserted. There was no trace of Tutankhamun.

24

'Come quickly, sir! This is serious, most serious!'

The *gaffir* was upset. A column had just collapsed in the tomb of Seti I, the largest and the most beautiful in the valley.

Carter went to the site to note the damage and take emergency measures. Once again, he was dazzled by what was in effect the Sistine Chapel of ancient Egypt. The splendour of paintings which seemed to have been completed just the previous day, the perfection of hieroglyphs telling of the dangerous journey of the sun in the underworld and the presence of divinities helping Pharaoh to come back to life aroused intense emotions. He often came to meditate in front of Nut, the goddess of the sky, a huge woman with a body studded with stars. In the evening, she swallowed the day star to which she gave birth in the morning.

This time, however, he did not have the leisure to study the frescoes. He had to prop up the part that had fallen in with wood logs, close the tomb to the public and hurry to see Maspero.

Weary of the town, the director of the service had set up his headquarters on a houseboat, a *dahabieh* named *Miriam*. Like the ancient Egyptians, he could now easily sail on the Nile from one site to another. In his tiny office stacked with piles of files, Maspero seemed in a bad mood.

'So what is going on in the valley, Carter? I heard that the tomb of Seti I has been half destroyed!'

'The incident has been slightly exaggerated, but the matter

is quite serious: a collapsed column. The renovation has already started.'

'And what about the tourists?'

'All visits have been forbidden.'

Maspero leaned forward in his armchair. 'Ah, tourists! What a mob . . . Two thousand people a year invade the valley. They form a real colony in Luxor from December to April. They are talkative, restless, crazy people who come to enjoy the sun and damage the monuments!'

He adopted a more imposing position and gazed serenely at his inspector. 'Is that your position, Carter? Are these your words?'

'To the letter as well as the spirit. These people only think of showing off in luxury hotels, flirting, exchanging visiting cards. They go from one party to another, play tennis and bridge and constantly invent new entertainment. The inevitable picnic in the Valley of the Kings and a visit to the tombs are high on their agenda. Yet they do not have the slightest interest, least of all respect, for them. Guides blacken the walls with the smoke of their torches and everybody has fun touching the reliefs. Drastic measures are necessary, sir, if you want to save these invaluable treasures.'

'Are you in any doubt?'

'We must do something.'

'Do something, do something! It's easy to say! Are you planning to forbid access to the valley to the tourists?'

'Why not? Just to give us time to dig there.'

'The valley has already been excavated, Carter.'

'Perhaps the discovery of tomb 42 with that of the three singers of Amon, which will now be number 44 on my list, proves that there is more to do.'

The argument unsettled Maspero, but he quickly regained his composure. 'The vaults have been violated and used again. They have neither furniture nor beautiful objects . . . Only people with a passion like yours are interested in such modest discoveries! Bear in mind that hundreds of pillagers have been here and only left scraps. What would you suggest we do about the most visited tombs in the valley?'

'I suggest that we build walls to preserve the entrances from falling stones and heavy rain, lay out paths to channel the visitors and set up banisters in the tombs to prevent people from holding on to the walls.'

Maspero opened a file. 'Mmm . . . we could do that. The budget would allow for that.'

'That is not all. The most important things remain to be done.'

'The most important things will have to wait. I have no more money.'

'But we have to fight the lampblack.'

'How?'

'We could use electricity in the main tombs.'

'Electricity? Who would supply you with electricity?'

'A generator in the valley.'

Irritated, Maspero broke his pencil. 'You are a revolutionary, Carter. Now, let me work in peace.'

'Do my suggestions meet with your approval?'

'Don't harp on about it.'

As soon as the news spread, tourists flowed in. Thanks to the electric light, it was now at last possible to admire all the bas-reliefs. Carter had not put off the mass of curious people, but the banning of torches and the provision of guard-rails ensured the preservation of the monuments. For a few hours he had to become a martinet to steady the excited people.

Calm returned with the night. Sitting on one of the mounds overlooking the royal tombs, Carter enjoyed the solitude and the moments of grace when he felt united with the soul of kings who had triumphed over death.

The wardens did not venture into the darkness of the valley, which they believed was haunted by demons who made people mad, blind or mute. They felt unprotected without the magic hieroglyphic formulae.

Sometimes an owl or a bat brushed against him, or a fox hurtled down a slope in search of a prey. His hope was increasing. Because of the lack of graffiti, he knew that no Greek or Roman traveller had visited tombs 42 and 44, which had been closed since antiquity. As a consequence, important vaults were still hidden under the sand. People had merely dug hastily and been satisfied with spectacular results, for it had been arbitrarily assumed that the valley would now remain mute for ever.

As he looked closely, he realized that there was almost nothing natural in the grandiose landscape. He could see 30 feet of broken pieces of limestone, rocks that had been turned upside down, paths that had been laid out by builders, the huge rubble of modern diggers . . . the gigantic cliffs, the overlooking pyramid. Hadn't all these features been hewn by the hands of men?

How many tons would he have to move away before he could bring to light the portal of an unviolated royal tomb which might exist only in his imagination? The doubt was heartrending. He was not yet worthy of the valley.

25

Golf, photography, walks with his wife and children, long rests and reading in the library of Highclere . . . Carnarvon's life weighed down on him as the days went by. Contrary to the physicians' claims the after-effects of his accident remained. His jaws and his back were painful, he limped and he could not sleep at night.

Almina remained gentle and patient, even though her husband's temper deteriorated. He did not joke any more, and he had stopped playing with his son and daughter. He would remain silent for hours. The young woman took advantage of a ray of sun illuminating the park to pour out her heart.

'Do you feel imprisoned, darling?'

'I'm beginning to hate myself, Almina.'

'Because of your injuries?'

'A crippled man does not deserve to live any more.'

'You are talking nonsense.'

'I'm a cripple.'

'You keep going.'

'Can you say that I can still captain a yacht, drive a racing car or bring down a wrestler in a funfair?'

'These things are meaningless. Lots of mediocre people are able to do them. Whereas it is a major task being the fifth Earl of Carnarvon, isn't it?'

Carnarvon gazed at the sun until he was dazzled.

'You recovered the full use of your eyes. That should

encourage you to fight. The Carnarvons have always braved adversity with remarkable courage. Are you an exception?'

George Herbert bent his head. Moved, his wife came near him.

'Forgive me, I hurt you.'

'You are right. I behave like a coward.'

'Don't be unfair to yourself. You must know that I admire you.'

Lord Carnarvon turned to his wife. 'I would have given up without you.'

'If my presence hastens your recovery, don't hesitate to use it.'

'I need solitude, Almina. I draw strength from it.'

'I shall respect your wishes, on condition that you keep your promise to improve your golf handicap.'

In spite of sometimes acute pain, Carnarvon forced himself to play and to walk the long distances from one hole to the next. His rigorous approach to the game dismissed his gloomy thoughts. Aiming to recover some degree of mobility restored his spirits. The pleasure of the game and a good series of performances added spice to the effort.

It was a surprise when a government emissary came to see him again. 'Congratulations, Lord Carnarvon. You are becoming an excellent golfer.'

'There is too much nervousness in my approach and my drive lacks precision. But I haven't given up hope.'

'Such a pleasant day calls for some thought for the future.'

'My future is behind me.'

'Permit me to disagree. Even if you give up the idea of a political career, there are many other ways of serving your country. What about your knowledge of the Orient?'

'You would probably prefer my political analysis.'

'The Foreign Office might. They consult the best experts, and the Secretary of State would like to have lunch with you.'

Before his accident, Carnarvon would have answered with an ironic comment. Now the invitation entertained him.

When her husband agreed to lead a hunting party and allowed her to arrange a large dinner at Highclere, Almina realized that the fifth Earl of Carnarvon had recovered his wish to live. Although he persisted in refusing to wear a dinner-jacket and appeared in his favourite blue serge jacket, he made witty remarks and caustic comments with his usual talent.

'What would you like to be if you were not one of the richest noblemen in the country?' asked a baroness.

Carnarvon did not think long. 'Someone like Schliemann.'

'Is he a painter or a jockey?'

'Neither. He's an archaeologist.'

'What an awful profession! Dust, heat and sweat . . . What did your Schliemann discover?'

'Troy.'

'The town Homer wrote about?'

'In a way.'

'Would you be able to discover a whole town like that, full of gold, hidden in the sand?'

'At the risk of disappointing you, baroness, I fear I would not. Your question was asked in fun, and my answer is just a dream.'

Her husband was late for dinner. After a time, Lady Almina began to worry. As it was the butler's evening off, she had to go to the library to find him.

'Have you forgotten the time?'

'I'm afraid so.'

'What is keeping you?'

'A big book by a Frenchman on ancient Egypt.'

'What is his name?'

'Gaston Maspero.'

'Do you intend to invite him to Highclere?'

'He lives in Egypt.'

'How awful! It must be insufferable . . . People say that winter is pleasant there, but the other seasons are scorching. How can people stand such inhuman climates?'

'I don't know, Almina. I don't know Egypt.'

'You went around the world several times.'

Carnarvon closed the book and stood up.

'An evil genius kept me away from that magical country.'

'"Evil genius", "magic" . . . are you becoming super-stitious?'

The Earl offered his arm to his wife. They walked slowly through the corridor towards the dining room. 'Our world is more mysterious than it seems. Occult forces pervade it, even though our eyes do not perceive them. The Egyptians studied them the way our scientists do.'

'That book is dreadful! Not only does it make you late for dinner, but it also gives you strange ideas. Forget about this Maspero, Egypt and its demons. Come eat your salmon.'

His mind elsewhere, the Earl did as he was told.

26

'Carter,' announced Maspero assertively, 'we are going to make some changes which will enhance the reputation and prestige of the Antiquities Service. The new Museum of Cairo will incorporate all the existing collections in Egypt, and with the creation of a general catalogue, we will make an assessment of all the ancient objects, from the tiniest statuette to the colossus.'

'What a brilliant plan!'

'I'm glad you agree. A catalogue is indeed most essential!'

Carter did not share this opinion. In a country like Egypt, the most important thing was to dig and discover. But Gaston Maspero stuck to his view. 'As the inspector for the Thebes area, I entrust you with two priorities. The first will be to escort the royal mummies concealed in the tomb of Amenhotep II to the Museum of Cairo.'

'So they will be part of the collection.'

The comment annoyed the director. 'Are you by any chance unhappy about my decision?'

'So what about the second mission?'

'An authentic king has immeasurable worth on the antiquities market. Amenhotep is not in his original sarcophagus, so take care to put him back there so that tourists can admire a real pharaoh in his real vault.'

Caught off his guard, Carter stammered, 'You . . . you give me great pleasure!'

Surly, Maspero immersed himself in a file. 'Hurry up! Even mummies hate to wait.'

The burial of Amenhotep II, the king with a strong arm and incomparable bravery, was a moment of lasting happiness for Howard Carter. Outside, the sky was a tender blue, bathed in a soft light that encouraged meditation.

With the help of Ahmed Girigar and some wardens, he silently followed the path used by the Pharaoh 3,500 years before. They carried this close and distant ancestor, human being and god, with great respect. Their steps raised a fine dust, which was blown away by the north wind. Not a word was said until they reached the entrance to the tomb. The wardens may have recited Muslim prayers to themselves, but Carter's thoughts turned to the ritual opening of the mouth, which revived the departed by restoring his power of speech.

Still silent, the procession entered the dark sepulchre. They slowed their pace as their eyes grew accustomed to the darkness. Carter had allowed only one torch, produced in the ancient way with an old cloth dipped in sesame oil, so as to avoid lampblack. When they laid the coffin in the sarcophagus, he held back his tears with difficulty. As he celebrated the timeless funeral, he felt that he was doing something right.

A long time after the end of the ceremony, alone in the shadow, he dreamed of the splendour of a time when death was a transcendence towards the light.

Not far from the temple of Luxor, there was an old mansion that had housed one of the last harems in Egypt. Inhabited by lascivious women in the past, the place had received the attention of the local potentate. But it was now becoming visibly dilapidated. Paint was flaking away on the *mucharabiehs*, and stuccoes had become porous. Howard pushed the door on its rusty hinges. He was convinced that he would stumble upon a eunuch with a club. But there were only a dozen poor wretches smoking hashish. An awful smell of fried onions indicated that they also cooked there.

Why had Raifa suggested that they meet in such sordid surroundings? Again he read the note a young boy had brought to him: there was no doubt about the place. He tried to question the tenants. Stunned by drugs they did not answer. Annoyed, he was retracing his steps when the door opened on Raifa.

Her eyes as green as water, her soft face and her elegant gait caught him in the web of charms she displayed so well. The shabby harem turned into a palace of wonders with sparkling gilded furnishings.

'Come,' she said as she took his hand.

They ran to the first floor.

She took him to a bedroom hung with red velvet where a four poster bed stood, illuminated by a ray of sun filtering through the *mucharabieh*. 'Nobody will bother us here. Gamal does not know the place.'

'I love you, Raifa.'

'Prove it, Howard.'

The challenge evoked a swift reaction. Raifa did not resist for long.

By order of Maspero, Carter had had to inspect the south of the Theban province in order to locate any archaeological remains. The meticulous work took him away from the valley and Raifa.

One month after the start of the mission, however, a cable surprised him: the director of the service requested him to return to Luxor immediately.

Omitting their usual greetings, Maspero received him on his boat. 'This is serious. The tomb of Amenhotep has been desecrated: the door has been broken and the mummy damaged.'

Carter was mute with indignation.

'So here are the first pillagers of the twentieth century . . .

It's crazy! Are there really people so irreverent they would profane such a venerable corpse? Of course I called the police. The investigation was speedy and disappointing as the warden did not see anything. Nor were there any witnesses, rumours or leads. Repair the mummy, Howard.'

'The culprit . . .'

'Forget about the culprit. We won't find him. We already look ridiculous.'

The tragedy had at least enabled Carter to come back to the valley, even though under dreadful circumstances. Before he even stepped over the threshold of the tomb, he had decided to start the inquiry again.

Spring drove away those tourists who were afraid of the heat, which very quickly became unbearable. The few visitors left crowded the entrance of the sepulchre which had been robbed, as if they were expecting some new tragedy to happen. With the help of Ahmed Girigar, Carter chased them away so as to be able to examine the scene of the crime at leisure.

The iron door provided by the service had been forced by an instrument which was easy to identify as a jemmy.

'Who in Gurnah has something like this?'

'The blacksmith,' answered the *reis*.

They questioned the man, who declared that he had been robbed, and then claimed that he did not know the identity of the culprit. Carter went back to the tomb and, under the astonished gaze of Ahmed Girigar, took a cast of some rather suspicious footprints.

'Do you know anyone who could identify these?'

'There is a camel driver who has been travelling across tracks in the desert ever since his childhood and usually rests in Gurnah in between trips. His favourite hobby is studying footprints, be they of animals or human beings.'

The expert did not disappoint Carter. His diagnosis was positive. To check it, he told him that he only had to walk in front of the house of the Abd el Rassul clan. Carter did not hesitate. His investigation disturbed the members of the clan and he was invited to show the casts to their chief.

'What is the point of this game, Mr Carter?'

'To demonstrate that you were at the head of a gang of pillagers who desecrated the tomb of Amenhotep II. This is why all the witnesses remain silent, including your accomplice, the warden.'

Abd el Rassul's face hardened. 'Don't persist. You won't succeed.'

That very evening, just after prayers, Carter came back with a group of policemen who proceeded to a proper search, whose result exceeded his hopes: necklaces, funerary figurines, bandages of mummies, fragments of relief cut with a saw from several tombs proved that the clan was guilty.

Abd el Rassul did not deny it.

The trial took place a few days later. The court in Luxor was full. Carter appeared as a witness. The presiding judge questioned him for a long time. He described the various stages of the enquiry which had led him to discover the culprit.

'Where is the evidence, Mr Carter?'

'In the hands of the police, Your Honour.'

'You are mistaken.'

'I was a witness, your Honour . . . a number of archaeological objects were found in the cellar of Abd el Rassul.'

'This is not true. The report does not mention them.'

'Your Honour—'

'On the grounds of lack of evidence, the court declares Abd el Rassul not guilty.'

Maspero and Carter put the corpse of Amenhotep II back into his sarcophagus. Now visitors standing over the vault could see the Pharaoh in an upright position, ready to leave for the other world.

'Don't be disappointed, Carter. Nobody has ever been able to put the clan under lock and key and nobody ever will.'

'I cannot bear injustice.'

'Adopt a better strategy.'

'What do you mean?'
'When you cannot shoot your enemy, it is better to make an alliance with him.'

27

It was 1902, and Debussy's *Pelléas* was revolutionizing music. Highclere was becoming a centre of British cultural life. Piqued at not being able to recover more quickly and unable to embark on long trips around the world, Lord Carnarvon brought artists, writers and historians to his home. His wife insisted on also offering hospitality to politicians, financiers and dignitaries who were glad to engage with the sharp mind of their host.

A retired colonel, a great amateur sportsman and a specialist in military engineering, began to praise Britain's conquests.

'We are guarantors of world peace. When we do not fight to preserve it, we build. That is why in Egypt—'

'Are we erecting a new pyramid?' enquired Carnarvon.

'Much better! A dam.'

'The dam is in Aswan, isn't it?'

'Thanks to this structure, the people's well-being is assured.'

'I am not sure of that.'

Indignant, the colonel laid down his fork. 'How can you doubt it?'

'As Egypt moves from the natural cycle of floods to permanent irrigation, we abruptly change customs that are thousands of years old and replace them with techniques that will be misunderstood and ill-applied.'

'That is progress, Lord Carnarvon, progress!'

'Do you really think that the human race is progressing? Do

Christian Jacq

you believe that the sordid areas of London are an improvement on the temples of antiquity? Do you believe our thinkers are superior to Plato, Lao-Tzu, Buddha or the builders of the great pyramid?'

The colonel tugged at his starched shirt collar. 'These are . . . revolutionary opinions.'

Almina diverted the conversation by mentioning the latest performance of *A Midsummer Night's Dream*, where the Royal Shakespeare Company had once again lived up to its reputation.

When the guests had left and she was alone with her husband in front of the blazing fire in the great living room, she felt she needed to say something.

'Don't you think you went too far?'

'The world is absurd, my dear, and Great Britain is in a delusion.'

'Isn't it in the heart of an extraordinary empire which guarantees the welfare of its people?'

'Not for much longer.'

'What do you mean?'

'I'm as interested in the future as in the past. In the course of this endless convalescence, I have time to read the press and specialized studies. The empire is chaffing at the bit, Almina. Tomorrow it will disintegrate and our colonies will claim independence.'

'Our army will silence those who cause trouble.'

'Alas, it will try!'

'Alas?'

'It is stupid to oppose a river in flood. It is better to channel it. But politicians only think of their present interest. As usual they become aware of reality too late.' Carnarvon laid a log in the fireplace, where the flames moved in an ever-changing dance.

'What awful thoughts you have, my dear. No wonder they depress you.'

'On the contrary.'

120

'You . . . you're not going to start an opposition party?'

The Earl hugged his wife tenderly.

'Britain is a small island which likes to think it is a continent. You know how much I hate narrow-mindedness. So I shall not do anything here.'

'That does not reassure me at all. Do you have another plan in mind . . .'

'A crazy one perhaps, but not yet. My physical state prevents me from planning a new trip around the world on my own, but I cannot keep still, like stagnant water.'

'You shouldn't talk like that. Think of your children, your estate and me.'

'I am both happy and unhappy, Almina. That is my tragedy. I love you. I love the children. I love this land . . . and yet there is another love in me which I cannot name and which will stifle me if I do not succeed in expressing it.'

'It's so difficult to understand you, my dear.'

'I'll grant you that. It is a superhuman task even for me.'

Almina snuggled up to her husband.

'Promise that you won't leave Highclere any more.'

'I can't; a Carnarvon has never been guilty of going back on his word.'

Almina held back her tears. It was possible to fight an avowed enemy, be it a mistress or an ambition, but how could she fight the invisible presence which was gnawing at George Herbert's soul? Like him, she felt that unexpected events would upset the peaceful existence she was clinging to with all her strength.

She fell asleep in his arms.

The Earl remained awake and thought of the distant horizons he had lost with the stupid accident. In his need to forgo adventure he had immersed himself in family comfort without mental reservation. Yet his common sense compelled him to realize that this was a failure. The answer, the only answer he expected from life was still escaping him: to know what was to be his destiny.

28

'I refuse.'

Maspero turned red with anger.

'You're not in a position to refuse anything, Carter! I am the one who runs the service and I am the one who takes the decisions!'

'As the inspector for the Theban area, I think I'm entitled to have my say in the matter.'

'You carry out my orders and nothing else!'

His tweed jacket, flannel trousers, starched shirt and spotted bow tie gave Carter sufficient composure to resist Maspero. Aged twenty-nine, he had now become a personality in the Luxor smart set and he did not react like a frightened boy any more.

'Even when you are wrong?'

As cold as an iceberg, the director of the service stood up, walked around the desk and faced him. 'Make yourself clear, Mr Carter.'

'As a scientist, you assume that it is useless to dig in the Valley of the Kings.'

'Yes.'

'So why do you give permission to Theodore Davis, an inexperienced amateur?'

'Because the man possesses a major quality: wealth. The service won't have to lay out a penny. On the contrary it will receive some money as a tribute and it will keep its share of possible funds.'

'Money . . . is that the only criterion? If the man ruins the site and makes it unsuitable for any further scientific investigation, what shall we earn?'

'Your wild imaginings are groundless. You feel uncomfortable, Carter, because what really bothers you is the fact that the man is an American: as an Englishman you hate the United States. As for me, I need to ensure the financing of the service.'

'At the cost of the destruction of the valley?'

'Certainly not, because you are the inspector and it is your job to make sure that does not happen.'

'What does that mean?'

'It means that you will take part in Davis's excavations.'

'That is out of the question.'

'Don't be stupid, Carter.'

'A professional cannot submit to the whims of an amateur.'

'This is not a question of submission, but of collaboration.'

'That is even worse. I won't collaborate with the enemy. Permit me to take my leave.'

Shut up in his office, Carter wept with rage. Not only had the valley escaped him, but it had fallen into the hands of an American lawyer eager to spend his retirement chasing the shadows of the pharaohs. Carter was experienced. He felt ready to explore the sacred land with love and care, and now, with the support of the authorities, an intruder was stealing the goal of his entire existence. Even Raifa had not succeeded in cheering him up. Unable to forget the catastrophe, he had been a mediocre lover. He had rudely slammed the bedroom door and probably put an end to their affair by leaving her naked and in tears in the disused harem.

His life was collapsing.

Only Ahmed Girigar could still enter his den. He brought him water, fruit and bread, at which he nibbled.

One visitor did manage to force his way in, however.

'Professor Newberry!'

'Glad to see you again, Howard.'

'Have you been sent by Maspero?'

'Your obstinacy is ridiculous, Howard. Egypt needs you.'

'But the service needs Davis.'

'I know him and I want to arrange a meeting. I may as well warn you that he is not an easy man, but please accept. You will be able to save the valley by controlling his activities. But this requires that you forget your vanity.'

'Have I deserved such unfairness?'

'It doesn't matter. Fight with what you have.'

The stories about the American's bad manners were true. Theodore Davis shook hands with Carter with the assurance of a hunter convinced that during his first shoot he would find and kill his prey.

'So, you are the scientist? You really look like it.'

Of average height, Theodore Davis gave an impression of weakness. He did not move without a stick, hid his throat with a white scarf and covered his head with a wide-brimmed hat. His jodhpurs and puttees made him look like a rider without his horse. A thick moustache spread like the wings of a bird covering the lower part of his face. His gaze was aggressive behind the round lenses of his tiny spectacles.

'I'm sixty-five and I have no wish to become an archaeologist, Mr Carter.'

'In that case, the Valley of the Kings won't attract you very much.'

'I am bored by law. But I am amused by the prospect of digging. I intend to bring to light a large number of tombs full of statues, sarcophagi, mummies and magnificent objects. You will help me. But you should know that I am used to being obeyed and that I hate to argue with my subordinates.'

Newberry thought he ought to say something.

'My dear Davis, Howard Carter is not really your subordinate. Assistant would be a more appropriate term. The Antiquities Service insists on helping you in your generous endeavour.'

'Generous, but not extravagant! I paid my share, so I want results. Now Carter, here is what you have to do: have a house built for me near the site. In the meantime I shall live on a ship on the Nile. I shall have a breath of cool air and I shall be able to sail as I like.'

'What is your plan for the excavations, sir?'

'Plan? Why, do as you please . . . While I am waiting for the first finds, I shall wait in Aswan. They say it is an attractive town.'

At the end of the winter of 1902, Carter headed a team of some sixty workers digging for Theodore Davis. Taking advantage of the labour force, he cleared the two sides of the road to the Valley of the Kings, which was too narrow for the increasing number of tourists. Then he started digging an area of 100 yards or so between the tombs of Ramses IV and Ramses II.

Luck smiled on him. He discovered vaults containing male and female mummies damaged by water. At the bottom, he found canopic jars and a yellow box containing a leather kilt worn for war. Duly informed, Davis came back from Aswan and had a row with Maspero. The director of the service asked for the objects so as to send them to Cairo. Davis refused. According to custom, they came to the man who had found them and he wanted to give them to an American museum. Maspero ranted and raged. Davis paid. The service needed money.

Now rested, the American had devised an absurd plan, notable for its total lack of method, for the excavations. He attempted to manage the team himself, gave incoherent orders, became restless and only succeeded in covering his black suit with dust. Carter followed him like a protective and discreet shadow. Neither he nor *reis* Ahmed Girigar protested. Davis went about things in a way which was stupid but innocuous. Spring and the heat soon crushed his enthusiasm.

Maspero could not believe his eyes. For the third time he

reread Carter's confidential report on the summer he had just spent in England.

'Is this a dream, Carter?'

'No, sir. We've been granted a subscription by Mrs Goff to renovate the tomb of Seti II and another one by the industrialist Robert Mond for the tomb of Seti I.'

'Are they in love with Egyptian art?'

'I managed to show them how interesting our work is.'

'So you're turning into a diplomat! For my part I give you electricity for Abu Simbel.'

Disappointed by the lack of results – a small tomb with two female mummies and mummified ducks – Davis went into winter quarters in Aswan.

At the beginning of January 1903, Carter was taking a long ride at the Deir el Bahari site. Suddenly his horse's front legs sank in the sand and he turned head over heels. Neither he nor the animal was injured, but he only had eyes for the miraculous hole which had appeared. He very soon asked his team to enlarge it.

A hundred and fifty yards from the entrance to the corridor they found a sealed door. On the other side was a vault which contained only an empty wooden coffin and a block wrapped in cloth. Carter removed it carefully: it protected a large statue of Mentuhotep II in a white dress with a red crown. The last dwelling of the pharaoh with the severe face immediately received the name Bab el Hosan, 'the tomb of the horse'.

In Davis's absence, Carter tried an experiment. Ahmed Girigar had indicated the location of two wells full of minute objects, tools and pieces of crockery bearing the name of Tuthmosis IV: a storeroom! Such a discovery meant that the tomb should be nearby. Yet it did not figure in the only exhaustive report on it that had ever been made. A systematic search of the area should bring some results.

On 18 January 1903, he cleared the wide stairs and a door. In spite of his wish to move further, Carter respected the agreement he had made with the official excavator: Davis was to enter first. The archaeologist vainly tried to get in touch with him. He had gone on an outing, and it was impossible to find him. Nobody knew where he had anchored his ship. Considering himself free of all moral obligations, therefore, Carter walked down into the tomb.

The width of the artistically cut corridor gave a hint of marvels to come. The quality of the paintings confirmed the first impression, which, alas, quickly turned into disappointment: thousands of fragments were scattered on the floor. Between pieces of blue faience lay the rope the robbers had used. Carter went beyond the well, progressed through a mass of debris and stopped horrified in front of a child with blackened flesh who was standing there motionless! It was not someone who had left the slumber of death. Nor was it a vengeful spectre. It was just an unfortunate mummy deprived of its bandages and thrown back against a wall. Upset, Carter felt nothing but hatred for the profaners who had vandalized the little prince.

The official opening of the tomb of Tuthmosis IV took place on 3 February 1903, in the presence of Maspero. Carter's workers had to hold back a crowd of onlookers. Davis was strutting about.

'This is my first tomb, Mr Maspero.'

'Congratulations.'

'You put your trust in the right place. I was sure that I would achieve results. By the way . . . where is Carter?'

'Just behind you.'

'Well, well . . . is everything ready for our visit?'

'I boarded up the antiquities,' indicated Carter, 'but our progress may be uncomfortable because of the dust.'

'That is most unfortunate. Are we likely to encounter any other disturbances?'

'Just the wandering soul of a little prince whose last sleep was disturbed by pillagers.'

Davis looked ill at ease.

Christian Jacq

'Carter is joking,' declared Maspero. 'Mummies have no evil power whatsoever.'

The American cast a murderous glance at the Englishman.

29

'Is it sensible, doctor? Such a long journey!'

'It is necessary, Lady Carnarvon. The Earl will recover more quickly if he can benefit from a warm, dry climate in the winter. Egypt will offer him a real cure. He must avoid all risks of bronchitis, otherwise his breathing will become worse and I won't be responsible for his health any more.'

Lady Carnarvon yielded. Up to now, she had always managed to repress her husband's desire to wander. Now that his life itself was at stake, she could not prevent him from leaving.

An icy rain was falling over Highclere. On the previous day, snow had fallen on the high branches of the cedar trees. In the hall of the castle, the Earl was making an inventory of his travel trunks. He was amused to see that his wife had equipped him for an expedition lasting several years.

From a vantage point behind a hanging, she looked at him. His dishevelled sandy hair contrasted with his perfectly cut moustache. His elegant face was lively with obvious delight. The Earl's real mistress, adventure, had reappeared, adorned with a thousand appeals which not even the most affectionate spouse could claim. Nor could the two young children, nor the most beautiful estate in Britain. Carnarvon tightened the belt of his coat. As he kissed his wife, she felt that his mind was already in the land of the pharaohs.

*

Christian Jacq

Opened in 1895, the Bristol was one of the most beautiful hotels in Cairo. Its architecture was like a Victorian cake. It boasted a showy entrance with a colonnade and it met British requirements for comfort and elegance. Throughout his stay Carnarvon had been living a dream worthy of the Thousand and One Nights. His pain was decreasing, his eyesight was improving and his strength was increasing. He enjoyed the air and the sun as if they were delicacies. He spent hours in the streets of Cairo, on foot or in a barouche.

He took part in the Ramadan fast from sunrise to sunset, abstaining from eating, smoking, quarrelling, swearing, lying and envy. The asceticism raised the soul from the material world and opened it to spiritual thoughts. The Earl was not disappointed: a new wish to live took possession of him. He impatiently waited for *iftar*, the end of the fast, when shops closed very quickly and streets emptied while the hundreds of mosques in the town lit up. Lights in the shape of triangles, diamonds or crescents illuminated cupolas and minarets.

Carnarvon stopped in front of an open-air kitchen, lit a cigarette, drank apricot juice and ate heartily of rice with meat, salad and bread full of hot broad beans. Around two o'clock in the morning he was not averse to savouring angel hair or a pistachio pastry, before going back to the hotel and having a lie in, indifferent to the drummers who woke the people so that they could take food before daybreak.

Two days before the end of the Ramadan, an old lady approached him in the hall of the Bristol. 'Are you by any chance the Earl of Carnarvon?'

'I have that honour.'

'Ah! So, my memory is as good as ever . . . I knew your father very well and you look very much like him. What a strange country here, don't you think? Sparse lawns threatened by drought, a tragic absence of showers and a chronic shortage of fog. Do you know Cairo?'

'This is my first visit.'

'You'll come back each year. My dear friend, the town is

130

like a drug. Of course it has changed; there are now too many tourists . . . But tell me, why are you spending the winter here?'

'To heal myself and to give meaning to my life.'

'You should go and excavate! It is said that the ground here conceals marvels. A young man should have an aim and stick to it, even in his leisure time. An idle Englishman betrays his country.

Excavating forgotten treasures – the idea had crossed Carnarvon's mind ever since his childhood, yet he had never succeeded in expressing it clearly. Was the old lady his destiny in disguise? Her words obsessed him. Neglecting streets and festivals, he went round ministries and administrations to enquire about excavations. He very soon realized that only money mattered. A wealthy American, Theodore Davis, had just been given a concession for the Valley of the Kings, although he had no archaeological experience whatsoever.

The Earl was savouring a Nile perch at his table at the Bristol when a colossus with a beard seated himself in front of him, without asking permission. A black frock coat, red trousers and boots with spurs gave him a martial appearance.

'I am afraid you have the wrong table.'

'You are Lord Carnarvon and my name is Demosthenes, at least today. In my job it is wise to change names.'

'Do you mind if I have you chased away?'

'I hear you want to excavate. You don't have a chance.'

Demosthenes' face was yellow and flaccid. His hands were trembling and he sometimes gazed off into the distance. Carnarvon knew the symptoms, having seen them in low-life bars: the man was addicted to hashish.

'If you want to purchase rare objects, get in touch with Demosthenes.'

'Are you well versed in archaeology?'

The colossus stifled a throaty laugh. 'I was an Anglican priest in Cairo. I sold doctored brandy in Alexandria. Now I have discovered a much better occupation: I sell mummies. In good condition too, they come from authentic tombs. They are expensive, but they are worth their price.'

'I don't doubt that. Where do you "discover" them?'

'Careful, prince! My sources are sacred. Let's discuss prices!'

'I agree, but not here.'

'Where?'

'At the nearest police station.'

His lips suddenly bloodless, Demosthenes stood up. 'We have never met. Don't attempt to cause me trouble. We are in Egypt here, not in Britain. Life does not have the same price here.'

'Authentic mummies . . . do they still exist?'

The colossus strode across the restaurant. On his way he bumped into the head waiter, who was bringing some pudding to Carnarvon.

'If I may give you some advice, my Lord, you should not trust this man. He is a corrupt Greek, a robber, a police informer and maybe a murderer.'

'He's been the second good angel in the day. The Greek and the old English lady deserve my eternal gratitude.'

The head waiter left the pudding. In some circumstances, it was better to stick strictly to his job.

Lord Carnarvon pushed away the dessert and gazed at a candle until long after midnight. How sublime it was to see his life move from emptiness and take meaning at last.

30

In 1903, specialists and tourists alike talked only about the discovery of a cache in a courtyard of the temple of Karnak. The French architect Legrain thought it would take several years to bring back to the surface this mass of buried objects once used by the priesthood. The success of the find confirmed Davis in his belief that a really spectacular find was within his reach.

He summoned Carter on his ship, which was moored in Luxor. Nervous, he walked back and forth, pounding the floor with the heels of his boots.

'What really matters, Carter, is the queens of Egypt. If the tombs of their husbands have been plundered, theirs may have remained untouched.'

'Ask for the concession for the Valley of the Queens.'

'It's already ruined. I'm referring to the queens buried in the Valley of the Kings. Are there any?'

Carter nodded.

'The great Hatshepsut fascinates me. It is said that her vault was never properly explored. Is that true?'

Again, the Englishman agreed.

'Enter it, Carter. I am sure it contains a treasure.'

The American had underestimated the difficulties, however. With his team of workers, Carter dug 630 feet under the rock, through an endless corridor, in dust and darkness. Clearing their way with adzes they progressed through a mass of broken pieces which blocked the narrow gallery. The disappointment was as great as the effort had been. In the ruined burial chamber there were only two empty sarcophagi, one for the queen and one for her father Tuthmosis I. When Davis was able to join Carter, thanks to an air pump, the latter was painting a watercolour which gave a faithful reproduction of the derelict appearance of the sacred place.

'It is a great achievement, nevertheless,' he commented. 'I shall publish something about the tomb and mention your courage.'

They shook hands in the American way. What really mattered for Carter, however, was the fact that he had an increasingly well-qualified team of workers at his disposal, whom he could train according to his own views, even though Tutankhamun still escaped him.

'I want to get married,' said Raifa. 'I have talked to my brother for a long time and he has given way to reason. Love cannot be fought.'

'I'm afraid it can be resisted,' objected Carter.

'I have worked and I have the elements of my dowry: pieces of furniture, household goods and sheets. I shall bring all this and you won't be ashamed of me. If you were very poor, you could content yourself with 25 piastres. But you are a respected person, Howard. I owe you a good dowry.'

'On that point, I—'

She laid a finger on his mouth. 'I shall have all hair removed on the eve of our wedding. My brother will play the role of father and ask you to protect me. After your oath, he will give me to my future husband and we will take our places on thrones. In front of us, flowers, pastries, roast meat, spices will be displayed. I want many singers and dancers! This will be the most beautiful wedding ever celebrated in Luxor. People will still mention it in a thousand years.'

She snuggled up to him. The bedroom of the disused harem had been turned into a palace where the most beautiful dreams carried the two lovers away on a bed of roses.

'Are you sure you have convinced Gamal?'

'What does Gamal matter?'

'Remember that he has to play the role of the father.'

'He'll do that. Nobody can resist a woman in love. Not even you, Howard Carter.'

'In the end—'

His questioning face aroused her anger. 'Please take this seriously.'

'I suppose I must.'

Mena House, an old hunting lodge of Khedive Ismail was transformed into a luxury hotel during the celebration of the opening of the Suez Canal in 1869 and welcomed the wealthiest families of Cairo and other distinguished guests. Britain had promoted it to the rank of colony, and the subjects of His Majesty had a doctor, a chaplain and a British nurse as well as a 600-volume library at their disposal.

On a spring evening, Carter was invited to Mena House to celebrate his triumph. The inspector's fame had reached Cairo, where the cream of society had arranged a dinner in his honour. The humble Norfolk draughtsman had become a well known and envied archaeologist, whom dignitaries liked to welcome at their table. The clearing of the great tombs of Queen Hatshepsut and King Meneptah, performed with as much speed as scientific rigour, had turned Howard Carter into the best excavator in operation. He was both proud and sad: proud of the work achieved and of the career ladder he had climbed, proud of practising a profession he adored, but sad to waste his time on society life when his dialogue with the valley was just starting and his search for Tutankhamun demanded all his efforts.

Before going to Mena House, at the foot of the plateau of Giza, he walked towards the Great Pyramid. With a few curt sentences he pushed aside men selling fake antiquities and

Bedouins who wanted to hire out their donkeys and camels. As he raised his eyes towards the summit of the fabulous monument, he remembered the words of Chateaubriand which Newberry had read to him:

> Men did not erect such a sepulchre because of their experience of emptiness, but because of an intuition of their own immortality. The sepulchre is not a monument to a short-lived career. It marks the beginning of life without an end. It is a kind of eternal gate, built on the borders of eternity.

He reluctantly left the great pyramid for the dinner party. He was begged to talk about his feats and people sympathized with him for having to swallow so much dust.

A British lawyer raised a glass of champagne. 'To our new Archimedes! Have you been informed of the latest fabulous find?'

'No, where is it?'

'In Luxor, my dear. It happened in your absence!'

Despite his fear, Carter put up a good show.

'Well, it would be cruel to let you wait any longer. It is a tomb.'

Carter nervously clutched his napkin. 'In the Valley of the Kings?'

'Precisely.'

The whole table became silent.

'Is it a royal tomb?'

'I don't know, but it had never been opened.'

'Do people know what it contains?'

'Yes they do.'

The lawyer went on pompously. 'They do, thanks to three white camels which came out of the vault carrying heaps of gold and jewels!'

Delighted, the audience burst into laughter.

Carter put down his knife and fork and stood up, deathly

pale. 'Excuse me for leaving so early. Stupidity spoils my appetite.'

Drowsy, Raifa coiled up against Carter who stroked her hair and kissed her neck.

'When are we getting married, Howard?'

'Soon.'

'Tomorrow?'

'There are still a few details to settle.'

'My dowry?'

'Maspero. I must talk to him.'

Gaston Maspero was in a jovial mood. He was drinking a cup of coffee and eating bread filled with onions and beans.

'Glad to see you, Carter. Because of you, I haven't slept.'

'May I know the reason for such a misfortune?'

'The quality of your work. You are the most brilliant of my inspectors and your contribution to the service is absolutely remarkable. Your success comes from your relentless work, your excellent training, your knowledge of the field, your command of Arabic, your gift for handling the workers and your acute artistic sense.'

'So many compliments worry me.'

'What do they mean? A promotion, my dear Howard! At the age of thirty you are the right person for a key position: chief inspector for Lower and Middle Egypt. The pyramids are yours!'

31

After six months of relentless work in Saqqara, it was his first evening off. How many acres remained to be excavated in the huge necropolis where Maspero had discovered the first pyramids with secret chambers covered with hieroglyphs? From the modest inspector's house, where he had settled, Howard Carter enjoyed an unequalled view. On one side he could see the desert and the eternal monuments, and on the other the palm grove of ancient Memphis. It was often painful to tear himself away from meditation to immerse himself in the complexities of everyday life. But he was aware of his task and he was intent on fulfilling it to the letter, even though his distance from his dear valley made him suffer.

On the day before his departure for the north, Raifa had thrown herself into his arms in tears. He had not tried to comfort her. They both knew that the separation would be long. Of course Carter would return to Luxor during his holiday. But he could not promise to marry her. Vexed, she promised to be faithful to him. He refused her undertaking, but she did not cancel it.

Solitude suited the site of Saqqara, overlooked by the stepped pyramid of Djoser, the first stone monument erected on Egyptian land. Pharaohs and nobles had been resting here for over five millennia, an invisible community with a lasting reality which could still be perceived.

Seated on a chair, sheltered from the wind, Carter was

thinking of Raifa and of the sweetness and abandon of her embrace, when a warden ran towards him.

'You must come immediately, sir.'

'What is the matter?'

'French people . . . they want to visit the Serapeum.'

'Remind them that the site is closed.'

'They refuse to listen to me.'

'What do you mean, they refuse?'

'I believe . . . that they are out of their minds.'

Annoyed, he sped towards the Serapeum, a network of underground galleries with huge sarcophagi of sacred bulls. In front of the entrance, two wardens were quarrelling with some merry tourists. One of them, a drunk man of some fifty years, called one of them 'dirty Arab' and 'son of a bitch'. Before Carnarvon even had time to intervene, a warden jostled him. A general fight followed to which he put an end with great difficulty.

'Who are you?' asked an aggressive woman with brown dishevelled hair.

'Howard Carter, antiquities inspector.'

'I'm glad to meet someone who is in charge, at last! We wanted to visit the Serapeum when these apes attacked us. They even wanted us to pay for admission.'

'I beg to correct you, madam. The wardens are my subordinates and they obey my orders. You are not allowed to be on the site at this time of the day.'

'You've got an absolute nerve! We are Europeans and our friend has been wildly attacked! We order you to have these savages arrested!'

A man with a moustache, red with anger, shouted like an ill-tempered little back street child. 'I paid and I want to be refunded! It is pitch black inside and we were not even given a light!'

'Go back home and take a cold shower, all of you.'

'I shan't let it rest, Mr Carter! We'll lodge a complaint.'

*

Maspero seemed very embarrassed.

'They lodged a complaint against you, Carter. Aggravated assault . . . this is serious.'

'It is also untrue. My wardens react in the way anyone would if insulted in that odious way.'

'Would anyone attack a French tourist?'

'A dangerous drunkard who was hardly even jostled. I testify in favour of my team.'

'That is no use. Your adversaries have already obtained the support of the Consul-General of France, who demands reparation.'

'I'm afraid I do not understand.'

'It is very simple. Thanks to my intervention, we shall avoid a trial. You will just have to apologize to the Consul and the group of tourists and dismiss your warden.'

'That is out of the question. The drunkards should apologize to the warden. That would be justice.'

'This is not a matter of justice, but of diplomacy! Make my task easier and do not persist.'

'I have no intention of humbling myself before liars.'

'Don't take it like that, damn it! I just beg you to say a few words and nothing else.'

'That is far too much, sir.'

'Don't be stubborn. The matter could get worse.'

'I do not feel I am in the wrong; justice will triumph.'

As Maspero could not obtain Howard Carter's surrender, the plaintiffs requested an interview with Lord Cromer, the British high commissioner, the most powerful man in Egypt. He gave credit to the lie and took sides against Carter. The young archaeologist was not really liked in the higher ranks of his own society.

When Maspero summoned him again, he was very gloomy.

'I have received strict instructions: you must immediately dismiss your warden and present your apologies. Lord Cromer will be here in a few minutes to listen to them.'

'So I shall be able to tell him the truth.'

'He won't listen to you. He's already made up his mind.'

'So he is stupid.'

'Carter! You're not aware of the seriousness of the situation. You must yield, otherwise . . .'

'Otherwise?'

'I shall be obliged to accept your resignation.'

Carter was dumbfounded. 'Gaston Maspero, you're not going to commit such an infamy!'

'It's just a few words, Howard, just a few conciliatory words and we will forget this absurd tragedy.'

Lord Cromer burst into the office. He did not even glance at Carter, but shouted at Maspero, 'Is the matter sealed?'

'Almost, sir.'

'Carter should immediately present his apologies which will be put down on paper and handed over to those concerned.'

There was a heavy silence. Lord Cromer only bore it for a few seconds.

'Are you making a mockery of the authority I represent, Mr Maspero?'

'Howard Carter is ready to acknowledge his wrongdoings, but injustice—'

'My opinion is based on facts and not on feelings. Any further discussion would be superfluous. Carter should either yield or resign.'

Lord Cromer did not hear Howard Carter's voice, but he gave a start when the door slammed.

32

As the cold weather set in at Highclere, Carnarvon's character changed. Usually morose, he whistled as he read or went for a stroll, joked at meals and played more often with his children. Freezing fog and rain made him happier. His pain disappeared and he walked for several hours a day in the park, despite his doctor's protests.

On his return from one of these outings, his wife was not able to conceal her concern any more. 'Your bath is hot. Hurry up and get into it.'

'What care, my dear. According to the peasants, the winter will be very harsh.'

'Why do you take so many risks? Cold and damp are not good for you.'

The Earl lowered his eyes. 'I have to trust you with a very precious secret, Almina.'

'It is not usual for you to be so cautious.'

'The situation requires me to be careful how I express myself.'

'I do not understand . . .'

Carnarvon turned away. 'I have fallen in love. Desperately in love.'

Lady Almina closed her eyes. 'God is asking me to undergo a terrible ordeal, but I accept it. What is her name?'

'She is no longer young.'

'Is she from a noble family at least?'

'From a royal family.'

'But . . . what is her name?'

'Pharaonic Egypt.'

'You had no right to tease me like that.'

'This is extremely serious, my dear. As my excellent doctor advises me, I'm leaving tomorrow for Cairo.'

At the end of 1904, Lord Carnarvon walked again with pleasure in the lively, sweet-smelling streets of Cairo. He had been impatiently waiting for this stay, which now illuminated his existence. It enabled him to escape the numerous social duties of London and to avoid performances of *Madame Butterfly* by Puccini, a whimpering and garrulous musician whom he hated.

The Earl wanted to finalize an excavation plan, but he had no experience whatsoever in the field. Therefore, he consulted the High Commissioner's office, the real master of Egypt, thanks to the Entente Cordiale between France and Britain, which decided the division of North Africa and the Middle East. France had been allotted Morocco, which it occupied in complete freedom, and Britain, Egypt. There was only one restriction, and a considerable one: the position of Director of the Antiquities Service was reserved for a Frenchman, as in the past.

Carnarvon made an appointment with Maspero.

'I would like permission to excavate.'

Maspero wiped his glasses. The nightmare was starting all over again. Once again he would have to bow before a wealthy amateur whose main scientific argument would be the importance of his bank account.

'Nothing is more simple. You only have to sign a form.'

'What are my duties?'

'You have to excavate a piece of land belonging to Egypt, with no buildings, nor cultural interest, free of taxes, outside of a military area, that has not been designated for public utilities. If you make an important discovery, like for instance a tomb, you must inform the service.'

'May I be the first to enter it?'

'On condition that an inspector comes with you. You have two years to give me a report on your activities.'

'What happens to the mummies?'

'They remain the property of Egypt, as do sarcophagi. As for other artefacts, we would make a fair division.'

'What do you mean by "fair"?'

Maspero restrained his anger with difficulty. Of course, a clause in the contract specified that the contents of an undesecrated tomb would not be shared between the man in charge of the excavations and the State. But no untouched tomb would ever be discovered and, in the event of a miracle, the clause would be inapplicable.

'Well . . . depending on the importance and value of the objects, we would come to a gentlemen's agreement.'

'Nothing seems fairer,' conceded Carnarvon.

'I forgot the main point: the excavations will be done at your own expenses and risks.'

'Agreed.'

'One last detail: which site do you want?'

The Earl was caught off guard. 'You won't believe it, but I haven't even thought about it. This is my second winter in Egypt and I only know Cairo. Can you suggest a suitable place?'

Maspero was dumbfounded. 'Anywhere, sir. You could dig anywhere . . . Luxor is an attractive place, much liked by your fellow countrymen, and the region is not lacking in unexplored areas.'

Carnarvon followed Maspero's advice. He loitered in the ancient city of Thebes. Like other visitors he was reduced to the state of a Lilliputian in front of the huge columns of Karnak. He enjoyed the light of Luxor, sailed the Nile in a felucca, meditated under the acacia of the Ramesseum, experienced the greatness of the pharaohs in Medinet Habu, and marvelled hundreds of times as he looked at the paintings in the tombs. Egypt penetrated him, moulded his soul and brought forth a new sensitivity. Before he began excavating, he wanted to absorb the beauty which time could not erode and which offered unequalled nourishment.

He was savouring a mint tea in a tavern on the west bank, when a colossus with a beard greeted him, doffing his white hat.

'Mr Demosthenes, what a pleasant surprise!'

'May I sit down?'

'I can see that you've learnt some manners.'

With his black jacket, his red trousers and his high boots, the antiquities trafficker could hardly escape notice.

'You are a man of his word, sir, because you haven't caused me any trouble.'

'I am indebted to you.'

'I didn't lend you any money.'

'This is a moral debt.'

'Ah . . . this is unimportant. Did you come to buy mummies?'

'I came to find some.'

'Where?'

'In the depths of the earth.'

'You want to dig! Are you joking? You'll lose your money. I have everything you might need and at a good price. This country is rotten.'

'Britain will clean it up.'

'Certainly not. The new law enforces the closure of insalubrious and dangerous premises . . . that is to say it will cause general bankruptcy! Local manufacturers and workshops are done with. International organizations will take their place and provoke a discontent which will turn out badly. Trade, that's our future! Enjoy your winter holiday. Egypt won't be British for ever. Please forgive me, I am expected elsewhere.'

The increasingly fat Demosthenes stood up like an elephant and walked away, swaying from side to side. Was he a madman or a visionary? Nobody shared his views at the Foreign Office. But do not diplomats spend their time being wrong?

33

Lying near some slumbering beggars, Howard Carter was no longer an inspector in the Antiquities Service. Lord Cromer had demanded and obtained his head, compelling Maspero to dismiss him. Fifteen years of relentless work was abruptly ended in this knockout blow. Unemployed, with neither money nor savings, unable to find another job, Carter felt crushed. The loss of his position took him away from the Valley of the Kings and Tutankhamun for ever. His dream was crumbling and his life was losing its meaning. Yet he did not regret his attitude. Injustice was evil and he would never accept it.

A man of middle height, dressed in the Western fashion, with a round face and a moustache, stopped in front of him. 'Are you by any chance Howard Carter?'

'I am nothing now.'

'My name is Ahmed Ziuar . . . You were my guide in Saqqara. You know my country better than I do. I almost believe you love it more. I heard about your misfortune. Allow me to express my admiration of your courage, Mr Carter.'

Incredulous, the Englishman raised his eyes.

'Where do you intend to stay in Cairo?'

'I don't know.'

'I am only a humble civil servant, but I have a spare room. I would be very happy to offer it to you. You will be able to sleep, regain your strength and prepare for the future. When God closes a door, he opens another one.'

Carter stood up. He had no right to appear unworthy in front of a man of such quality.

At the corner of a street, Carter observed the comings and goings of the people of Cairo, a water carrier, a man selling bread, a housewife with a basket on her head and a baby in her arms, a donkey loaded with alfalfa. In an attempt to forget himself, he painted these trivial scenes, a precious testimony to a monotonous but reassuring life. Strollers and boys gathered round him and looked at him while he was working. A European man even offered him some money. After some initial reluctance, he accepted it. Now a genre painter he earned the money necessary to pay the rent for his little room in a poor area. On the top floor of a flaking building, it offered a haven of peace after a day spent in the constant noise of the town. Barking dogs often disturbed the night. Lying on his bed with his eyes wide open, he remembered the marvellous time when he worked on grandiose sites and he was overwhelmed by nostalgia. He went back to Saqqara, painted the stepped pyramid, the desert, the beautiful scenes in the tombs of the Old Kingdom. Tourists liked his paintings and watercolours. Not content with selling these insignificant works, he guided them in places that were formerly under his protection. His reputation increased and he was soon a mentor appreciated by the most attentive visitors.

His art and tips did not turn him into a millionaire, but he learnt to make do with little and dressed impeccably to conceal his poverty. He often wrote to Raifa and tore up the letters, for he could not bear the idea of telling her the truth. He wanted her to retain in her memory the image of a happy and respected Carter.

As the months went by, another occupation developed. Credulous buyers asked him to assess statuettes or fragments of relief they found in the souks. Most of them were forgeries, but some were authentic. Carter's reputation spread. He was even consulted during transactions.

He spent most of his spare time at the foot of the stepped pyramid, fascinated by the austerity of the mother of all Egyptian architecture. His numerous sketches did not satisfy him. How could he express the vigour of the huge stone steps stretching out to the sky?

The sand crunched. What sounded like a tourist came and stood behind him.

'Your talent has remained, Howard.'

Gaston Maspero's voice made him shiver.

'How are you, sir?'

'I have been told that you survive.'

'You've been well informed. Is the service developing well?'

'It is at a virtual standstill without you. Amateurs get the better of us.'

'Are you referring to Theodore Davis by any chance?'

'His team is proud of his latest feat: the discovery of an untouched tomb.'

The brush quivered. 'With a treasure?'

'A beautiful funerary set of furniture: chests, chairs, vases and two large coffins containing the well-preserved mummies of the parents of Queen Tiy.'

Queen Tiy, the wife of Amenhotep III and the mother of the heretic king, Akhenaton . . . these people had met young Tutankhamun, whose shadow had just brushed against him. Tiy may even have been his mother.

'Davis wants to publish something, but he can't. This is why he asked me to help him. I agreed, but I need a draughtsman. Would you accept the task, Howard?'

Davis and his team, among whom figured a young archaeologist called Burton, occupied a small house at the entrance of the little west valley of the Valley of the Kings. Built in stone and adobe, in the shadow of the cliff, it was invisible to the eyes of visitors. Four little bedrooms, a dining room, a storeroom for antiquities, a darkroom, a study and a kitchen formed the dwelling over which a warden constantly kept watch. The American received Carter in one of the cells without water or electricity. Dressed in black, he looked like an exterminating angel.

'You owe it to me to return to Luxor. In exchange, I ask for the utmost discretion. You will draw, but you won't intervene in the excavations. You are no longer an inspector and I have formed a skilful team which does not need any advice. In addition, I do not want any trouble. The British authorities would not appreciate your presence here. Shut yourself up in the study Maspero has put at your disposal and content yourself with reproducing faithfully the objects my assistants will bring you. Any comment?'

'No.'

The winter of 1906 was similar to all other winters: mild, quiet and sunny. Carter's wealth did not improve. Some expert evaluations in transactions concerning artefacts of more or less licit origin brought him enough money. His main, unpaid, occupation consisted in drawing the sumptuous pieces of wooden furniture discovered by Davis in the tomb of the in-laws of Amenhotep III. He did not expect these high dignitaries of humble origin to be present in the valley, which had been reserved for pharaohs. This anomaly reinforced his idea that the Egyptians had given great emphasis to the period preceding Tutankhamun's coming to power. Why had his reign been eclipsed and his tomb concealed with so much care?

When the nights became cold, he wrapped himself in a woollen blanket and read the scientific documents which Maspero had put at his disposal. He was often furious at the poor workmanship of other archaeologists. As for historians, they seldom checked their sources, contenting themselves with an accumulation of publications so as to obtain the academic chairs distributed according to their production of printed paper and their social relations. Competence, courage and honesty were stupid virtues which led to social mediocrity.

Someone knocked on his door.

'It's open.'

She entered, as beautiful as ever. Her eyes made up, her lips glistening with a light red, her black hair spread in curls over her shoulders, she stood still on the threshold. 'Are you pleased to see me?'

'Raifa . . .'

He was unable to move. She stepped forward without stopping to look at him.

'Am I pretty?'

He took her in his arms and hugged her tightly.

'I am nothing, Raifa. I have lost my position as an inspector and I am poor.'

'I don't care . . . If you only knew how little I care!'

'Gamal will never accept a beggar as a husband for his sister.'

'I shall content myself with being your mistress . . . I love you, Howard.'

Words gave way to hugs. How many hours of love had they lost because of his vanity?

The worker leaned forward, took away a big stone and dug slowly with his hand. At the foot of the rock, in a hollow, he had seen something like a flash of lightning. The rays of the sun had been reflected on a glistening surface. As he bent, he believed that he had seen a blue line between two pieces of limestone. Once cleared, it turned out to be the rim of a glazed dish, once covered with gold.

The worker called his boss, who informed Theodore Davis. The American considered the artefact disdainfully.

'It does not deserve a photograph. Take it to Carter. He will make a drawing. Then we shall send it to the Museum of Cairo. We should present them with something from time to time.'

Leaving the group of tourists with which he had mingled, Carter examined the place where the blue faience dish had been removed from the earth. To his mind, it had probably contained balls of natron, used as a purifying substance in the ritual of the opening of the mouth which restored life to the mummy, that is to say during a royal funeral! His first investigation confirmed his conviction: it was a cache. A priest had taken the trouble to conceal the precious object under a rock.

He had been vainly trying to draw it for the last three days, but his hands trembled too much. On the dish figured a text: 'May the perfect god give life.'

The hieroglyphs in the cartouche[5], the sun, the basket and the scarab, followed by the three sticks of the plural read: 'Divine light rules transformation[6].' Insignificant as they were to Davis, these few signs disturbed Carter to the point that he could not sleep; were they not the enthronement name of Tutankhamun?

Now his personal conviction began to look more scientific. The modest artefact proved that the mysterious pharaoh's funeral had taken place in the valley and that he was buried there, somewhere under the sand.

[5] Cartouche is the technical term for the more or less oblong oval, in which is written the name of the Pharaoh.
[6] Technical transcription: *Neb Kheperon Rê*. This is one of the names of Tutankhamun, each pharaoh possessing several names indicating the meaning of his sacred mission.

34

Lord Carnarvon attended the opening of the Winter Palace, the latest luxury hotel in Luxor. Built in the heart of the little town, in front of the Nile, it pretentiously displayed a yellow façade which stood out clearly against the green of palm trees and the white of the mosque and nearby houses. The Earl did not really appreciate the mass of stucco and plaster covering a metal frame. Luxor had become prey to salesmen and stupid hordes. A Baedeker guide in one hand, tourists invaded shops full of fake scarabs, fans and hats. Groups hurriedly disembarked from ships chartered by Cook-type travel agencies, rushed up and down temples at the double and, at the call of a whistle or a bell, climbed on board again and dressed for lunch.

Carnarvon, now nicknamed Lordy, contented himself with a yachtsman's jacket with copper buttons. It gave him a martial appearance belied by his kindness to the natives. Avoiding Europeans, he was the guest of all the local pashas. He learned to know Egypt from inside and was soon able to get by in Arabic. Such preliminaries seemed essential before he could launch into excavations properly.

'If you still want a concession,' declared Maspero, 'I can offer you one: an unexplored site at the top of the hill of Sheikh Abd el Gurnah. With a bit of luck, you might be able to discover a small tomb. Don't forget to inform me.'

'Luck is smiling at me,' answered Carnarvon. 'When can I start?'

'As soon as next week, if you want.'

'All right. I'll cancel an appointment and go immediately to the west bank.'

The Foreign Office civil servant who worked in Luxor under the cover of a grain merchant was angry at what he felt to be a waste of his time. It was not that the Earl refused to pass on his impressions about the country, but that he did not agree to be in his pay.

Lordy was not charmed by the Sheikh Abd el Gurnah site and there was nothing engaging about the hot sun, the dust, the sand-filled wind or the amused smiles of the villagers. As he started to dig, the aristocrat realized that it was not easy to act as archaeologist. Why should he choose this place rather than that one? Relying on his instinct, he gave the order to his two workmen to remove a big flat stone and to drive the iron part of their spades, the *fâs*, into the slope. When they were tired, he took their place.

Handling the tool almost broke his back, but it attracted the workers' friendship. After they had shared bread, onions and tomatoes, they displayed a new enthusiasm. In addition, Lordy had a valuable ally: his female terrier Susie, who had refused to leave her master. Carnarvon had taken her to Egypt so as not to betray her affection. He relied on her sense of smell and her ability to follow a prey as far as its den. But Susie, with her ears flapping near her cheeks, had lost all aggressiveness and did not like anything so much as settling comfortably against Lordy's legs, while he sat in a wicker chair, sheltered from the dust. Extremely jealous, she did not allow anyone to approach him without her consent.

Shortly before sunset, the *fellahin* came across what looked like the opening of a funerary pit. As excited as the Earl, they could hardly restrain their enthusiasm to dig deeper. By the following morning, a delegate from the Antiquities Service had come. As disappointed as Carnarvon, he saw that the unfinished pit appeared to lead to an empty hole.

But since fate had given him a sign, the Earl did not lose

heart. For six weeks, he worked relentlessly at the site of his first success. The pit was linked to a tomb and, despite clouds of sand, profuse sweat and a certain stiffness, the Earl slid into the cavity. A workman handed him a torch, which shed light on a small coffin with the mummy of a cat inside. Susie showed moderate disapproval.

Carnarvon was aware of the insignificance of his feat. Hundreds of feline corpses already cluttered the storerooms of museums. Yet this insubstantial beginning prompted him to pursue his investigation in the great flat expanse in front of the temple of Deir el Bahari: he dug holes here and there, under an increasingly oppressive heat, without the slightest result.

'This will be the fourth winter you've spent in Egypt, my dear . . . Aren't you weary?'

'On the contrary, Almina.'

'What attracts you?'

'A most important task.'

'Those amateur excavations?'

'Amateur . . . you're right. I should put an end to such a ridiculous practice.'

Lord Carnarvon's wife seized his arm. 'Does that mean that you will forget about your trip and stay at Highclere?'

'It means that I want to become professional.'

'Are you satisfied with your archaeological occupations, sir?'

'Not at all, Mr Maspero.'

The Director of the Antiquities Service frowned. Worries had been cropping up over the last few months. The new inspectors did not have Carter's qualities and the antiquities traffic was picking up. There were numerous criticisms of the French scientist. People accused him of giving too much importance to history, neglecting archaeology, granting permission for wild digs without checking the qualifications of the applicants, and letting artefacts leave for foreign museums.

'Have you been bothered by anyone?'

154

'I think you overestimated me. Despite being the Earl of Carnarvon, I do not possess the knowledge and, least of all, the necessary technique to carry through my endeavour to a successful conclusion. I am not satisfied with unearthing cats' mummies. I intend to work in a serious professional way.'

'Your team of workers . . .'

'They obey my orders. As these are worthless, they content themselves with digging holes which lead to nothing. Forget I'm a wealthy aristocrat for a moment and give me the technical assistance I need.'

Maspero took his glasses off, wiped them slowly and scribbled a name on a piece of blotting paper. He hesitated to utter it. Did Carnarvon feel a real passion or was he just a butterfly fluttering from one occupation to the next?

'I know an Egyptologist who might be useful to you.'

'Is he experienced?'

'He's been working in Egypt for over fifteen years. He speaks Arabic, he is able to command teams and he knows everything about local customs.'

'What is the name of this gem?'

'Howard Carter.'

'One thing intrigues me. Why is such a brilliant man not one of your collaborators?'

'He was, I am proud to say. Carter was destined for a great career, but his stubborn nature and lack of tact led him to go too far.'

'Did you dismiss him?'

'I did, under protest, because he refused to submit to an administrative obligation.'

'What kind of administrative obligation?'

'He was told to apologize to a group of French tourists, who had been guilty of loutish behaviour, but who enlisted the support of the British high commissioner.'

'Your Carter sounds rather likeable. Do you think there is a chance he might take to me?'

'I cannot guarantee that.'

'How does he survive?'

'Rather poorly. He sells a few paintings, does expert evaluations and contributes to scientific papers for the glory of it. But do not consider him as easy prey.'

'Where does he live?'

'In Luxor. Do you want to see him?'

'Yes, today.'

35

Shortly after 6 p.m., Carter entered the hall of the Luxor Hotel. Maspero had insisted he leave his study to come there at the invitation of a certain Lord Carnarvon. According to the director of the service, the rich aristocrat needed him. Carter did not believe a word of it. He was probably one more pretentious amateur, greedy for statues and mummies, who wanted technical advice on his latest purchases. Carnarvon was no better than Theodore Davis, who was becoming increasingly incompetent as his excavations in the Valley of the Kings progressed without any real plan.

A frail, almost emaciated man in a blue suit approached the archaeologist. 'I presume that you are Mr Carter. I am the Earl of Carnarvon.'

Beside the aristocrat was a rather hostile-looking black and white terrier.

Carter nodded. The tired-looking man leaned on a stick. His right hand slid in the pocket of a crumpled jacket, he talked with some difficulty. The lower part of his face bore the mark of an old injury.

'Let's sit down.'

'I appreciate your invitation, but I would like our meeting to be as brief as possible. My work is waiting.'

'Thank you for giving me a few minutes of your precious time, Mr Carter. I hope that you won't be disappointed.'

The Luxor Hotel was a British enclave where tourists

enjoyed the services of a British doctor and nurse, could play British billiards and ride bicycles seated on British saddles.

The waiter brought two glasses of port and a bowl of water for Susie.

'You are the best archaeologist in your generation, Mr Carter, and the one who knows Egypt best. It's unfair to see you deprived of excavations.'

'Doesn't injustice rule the world? Maspero must have told you my story.'

'Talent deserves to be rewarded. Would you like to work with me?'

'I don't think so.'

Carnarvon remained calm. 'I may as well tell you that I am a cripple, Mr Carter. Before my car accident, I sailed the seas and I did not shrink from any adventure. Now I am unable to manage on my own.'

'Do you need a porter for your suitcases? In that case, I'm afraid I will be unfit for the position.'

'I can see you're not a man to kowtow.'

'I'm getting worse as time goes by.'

'Yet will you agree at least to listen to me?'

'My expert evaluations are not free.'

'I am not a tourist. Egypt has become a passion which illuminates my existence. I spend each winter here. And I love it more each winter.'

'I'm glad for you.'

'That is not enough for me. I'm convinced that there are still treasures buried under the ground.'

'Here we go . . . Do you like digging holes?'

'I started to do so, but I need an expert like you, Mr Carter.'

'What is your real aim?'

'I want to create the most beautiful private collection of Egyptian antiquities. My castle in Highclere is worthy of sheltering works of art unearthed from this unrivalled land. I want the best as well as the most beautiful things.'

'That would be a considerable investment.'

'It is easier to get money than an authentic statue. I have scoured all the shops and I have only found fakes or knick-knacks. As robbing the Museum of Cairo is not in line with my principles, the only thing I could do was to obtain a concession.'

'Where?'

'On the west bank. Sheikh Abd el Gurnah, Deir el Bahari . . . it was a fiasco.'

Carter smiled. 'That is just a lack of technique, sir. The bank of the dead is wild and implacable. You must tame it and learn its language without disturbing its serenity.'

'You are becoming mystical.'

'If you do not understand that, go back to England. Egypt is a secret, four-millennia-old world. We are intruders. We are in too much of a hurry and we do not know anything. Forget about your collection.'

Carter stood up.

'You're not drinking your port. It is an excellent vintage.'

'Life is not easy on excavation sites. I caught a stomach complaint and I do not drink alcohol before dinner.'

'We agree on that point. My physician forbade me to drink before dinner. Maybe we could chat by the Nile. You'll forgive me for my slowness; I limp.'

Lord Carnarvon was already standing. Susie showed her agreement to a walk.

They moved slowly along the divine river.

'I know about your passion, Carter.'

The attack surprised him.

'Have you made inquiries about me?'

'I do not hire a collaborator without giving the matter proper consideration. Your colleague Georges Legrain has just unearthed a document which should interest you: it is a stele whose text was composed by Tutankhamun. The unknown monarch states that he came back to Thebes after

159

the heresy and restored traditional religious practices, so as to bring back happiness and prosperity.'

A long silence set in, as they walked slowly along the bank. The revelation confirmed definitively the existence of Pharaoh Tutankhamun, which some Egyptologists continued to deny. He even appeared to have been a powerful monarch, who was able to rule and be obeyed.

'The tomb of Tutankhamun – that is your obsession, Mr Carter. Everyone knows about it in Luxor, but everyone mocks you.'

'Do you follow them?'

'Please agree to work with me; you can search for your tomb and for beautiful objects for my collection.'

'That is unrealistic.'

'Why?'

'Because my tomb lies in the Valley of the Kings, whose concession has been granted to Theodore Davis.'

'That is merely an assumption, Mr Carter. Your Tutankhamun may be elsewhere. That is probably why his last dwelling has not yet been identified.'

These were precisely the words Carter was afraid to hear.

'Our life has meaning only if it is devoted to some impossible task. For you, that is a vanished king and for me buried treasures. If we combined our passions, we might have lives which make sense.'

The river was slumbering and, in the darkness on the west bank, the summit was watching over the valley.

'I shall go back to my painting. The rest does not interest me any more.'

'What a peculiar man you are, Carter! Theodore Davis is a pretentious and tyrannical man. You believe that I am like him. You're wrong.'

'You are rich and I am poor.'

'You are very knowledgeable and I do not know anything. I shall take care of finance and you will take care of excavations.'

'Davis hired a young archaeologist who has to obey the whims of his employer.'

'It is meaningless to compare a New World billionaire with a British Earl, brought up in the first tradition. I must repeat to you that you are the one who will manage our team. Nobody else will do it. But I need results.'

Carter shook his head. 'I don't believe in miracles any more. My watercolours are enough for me.'

Carnarvon put his stick in front of Carter, preventing him from moving any further. Susie sat between them.

'Your refusal means that you have no confidence in your ability.'

The archaeologist turned red. 'I know the west bank better than anyone else. It has become my homeland.'

'Prove it.'

When Carter had played in the countryside with his young companions, they viewed all noblemen liars and exploiters. He had promised himself that he would never become the servant of one of these people.

'You are blocking my way, Lord Carnarvon.'

'I beg you to cease your stupid internal dialogue and to fulfil your vocation.'

'I beg you' – the owner of Highclere Castle was 'begging' him, Howard Carter, a painter and a dismissed archaeologist, an exile without wealth!

'With a character like yours, life must be a daily fight. I like that, Mr Carter. Go on being uncompromising and ruthless with yourself. Otherwise I shall find you boring. Director of the Carnarvon mission: how do you like the title?'

The prospect of being able to excavate again, of not collapsing under the weight of material worries, of demonstrating that his methods were adequate and being able to search for Tutankhamun again . . . Carter bit his lips, avoiding answering. Susie moved away from her master for a while and laid her nose against Carter's right calf. The Earl smiled.

Christian Jacq

'There is a last point, and a major one,' he continued. 'I have a weapon which you lack from time to time. Without it, you are condemned to decline. I am ready to offer it to you.'

'What is it?'

'Luck.'

162

36

The cedarwood ceilings were decorated with hundreds of Koran suras. The extraordinarily fine designs were the work of a dozen sculptors who had worked themselves to death for more than fifty years.

'Do you like my house, Mr Carter?'

'I admire it.'

Touched by the compliment, Ahmed Bey Kamal put his right eye to the astronomical telescope which enabled him to look at the moon rising during Ramadan.

'This old house is propitious to meditation. That is why I keep the books and documents here which I inherited from my family.'

Ahmed Bey Kamal was a modest, erudite man who delighted in the study of rare documents. Rather taciturn, he seldom opened his door to visitors.

'Why did you come to disturb my solitude, Mr Carter?'

The Englishman hesitated. Under certain circumstances, sincerity might be confused with boorishness. But he did not know how to lie. 'Rumour says that you are about to publish a surprising book.'

'Here is its exact title: *The Book of Buried Beads, the Mystery of Vital Information, Caches, Finds and Treasures.* Rumour also claims that you are a tomb robber.'

Carter stood up, outraged. 'I'm an archaeologist and I want to bring a forgotten pharaoh back to light. Is that a sin?'

Ahmed Bey Kamal's tone softened. 'What do you want to know?'

'Does the book mention the existence of a carefully concealed royal tomb?'

The scholar consulted his manuscript. 'Tradition refers to a tomb hidden in the mountain. Whoever reaches the place will have to fumigate it and dig into the ground. He will discover a plate with a bronze ring which he will lift. Then he will walk down a gallery through three doors. The last one opens on to a spacious room with twelve cupboards full of silver coins, weapons and precious artefacts. In front of the largest one, a gem sheds light as if it were a lighted lamp. There is a key near it. Whoever uses it to open the cupboard will experience heavenly joy. A king will appear to him on an ebony bed decorated with gold and inlaid with pearls. All the riches of Egypt will be gathered around the corpse.'

Carter's hands were trembling. 'Is the manuscript more specific?'

'I'm afraid it isn't.'

'Is there any geographical clue? A name of a pharaoh?'

Ahmed Bey Kamal shook his head negatively.

Carter set up house on a platform overlooking a crossroads, some twenty minutes' walk from the Valley of the Kings. The modest square brick dwelling opened on to the site of Dra Abul el Naga. Built in the desert, tombs and temples retained the memory of a vanished splendour. The peasants respected the limit of arable land as if it were a sacred boundary.

The archaeologist woke early. He left his bedroom with its dome-shaped ceiling and opened the door, an authentic piece of furniture from an English cottage with a trusty Suffolk lock. When he had fed on dried fruit, tea, bread and a sunrise he never tired of, he walked to Deir el Bahari which he had elected to be the first site for Carnarvon's excavations.

On this morning of the tenth day of work, the slow procession of people bearing baskets of rubble started again.

On Carter's orders, they dug, cleared away and tipped the broken pieces away from the excavation ground. Carnarvon arrived by mid-morning. Leaning on his stick, his right hand in the pocket of his grey suit, he observed the comings and goings of the workers. With military rigour, Carter summarized the work of the previous day.

'This country will never lack for dust.'

'Nor tombs, Lord Carnarvon. I believe that we are getting close.'

'Near a vault already?'

'Didn't you ask for results?'

'I have learnt to be patient. Should I admit that you surprise me?'

'Don't be too optimistic. The entrance has just been cleared. May I ask you to enter an intact tomb as its rightful owner?'

The vault held several sarcophagi: one of them, a shiny white, was covered with a veil. At its foot was a wreath of flowers. Moved, Carnarvon picked it up.

'It means that the deceased's resurrection was successful,' explained Carter.

'Mine too.'

Carter hurried his donkey into the Valley of the Kings. The year 1907 was beginning badly, for Theodore Davis's team was boasting about the discovery of an extraordinary tomb. Whenever he heard that sort of news, Carter immediately went to the site.

In his dusty suit, Davis was standing in front of the entrance. Planted on his short legs, with his fierce moustache, he shouted at the intruder. 'Unless anything has changed, Carter, you are no more an inspector in the service. Your presence here is unnecessary. Don't you know that you have been replaced by Weigall?'

'He is incompetent. Whose tomb is it?'

The American's round face smiled. 'I like queens and queens like me. Look, my friend, look!'

The former lawyer nervously cleared broken pieces of stone and ducked to enter a corridor where wood panels covered with a thin layer of gold lay.

'These are extremely damaged. They should be renovated urgently, otherwise they will crumble to dust.'

'Let's move on, Carter. There are more interesting things to see.'

A gold coffin was resting on the ground of the burial chamber. Inlaid with semiprecious stones, it had lost its face. People had been careful to prevent any identification.

'This is Queen Tiy, the royal wife of Amenhotep III and the mother of the heretical Akhenaton! This is the most beautiful thing ever found in the valley!'

'That is a hasty conclusion, Mr Davis. You should note the position of artefacts and photograph them without neglecting the slightest detail—'

'I am in charge and this is my tomb. Clear off.'

Carter gave the tomb the number 55. Despite his advice, Davis had run the excavation disastrously. He had made no archaeological report, no attempt at renovation and, to crown it all, he had even proceeded to 'tidying up' before taking photographs! This was an official type of vandalism which Maspero and his inspectors did not punish.

When a petty thief in Gurnah offered him a jar full of gold leaves and part of the golden necklace of the mummy, Carter knew that he had an opportunity for revenge. He bought the objects at a good price and went to see Davis, whose rest he disturbed.

'You annoy me, Carter!'

The Englishman put the precious relics at his foot. 'These are for sale.'

'Where did you get them?'

'Members of your team rob you and plunder the tombs you are excavating. I'm bringing back your possessions.'

Davis lit a cigarette and burnt his forefinger as he forgot to blow the match out. 'I . . . I'll buy them from you!'

'Your contribution is most welcome.'

When Carter turned on his heel and walked away, the American attempted to keep him.

'I rely on your discretion.'

'Why?'

'My reputation . . . that of my team . . .'

Carter turned back and looked him straight in the face.

'I need the truth. Who is in the sarcophagus?'

Davis clenched his fists.

'Experts contradict themselves. Some of them think it is the body of a man. Others think it is the body of a woman . . . As for me, I am sure that it is Queen Tiy.'

Carter seized Davis by the lapels of his jacket. 'Is there any proof, anything at all, which makes it possible to identify Tutankhamun?'

'Let go of me! No I swear to you there isn't!'

Carter released his grip.

'Will you keep silent?' asked the American in a broken voice.

'I despise you, Davis.'

Carnarvon dusted off his suit and struck a pose. 'Do I look acceptable?'

'You look perfect, sir,' said Carter. 'Let me know as soon as you become too warm.'

'I may not have time to do that. If I fall, you'll know that I have collapsed. Susie will alert you.'

Sitting at his easel, the Englishman was sketching a portrait of his employer on the site of Deir el Bahari, by the side of the second tomb he had just discovered for the owner of Highclere. According to Carnarvon, it was only a kind of cowshed where a small landlord had stored his account books and sheltered his donkey from the sun. But it was a promising beginning.

37

Carnarvon and Carter had dinner at the Luxor Hotel. The autumn of 1907 was mild and luminous.

'The pigeon is a bit hard, isn't it, my dear Howard? And you have no appetite. Does the Valley of the Kings weigh down on your stomach?'

'Davis is an iconoclast.'

'His reputation keeps growing. A new tomb a year is a good score.'

Carter stuck his knife into the grilled pigeon. At this rate, he was afraid that the American might accidentally find Tutankhamun's tomb and spoil it with his usual carelessness.

'Davis accumulates a number of broken pieces and he has no respect whatsoever for Egyptian art. If he goes on, he will end up destroying the whole site.'

'Why don't we ask for the concession for the valley?'

'Maspero will never give it to us. Davis pays far too much money and he gets excellent results.'

'You're still obsessed by your Tutankhamun . . . Incidentally, what does his name men?'

'"Living symbol of the hidden god".'

'"Living" sounds rather encouraging, but hidden is more annoying. How long did he rule?'

'Nine or ten years.'

'Was he married?'

'To a daughter of Akhenaton.'

168

'Did they have children?'

'Probably not.'

'Any outstanding deeds?'

'Nothing that is known, except the stele discovered by Legrain, this year. Tutankhamun is represented as a powerful, fair and generous monarch.'

'The usual praise . . . Why did he disappear from history?'

Carter had again come up against this insoluble problem. 'I am sure that he rests in the valley.'

'Without diverting you from your ideal, dear Howard, I would like you to think more about our mutual exploration. I am impatient to see some beautiful statues in the corridors of Highclere.'

While his archaeologist was running the excavations, the Earl of Carnarvon was meeting a starchy tourist from London in a reception room of the Winter Palace. He was the only one who knew that the man was from the Foreign Office, an affiliation usually displayed with ostentation. The interview the man had asked for was well justified. In a village in the Delta, some British officers who had come to shoot pigeons had missed and killed an old peasant woman. The incident had given rise to a riot, followed by severe repression. Calm usually returned fairly quickly in these cases. But this time, people's reactions were hardening and relations between the Egyptian government and the British administration were worsening. Mustafa Kamil, a journalist with a French – that is to say an anarchist – training, had begun reorganizing a National Party, which demanded the evacuation of British troops. Fortunately, he had died before he had been able to spread further unrest.

The man's account of these events gave Carnarvon cause for concern. As for Susie, she was baring her teeth.

'Such tragedies augur serious trouble,' he prophesied.

'But our high commissioner, Lord Cromer, restored order.'

'With an unacceptable level of violence which will generate further violence.'

'Do you think that his action—'

'Cromer is narrow minded and he does not understand anything about the development of the country. His departure would be excellent news.'

'The idea has been considered in high places. As an expert . . .'

'I am very much in favour of it.'

'What do you advocate for the future?'

'Make concessions.'

'Latitudirianism is no policy.'

'Nor is repression.'

Disturbed, the emissary cut short his holiday. The situation seemed more dangerous than he had imagined.

Theodore Davis' assistants called their employer. Having cleared a vault which, as the result of the heavy rains that sometimes lashed the valley, was full to the ceiling with dried mud, they had just extracted a figurine and a wooden box without any writing. Even though it was broken, it was the American's privilege to take out the gold leaves it contained.

Davis pulled a face. A minute tomb, a modest treasure . . . As he gathered the pieces of gold leaf, a pharaoh appeared on his cart and then he saw the same king smashing the head of a Libyan with his club under the encouragement of his wife.

'This is rather mediocre work,' he reckoned. 'What do the hieroglyphs mean?'

Nobody was able to decipher them.

'We could ask Carter to help,' suggested one of his assistants.

Davis did not hesitate. He had promised the Englishman he would inform him of the most important discoveries, so it was better to let him know without delay. Moreover, he would be able to translate the text.

Howard Carter rushed up. As he looked at the gold leaves, he immediately identified work of the Eighteenth Dynasty.

His voice caught in his throat when he read the name of the pharaoh who was both a warrior and a hunter.

'Tutankhamun . . .'

For the tenth time, Carter explained to Carnarvon that the statuette, the wooden box and the gold leaves had been stolen from the tomb of Tutankhamun and dropped in a disused vault, to which the archaeologist had given the number 58.

'Here are Tutankhamun and his wife, splendid and beaming, under my very eyes . . . There is no doubt this time! The king is in the valley. And it is the incompetent Davis who is getting nearer to him!'

'I do not want to shake your faith, Howard, but these small gold artefacts tend to prove that a royal vault has been plundered rather than preserved. To my mind, this is a false clue.'

'Can you even dare think that?'

'I'm afraid I may be right.'

'I cannot believe that you are.'

In the days that followed, Carter displayed an energy which exhausted his workers. Baskets were filled and emptied in vain. After a promising beginning, the expedition was becoming bogged down. As he tackled the lower part of a hill where masses of broken pieces of limestone made him expect a filled up grave, Carter came upon the mocking Davis. His hat stuck on his head and his white scarf contrasting with his black suit, the American swayed from side to side, as if he were drunk. Carter straightened his bow tie and faced him. Davis played at tracing circles in the sand with his stick.

'You are a good sort, Howard. Since you held your tongue, I am keeping my promise.'

'Have you discovered a new tomb?'

The American smiled fiercely. 'What excellent intuition you have.'

Beads of sweat formed on Carter's forehead. 'Is it intact?'

'More or less.'

'Is it a king?'

'This one.'

Davis pulled out of his pocket a piece of cloth on which was written: 'Tutankhamun, in the year 6'. The mysterious pharaoh was gradually emerging from the darkness.

'Where does this cloth come from?'

The American lifted his stick, like a music master. 'Haven't you understood yet? From the tomb of Tutankhamun, of course!'

'That is impossible!' shouted Carter, wounded to the depth of his heart.

'Come on, you must face facts. Come and visit your famous tomb. I'll go first.'

38

Suddenly as agile as in his best years, Davis took Carter to the hill overlooking the tomb of Seti II. Workmen were keeping watch by the side of his new tomb.

As nervous as he was intrigued, the Englishman held back tears of despair.

'Come in Howard, and look for yourself.'

Carter stepped forward. By accepting the American's invitation, he was acknowledging his success. He was surprised by what he saw.

'But . . . this is a simple cache!'

'At first sight,' retorted Davis. 'Be more scientific, my dear man.'

Carter went further into the little room dug in the rock. It did not measure much over a yard on each side with a height that hardly reached 2½ yards. On the ground lay pottery and bags.

'This is not a royal tomb,' said Carter with relief.

'On the contrary! Look at the lid of this jar.'

The Englishman read the hieroglyphs: the modest artefact was sealed with the name of Tutankhamun.

'Let's agree,' suggested Davis. 'I've just discovered the tomb of the petty monarch and in this way solved an annoying enigma.'

Carter flared in anger. 'That is stupid! This is just a cache, Davis, and nothing more! No royal tomb looks like this!'

173

'Calm down and recognize that you have failed. Isn't fair play a British characteristic?'

'Where is the seal of the royal necropolis? Where is the sarcophagus? If you go on defending your ineptitudes, the most ignorant Egyptologists will laugh in your face. Let me see the content of these jars.'

Davis blocked the way. 'That is out of the question. Come tomorrow to the party at our house and you will know the treasure of Tutankhamun at last!'

Davis had not laughed so much for twenty years.

The rooms of the house had been cleaned, the office and the antiquities storeroom tidied, the kitchen and the dining room washed down without the slightest regard for the value of water. The entire Davis team was standing to attention in front of the warden's office.

The American was chain smoking as he was walking to and fro. He flicked off his cigarette ashes, which constantly dropped on his black suit. Lord Cromer's successor, Sir Eldon Gorst, was already half an hour late.

Howard Carter was standing back. He was the first to see the barouche slowly climbing up the road. Theodore Davis rushed to meet the unofficial master of Egypt. With his support, he would become the most famous archaeologist and he would be able to transfer to the United States the most beautiful artefacts unearthed in the desert.

He introduced the members of his team to the high-ranking visitor, avoiding Carter, and then complimented a figure whom the Englishman was meeting for the first time. Herbert E. Winlock, deputy curator of the Egyptology department of the Metropolitan Museum of Art of New York, had come to negotiate the purchase of some Egyptian antiquities. Almost bald, with short legs and very lively eyes, he was restless. Some of his colleagues compared him to a gnome and feared his critical mind and sharp retorts. Winlock praised with good humour the excellent relations between his country and Britain and expressed the wish that the meal would please the guest's palate.

Davis, Winlock and Gorst exchanged trivialities at the table of honour, set up outside of the house, while Carter nibbled without appetite with the members of the American team. As soon as the banquet was over, Davis ordered servants to bring the jars and bags stored in the tomb of Tutankhamun which he had described to Sir Eldon Gorst.

The American launched into an embarrassing speech in which he congratulated himself on being the first to unveil an antique treasure in front of an official personality who, because of his culture, was able to appreciate the event and its real value. He took off the lid of the first jar, which had been sealed with dry mud and pieces of papyrus. He extracted a small mask painted in yellow to imitate the colour of gold. Some applause burst forth. Encouraged to go on, Davis emptied a second jar, which contained only strips of cloth. The American quickly moved to a third one, out of which he drew fragments of the bones of birds and small animals. Embarrassed, he went on quickly. The next results were also meagre: the remains of plants, pieces of earthenware, rags, necklaces made of flowers, natron. There were no gold jewels.

'Archaeology is an art,' said Gorst. 'Sometimes it leads to success and sometimes to failure. You will probably be more fortunate next time, Mr Davis. I shall, however, retain one memory from my visit: the meal was good.'

When the barouche had disappeared in a cloud of dust, the American threw his hat on the floor and trampled on it.

The sun was setting over the house, which had now been deserted by Davis and his team. Herbert E. Winlock leaned over the scanty treasure despised by Sir Eldon Gorst.

'Are you going to buy these corpses?' asked Carter.

'I'm not your enemy. I appreciate your work. Davis only likes things he can show off. These poor objects tell a story, and you are the one to understand it.'

Intrigued, Carter knelt down near Winlock. 'Look carefully . . . the strips were probably cut to wrap the royal mummy.

With the rag, a priest would have wiped away the native soda used for the mummification. During the ceremony, vases were broken to annihilate evil forces in a magical way.'

'The funeral of Tutankhamun . . . this is evidence of it.'

'That is my opinion. The remaining writing makes the identification certain.'

'What about the rest?' Winlock reflected and felt the weight of a few bones. 'Could they be the leftovers of a meal? In the banquet for those who took part in the funeral, the guests ate fowl.'

Carter considered the flower wreaths, the acacia twigs and the cornflower in a different light. 'Plant ornaments were always part of the ritual . . .'

'Even the last detail is not missing.' Winlock showed a reed broom.

'When the banquet was over, a priest used it to erase the guests' footprints and abandon the place to eternal silence.'

The sunset suffused the hills close to the Valley of the Kings with a pink and orange light.

'This is a unique discovery, Carter: the leftovers of the last meal in honour of your dear Tutankhamun. I shall take them to New York and prove the soundness of our assumption.'

'Our assumption?'

'Carry on, old boy. We now know for sure that Tutankhamun was buried in the valley.'

39

Howard Carter leafed through Davis' work, burst out laughing and threw it out of the window of the hotel room where Carnarvon had invited him to tea.

'You shouldn't have done that, Howard. On the one hand you might injure an innocent passer by, and on the other a book deserves more respect.'

'That is not a book, it is just a jumble of stupidities! Did you read the title? *The Tomb of Tutankhamun*! The stupid American persists! And that is not all: he even obtained the collaboration of Maspero!'

Carnarvon savoured a muffin of acceptable quality. 'He merely wrote a note on the life of Tutankhamun, that is to say on emptiness.'

'Anyway I want to see him and tell him about my ideas.'

'Your tea is getting cold.'

'Lies are unbearable.'

'Humankind is unbearable too, Howard. You should be prepared to make a sacrifice. Your enemy is at the climax of his glory. Maspero will acknowledge that he has discovered some fifteen tombs since 1903.'

'Is that any reason to open a Theodore Davis Room in the Museum of Cairo?'

'The finds had to be exhibited somewhere. Instead of bothering our good Maspero and slamming doors, shouldn't you think about our own excavation campaign?'

Carter lifted his cup to his lips.

'Be objective, Howard. Davis is a colossus with feet of clay. Gorst did not exactly enjoy his failed performance. You do not invite someone like that to see a plaster mask and old rags. If the American does not continue to clear at least a tomb a year, his credit is in danger of being damaged.'

Scientific circles despised Carter and hated Davis. They condemned the latter for the hastiness of his publications and for his ridiculous last book. It was obvious that the tomb could not be royal, and certainly not that of the obscure Tutankhamun. It was generally thought that the American had gone too far.

Carter ran his own team energetically. His efforts had not met with any noteworthy success. He had, however, unearthed a wooden tablet with a text on the war of liberation led by King Ahmose against the Hyksos, Asian invaders who had occupied his country at the end of the Middle Kingdom. The historical value of this modest relic, to which Carter gave the name the Carnarvon Tablet amused the master of Highclere for a while. He was dividing his time between brief stays at the excavation ground and long appointments with Egyptian dignitaries. 'Lordy' was gradually becoming a key figure in the country. Everybody appreciated his sense of diplomacy, his ability to listen and his knowledge of administration. Although sometimes offended by his independent mind, the Foreign Office enjoyed his frankness and lucidity.

The fact that an observer of his quality kept an eye on the dealings of Sir Eldon Gorst satisfied some members of His Majesty's Government. High-ranking civil servants posted abroad sometimes acted like tyrants.

Carter's network of spies worked perfectly. Thanks to the wardens of the valley whom he had known for a long time, he followed the excavations of an increasingly restless Davis step by step. The American had not recovered from his disastrous performance. In retaliation, he had dismissed several members of his team and dug relentlessly into each hillock. He wanted to prove, one more time, that he was the best, and the only one who was able to discover new tombs.

February 1908 was drawing to a close, when a panting *gaffir* told Carter that Davis' team was about to enter an undesecrated tomb. The Englishman left his own excavation ground and hurried to the valley.

With a cigarette between his lips, Davis considered him disdainfully. 'Here you are, Carter! Be happy. I have found your damn kinglet this time!'

The American ordered that the gold leaves found on the threshold of the hypogeum be brought. Carter read the names of Tutankhamun and his successor, Ay, whose vault had already been identified.

'This does not prove anything.'

'Wait and see!'

Three days were needed to remove the broken pieces of stone filling the large vault to which a wide staircase gave access. As workmen removed the rubble, Davis brought to light extraordinary mural paintings with unfaded colours. Their brightness and freshness made them look as if they had just been finished. But the American saw one detail: the name of the pharaoh who owned the place was not Tutankhamun, but Horemheb, and there was no treasure.

Carter was jubilant. Horemheb, a general under the reign of Akhenaton, had continued to occupy his post when Tutankhamun was enthroned. Still powerful in the short two years when the old sycophant Ay became the master of the Two Lands, Horemheb had ascended the throne. He had not destroyed the tomb attributed to Akhenaton nor the tomb of Ay, so why would he have taken blind revenge on Tutankhamun? If the young king had been guilty of some infamy it might have justified the obliteration of his name and the destruction of his monuments.

Davis was piling mistake on mistake. Not only did he not write scientific reports on his excavations, but he also forbade his assistants to publish any. Increasingly numerous voices rose in protest against his hasty methods.

The winter of 1909 had begun badly for Carnarvon. Yielding to a request from Carter, who was convinced that he had exhausted the site of Deir el Bahari, he had agreed to start new excavations in the Delta, where splendid statues were sometimes unearthed. This had been a waste of time, because of a cold and wet season in a region where temples had been dismantled stone by stone. With the returning heat, the team had tried to work near Sais, but a cobra invasion had persuaded them not to do so.

While Carnarvon went back to England after numerous meetings with politicians from Cairo and Alexandria, Carter returned to Luxor. There had been no message, so he knew that, for the first time, Davis' excavation season had been totally unfruitful. Abandoning the centre of the valley, the American had explored the ravines and cliffs bordering the west before he got lost in small hollows in the terrain that turned out to be just as barren.

Piqued and gloomy, Theodore Davis told those who were close to him that the Valley of the Kings now only held sand hillocks.

Lady Carnarvon saw the end of autumn 1910 approach with fear. George Herbert would soon again order his trunks to be prepared.

'Did you like the concert?'

'I was exasperated. Mr Stravinsky and his *Firebird* make a din which has little to do with music. My ears are still ringing.'

'You look tired.'

'The dampness is gnawing at me. It is time for me to go back to Egypt.'

'Your daughter will complain about the long absence.'

'Evelyn is sensitive and intelligent. She will understand my innermost reasons.'

'I'm not so sure of that.'

'Wait and see . . . One day she will share my love of Egypt.'

Lady Carnarvon stopped fighting. Nobody was as stubborn as her husband.

Carter was waiting for his employer on the platform of the railway station of Luxor. His sparkling eyes told the Earl that he had been successful. For a long time, the two men had avoided trivialities. A mere look was enough for them to understand each other. Susie expressed her joy by licking Carter's hands.

'Is it a tomb?'

'It is the tomb of the man who founded the Valley of the Kings, sir. I studied the Abbott Papyrus carefully and I became convinced that the tomb of Amenhotep I is within reach. It would be a fantastic discovery.'

'Are you forgetting Tutankhamun?'

'We shall find *two* undesecrated tombs.'

'What an optimist you are. What is stopping you?'

'Informers . . . difficult to handle.'

Carnarvon frowned. 'You mean pillagers. Take care of yourself, Howard. Susie has got used to your company and she would not like to lose you.'

40

The back room of the café was smoky and stank of garlic. Carnarvon sat at a table where two customers had abandoned their coffee cups. With his blue serge jacket and his crumpled trousers, the aristocrat could not be mistaken for a wealthy tourist. He ordered a mint tea he had no intention of drinking and waited for Demosthenes' arrival.

The bearded colossus appeared, complete with white hat, black frock coat and red trousers. A waiter immediately brought him a drink made of hemp seeds and blocked the entrance of the room with chairs.

'We're now safe, Lord Carnarvon.'

'Why did you want to see me urgently?'

Demosthenes took a sip of his favourite drug. His hands trembled. Swollen eyelids emphasized his sickly appearance.

'Because your life is at risk.'

'What an unpleasant piece of news. Is that an assumption or a certainty?'

'You are upsetting everything, sir. Some high-ranking Egyptians do not really appreciate your interference and some Englishmen with financial interests in the country appreciate them even less.'

'One is always betrayed by one's kin, dear Demosthenes. Did you get wind of more . . . precise intentions?'

'No, just persistent rumours. That deserves *baksheesh*, doesn't it?'

182

'Undoubtedly.'

A bundle of banknotes changed hands.

'Your commission will be more substantial if your information is more complete.'

'That is impossible, sir. I care too much about my own wretched life. I warned you, because I like you. The matter is now in your hands.'

Demosthenes emptied his glass and staggered out of the café.

Meanwhile, in an adobe house in Gurnah, Howard Carter was drinking coffee with one of the *gaffirs* of the Valley of the Kings whom Davis had hired to keep watch over his latest excavations.

Aged some fifty years, the man was one of the most formidable thieves of the Abd el Rassul clan. They provided him with efficient protection and thanks to their support he was able to dispose of some beautiful artefacts which the archaeologists had somehow left around.

'What is Davis doing?'

'He is exploring some of the valley's unknown recesses.'

'Is he successful?'

'He looks more furious each day. God has deprived him of his good fortune. Do you want to purchase these stones?'

The *gaffir* unfolded a large handkerchief. The stones looked like engraved shards and carnelians. On one of them figured a jubilee scene depicting Amenhotep III, Tutankhamun's father or grandfather, and his wife Tiy as a winged sphinx.

It was the beginning of trying time for Carter. The haggling would last several hours.

Carnarvon examined the little treasure Carter had brought him. It gave him real pleasure to hold these antique jewels in the hollow of his hand, to feel their weight, and to touch them with his fingertips.

'Congratulations, Howard. Is it an Amenhotep I treasure?'

'Unfortunately not. But it definitely comes from the valley.'

The Earl frowned. 'We're not allowed to excavate there, are we?'

'We are not forbidden to make purchases.'

'Does Davis allow that?'

'Davis is very depressed; he has not made a discovery in two years. He has a bad press and his team is splitting up. I think he is on the brink of throwing in the towel.'

Carnarvon twirled his moustache.

'If I follow you properly, Operation Valley of the Kings has now started?'

Carter smiled. 'An ideal is the only fire which never goes out. Give me the means to reach mine and I shall give you all that you may wish for.'

'What a strange speech, Howard. I am already a billionaire, am I not?'

'You forget that Tutankhamun and his treasures will soon be within reach.'

'And your famous tomb of Amenhotep I?'

'I am on the scent.'

Theodore Davis burst into the office where Maspero was talking to Lord Carnarvon. The French Egyptologist stood up.

'What do you think you are doing, Mr Davis?'

'Why is the Earl of Carnarvon here?'

'My appointments are my own business.'

'I'll tell you, Maspero. Carnarvon wants a concession for the Valley of the Kings and to take away my excavation grounds!'

'So what? You are a tired old man, Mr Davis. So many years in the valley have exhausted your curiosity.'

Theodore Davis' round face turned red with anger. 'That damned Carter is acting through you as an intermediary . . . He wants the valley, but he is not rich enough to buy it! Rest assured, he won't get it.'

Maspero tried to be conciliatory. 'What does it matter? There is nothing more to find there. Your excavations have proved it.'

'I don't care. I don't want Carter to touch a stone in the valley.'

'Why do you hate him so much?' asked Carnarvon.

The question surprised Davis. He lit a cigarette and walked to and fro. 'Because . . . because he is Howard Carter!'

'That is a bit lame,' answered Maspero.

'He disturbs the system, and keeps on about an insignificant king and a tomb which does not exist! The man is impossible. He thinks that the valley has always been his. His case is one for a psychiatrist.'

'He might be right,' suggested Carnarvon.

The American hit Maspero's desk with his fist. 'As long as I am alive, Carter won't dig up even a spade of sand in the valley! You have no rights to my concession, Mr Maspero.'

'That is true, but—'

'None of the tombs I excavated have been explored thoroughly. Therefore I shall start again. You want science? You'll get it! I shall investigate *my* sepulchres, yard by yard. Then Carter will understand that I shall never leave the place.'

Davis slammed the door as he left.

'I'm sorry,' said Maspero. 'I hoped he would be more understanding.'

'What can we do?'

'Unfortunately there is nothing we can do. The valley belongs to Davis.'

41

Carnarvon looked at himself in the huge mirror. Sitting in a comfortable armchair, his chest protected by a large white towel, he saw the barber bend towards his left cheek, cover it with lather and raise an English razor he had sharpened on a leather strap.

'Is Ibrahim ill?'

'He has a cold, sir. I am his replacement.'

The barber had a steady hand. The blade slid on the cheek and the lather dropped into an English-made shaving mug.

'It is a bit chilly today, isn't it?'

'You are under no obligation to make conversation with me, my good man.'

The barber spread the lather on the right cheek.

'I am not sure that the appointment of Lord Kitchener as Consul-General is appreciated by the Egyptians. He is a hard man, who will not understand our people's aspirations.'

'Are you a specialist in international politics?'

The blade rested on the neck. 'You should listen to me, sir.'

'Why?'

'Because a razor is a formidable weapon and you are defenceless.'

'The gun I'm pointing at your stomach is proof to the contrary. Don't make any awkward movements.'

'I shall be quicker than you.'

'Only time will tell. I'm listening to you.'

The blade stopped. The barber's voice became more muffled.

'As a friend of Egypt, sir, advise Kitchener against ordering the repression of those who support independence.'

'You credit me with a power I don't possess.'

'Even so, you should try. You have considerable influence. If you fight with us, we may avoid bloodshed. Otherwise . . .'

The blade cut into the flesh.

'Be careful, my good man. You're wandering from the point.'

The pressure relaxed.

'Who sent you?'

'The people, sir. Don't forget that.'

The fake barber took his leave.

Carnarvon removed the white towel and felt his perfectly shaved cheeks with his hand. If people kept bothering him, he would have to equip himself with a real gun, instead of making one with his fingers.

In 1912, which was to be remembered as the year when the *Titanic* sank, Egypt became British. It happened without obvious trauma, thanks to the discussions of a few men, among whom was the fifth Earl of Carnarvon.

Howard Carter had other worries. He was putting the finishing touches to a book which was also signed by his chief, *Five Years' Explorations at Thebes*. It proved to specialists that his collaboration with the British aristocrat had resulted in serious, if not spectacular, work. Carter proudly presented it to Maspero.

'This is excellent, Howard. I'm happy to see you again as a conqueror. I miss you.'

'Because of the thefts.'

'Exactly.'

'Tombs are plundered, bas-reliefs cut off and statues broken so as to carry the pieces more easily . . . Regular bands are more and more active. That is the deplorable truth! There are many wealthy clients.'

'I know that!' thundered Maspero. 'You would have been able to curb this traffic! There is corruption and laxity all around me. This is why I have decided to pass a regulation against illicit archaeological digs.'

'Do you believe it will work?'

'I shall have watchers on all the sites and the people working on them. The most simple measures are usually the most effective.'

'You can rely on me to help you.'

The two men shook hands.

Theodore Davis flew into a violent rage, calling his collaborators incompetent idiots and taking refuge in his bedroom. Nobody dared enter the house, where there had been a bad atmosphere for the last two seasons.

Davis had had no further success in discovering unknown tombs. He had had to satisfy himself with clearing vaults which had been known for a long time and settling insignificant archaeological matters. The famous financier was becoming a laughing stock among opponents and colleagues. Even members of his own team were beginning to criticize him. Quarrels broke out every day for no reason at all. His great successes were things of the past.

But could a man like Theodore Davis give up?

Carter had not heard anything about the valley for a fortnight. Only tourists haunted the famous site, where all archaeological activity seemed to have stopped. His informers were silent. He was no longer in touch with the *gaffirs* who pretended to know the location of the tomb of Amenhotep I.

He had lunch with Raifa at their painter friend's. In spite of his insistence, the young woman still refused to sit for him. Being painted seemed to her to be a fate worse than death. She did not mention marriage any more. She contented herself with the faithfulness of her lover, with moments of tenderness stolen from his work and his dream, and with a sincere love which time did not erode. In the winter she did not try to meet him. Carter was devoted to Carnarvon and worked relentlessly with a steadfastness that frightened his colleagues. When the heat became unbearable, excavations stopped in favour of reports and archive work. But he agreed to forget them for a while and to become more available. She managed to take him for long walks, in the course of which he gradually confided in her and confessed his bitterness, doubts and hopes.

Thus their life together passed at the pace of the Nile, and their passion developed under the gaze of the spirits of its west bank.

'You look worried.'

'It is just a touch of tiredness, Raifa.'

'I don't believe you.'

'You're right, I'm worried.'

'What are you afraid of?'

'The valley flouts me. It is here within my reach and yet it rejects me. It knows that I know it better than anyone else. Is the valley dead, Raifa? Has it given away all its secrets?'

Their host interrupted them. 'A man is asking for you, Howard. He says it's urgent and important.'

'Is it someone from Gurnah?'

'No, it's a European man.'

Carter apologized to Raifa. The unexpected visitor was none other than Theodore Davis. With his had stuck to the middle of his forehead, his threadbare black suit, dusty jodhpurs and puttees, he almost inspired pity.

'Forgive me for disturbing you . . . I would like to talk to you.'

Carter was not used to so much courtesy.

'Let's walk towards the hill. We'll be alone.'

The sun shone high in the sky. The brisk air made their cheeks glow. Under their footsteps crunched sand, stones and broken pieces of limestone.

'I'm seventy-five. I am ill and tired. The valley has

189

exhausted me. It may be taking revenge on me for having unveiled all its mysteries.'

'You know very well that this is not true.'

'You know very well that it is true, Carter. All the royal tombs have been discovered.'

'Not Tutankhamun's tomb.'

'A mere cache for a kinglet . . . the gold leaves prove it. In spite of the fact that we are rivals, I hold you in high esteem and I'm telling you without holding anything back that this is my final conclusion. Tutankhamun was indeed buried in that modest vault. Pillagers destroyed the sarcophagus and the mummy. Don't persevere in a useless quest. Your talent deserves better. There are fifty unexplored sites waiting for you.'

'I have an appointment with Tutankhamun and I shall stick to my commitment.'

'As you please . . . But I am giving up.'

Carter stood still, dumbfounded.

'I have taken the decision to leave Egypt and give up my concession. Rest suits my age better.'

Carter restrained his joy with difficulty. 'The valley . . . Is the valley free?'

'Be patient. There are still some formalities to complete. But it will soon be free.'

The Englishman closed his eyes. 'This . . . this is fabulous!'

'Don't rejoice too quickly. For one thing you may not be granted my concession, and if you are you will only get an empty shell. The valley has given away all its treasures.'

'That is impossible.'

'Well, don't say I didn't warn you.'

42

'Lord Carnarvon cannot see you,' declared the English nurse disdainfully.

'Is he very ill?' asked Carter.

'What right do you have to question—'

'I am his main collaborator.'

The nurse shrugged her shoulders. 'Visits are forbidden.'

'That does not apply to me. Will you please announce me!'

'That is out of the question.'

Exasperated, Carter shoved aside the fierce nurse, opened the bedroom door and planted himself in front of the bed where Carnarvon was lying. Susie was keeping watch at his bedside.

'Leave immediately,' howled the nurse.

Feverish, with a weary look on his face, the Earl sat up.

'Please be quiet, nurse. Doctor Carter was expected.'

Vexed, she gave up the fight.

'I have a great piece of news!'

'Have you found the tomb of Amenhotep I at last?'

'Even better. I have found the valley! Davis is giving up. The valley is ours.'

With arms dangling, Carnarvon leaned his head back. 'I'm afraid I'll have to give up too.'

'What are you suffering from?'

'From some strange infection. The doctors don't understand it.'

191

'Trust me.'

Two hours later, Carter came back with Raifa. The nurse cast a doubtful look at them, but she did not dare stop them.

Carnarvon was too weak to protest. Raifa made him drink water over which a dervish had blown. She rubbed his forehead with fragrant herbs and laid an amulet with a sura from the Koran on his chest. Then she closed the shutters, drew the curtains and, without uttering a word, left the room.

The Earl savoured his second kebab with a hearty appetite and emptied a mug of brown beer. Susie enjoyed the grilled mutton.

'My appetite is coming back, dear Howard. Your healer has been wonderful.'

'Please excuse my impatience . . . What was the result of your interview with Maspero?'

'There was no result.'

'What do you mean?'

'Davis' promise has not come true. Officially he keeps the concession, even though he does not plan any more excavations in the valley.'

'Did he at least confide in Maspero?'

'He only confided in you. Only in you. Maspero is convinced that you dreamed it.'

'I swear it . . .'

'This is useless, Howard. Davis gave you false hope.'

'He seemed sincere.'

'You are a great archaeologist, but a mediocre expert in human nature. Your opponent tricked you.'

'I am sure he didn't. Davis is worn out. He does not want to struggle with the valley any more.'

'Let's hope that you are right.'

During the 1913–14 winter season, Carnarvon was very busy in Cairo. He kept a close eye on political developments in Egypt, which, thanks to a well constructed law, had been granted a legislative assembly composed of sixty elected members and twenty-three members appointed by the Government. Of course it had only one power, that of levying direct taxes. But it was a step towards independence, whose champion, Zaghlul, no longer hesitated to assert his convictions. To avoid direct confrontation, Carnarvon increased his confidential meetings and favoured contacts between those in charge on both sides. Initially Great Britain was attentive and conciliatory, but the situation deteriorated in 1914 and the authorities hardened their position. Several contingents of soldiers reinforced the military presence and barracks were given modern military equipment.

Quarrels between nations left people unmoved, but foreign soldiers, armed to the teeth, watching public buildings in large cities and arrogantly parading around caused more than a few murmurs of discontent.

Carter remained indifferent to the coming uproar. In the spring of 1914 he went to Theodore Davis' house to meet the last of his assistants still at work. Aged thirty-five, Henry Burton, nicknamed Harry, was British. Dressed in austere suits sent by his London tailor to 'H. Burton, Royal Tombs, Luxor', he looked severe. Nobody had ever heard him laugh or joke. Meticulous, even finicky, he was never seen without his black hair plastered down over his flat head and an immaculate white pocket handkerchief.

The introductions were ice-cold.

'I'm Howard Carter, Lord Carnarvon's archaeologist.'

'Henry Burton, I'm Theodore Davis' photographer. Please do come in.'

On the walls were pinned photographs of the sphinx, pyramids, tombs and English landscapes with green lawns sprung from generous rainfall.

'The house is somewhat untidy. I have not had time to have it cleaned.'

'Please excuse my unexpected visit. I acted on impulse.'

'Accepted. Do you want to see the darkroom?'

'It would be a pleasure.'

Carter admired the material Burton had set up. There was no doubt that he was the best professional photographer in Egypt.

'May I offer you lunch, Mr Carter? I have just received Oxford sausages, rabbit with mushroom, German beer and a good supply of bicarbonate of soda.'

The meal was cordial. Burton revealed proudly that his shots had been published in the *Illustrated London News* and that he intended to join the Metropolitan Museum expedition in Deir el Bahari.

'Will Davis return to Egypt?'

'No, he has retired to his Newport residence from where he has sent his orders: we should dig in the area between the tombs of Meneptah and Ramses VI. I took a few soundings at my own expense. I have neither the men nor the necessary equipment. But it's all too late . . . the Davis mission is over.'

Carter restrained his excitement with great difficulty. Davis had not lied to him.

'Have you read the latest editions of the *Daily Mail* and the *Westminster Gazette*? Disastrous news. Tensions are increasing around Europe. I hope the governments concerned will be wise enough to avoid conflict.'

'What about Davis' message? Was it his last one?'

'There is no doubt about that.'

A strange noise intrigued the two men. They first thought that they must have made a mistake. Then they realized that it was rain: a lashing rain was pouring down with incredible violence over the Valley of the Kings and forming into furious torrents, washing mud and loose stones along with it. Within less than an hour the tombs of Ramses II and Ramses III were flooded and blocked by a mass of debris.

'I won't have time to clear them,' declared Burton, shattered. 'The place is cursed.'

Carter was meditating by the entrance to the valley when two downcast-looking men came towards him. One of them,

Mohammed Abd el Gaffir, was one of the informers who had declared that they knew the location of the tomb of Amenhotep I. He stopped a yard away from the archaeologist and showed the contents of his basket: fragments of an alabaster vase.

'I am selling them,' he declared gravely.

'Where did you find this treasure?'

The pillager pulled a sour face. He expected Carter to help him.

'Does it come from the tomb you promised?'

Abd el Gaffir lowered his gaze.

'Is there a pit?'

'Yes, in the middle.'

'Is it deep?'

'Very deep indeed.'

Carter was exultant. So it was a royal tomb!

'Take me there.'

'You'll have to pay.'

'You'll be rewarded.'

'You'll pay for the vases and you'll pay for the tomb?'

'All right.'

A brief negotiation enabled them to fix prices. Then Abd el Gaffir guided Carter to a steep path behind Dra Abu el Naga. The vault had been dug in a dark and lonely little depression at the back of the valley. A block of stone concealed the entrance. The archaeologist and the pillager removed it painfully. The effort calmed Carter, who was excited at the prospect of penetrating the undesecrated sepulchre of Amenhotep I, the creator of the Valley of the Kings.

As soon as the torch illuminated the tomb, Carter cursed himself for his gullibility. Thousands of broken pieces of ceramic and alabaster vases were scattered on the floor. Abd el Gaffir and his associates had engaged in some real plundering before they had converted the royal skeleton into cash. Amenhotep I had not escaped the rapaciousness of the human vultures.

Vexed, Carter bought some of the most beautiful pieces Abd el Gaffir had in his possession as a gift for Carter and sent it along with a report to his employer. He emphasized the archaeological significance of the find as well as the fact that they had identified the secret location of the last dwelling of an illustrious pharaoh.

43

Completely bald and stout now, with a white moustache, a severe look and plump hands, Maspero did not conceal his weariness.

'My wings have been braving the air for almost sixty-eight years, but they are getting tired, my dear Howard. I can see the moment approaching when I shall have to fold them back. Because of this feeling of the inevitable end, I'm trying to complete, if not all the things I thought I would do, at least some of the things I started. Unfortunately, there are only twenty-four hours to the day and administrative chores shorten them so much that I have great difficulty to find the few hours I need to finish all these tasks. What will probably happen is what usually happens in human affairs: a lot of ambition is carried out to little profit. I hope that time will show that I encouraged people and that I made sure that any true vocation here could be carried out with a minimum of pedantry and interference from authority.'

'In that case, you should encourage my vocation.'

'What more do you want, Carter?'

'The valley.'

'The valley, always the valley!'

Maspero stood up and looked through the window of his boat, still anchored near the Museum. There he had accumulated books, administrative documents and notes taken during all the years when he had ruled as undisputed master of the

Antiquities Service. This was his favourite office. It gave him the impression that he was always on the go, that he was not trapped in the respectability of a scholar laden with honours.

'Davis owns the concession.'

'He is giving it up. I want it.'

'Why, Carter?'

'Because the valley is my life. I believe in the valley.'

'You're talking about faith now! As for me, I have lost my faith . . . In the beginning I really believed in the unity of the Egyptian god, in his immateriality, in the sublimeness of the teachings delivered by the priests. Everything was like the sun to me. Now I have become sceptical; facts, only facts matter and all religions are equal!'

'I'm sorry to disappoint you, but my faith in Egypt has remained untouched.'

'You are young. You will abandon your illusions.'

'I shall never give up the valley.'

Maspero grabbed a notebook and waved it in Carter's face.

'My notes are definite! The sand of the valley has been completely turned over. Not a single royal tomb is missing.'

'Only that of Tutankhamun . . .'

'That is a dream!'

'I'll find it, even if I have to move tons of soil and rubble.'

'You have no proof of its existence.'

'Of course I have: a faience dish with the name of the king, a gold leaf bearing his effigy and part of the material used during the funeral.'

'You'll waste time and money if you start to dig in the valley again. I know that Carnarvon saved you from hell, but your collaboration is now meaningless.'

'He is my friend. He needs me and I need him. Several areas of the valley have been buried under old or recent debris and not properly explored.'

'You'll only discover small insignificant artefacts. They won't refund Carnarvon's capital outlay. Davis' conclusion is positive: the valley is now stripped of its secrets.'

'There is still that one king missing: Tutankhamun. Why should you deny the evidence? In the chain of kings, he is the only missing link.'

'A kinglet without power and a tomb . . . That is the truth.'

'You have written to the contrary yourself. Give me the concession. You won't regret it.'

'I already regret it. You deserve better than an obsession. The papers are on the table, to your left.'

Carter clutched the precious documents against his chest. In June 1914, he became the official owner of the Valley of the Kings. At the age of forty-one, he was fulfilling what others thought to be his insane dream.

'I'm going back to France,' declared Maspero. 'We won't see each other again.'

Carter entered the house of Theodore Davis, which had recently been abandoned. Burton had taken on the Deir el Bahari American team. Everything was empty, the bedrooms, the study and the dining room . . . The photographer had taken his snapshots and left bare walls. He had only forgotten a calendar. Each day had been checked off to the end of June.

The hot summer did not disturb Carter. Of course, he would have to wait a few weeks before he received the official permit all archaeologists dreamed of, and which would allow him to dig wherever he wished in the valley. But all the *gaffirs* already knew the name of the new master of the place.

The setting sun of a July evening caressed Raifa's forehead as it rested on Carter's shoulder. They had made love with the continuing passion against which the Egyptian woman's brother fought in vain.

'I would like to have a child, Howard.'

'The valley is waiting for me.'

'How can you compare this mass of dead stones with the little being that will be born of our love?'

'They are not dead . . . In them quivers another kind of life which time cannot erode.'

'The site is making you crazy.'

'It is my destiny. I have no right to try to escape it.'

'You only love those vaults, those vanished kings, that silence which I can tell you frightens me . . .'

He hugged her more closely. They were both silent. Never would Raifa protest again. Never would she ask anything other than what he asked from himself. She should have left him and married a man from her own land and borne numerous sons. But the Englishman from a planet far from her own had fascinated her. As exacting with himself as he was with others, refusing dishonest compromises and base acts, relentless in his pursuit of an insane ideal at the risk of his own life, her lover was a man under the orders of fate, one of those people who are called to play a role that transcends their own being on this earth. Carter could not leave the eternal path that had been traced before him and for him. If he moved just one step from it, he would grow weak, like a wilted flower. That was his fate and it would not change. How could she fight against a three-millennia-old mistress, as young as the early morning sun, with a name like the Valley of the Kings?

The British military advisers looked at each other questioningly. The colonel presiding over the meeting understood what they were thinking.

'Come on, gentlemen! The Earl of Carnarvon is a voluntary adviser. He has no other aim than the good of the British Empire.'

'In that case,' protested a young officer, 'why does he inundate us with stupid reports? It's like reading the prophecies of a crank!'

The Earl remained calm. 'I have been warning you for a year. The war will take place and Egypt won't escape the conflict. Yesterday the heir to the Austrian throne was assassinated in Sarajevo. I feared such an incident. The

Balkans will be ablaze, and that in turn will kindle the great powers.'

Protests erupted, with exclamations of 'ridiculous', 'shameful', and 'stupid'.

The colonel decided to put an end to the confrontation. 'Pessimism is a bad adviser, Lord Carnarvon. But we thank you for your collaboration.'

On 28 July 1914, Austria declared war on Serbia. Unable to wait any longer, Carter had taken the train to Cairo. It was not until 1 August, the day when Germany declared war on Russia, that Carnarvon could receive him. Although the Earl looked extremely worried, Carter managed to convince him to go and see Maspero and get from him the last form, which would at last enable them to dig as they liked. His enthusiasm decided Carnarvon. The Valley of the Kings offered distractions from visions of the battlefields where the aristocrat could already see European youths tearing each other to pieces because of the vanity and foolishness of blind politicians.

Maspero was pale. 'I'm ill. France will cure me. I really thought I would never see you again. Tomorrow I shall leave this office, the Antiquities Service and Egypt.'

'We will miss you,' said Carnarvon, moved. 'Before your departure, would you agree to sign the last document that is missing?'

Gaston Maspero sat at his desk. 'At the end of fourteen years at the head of this service, during my second mandate, I put an end to the British–French rivalry in the field of antiquities. How could I refuse to crown such a task? Therefore you will benefit from my last official action.'

On a sheet of paper the scholar wrote a contract between the service and Lord Carnarvon. For ten years, the aristocrat, who was entrusting the scientific management of excavations to Carter, was allowed to explore the Valley of the Kings as he pleased. If undesecrated royal tombs were discovered, they would remain the property of Egypt. But the Earl would keep

Christian Jacq

works whose worth would be in line with his expenses.

On the evening of 13 August, Carnarvon received a fiery Carter, who had just completed his work plan. He would need no less than three hundred men to clear the masses of sand, stones and debris covering the untouched parts of the valley.

The Earl read the report carefully. 'It is too late, Howard.'

Carter turned pale. 'But we haven't even started . . .'

'Unhappiness is flooding the world, my friend. Today Great Britain declared war on Austria.'

44

Carnarvon had followed the advice of Kitchener, who had begged him to leave Egypt as soon as possible and go back to Highclere to turn his huge estate into a field hospital. Back home, he realized that 253 people depended more or less directly on him. His first duty was to support them. Happy to see her husband again, but worried about the future, Lady Carnarvon feared a shortage of supplies. So the Earl ensured that there were potatoes in the fields and wheat in the barns, and he converted pasture into arable land. He established a rationing plan and solemnly told his people to avoid any plundering, on pain of dismissal.

When the first officers injured in the battles arrived, Highclere was ready to welcome the. Carnarvon was thinking of Egypt, of Howard Carter's insane dream broken by a world war, of the valley which once more escaped them. But he dismissed these thoughts so as to concentrate on a single task: the struggle against the German barbarity threatening the whole of Europe.

The taxi stopped in front of the entrance. Almina tried to hold back her husband.

'This is sheer madness, darling. I beg you to give up the idea of leaving.'

'I want to fight.'

'Your physical condition is too bad and you are over the age of conscription. The Army cannot accept your contribution.'

'I have an appointment at the Ministry of War. Thanks to my command of French I shall make an excellent liaison officer. My friend, General Maxwell, will take me to the front.'

'Are you forgetting your children?'

'Not for a moment. They would never accept that their father refused to fight.' Carnarvon kissed his wife and climbed into the back seat of the car.

Not far from London, a searing pain shot through his stomach. With sweat on his forehead and strained lips, he tried to resist. But the pain was too strong. Furious with himself, he asked the driver to drive him back to Highclere, where his wife welcomed him with utmost tenderness. Having made up his mind to leave again as soon as possible, he consented to rest a few days.

One week later, the pain recurred, even more violently. As the injured soldiers had been transferred elsewhere, the castle was empty. The symptoms enabled Almina to identify an acute attack of appendicitis. She managed to find a car and, with the help of a servant, accompanied her husband to the capital. At the hospital peritonitis was diagnosed. Almost unconscious, Carnarvon was immediately taken to the operating room.

'I don't know whether your husband will survive,' declared the surgeon.

'Your name is Howard Carter, isn't it?'

'That is true.'

The field officer did not appreciate the proud attitude of the man dressed in a jacket and flannel trousers. He had the appearance of an aristocrat isolated from the trivialities of the world.

'You're too old to go to the front and fight, Mr Carter, but you can still serve your country.'

'I'm at your service.'

'You're appointed as a king's messenger and you will fulfil

this duty in the Middle East. The Foreign Office will entrust you with various missions.'

'As you please.'

'That is no soldier's response.'

'I'm an archaeologist.'

The field officer wrote a comment in the column reserved for the military administration: 'Independent mind. Inclined to discipline. Should be watched over.'

On 18 December 1914, Great Britain declared that Egypt was no longer a vassal of Turkey, an ally of the Germans, but a British protectorate. On 19 December, Khedive Abbas II Hilmi, whose nationalist tendencies were too strong, was deposed and replaced by Husayn, who in spite of the grand title of Sultan, would obey the orders of the British high commissioner. Cairo would become an important operational base and a war effort would be bluntly imposed on the Egyptian population. Martial law would be implemented, if necessary.

Summoned for 8.30 a.m., Carter arrived shortly after eleven. The field officer shouted at him, 'This is intolerable, Mr Carter! You haven't fulfilled any of the missions entrusted to you, and you have no respect for authority!'

'I'm being given ridiculous orders.'

'How dare you—'

'The civil servants who give them are stuck in their offices and they don't show their face out of the window.'

'Discipline and obedience are what are required of a soldier. You do not criticize orders. I expect an apology.'

'You should acknowledge your mistakes. Then I shall fulfil my mission as it suits me and in my own way.'

The field officer stood up. 'Consider yourself removed from office, Carter.'

A few months after the beginning of the conflict, there was no winner. In Europe, an endless trench war was beginning.

Soldiers died in awful circumstances. In the Middle East, the Turks had closed the straits.

Free to do whatever he pleased, Carter returned to Luxor where he shared his time between Raifa and the still popular visits to the royal tombs. Smiling Egypt was sinking into sadness and anxiety. Most of the excavation sites were now closed. Many young archaeologists were killed in action, far away from the sun of Upper Egypt and its luminous stones.

Carter spent long lonely hours in the valley, the valley that belonged to him and that he was unable to dig with his bare hands. Discouragement overwhelmed him. Without Carnarvon's presence and his conquering magic, he felt abandoned. Why was fate so cruel? Just when he was about to savour the fruit he had been coveting for so many years, it was brutally taken away.

Some people predicted that the war would last ten years, maybe even more. Egypt would be invaded by hordes of Turks and Germans. Monuments would be razed to the ground and tombs would serve as storerooms for ammunition.

On a brisk December morning, Carter thought he might give up. He would write a long letter to Carnarvon to explain that the valley was refusing him. Heartbroken, he entered the huge vault of Seti I for the thousandth time and let himself be enraptured by the ritual scenes and esoteric text covering the walls. As his gaze rested on hieroglyphs, gods and goddesses welcomed him and uttered the words of life engraved in the stone. Without knowing it, Carter identified with the sun plunging into the other world as he faced the mysteries of the hidden vaults of rebirth. The dying star went through twelve terrifying regions where darkness ruled. There were aggressive genies and a snake intent on destroying the light. The traveller went through the gates and walked over the deep pit from which arose the energy of a primeval age. On the walls he read the Book of the Day and the Book of the Night and recited the formulas for the opening of the mouth.

He penetrated into the golden room where the soul of the

sun and the spirit of Pharaoh, his messenger, presided. Taking the sarcophagus of Seti I to England had left a cruel emptiness. Carter swore to himself that he would never change the nature of a tomb by stealing its heart, the stone of regeneration, which Egypt did not call a coffin but 'provider of life'. As he raised his eyes, he admired the representations of the sky goddess, the stars, the planets and the decans. Those who triumphed over death returned to the light from which they came and merged with the origin of the universe.

Overwhelmed, Carter wrote to Carnarvon:

A superficial study of Egyptian mythology or religion might imply that we have made progress. But if we have the ability to admire and understand their art, we lose all feeling of superiority. No sensitive person would deny that Egyptian art embodied what is essential. Despite all our progress, we are unable to see that. Egypt is an eternal horizon, the valley retains the secret. That is why we must go on. I will stay here and wait for you.

45

Lord Carnarvon was reading newspapers and dispatches. Things were getting worse. German submarines had managed to blockade Great Britain and ill-prepared Allied offensives did not produce any large-scale success. Among the flood of bad news, Howard Carter's letter about the valley brought some light. Now the Earl kept dreaming about it. It represented an unreachable heaven where the madness of human beings subsided before eternal dwellings.

'Darling! You promised me that you would not get up.'

Her patience sorely tried, Lady Carnarvon tried to persuade her husband to go back to bed.

'I need to do some work.'

'When you have pleurisy, you mainly need rest and warmth.'

'I'm not ill.'

'You're not sensible! Take care of your health.'

The butler interrupted the discussion. 'An urgent letter, sir.'

'Who from?'

'The Ministry.'

Carnarvon read the document. Shattered, he slumped in an armchair.

'What is the matter?' asked his wife.

'The Turks and the Germans have just attacked the Suez Canal. Tomorrow they will invade Egypt.'

*

Howard Carter completed the assessment of artefacts found in the tomb of Amenhotep III and completely cleared the inside of the vault. Here as elsewhere, Davis had contented himself with basic work. Thanks to a meticulous and systematic exploration, Carter had found five intact dumps from the original foundation work in front of the tomb. Hundreds of minute tools had been piled up in pits dug in limestone, mixed with sand and covered with stone debris. Curiously, the inscriptions did not mention Amenhotep III, but his father Tuthmosis IV. However it was a lead towards his son.

The rumour of the German–Turkish attack on the Suez Canal hardly reached Carter. Having no doubts about the British troops' victory, he heard without surprise that they had repelled the invader and were pursuing them in the Sinai and Palestine.

While maritime communications were broken and the slump in cotton sales and export prices drove Egypt to the brink of misery, Carter had resolutely engaged in an unbroken dialogue with the Valley of the Kings. It would now be his sole preoccupation and his whole life.

At the end of February 1915, he unearthed the humble remains of the funerary furniture of Queen Tiy, the famous wife of Amenhotep III and maybe the mother of Tutankhamun. As he was holding two alabaster figurines bearing the effigy of the queen, he heard of the death of Theodore Davis, who had been so much enamoured of this great queen. The American had not survived his departure from the valley very long. More exacting than the most jealous mistress, the valley imposed absolute faithfulness on its lovers.

Howard Carter forgot the outside world. While European countries tore each other to pieces, he wrote to museum curators and drew up a catalogue of the artefacts discovered in the royal tombs. He gathered books and articles on the valley, read early explorers' accounts and studied ancient maps.

Nothing that had happened on the site escaped his attention. He questioned people in Gurnah, chatted with thieves, perused masses of excavation reports. Day after day he perfected his working tool: a huge map of the Valley of the Kings with the locations of all the tombs. He breathed in rhythm with the valley, became sensitive to its slightest noises and watched its most intimate changes. He had died to himself. In his marriage with the mystery he had offered his whole being.

At the beginning of spring 1916, Lord Carnarvon had been elected Chairman of the Camera Club and he was hoping to go at last to the front as an adviser to the Royal Flying Corps on aerial photography. Of course he would not fight with weapons, but by detecting the enemy's presence on the field, he might help the progress of the Allies. Meanwhile the terrible battle of Verdun went on, during which the French managed to block the German offensive at a cost of many thousands of deaths.

Egypt, whose currency had been linked to the pound sterling, seemed to avoid chaos, even though the people suffered increasing hardships.

The most barbaric destructive war ever fought in the history of humankind must end as soon as possible. Carnarvon was ready to offer his life to save thousands of young men from the slaughterhouse.

Once again, his health weakened. Only three days after his enrolment, he was compelled to go back to Highclere. Depressed and on the brink of despair, he relied on the affection of his wife and children. But it was Carter's letter which cheered him up: his distant friend had just pulled off a feat.

In deserted Luxor, empty of dignitaries and officials, the most trivial event took on extraordinary proportions. When rumours of the discovery of a fabulous treasure in a lonely place close to the Valley of the Kings circulated, people's imaginations were fired. Waverers contented themselves with dreaming, but professional pillagers insisted on verifying the rumours and, most important, on trying to grab some of the treasure.

The Tutankhamun Affair

After informers had yielded to the first tortures and talked, two rival gangs arrived at the same time at the coveted location. There was a violent fight and blood was shed. Panic-stricken at the idea that the conflict might degenerate to the point of setting the west bank ablaze, the councillors warned Carter. The latter did not hesitate a moment. He engaged a dozen new workmen, and despite the fact that it was already dusk, he went straight ahead with the expedition. They had to make their way over difficult ground to reach a crack at the bottom of a little valley between steep rock faces over a hundred yards high.

Carter bumped into a rope that was hanging in the fissure. Pricking up his ears, he heard noises that were easy to interpret: thieves were at work. The Englishman decided not to put his companions' lives at risk. He cut the robbers' rope and substituted another one, with which he was also able to descend. Once at the bottom of the sepulchre, some 200 feet beneath the entrance, he followed a sloping corridor and bumped into eight armed men who looked at him in amazement.

'You have a choice,' he said in Arabic. 'Either you go up on my rope and disappear, or you stay here and die.'

The robbers hesitated. They were aware of Carter's reputation and they knew that he would not shrink from anyone. They climbed up one after the other, leaving their torches behind.

The archaeologist remained alone. At last he had time to think about the amazing location of such a well-concealed tomb. It probably led to a treasure coveted by all the thieves in Gurnah. He walked further into a 16-yard long corridor ending in a small square room. There he turned at right angles and followed a second steep corridor, leading to a funerary chamber full of rubble. The plunderers had dug a gallery, into which Carter crawled.

Tutankhamun – would the name he had been hoping for for so long be engraved on the sarcophagus?

Twenty days were needed to clear the sepulchre. Carter had had a system of pulleys set up with a net which enabled him to go down into the vault. There was no treasure, no precious artefact, just a sandstone sarcophagus to 'Hatshepsut, ruler of all lands, king's daughter, king's sister, wife of the god, great wife of the King, mistress of the two countries'. He had just discovered another of Queen Hatshepsut's vaults, which had been dug for the great lady before she became a pharaoh.

Tutankhamun remained out of reach, but the valley kept talking.

46

On 30 June 1916, two years after he had left Egypt, Gaston Maspero presided over a meeting of the Académie des Inscriptions et Belles-Letters, to which he had been appointed secretary. He thought of the marvellous years he had dedicated to the study of monuments and to the reorganization of the Antiquities Service. Haunted by the memory of his son, who had been killed in action, he was also thinking of the unruly archaeologist, Howard Carter, who had been obsessed by an insane dream ever since his adolescence. He was probably mistaken, but how many times had Egypt unveiled its mysteries to men of this calibre?

Suddenly, he collapsed.

'My dear colleagues,' he said in a quavering voice, 'I beg you to excuse me . . . I do not feel very well . . .'

A few moments later, Gaston Maspero was dead.

In autumn 1917, Lord Carnarvon was at last able to go for long walks in the park at Highclere. At the foot of the cedars of Lebanon, he became certain that the Allies would win the apparently endless war. At the end of 1916, the German offensive had resulted in a failure in Verdun. Some 360,000 French soldiers had been killed, almost as many as Germans. When on 6 April 1917, the United States had declared war on Germany, the Earl had had no more doubt about the final outcome.

Egypt, though, was suffering. Of course it was no longer threatened by the enemy. The British forces, who had remained in control of the ancient land of the pharaohs, would soon take Baghdad and Jerusalem. But the war economy was causing the people great distress. Huge inflation resulted in ever-increasing hardships. The British had seized production plants and aroused a feeling of rebellion whose real significance the servicemen did not fully appreciate. In a country where, because of the conflict and of poverty, deaths outnumbered births, the worst turmoil could be yet to come.

But Carnarvon had taken his decision. In spite of various warnings, the Earl encouraged Carter to begin the excavation campaign he had proposed in August 1914.

While, worried and fascinated, Europe witnessed the collapse of the Tsarist regime in Russia and the Bolshevik revolution, indifferent to anything that happened outside the valley Carter crossed the Nile to the west bank. Under the protection of a rocky summit, pink and blue at sunrise, gold at noon, red and orange at sunset, the archaeologist embarked on the adventure he had always wanted with ever-increasing passion: the opening of his first excavation campaign.

He walked up towards the house in which he would stay, at the top of a hill overlooking the Nile and the valley. At its foot was a dilapidated fountain. He climbed up marble steps and opened the door with a wooden key. Inside were a British clock, a piano, cushions, mats, carpets, a paraffin lamp, a brazier, a clay oven and a metal bath, all the necessary comforts. There were a few holes in the roof, needing repair. But he had a more urgent task: he had to choose a *reis*, a brave and competent foreman.

There was a knock at the door. Carter opened it. 'You . . . Ahmed Girigar, my friend!'

'I have survived, and I'm ready to work with you.'

'Luck smiles again on me.'

'You need to organize your life here: you will need a secretary, a groom, a cook, a porter, a water carrier and—'

'No, Ahmed, I don't need any help.'

'That is not really suitable. But since I won't succeed in changing your mind, I shall take care of you. It's useless to try to persuade me not to. I'm as stubborn as you are.'

The two men hugged each other.

'From tonight on, you should put away your clothes carefully and don't leave them inside out! Night demons might enter them and prevent you from getting up.'

'*E' shams, effendi*! The sun, sir!'

Ahmed Girigar brought in coffee and a pipe to help Carter start the day right. The archaeologist was so impatient that he gulped his breakfast. After a quick wash, he climbed on the donkey which was to take him to the valley. The new master of the site had taken care over his dress for his first meeting with his workmen. He wore a woollen three-piece suit, a spotted bow tie, a white pocket handkerchief, a wide-brimmed hat and a cigarette holder. Ahmed Girigar had been equal to his reputation. A long procession of people carrying baskets was waiting for orders at the entrance to the valley. They had not yet taken off their *galabiehs*. They were singing and talking loudly.

'I negotiated six days' work per week,' explained the *reis*. 'Friday will be a rest day. Where do you want to dig?'

Carter thought of the abandoned map he had picked up in Davis' house, now turned into a storeroom for antiquities. Thanks to the American's team's notes he had completed his own map, contemplated for a long time and taken the decision to start excavating where Davis had stopped his own exploration, that is to say in the triangle between the tombs of Ramses II, Meneptah and Ramses VI. He was convinced that he would find numerous artefacts for Carnarvon's private collection in the masses of debris accumulated during the excavations, and maybe some clues to guide him to the tomb of Tutankhamun.

Sensitive to Carter's arguments, Carnarvon gave his

agreement. It restored his stamina to know that the most beautiful and insane adventure of his life was now starting in that distant land, under the sun of the gods.

Despite the present turmoil, the horizon was clearing. An intense emotion took hold of Howard Carter as he saw the long line of loinclothed workers going to work. Some of them filled baskets with rubble while others emptied them. A full skin on his shoulder, a water carrier went from one workman to the next. Songs punctuated the slow and steady progress, overseen by the *reis*, whose orders were followed to the letter. Barefoot, their bodies covered with sweat, the men earned a few pennies a day and thought they were well paid. The most experienced used spades to dig into man-made mounds. Carter had obtained a narrow-gauge railway from the Antiquities Service, still in an orphan-like state after the death of Maspero. On prefabricated tracks, workers pushed an open wagon. The small line could easily be moved elsewhere, according to the needs of the excavations. It made the removal of debris easier, away from the area and out of the valley. Rubble, rubbish and unnecessary blocks – that was what Carter had feared. His predecessors had only been concerned with digging hastily and blindly, without bothering about cleaning the valley, which was now cluttered with masses of sand and loose stones.

The first month's work took place under difficult circumstances, with brisk cold in the morning, oppressive heat at noon and dust sticking to the clothes and skin. Carter was not discouraged by an approximate calculation which showed that he would have to remove several hundred thousand cubic yards of sand and rubble to achieve a feat no archaeologist had ever attempted before him: to reach the rock itself, the mineral floor of the valley and thus make sure that no tomb entrance escaped his notice. As soon as an artefact was found or an ancient fragment emerged from the muddle, Carter wrote down its description on what was in fact the first exhaustive list ever drawn up in such a precise way by an archaeologist.

Unfortunately the *ostraca* had not registered any information about Tutankhamun.

At the beginning of 1918, the excavation site looked perfectly organized, but Ahmed Girigar had a worried face. Carter questioned him.

'Some workmen want to stop work.'

'Why?'

'You are here too much . . . Usually, archaeologists do not come so often nor stay so long on the site.'

'They will get used to it. Is there anything else?'

'Objects . . . Usually they take some and resell them. Your colleagues turned a blind eye.'

'I'm different. They'll have to give up stealing.'

'You'll have to negotiate.'

'That is impossible, Ahmed.'

'Then, you should raise their salaries.'

'Fix the right amount and tell them the good news.'

47

Carter shuddered as he examined the ancient map of a royal tomb, drawn by the very man who had built it. The hieroglyphic text and the captions mentioned the 'house of gold' which rested the Pharaoh's 'light body'. Brightened by the colours of frescoes and the presence of nine divinities, the house held a sarcophagus protected by chapels. How could he imagine the treasures which might have accumulated, since all the tombs of the valley had been desecrated?

All but one.

Carter had questioned many antiquities salesmen, from petty thieves in Gurnah to prosperous and highly respected antique dealers. No artefact of Tutankhamun's funerary furniture had ever been seen. Consequently nobody could have violated his vault.

The archaeologist did not sleep much. He usually thought about the work he would do on the following day, about putting strings and stakes to better use, the way the ancient people did, so as to respect proportions and the distance between monuments and better understand the peculiarities of the valley. Each day he had to learn to think like an Egyptian architect and to experience the soul of stone as such a man did.

Sitting on the terrace of his house, he caught a glimpse of a strange figure climbing up the path in the setting sun. The bearded colossus was panting. The last rays of the sun made his red trousers glow. His sinister black frock coat evoked the image of a predator in search of a prey. Labouring, he stopped a few yards away from Carter. 'I'd like to talk to you.'

'I have come across you in Luxor . . . Who are you?'

'My name is Demosthenes, I'm an antique dealer.'

Carter offered him a seat. 'Would you like a drink?'

'Something strong.'

'I'm sorry. I only have water.'

'It doesn't matter.'

'I'm busy, Mr Demosthenes. Would you please explain the purpose of your visit?'

'Everything is so calm and peaceful here . . . You'd never believe that you are in danger.'

Carter straightened his bow tie. 'Threats?'

The colossus protested good-naturedly. 'I'd rather say confidential information. You do not only have friends.'

'That comes as a surprise.'

'I am your friend. You can trust me.'

'What dangers are you talking about?'

Demosthenes looked embarrassed. 'You are harming business at all levels. Your team of workmen is incorruptible, your *reis* swears by you and business is now forbidden in the valley. That is an extremely embarrassing situation, Mr Carter. If we reached an agreement, I might be able to save you a lot of trouble.'

'I do not really understand your position . . . Do you want me to hire you as a workman?'

Demosthenes frowned. 'You won't get off so lightly, Carter. If you sell me some artefacts, then I shall keep the competitors silent.'

'Scientific morality won't allow me to do so.'

'There has never been any morality in archaeology. Everything can be bought and sold.'

'Except me, sir. Please leave as soon as possible. Even though we are different weights, I would still bet on my speed and on the precision of my fists.'

219

Demosthenes stepped back. 'You're wrong, Carter. In this world, integrity never triumphs.'

'Even with little success and dashed hopes we will go on trying anyway.'

'You'll be broken.'

The workmen bowed low towards Mecca, brushed the ground with their noses and foreheads and uttered the ritual words: 'God is great, I praise his perfection.' Then they cast a glance behind their shoulders to venerate the fallen angels.

A well-built man, refined and elegant, with a face reminiscent of antique beauty, and white hair, beard and moustache, waited for the end of the prayer before walking across the site to greet Howard Carter.

'Congratulations. You are extremely tolerant.'

'I'm afraid we haven't met.'

'I know you well, Mr Carter. My illustrious predecessor, Gaston Maspero, often talked about you.'

Carter stiffened. So the man with the lively eyes deep in their sockets was the new Director of the Antiquities Service, Pierre Lacau, whose recent appointment he had heard of. There were various rumours about him. The Jesuits' henchman, a lover of bureaucracy and regulations, a scholar with an extraordinary memory, he could read the most difficult texts with disconcerting ease. Smooth-mannered, meticulous, unshakeably calm, he little resembled Maspero, who had none the less appointed him as his successor because of his technical skills.

Carter immediately sensed that Lacau would be a formidable enemy. His coldness repelled him straight away.

'I was told that you had planned a large campaign.'

'As you can see for yourself.'

'What are your objectives?'

'I want the valley to talk.'

'Do you believe in the existence of an undesecrated tomb?'

'There are speculations.'

'If one is discovered, I should immediately be informed.'

'This is simple courtesy.'

'No, my respected colleague; that is a professional duty. My position is . . . extremely delicate.'

'Why?'

'Maspero was a generous man, too generous . . . I do not question your permit, but times change and I must look after the treasures unearthed from Egyptian soil.'

'Be more specific.'

'Well . . . the sharing of historical works seems an heresy. The content of a royal tomb, be it desecrated or not, should belong to the service, shouldn't it?'

'Lord Carnarvon's investing a lot of money in the excavations I am running. He was promised some compensation in the form of works of art.'

'Of course, of course . . . But such deplorable customs must stop. Even duplicate artefacts will stay in Egypt.'

'What do you intend to give to the Earl?'

'Prestige, Mr Carter . . . prestige. That is a lot, is it not?'

'I'm afraid he won't be very happy with your proposed regulations.'

'Proposed . . . but soon to be implemented. I shall rely on you to have them scrupulously carried out.'

'Otherwise?'

Pierre Lacau's gaze became piercing. 'You're not well regarded among Egyptologists, Mr Carter. People consider that you are too independent, indeed even revolutionary . . . and your route appears rather chaotic. Nobody denies your competence, although your projects seem a bit . . . eccentric.'

'Have you been closely following my career?'

'I keep lists and I write cards, many lists and many cards. That is the only scientific method that enables one to keep informed.'

'You would never have granted me that concession, would you?'

'Gaston Maspero was too liberal with foreign archaeologists, but what has been done cannot be undone. What now matters is to respect the new regulations. I am convinced that our collaboration will be fruitful. We'll meet again, Mr Carter.'

48

Carnarvon paid a lot of attention to Carter's reports, and he was not slow to react. As the Antiquities Service, inevitably run by a Frenchman, attempted to go back on its word, it was advisable to explore other alternatives. He therefore met the Director of the Metropolitan Museum in London and talked with him about the future of his private collection. Because of his wealth, his knowledge of Egypt and his great projects, the Earl appeared as one of the major collectors of the century. He revealed to the American that he and Carter had begun to gather a real treasure through previous archaeological digs and fierce negotiations with the antique dealers of Thebes. They did not want to keep these magnificent artefacts, the most beautiful of which had belonged to princesses of the Egyptian court. Therefore he suggested that the Metropolitan Museum purchase them, in the utmost secrecy. He would of course have to convince Carter, but there was a most suitable man for the transaction: Herbert Winlock.

At the end of January 1918, a large number of tourists came back to the ancient town of Thebes, as if the war had ended. Yet the German army was not retreating and some people forecast a new deadly offensive.

Howard Carter had made progress. Near the tomb of Ramses VI, in the eastern corner, a hole of a depth of some 50 feet testified to the continuous activity of his team which, after considerable effort, had reached the bare rock. For the first time it was possible to see the soil of the valley as it was originally. Cursing the onlookers who leaned over the edge at the risk of breaking their necks, Carter ordered that small protective walls be built around the pit.

Twelve feet below the level of the entrance door to the tomb of Ramses VI, they made a strange find: stone slabs covered with branches and reeds, which had undoubtedly been workers' houses scantily built on blocks of flintstone. The archaeologist unearthed some *ostraca*, one of which dated back to the rule of Ramses II, glass beads, fragments of gold leaves and a vase containing the dried body of a snake, considered as the protector of homes.

The living arrangements proved that craftsmen had worked at the construction of a tomb which must be hidden beneath the slabs. Once the houses had been explored, they would have to go on digging.

As he was preparing to approach this new phase of the adventure, Carter received a visit from a civil servant from the Antiquities Service. Because of the crowds of tourists, and their economic importance, he was asked not to forbid access to the tomb of Ramses VI, one of the most beautiful and most visited in the valley.

The hot season was approaching and the workmen were tired, so Carter agreed to stop digging.

'Glad to see you again, Howard.'

'Me too, Herbert.'

Winlock and Carter were lunching in the house on the west bank from which, with ever-increasing joy, the Englishman contemplated the magical sites which bewitched him.

'Does my proposition meet with your approval, Howard?'

'I have received instructions from Lord Carnarvon and I shall follow them.'

'You're becoming very obedient . . . I have the impression that Lacau did not really appeal to you, and that the valley war between Great Britain and France is about to start again.'

'It won't be through my doing.'

'The Metropolitan Museum has decided to purchase the most beautiful of the artefacts you are gathering for Lord Carnarvon.'

'They are all magnificent.'

'Well, then we'll buy them all. The Earl mentioned necklaces, armbands, dishes, scarabs, mirrors . . .'

'You'll have a chance to look at them at your leisure.'

'I have been ordered to negotiate directly with you and to keep the deal secret until all the objects are exhibited in the Metropolitan.'

The two men sealed their agreement by raising their glasses.

'What about Tutankhamun?'

'There is no serious lead, alas! But he is here; I have the feeling that he is very close by.'

On 21 March 1918, the Germans launched a terrible offensive in Picardy. Glad to have secured Carter's financial position through the commissions he would earn by gradually selling artefacts from his collection to the Americans, Carnarvon was worried when the enemy progressed in Flanders and on the Marne. The fate of the war was at stake.

In his house, which was watched over day and night by men whose honesty Ahmed Girigar guaranteed, Howard Carter spread out his map of the Valley of the Kings. He contemplated it for hours, checking his annotations over and over again, making sure that he had ticked off areas where people had dug on a large or small scale. How could he escape the overwhelming reality? He would have to dig every tiny recess, so as to leave no inch unexplored. He would therefore have to divide the valley into sectors.

With the affection of a father, Carter watched over the valley so as to spare it any damage. He made sure that the wardens performed their duties as thoroughly as possible and made unexpected rounds of inspection. On the previous day, he had expelled an American who, a jar of tar in one hand, was writing his name on the walls of a tomb. The vandal deserved to be sent to jail. In the past the defacing of a sacred monument was considered to be a serious crime.

Spring saw the gentle Raifa return. With the patience of Oriental women she endeavoured to conquer her lover again. But he looked more distant, almost inaccessible, even though his passion seemed unchanged. The Egyptian woman began to doubt her own beauty. She took more care of her make-up, displayed tricks of seduction and became as tender as a fiancée come from heaven. Carter cherished her, but his mind was elsewhere. She understood that her most formidable ally, the Valley of the Kings, had taken hold of the heart of the man she would keep trying to rid of these ridiculous ties. How could a man make love with stones, sand and tombs?

Carter was examining the location of his future excavations, when he saw Ahmed Girigar running towards him. The *reis* was not usually in a hurry. Something serious must have happened.

'Come quickly.'

'What is the matter?'

'Something has happened in your house . . . I do not know the details.'

The two men climbed to the house. On the threshold, one of the two wardens was wiping blood from the head of his colleague.

'We caught a thief in the act,' he explained. 'He came in through the back entrance. We fought, but he managed to escape.'

'Did you identify him?' asked Carter.

'No.'

'Where was he?'

'In the large room. He had begun to roll up the map.'

'Thank you for your courage.'

'*Malech*,' answered the warden fatalistically. 'May God avert evil!'

Tense, Carter noted the damage. There had been no theft and the map was intact.

'I shall pay for any medical care the injured man needs and I want an additional warden behind the house,' he instructed the *reis*.

'Who was the culprit?'

'That is not difficult to guess. The map can only be of interest to one of my dear colleagues. Someone wants to intimidate me and stop me from carrying on.'

'Why is there so much hatred in the hearts of men?'

'*Malech*,' answered Carter.

49

In Gurnah, the clans and families spied on each other. The
village had its own laws and hierarchy. Calm prevailed as
long as everybody received what he was entitled to. When
there was a conflict, gang leaders applied rough justice. That
was why usually nobody dared depart from the existing
social order. Yet old Mahmud, who already had difficulty
supporting his wife, had just taken a second wife. In other
words, he had made a fortune and nobody knew how.
Remembering that Mahmud had worked in a team in the
Valley of the Kings, one of the police informers thought it
right to warn his superiors, who immediately let Carter
know. Mahmud's wealth could only originate from
plundering and, even worse, he was the only beneficiary of
his theft. Accompanied by a policeman, Carter paid a visit to
the old man. As he refused to answer questions, the
investigators decided to ask his new wife, who was working
in a field. She escaped and tried to reach the pier, where a
civil servant caught up with her. Hysterical, she howled for a
good ten minutes. When she had calmed down, Carter talked
to her kindly.

'Are you Mahmud's wife?'
'Yes, yes.'
'Why don't you let go of that basket?'
'It's mine!'

'I would like to see what is in it.'

'No, it's mine.'

The policeman was forced to intervene, and he snatched the precious object from her. Inside was a small wooden figurine. Carter examined it carefully.

'It is authentic. Who gave it to you?'

'Mahmud.'

'Did he tell you to sell it?'

'Yes.'

'Where did Mahmud find it?'

'I don't know.'

Carter and the policeman took the woman back to Gurnah. Her husband retreated into a silence nothing could apparently break. The archaeologist resorted to the ultimate weapon: appearance before the Mudir, the governor of the province. His reputation frightened the people: it was said that, in order to get rid of gangs of thieves, he had the entrances of the caves where they hid blocked with bundles of sticks to which fire was put. Preferring death to torture, many of them suffocated in smoke.

A trembling Mahmud entered the house. At first he thought that the magistrate was absent. At the back of the large room stood a huge bath, out of which rose wisps of steam. Dripping with water, a head suddenly emerged. When the black eyes stared at Mahmud, the old man let out a shout of fright.

'You are a thief,' declared the Mudir, 'and I shall have your hands cut off.'

Mahmud knelt down. 'Please don't!'

'If you want to escape punishment, tell me the location of the tomb you plundered!'

Bending his head, the old man talked abundantly.

Carter and Ahmed Girigar climbed to the forlorn little valley. 'An undesecrated tomb,' the Mudir had said. 'According to Mahmud, it is full of treasures.'

The archaeologist decided not to tell anyone before he could check himself. At night, with the help of ropes, the two men ascended the rocky piton, which they had been able to locate thanks to the old man's precise descriptions.

They noticed that a stone slab had been laid over a hole in the rock. Girigar removed it. Carter roped up and started to descend. The pit had been dug coarsely and ended in a tiny room, where bats flew away. On the roughly hewn walls were neither traces of inscriptions nor paintings. The insignificant cavity had never contained an antique artefact. Furious, Carter climbed up again.

'Mahmud cheated us.'

Ahmed Girigar looked worried. 'I saw shadows there . . . let's take another way down.'

A shot rang out. The bullet skimmed past Carter's right ear. Taking his gun out of the pocket of his *galabieh*, the *reis* fired blindly to protect Carter's retreat.

The archaeologist knew who the culprits were. He had been wrong not to take heed of Demosthenes' warning and he had fallen into a well-organized trap. Old Mahmud had played his part to perfection. Who would have ever doubted his confession? The next day the plunderers would plan a new and brutal attack. To put an end to the threat, there was only one solution. He had to confront the leader of the bandits. He requested an audience with the head of the Abd el Rassul clan.

He was welcomed as ceremoniously as on his first day. The fearsome personality offered him grilled mutton, dates and fresh milk. During the meal, Carter contented himself with talking neutral topics like fishing in the Nile and the millennia-old trouble of irrigation. His host had to make the first move, which he did as he drew in the smoke from his hookah.

'I am honoured by your presence, Mr Carter. You are now the master of the valley.'

'A site which requires all my attention.'

230

'My family has been frequenting it for several generations. We have an owner's right.'

'The past is now past.'

'Whoever does not respect the past is not worthy of the present.'

'My role consists in preserving the valley from plunder.'

'You fulfil it very well.'

'Maybe too well for your taste.'

'You know my tastes very well.'

'Have I become . . . a nuisance?'

'Some people say so.'

'Don't they also say that it would be advisable to get rid of the intruder?'

'It's highly possible.'

'My death would not really annoy you.'

'Life and death are in the hand of Allah.'

'The hand of men often substitutes itself to the hand of God.'

'That is fate.'

'It would be improper to ask you if you are the actual author of the murder attempt I was subjected to, wouldn't it?'

'Yes.'

'You should know that I would rather die than give up.'

'Why are you so stubborn, Mr Carter?'

'Because the Valley of the Kings is my fate. This is where God's hand touched me. Leaving it would doom me to emptiness.'

Abd el Rassul seemed shaken by so much determination. 'If you prevent me from buying and selling, Mr Carter, how can I support my household?'

'It is generally thought that the valley is exhausted. No more treasures hide in its sand. Archaeological remains will not bring you any benefit.'

'I have a specific question to ask you: will you extend your power to the whole west bank?'

'I am only interested in the valley now.'

231

'Let's make an arrangement: my men won't intrude and nobody will dare attack you. But don't bother me outside your territory and don't call the police for help.'

'Let's agree on that.'

'May Allah be our witness!'

50

In the last week of September 1918, the Allies launched a fourfold offensive, in Champagne, in Argonne, on the Somme and in Flanders. This time, Carnarvon was convinced that the German troops would not resist and that the awful war, in the course of which over 8 million men had died, would soon come to an end.

Alas the Earl's health was not improving. He felt unable to bear the fatigue of a long journey. How distant Egypt seemed! Day after day, Carnarvon followed the course of the events which troubled that hungry and exhausted peasant society. When, on 30 October 1918, Turkey surrendered, the nationalist movement began to organize. The Earl emphasized its strength in his meetings with the Foreign Office emissary, who did not fail to consult him regularly. Cautiously, London began to disown some high-ranking British civil servants, who were too rigid. Old-timers with a starchy way of doing things were not suitable to prepare the future.

After the armistice was signed on 11 November 1918 at Rethondes, Egypt drew attention to the fact that it had remained faithful to the Allies. Sultan Fuad did not disguise his ambition to obtain independence quickly. Saad Zaghlul headed a delegation of patriots, the WAFD, which asked the British high commissioner for permission to go to London to request freedom for Egypt. In reply, he was deported to Malta.

Carnarvon, who was fighting as best he could against the

world epidemic of flu, deplored the decision and gave several warnings. Great Britain had broken an international order which some people had thought unshakeable and had deeply changed people's attitudes. What sort of turmoil now lay in store for Egypt?

'You have to compromise,' said Ahmed Girigar.

Carter restrained his anger with difficulty. 'Compromise . . . what does that mean? My workers are the best paid in Egypt!'

'This is not just a question of money.'

'I respect these men, Ahmed. Do I behave like a tyrant?'

'You are exacting, but you are fair.'

'In that case, why are they stopping working?'

'The whole country is in ferment. My fellow countrymen want independence.'

'I do not care about politics . . . and the valley does not either!'

'Repression has not killed people's aspirations. It has increased them tenfold. Riots have broken out in many places and a campaign of civil disobedience has attracted many participants.'

'How does all this unrest concern me?'

'You forget that you are a foreigner and an Englishman.'

'What do you advise me to do?'

'Slow down operations for a while. We'll get the team back to work when calm returns.'

'And if calm does not return?'

'God will decide.'

Even hashish was no consolation for Demosthenes. How could his plan have failed? But for the clumsiness of the gunmen, Carter would no longer be alive and the traffic might have been resumed, as in the past. The dealer would readily have persevered, but the orders of the Abd el Rassul clan were strict: the Valley of the Kings had now become the preserve of the Englishman. Still, there was no ban on ruining his reputation.

Demosthenes could not go and see Lacau. The director of the service would have refused to receive such a dubious individual. He had to infiltrate more subtly by winning the confidence of junior employees. The most accessible were the local inspectors, who were offended by Carter's character. To see him scuttle away would give them deep satisfaction, a satisfaction shared by a number of Egyptologists, who were exasperated by their colleague's independence and ability. Because of characters like him, scholars were being accused of shutting themselves away in their offices instead of getting some experience on the field.

Demosthenes' weapon would be venom. In the course of the next few months, he would initially spread insignificant false rumours, then more and more compromising ones.

His first prey was a middle-aged Egyptian inspector, whose career was at a standstill in a mediocre area in Upper Egypt.

The Greek slipped an envelope full of banknotes into his pocket.

'What is that for?'

'Your documentation on mummies has been useful to me.'

'Mere articles . . .'

'We are so badly informed in Luxor.'

'Yet you have the famous Carter!'

'A curious archaeologist actually.'

'Curious? You mean impossible! His scientific demands are unbearable. He publishes details about even the smallest artefact he finds.'

'He has other preoccupations.'

'What?'

'This is only a rumour,' whispered the Greek, 'but people assume that he sells artefacts for his own benefit, without telling Carnarvon.'

'Do you have any proof?'

'It's just a rumour,' repeated the Greek.

Raifa harboured no illusions. If Carter went for so many walks in the countryside with her, it was because the threats of a popular uprising were slowing his work in the valley. As soon as the unrest subsided, he would go back to his true love.

Saad Zaghlul's deportation had calmed a great number of people, who were aware that Great Britain would react with the utmost firmness as soon as the independence movement became too obvious. The new world order was not shaped in Cairo, but in Washington, London and Paris. Egypt would have to yield to decisions that would be imposed on it from outside, even though many passionate spirits like Raifa's might be bruised.

The heat of the summer 1919 overcame the last of the protestors. It seemed a utopian dream to get rid of the weight of the British administration. People continued to argue endlessly and even to plot, but revolution was postponed.

'When will you start excavating again?'

'In the autumn. The unrest has wasted precious time.'

'What you call unrest is the anger of a people, Howard!'

'Do not take me for a blind man, Raifa. I am aware of that. But you must understand my fight as I understand yours. My concession is limited and I must get the valley to give up its secrets.'

'Why, Howard?'

'This is a fire, deep within my heart, a demand I cannot escape. The valley constantly calls me and I cannot yet understand its message.'

'You frighten me.'

'Are we free to choose our own path?'

'Most people are. But you are at the service of an irresistible force.'

They sat under the shade of palm trees, near a well.

'Don't refuse my help, Howard. I feel you are so lonely sometimes. Are you going to waste all your energy in a fight with something invisible?'

'A pharaoh sleeps in the darkness of oblivion. Sometimes I believe that I hear his voice. Invisible . . . yes, you are right, I am attracted by the invisible, on the other side of walls and rocks and rubble. I shall overcome them, I promise you.'

Raifa did not need the promise. She coiled tenderly against Carter and enjoyed the mildness of the evening.

51

As her husband wished, Lady Carnarvon organized a dinner party for thirteen guests. The dining room was lit only by candles. She did not know any of the visitors and she thought that they looked rather strange: they were elderly women dressed in richly coloured clothes and men with beards. One of them wore a turban. When they had settled according to the table plan designed by the Earl, Almina dared question him in a low voice.

'Who are these people?'

'London's best mediums.'

'High spirits in Highclere? But why—'

Carnarvon laid his forefinger on his wife's lips. 'Let's concentrate, my dear. This is a serious matter.'

During dinner the flower of British clairvoyance behaved properly. The Earl, however, noticed a propensity to greed in some of them. Used to analysing others by concentrating on their attitudes or gestures, he quickly spotted two charlatans, several unbalanced people and a crazy man. A small dark woman who pushed impudence as far as looking like Queen Victoria in her old age intrigued him. She ate little, spoke even less and constantly looked at the flame of a candle, to the point of becoming hypnotized.

Once the table had been cleared, Lord Carnarvon displayed a map of the Valley of the Kings and a sheet of paper on which Carter had written Tutankhamun's names in hieroglyphs.

'Concentrate, my friends, and summon the spirits. Is the king whose name you see buried in this site? If he is, can you locate the place?'

A heavy silence descended on the gathering. Some people closed their eyes, others seemed to pray, while others concentrated on crystal balls or tarot cards. Queen Victoria's double continued to gaze at the flame.

'The monarch is a man from Atlantis,' said the man with a turban. 'His body is buried under the water.'

As Carnarvon had categorized him as one of the charlatans, his vision did not really disturb him. Other revelations cast in the same mould followed, without any relevance to the valley or Tutankhamun's rule.

Suddenly the small dark woman started to talk. She spoke in a low voice which arose from her stomach. 'A pharaoh . . . a pharaoh who died young . . . everything shines and radiates around him . . . his soul hides and escapes us . . . a sealed door . . . it must not be opened by anyone. Nobody is allowed in! That is the secret, the great secret!'

The seer fainted and fell to the floor. At the same moment, the butler entered the dining room.

'Sir . . . there has been a theft in the library!'

Carnarvon left the mediums and rushed to the scene of the crime. A quick look showed him that the thief had been at his collection of Egyptian artefacts. Leaving aside the most precious objects, he had only seized a gold leaf of Tutankhamun.

Panic-stricken, Lady Almina cowered against her husband. 'A theft in our home, this is horrible! But who—'

'It could be either the spirit of the Pharaoh or a specialist.'

According to recent information, an indiscretion had enabled the British Museum to learn of the secret agreement between the Earl and the Americans. Had the fury of the Egyptologists who denigrated the work of Carnarvon and Carter as that of a dreamer and a fanatic, been expressed in such a crude way? Used to perfidy and its innumerable manifestations, the master of Highclere thought the assumption plausible. Yet he preferred to believe that Tutankhamun's soul was rebelling at the prospect of being disturbed in his sleep and giving him serious warning. He found it all quite exciting.

The Foreign Office emissary was appreciative of the excellent port.

'It's a special vintage,' Lord Carnarvon reminded him.

'Remarkable.'

'Your visit, my dear friend, means that my last analyses have been taken into consideration.'

'They even created some fuss.'

'Pleasant or unpleasant?'

'Some people in charge of our service ground their teeth. To them, Egypt is a long way from independence.'

'They are mistaken. But if they were not usually wrong Britain would still rule most of the world.'

'That is an almost subversive opinion. Do you know that you have a lot of enemies?'

'Many British enemies and a lot of Egyptian friends. Those are the ones who will have the last word, believe me.'

'You should not forget that you are British, Lord Carnarvon, and that you must defend the interests of your own country before those of a distant people whose customs are so different from ours.'

'Is that a threat in disguise?'

'We praise your critical mind and your straightforwardness, but we do not want you to go beyond the bounds of what is sensible.'

'Where do you fix those bounds?'

'You should be cautious.'

'I'll take action immediately. Find me a means of transportation to Egypt.'

The emissary shuddered. 'Are you leaving again?'

'The war is over and my health is improving. Are you

forgetting that I have the concession for the Valley of the Kings?'

'That is an excellent cover, which will enable you to resume your numerous contacts with the Egyptians.'

'A cover? No, my dear man, it is more than that . . .'

'What do you mean?'

'How can one talk of vocation to a senior civil servant?'

Carter was walking to and fro on the quay of Alexandria harbour. The ship from England had been announced. On board was Lord Carnarvon, back in the land of the pharaohs after so many years of absence. Carter was even more nervous than usual because of the bad news that had been broadcast on the wireless. The ship did not really look like a liner. It was a troopship. It was mineproof but it had no comfort whatsoever. Narrow cabins had been hastily set up and there had been no time for proper cleaning and disinfecting. Several passengers had been seriously ill during the crossing over and even two deaths had been mentioned. Carter, aware of the Earl's poor health, was eaten away by worry.

Bad weather in the Mediterranean had delayed the ship and, for a day, the harbour authorities had even feared a wreck. But the ship's siren at last announced its arrival. The tugboat was detached and the first passengers soon disembarked.

Carter looked vainly for Carnarvon in the crowd. Families met again, parents kissed their children and wives their husbands. Joy burst out unrestrained. Almost an hour elapsed. The empty decks were a sad sight. If the Earl had not survived, the dilapidated tub formed a sinister shroud. Maybe he was lying in his cabin unable to stand up. Just when Carter was making up his mind to go on board, he saw him. He looked very frail. His gait was hesitant and his face bore the marks of intense fatigue. His right hand lifted a wide-brimmed hat, revealing sandy hair which fluttered for a moment in the wind. Lord Carnarvon still had the natural elegance which made him an irreplaceable character. Under the aristocratic armour

Christian Jacq

flowed generosity and passion. Susie ran towards Carter, who stroked her tenderly.

In spite of the happiness he felt at the reunion, another feeling invaded him. Carnarvon was no longer on his own. A radiant young woman was holding his arm.

52

The pair walked slowly down the gangway. A black cloche hat hid the hair of the young woman with the beaming face, who had hardly left childhood. Yet her heavy, austere grey jacket with large lapels was embellished with a décolleté suggesting a lovely figure. The long skirt and black stockings emphasized the excessively serious look of her dress.

'Glad to see you again, Howard. This is my daughter, Lady Evelyn.'

The large black eyes fascinated Carter. How could a woman be both so beautiful and so tender, so modest and so attractive?

'Well, Howard, have you lost your tongue in the valley?'

'Please forgive . . . my emotion.'

'I'm pleased to meet you, Mr Carter. My father talks so much about you in Highclere and about the mysterious king, whose name I forget.'

'It is necessary to travel to have a sound knowledge of humankind. This is why I decided to bring Eve. Susie wagged her agreement.'

'I insisted to the point of wearing down your legendary patience, didn't I?'

'That is too delicate a matter to be dealt with without proper consideration.'

A happy complicity prevailed between father and daughter. Carter felt clumsy and unable to find the right words. He hurriedly described his latest work in the valley while porters took care of the luggage.

'Does Lady Evelyn want to see the most beautiful sites in the country?'

'I am hot,' she conceded. 'But how can I dress differently? I read that women had to hide under thick clothes and even veil their faces.'

'Only peasant women dress very strictly in some remote areas. In town, European clothes do not shock anyone.'

'Marvellous! I was right to fill my trunks.'

'I chose to bring other things,' revealed the Earl. 'After all those years of hardship, I thought that even as exacting an archaeologist as Howard Carter would not despise more simple pleasures. Our house will soon be provided with French wine, brandy, English beer, tobacco and first-class coffee. When you fight against mystery, you must gain strength.'

From Cairo to Medinet el Faiyum, Lord Carnarvon and his daughter had a car driven by a chauffeur who was sometimes hesitant, sometimes daring. Then the Earl chose a barouche pulled by two well-kept horses.

'Where are you taking me?' she asked, lost in a noisy crowd.

'To heaven.'

As soon as the barouche had left the town and the stench of canals turned to drains, it followed tracks bordered by gardens. The young woman marvelled at the luxuriance of the landscape, embellished with date and lemon trees, oleanders and hibiscus. Her surprise became even greater when she discovered Lake Qarun, a huge water tank laid out by the pharaohs, from which the province of Faiyum derived its fertility.

'In the past,' explained Lord Carnarvon, 'the lake was twice as large and the vegetation was much thicker. Noblemen came to hunt in a preserve at specific times of the year.'

'Heaven . . . You're right. Heaven probably looks like this place.'

They had lunch near the lake. It contained excellent fish, and Susie tasted a variety of trout with obvious satisfaction. Suddenly Lady Evelyn stopped eating.

'There, near that small rowing boat, a man is bathing!'

Carnarvon looked up. 'There is no doubt about that.'

'But he is naked!'

'I have no bathing trunks to give him. Either you change places or you accept the local customs.'

'I thought nakedness was prohibited by Muslims, even for a bath.'

'That applies to women, but not to men, especially in this area, where old customs have been preserved. Under the rule of the pharaohs, people swam naked and worked naked in the fields.'

'The observation of surviving customs is part of a future archaeologist's training, isn't it? So I will stay where I am.'

The Earl took his daughter to sites unfrequented by tourists, such as the temple of Medinet Maadi, a wonderful remnant of a large city buried in the sand, and the Ptolemaic sanctuary of Kasr Karun, with its warm yellow stones. They wandered on the banks of the lake, quenched their thirst under the shade of palm trees and were offered bread and mint tea in several village houses.

'Mr Carter seemed annoyed to see you go away,' she commented.

'You have the wrong idea. He wanted to show you the valley as soon as possible. What am I saying . . . *his* valley.'

'When shall we go there?'

'Soon. I wanted to prepare you for the shock by letting you enjoy the marvels of the country. The valley is another world, fierce, hostile and grandiose.'

'You sound as if you were afraid of it!'

'I must confess I am a little. It suggests death and eternity, in such powerful terms that the soul is captivated.'

A few miles north of Medinet el Faiyum, peasants armed with pitchforks stopped the barouche and engaged into a very sharp dialogue with the driver. Carnarvon, who spoke Arabic badly but understood several words, was able to understand the gist.

'A riot. Freedom fighters have attacked policemen and they want to attack all foreigners.'

Lady Evelyn clutched her father's arm.

The driver proposed that they change their route and even go on foot, if necessary. In several of the towns the people's anger was bursting out. Paradise was becoming tinged with blood.

Lord Carnarvon was received by a close collaborator of Marshall Allenby, the High Commissioner ruling over Egypt.

'You won't control the uprisings much longer,' predicted the Earl.

'Don't be so pessimistic.'

'You should come to terms with the issues, or the whole country will be set ablaze.'

'What do you suggest?'

'Free Zaghlul.'

'Don't think about it.'

'You have turned him into a martyr. His followers' speeches are increasingly violent.'

'If he leaves jail, we won't be able to stop him any more.'

'On the contrary, he will tire himself out.'

'That is a rather dangerous bet.'

'It is the only possible way out. Zaghlul is much more fearsome in jail. And that is not our sole worry.'

Already annoyed, the civil servant bridled even more. 'Be more specific.'

'Egypt's debt remains huge. The defeated countries are no longer part of the trust managing it. Because of the revolution, Russia has withdrawn. Only the Italians, the French and we remain. If I'm not mistaken, the triumvirate won't last long. Someone will have to win.'

'That is a state secret, Lord Carnarvon.'

The Tutankhamun Affair

'It's an open secret. If Britain does not want to look ridiculous, we should first restore peace.'

Vexed, Carter felt lonely. Busy in Cairo, Carnarvon and his daughter did not pay any attention to his work. Yet the precarious calm that had been restored in Upper Egypt had enabled him to start his excavations again around the tomb of Ramses IV and later in front of that of Tuthmosis III. But the first borings did not bring any interesting leads.

At the end of a disappointing week, he was walking along the Nile in Luxor, when he was addressed by one of the most famous dealers in illicit antiquities on the west bank, a young man with a shaven head who belonged to the Abd el Rassul clan.

'I promised you a lot of scarabs.'

'That is true.'

'Now I am no longer afraid of being denounced, because you promised not to call the police.'

'On condition that no more objects leave the valley.'

'May he be cursed who betrays his word!'

'Where are your scarabs?'

'I do not have them any more. Another buyer offered a better price. If you want them, you'll have to pay me double the amount.'

'Who dared—'

'Don't be angry, Mr Carter. That is how trade goes. I'll wait for your answer till tomorrow.'

Dumbfounded, Carter followed the dealer at a distance. Who was playing around pushing prices up and interfering in long-established relationships which could save some artefacts?

The man entered the Winter Palace. A few minutes later he came out again with an American, whom Carter immediately recognized: Herbert Winlock! The Englishman continued to shadow the dealer and waited until the conversation came to an end before addressing his friend.

'Please forgive my directness, Herbert, but did this man offer you a set of scarabs?'

'Yes, but—'

'They belong to Lord Carnarvon.'

The American felt his cheeks, amused. 'In other words, the bandit is trying to interrupt the usual circulation and set us against each other.'

'I'm afraid so.'

'So I shall refer him back to you. The Metropolitan Museum promised not to disturb your employer's transactions in any way, on condition that the most beautiful part of his collection passes to us. I don't think you have any complaints about that, do you?'

'As I see it, it frees me from financial worries for some time.'

'That's good. Don't worry. The rule remains unchanged. Between ourselves, it amuses me to beat the British on their own ground and to discreetly take the British Museum down a peg or two.'

Winlock blushed.

'Excuse me . . . I was forgetting that you were British.'

Carter did not protest. Was he still an Englishman?

Carnarvon was modest about his triumph. The liberation of the freedom fighters' leader had pacified minds. Zaghlul spoke freely and vehemently. Interminable discussions replaced action. As he left the office of the High Commissioner, where he had been encouraged to pursue his task, the Earl felt his legs give way beneath him. His heart was pounding wildly and he breathed with difficulty. The guard came to his rescue. Susie barked.

'Call my daughter, quickly . . .'

On the ship back to England, Evelyn took care of her father, who was to undergo a small operation. She fought against the despair which threatened to overcome him.

'Carter must be disheartened,' he said. 'I came to give him

my support and we did not even go to Luxor.'

'It will wait for another time. We'll come back as soon as you are fit. I am as fascinated by Egypt as you are.'

53

During the whole of January 1920, Carter removed masses of rubble that was blocking the area around the tomb of Meneptah, the son and successor of Ramses II. Thanks to the narrow-gauge railway, work progressed quickly. In front of the entrance to the tomb of Ramses IV, he discovered five dumps from the original foundation containing minute objects, beads, faience slabs and four large closed pits. The arrangement gave hope of finding a cache. Alas, the pits were empty.

He was not making the progress he had hoped. As he lacked neither men nor material, he could only blame himself. He had expended so much effort for such meagre results. Despite his obstinacy and his sense of method, he was far from matching Theodore Davis' record. At times he despaired. Would he have to give in to the belief of most Egyptologists that the valley was exhausted? The deterioration in the Earl's health increased his feeling of failure. Everything was conspiring against him. Did Carnarvon still believe in his ultimate success? He had not even taken the trouble to bring his daughter to Luxor.

A cable received on 24 January made Carter regret having doubted his employer. Carnarvon announced that he would arrive by mid-February. The archaeologist immediately summoned Ahmed Girigar and asked him to work twice as fast. A special bonus would be given to the workers if they cleared the surroundings of the tomb of Ramses II, where precious artefacts might be hidden. When the Earl came to the site, Carter would not welcome him with empty hands.

As soon as Lady Carnarvon set foot on the land of the pharaohs, she disliked it. 'The most beautiful country in the world' according to her husband was just a huge breeding place for flies, where an unbearable sun beat down, and where there were dusty winds that caused headaches. What kind of charm could people find in the flat expanses, where spindly palm trees fought against drought, in the hot and inhospitable deserts, in the wretched and badly kept little gardens? What excuse was there for these lazy dirty people, who spent their time sitting smoking their pipes? The further south she travelled, the more Almina gave up hope of seeing rain or green valleys. Cramped in a woollen outfit, she constantly complained.

'Do we have to go to Luxor?'

'Fortunately we do.'

'Fortunately! I don't know how you and Evelyn can like this land and the savages who live there.'

'Do you know that they consider us uncivilized?'

Lady Carnarvon gave a start. 'What right do they have to do so? Good heavens!'

'To their eyes, we do everything the wrong way round. We walk with our shoes on in holy places and, mainly, we write the wrong way, from left to right whereas a scholar writes from right to left.'

'Such arguments are so absurd that I won't consider them.'

The surroundings of the Valley of the Kings appalled her. The chaos of rocks, the brutal appearance of cliffs overcome by sun and the mineral silence made her feel that she was leaving the world of the living and entering a resolutely hostile world where she had no place.

When Howard Carter came to meet her, she thought for a moment a demon was coming out of one of the tombs in the rock. The impeccable three-piece suit, the spotted bow tie and the man's appearance reassured her, however. She was addressing a fellow countryman, an islet of civilization in the desolation.

Greetings and introductions took place according to custom. Lady Evelyn remained slightly withdrawn. Then, Susie leading the way, Carter took the trio to visit the tomb of Seti I. He advised Lady Carnarvon to give her heavy colonial hat, wrapped in a veil, to a workman, but she refused drily. Dressed in an elegant patent leather suit and covered with jewels, she walked with difficulty in her high heels. Lady Evelyn, who had warned her mother that they were going for an outing in the desert and not to a garden party, had contented herself with a low-necked jumper, a tartan skirt and a parasol.

Carter enthusiastically described the journey of the sun in the other world and its successive transformations from apparent death to resurrection. Although dazzled and intrigued, Almina remained on the defensive. A good Christian and an aristocrat born in the most refined country in the world could not admire the barbarous works of a past religion.

The house revived her animosity. 'How can you live in such surroundings, Mr Carter? The house is unworthy of a gentleman!'

'That is why we must improve it,' declared Lady Evelyn softly. 'Tomorrow trunks full of carpets, mosquito nets, curtains and oil lamps will be delivered. I even thought of a small broom to dispel the dust of the vaults.'

'Our stay will be all the more pleasant,' said the Earl, 'as the food has already been sent.'

'Our stay!' retorted Lady Carnarvon. 'You're not going to make me stay here?'

'Of course not, my dear. Your suite has been booked in the best hotel in Luxor. But I shall spend a few nights in this house.'

Lady Evelyn did not dare express her own wishes. She would have liked so much to stay in the valley! She had inherited her father's taste for adventure and unexpected situations. When the fragrance of mystery was added to them, she felt a passion to conquer. Wasn't it a most incredible miracle to own the most famous site in the Orient at the age of twenty?

Howard Carter checked the crease in his trousers, tightened his tie, cut a rebellious hair which spoiled his moustache and walked down to the excavation site, where a fearsome ordeal awaited him. On this March morning, he had to show Carnarvon the result of the huge clearance work which had cost the Earl so much money. The archaeologist had only one certainty: he could not tell his employer of a concealed tomb with careful excavations already under way. Nor were there any statues, gold necklaces or funerary figures. What could he show to Lord Carnarvon but the rock, fragments of tools used by builders and the foundations of the small houses where they worked? The triangle delineated by the tombs of Ramses VI, Ramses II and Meneptah, from which Carter had expected so much, had turned out to be sterile. So he had not fulfilled his first mission which was to enrich the Earl's private collection.

On her daughter's advice, Lady Carnarvon had agreed to dress more lightly. She kept a dark jacket and a very strict grey skirt, but she had consented to change wool for cotton. There were times when she began to enjoy the sun of Luxor and even rides in feluccas on the Nile, but she tended to castigate herself for these carefree moments. Beside her, Lady Evelyn appeared radiant. A flowered hat, a white dress and a pearl necklace emphasized the full bloom of her youth. Leaning on his stick, the Earl looked at his watch.

'We are on time, Howard. Now show us your discoveries.'

In a few moments, Carter would have to face the shame. Of course he would attempt to demonstrate the scientific value of the excavations, but he was certain that the Carnarvons would soon yawn with boredom. A few steps away from the latest cavity dug by his team, Ahmed Girigar whispered a few words into his ear.

'Are you certain?'

'Yes, I am.'

More relaxed, Carter led his guests along the site. The two women were surprised by the scale of the work. The Earl remained silent. After half an hour of technical explanations, he interrupted the archaeologist.

'These heaps of rocks must have hidden some magnificent objects. We are impatient to admire them.'

Carter took them back to the deep hole, around which Ahmed Girigar had posted several wardens.

'We'll experience together the crowning achievement of our excavations,' he announced proudly. 'Deep down at the bottom is a cache. Do you want to be the first to go down, Lord Carnarvon, so as to bring out the treasure?'

'The privilege is mine,' declared Almina to everybody's amazement. 'I did not come that far for nothing. As we are spending a fortune in the area, I am the one who should appreciate our acquisitions.'

Intrepidly, she tackled the slope. Embarrassed and awkward, Carter tried to help her. She was quicker than him, however, and after a few slips, reached her goal.

'What should I do?'

'Well . . . use your hands.'

Without hesitation, she plunged her aristocratic hands into the venerable earth, which was a mixture of sand and fragments of rock. Very soon she freed the neck of a vase. Joyfully, she took it out of the gangue and brandished it exultantly.

'An alabaster vase. It's splendid!'

Carter picked up the masterpiece. Without waiting for his permission, she dug again. The cache contained three superb vases bearing the names of Ramses III and his son Meneptah. Fate had just saved Carter by offering Carnarvon the most beautiful artefacts discovered in the valley since he had begun financing excavations.

54

Pierre Lacau could not concentrate on the hieroglyphic text he was translating. Too many worries nagged at him. On 5 April, the League of Nations had allowed Great Britain to occupy Palestine. British influence was growing in the Middle East. When would it tackle the stronghold of the Antiquities Service?

Unfortunately the most famous and active excavator was this Howard Carter, who was once more being widely talked about. Had he not just unearthed thirteen alabaster vases in a remote area of the Valley of the Kings? Far from boasting, he had contented himself with photographing them, indicating their location and describing them in his own archaeological catalogue, and left the glory of the discovery to Lord Carnarvon.

The French scholar felt he was entrusted with an important mission: he had to play his role as the director of the service by defending the interests of both science and his country. Now, after a period of observation, which gave some substance to his reputation of passivity, he was going on the offensive.

'Lord Carnarvon has arrived,' announced his secretary.

'Show him in.'

Pierre Lacau stood up to greet the aristocrat. 'Thank you for coming, sir.'

'It is a privilege to meet you. You are, after all, one of the most powerful men in the country.'

Christian Jacq

'I'm a humble civil servant who tries to preserve a precious legacy. That's all.'

Coffee was brought.

'Your success is talked of everywhere.'

'Beautiful artefacts, I must say.'

'The term masterpiece has been used.'

'Here are Howard Carter's drawings.'

Lacau appreciated the artist's talent and the beauty of the vases. 'Rumour did not lie. On the one hand, it is marvellous; on the other very annoying.'

'Why?'

'These splendours are part of the Egyptian legacy.'

'The agreement with the Antiquities Service is clear. I finance excavations and the finds are my property.'

'The text is more ambiguous than that,' said Lacau. 'And I have introduced a major legal reform.'

'A law cannot be retroactive.'

'Of course, of course . . . I would not like to become embroiled in a legal battle. Yet . . .'

Carnarvon judged that the Frenchman was dangerous. His soft tone and courteous behaviour hid a will of iron and a rare obstinacy. In addition, the elegant man with the fine face and beautiful white beard handled trickery as easily as he breathed.

'So you thought we might come to a deal.'

'I am not a trader . . . But it seems to me that sharing would be an excellent solution.'

'According to what terms?'

'Seven vases for the museum and six for you. I will let you choose yours. Those with an ibex head would add prestige to your collection. As for scientific morality, it will be considered to have been maintained.'

'I hope this agreement will bring good relations between us.'

'Why should things be any different, sir?'

*

256

Carnarvon spent a peaceful summer in Highclere. His health was improving. His wife and daughter often mentioned their Egyptian trip and were already preparing for their next expedition. In the course of his long walks with Susie, the Earl thought of the positive developments in Egypt. By fixing the boundaries of a dismembered Turkey, the Treaty of Lausanne had definitely freed the old state from Ottoman influence. In spite of sporadic troubles, society was being restructured. The foundation of the Misr Bank enabled a middle class to re-emerge and enjoy the fruits of an expanding economy. Aspirations to independence certainly had not disappeared, but they seemed less aggressive and might even fade in the flow of prosperity.

'Are you lost in your dreams?'

'I cannot hide anything from you, Eve.'

'I like it when you use my pet name.'

'Beware of it, it turns you into a temptress.'

'Promise me again that you will take me with you this coming winter.'

'How could I say no?'

'Egypt is so beautiful, and I can understand your passion for the valley.'

'You make me so happy . . .'

'Do you believe that Mr Carter will discover his tomb?'

'He believes it. This is what matters.'

The heat abated with the first days of autumn. Howard Carter went to Cairo to meet Arthur Lucas, the director of the government analysis laboratory, to whom he had entrusted part of the contents of the vases. An experienced chemist, Lucas had a passion for the techniques of preserving and restoring antiques. His oval face embellished with a black moustache and thick brows, the scientist always displayed a seriousness of which his immaculately white starched collar was the best proof. Slow and meticulous, he had studied with pleasure the three-millennia-old material.

'What are your conclusions?' asked Carter.

'The jars contained a mixture of quartz, limestone, bitumen, resin and sodium sulphate.'

'Any traces of oil?'

'Yes indeed.'

Carter was disappointed. According to the inscriptions, the vases had been used to keep holy oils. They were not part of a funerary furniture which might have pointed to a nearby tomb.

'Are your searches going well?'

'I shall clear the whole valley if necessary.'

'I'd like to help you. If chemistry can ever be useful to you, do not hesitate to call on me.'

Ahmed Girigar and his workmen started work again enthusiastically. Every day on the site, Carter communicated his energy and his certainty of success to them. After the workers' houses had been cleared, he opened a new excavation ground in the ravine close to the tomb of Tuthmosis III. There again he had to remove rubble from Davis' digs to reach the soil of the valley at the time of the Eighteenth Dynasty, when it had been chosen as the burial ground of the pharaohs.

Marks and details continued to increase on the archaeologist's map. He clarified the location of small vaults, corrected his predecessors' errors, set up exact plans and thought over the builders' choices. All too often he forgot he had to bring to light artefacts worthy of a major collection. His only find was a series of fragments of canopic vases from tomb 42, the first he had ever explored in the valley, many years before.

When Carnarvon returned with his wife and daughter, there was no new miracle discovery. Carter had nothing small or large to present to them. His sole surprise consisted in turning the upper part of Ramses XI's tomb into a dining room, where they had their Christmas dinner with excellent champagne. Glad to see his daughter happy and his wife relaxed, Carnarvon did not question the meagre results of the excavations. Seated around a long table, the guests took part in an ageless celebration, thanks to the benevolence of a most hospitable pharaoh.

When the guests had left, Carter turned the light off and breathed the night air. He walked slowly and felt united with the valley he loved so much and which refused to give away its ultimate secret.

Some 15 feet away, a figure moved out of darkness.

'Raifa!'

'You have forgotten I exist, Howard.'

'Raifa . . .'

'Don't lie. I saw the young woman. I saw the way you looked at her.'

'Lady Evelyn is Carnarvon's daughter. I have no right—'

'Love does not care about prohibitions. I had no right either. But she is twenty and I am over forty . . . Am I not right?' Raifa stepped back.

'Don't go . . .'

'Don't hold me back, Howard. The valley has won. It has attracted the young woman and estranged us for ever.'

55

Deeply shaken by the end of his affair with Raifa, Carter immersed himself in a herculean task which exhausted his strongest workmen. In the middle of the valley, he explored the empty space between the disappointing tomb 55 and that of Ramses IX. Once again he reached the rock. His sole reward was a canopic vase from the time of Ramses.

Refusing to yield to disappointment, he attacked the other side of tomb 55 and had to content himself with a meagre cache containing bronze rosettes and bloodstone used to colour papyrus. Then he took his team to the little valley where, around the tomb of Tuthmosis III, he had already moved tons of rubble. Again the narrow-gauge railway went into action.

But it was all in vain. The valley remained mute.

Carnarvon and Carter looked at the sunset, under the canopy of the house.

'Still nothing, Carter?'

'Nothing of importance, it's true. The valley is probably the most barren of all sites, but when it gives away one of its secrets, we are rewarded a hundredfold for long years of tedious work.'

'I trust you, but I do have occasional doubts. What is your plan now?'

'I want to reach the primeval rock near the great tombs.

Vaults from Ramses' times were dug at a higher level than the tombs of the Eighteenth Dynasty to which Tutankhamun belongs. So not only do we have to dig under their debris, but also under the ground as it existed at the time of Ramses II and his successors.'

'That is a colossal endeavour.'

'Isn't it precisely the reason why you chose me?'

The Earl smiled. 'Content yourself with penetrating the mysteries of the valley, Howard, and not mine.'

Carnarvon stood up and walked slowly down the path with the help of his stick. Carter often wondered whether the aristocrat considered him as a real friend or just offered him the illusion of that privilege. He did not mind being tested by him, because his life had always consisted of a series of challenges. But he would have liked Lord Carnarvon to open his heart at least once.

Out of the last tongue of fire emanating from the setting sun on the slope of the valley emerged a black-haired woman in a white dress.

'I did not want to leave Luxor without saying good-bye,' said Lady Evelyn.

'I am touched by your consideration.'

'You are very lonely here.'

'I am surrounded by pharaohs.'

'But their words are silent, aren't they?'

'I must acknowledge that their voice is not as soft as yours.'

'Are you turning into a charmer, Mr Carter?'

'I am afraid I'm just the opposite.'

'I'm not so sure of that . . .'

'Will you come back?'

'There is no doubt about that.'

The white dress twirled and disappeared in the dusk.

Pierre Lacau closed the file. After mature reflection and without taking into account specific interests or sensibilities, he had taken decisions which had become irrevocable. He received Lord Carnarvon with cold determination.

'I'm sorry, but I have no treasure to share. The excavation season was fruitless.'

'You should change your archaeologist.'

'Howard Carter gives me complete satisfaction.'

'He has too ready a tongue, especially when it comes to criticizing the service and calling its director a mediocre and incompetent scholar.'

'That's just gossip.'

'I hear so much of it that I think it must be true.'

'Is Howard Carter the subject of our meeting?'

Lacau opened his file. 'Excavation permits are now obsolete. In the future they will include an obligation which must be respected to the letter: the permanent presence of an inspector of the service on each archaeological dig. He will keep an effective watch and intervene if necessary.'

'Aren't you afraid of creating a little . . . friction?'

'I don't take any notice of that.'

'Is that all?'

'The procedure for sharing newly discovered artefacts will be modified.'

Carnarvon's hands tightened on his stick. 'In what way?'

'The usual practice of sharing half and half is abolished. The service will get all the archaeological finds, or those parts which suit it and the needs of the museum.'

'This is a takeover by force, isn't it?'

'It is scientific necessity.'

'I shall have to accept it, then.'

'I strongly advise you to do so. There is another point, sir: your concession comes to an end in April 1923. Then the Valley of the Kings will return to the Antiquities Service.'

'This is not quite correct. Mr Maspero offered more time.'

'May God look after him. But he does not run the service any longer. You are going back to England, aren't you? So, let me wish you a safe journey back.'

*

In the early autumn of 1921, Lord Carnarvon listened to the first regular radio programmes on a huge receiver which disfigured his library. The world was becoming worse. China had allowed the creation of a Communist Party and Germany that of a National Socialist Party under Hitler. Bloody turmoil shook Russia and miners' strikes disturbed the serenity of Great Britain. And the Earl was worried about Egypt again.

Because of the rebellious climate, the British authorities had agreed to hold talks with the freedom fighters. But the negotiations had come to a sudden end because the High Commissioner had refused to make any concessions. Zaghlul had been used as a scapegoat and deported for the second time, this time to the Seychelles.

The green lawns of Highclere shone under the autumn sun. Through the library window, the Earl contemplated with delight a scene that had remained unchanged for several generations. A terrible war had devastated Europe, normally stable societies were shaking, but Highclere remained unchanged, like an immutable landmark.

After dinner, Lady Carnarvon stayed with her husband in front of a log fire. 'You look worried, my dear.'

'Our accountants have warned me that the value of the pound is falling, inflation is becoming more pronounced and our expenses are increasing. It will soon become impossible to support our 40,000 acres and numerous servants. If we want to retain our way of life, we shall have to think of ways of saving money.'

'How? We can't reduce the number of house servants, nor of gardeners. The hunt is indispensable. So we are left with . . .'

'. . . My excavations in Egypt.'

'You must agree that they have yielded poor results. And the sale of your collection won't reimburse your investment. Think about it, please.'

*

Christian Jacq

Carter regretted not having kept a stable job which would have enabled him to spend his whole life digging without being obliged to produced results. What a stupid thought, he immediately realized, because the hierarchy would not have allowed him to explore the Valley of the Kings! Carnarvon was the only man who offered the opportunity to make his dream come true.

He went to the appointment Herbert Winlock had arranged. In one of the reception rooms of the Winter Palace there was to be an exhibition of over 200 artefacts: necklaces, armbands, rings and dishes, all testifying to the art of the New Kingdom. As it also celebrated the Metropolitan Museum as the new owner of these most beautiful objects of the Carnarvon collection it caused great displeasure to the Antiquities Service and the British Museum.

The money received by Lord Carnarvon would compensate him for a large part of his efforts. As for Carter's final commission, it would enable him to end his days in a village in Upper Egypt, far away from a sham civilization whose values he did not share.

Winlock playfully remarked that the Englishman seemed to lack dynamism.

'The concession comes to an end in spring 1923 and I shall be nowhere near completing my task.'

'In New York, I examined closely the modest find that Davis had neglected . . . My assumption was confirmed. The seals of the royal necropolis and Tutankhamun's name prove definitively that a funerary banquet was held in his honour in the valley, where he is buried. I can even specify that there were eight guests. They wore flower wreaths and ate a hearty meal. The menu figured duck and mutton. They drank beer and wine and took the trouble to bury both the remnants of the exceptional meal and the crockery.'

Carter's eyes lit up. 'I was wrong to doubt. Tutankhamun is here, very close by. But why was he so carefully concealed?'

56

Demosthenes was agitated. Because of Carter, the antiques trade had been steadily deteriorating. Private tombs could still be plundered, of course, but nothing came from the Valley of the Kings any more. Scarcity drove art lovers to pay more and more for any artefacts, however insignificant, which came from the illustrious site. This also caused the Greek to increase his meetings with the inspectors of the service, who appreciated his generosity. It turned their meagre salary into something more acceptable and made them amenable to the rumours he spread.

Everybody knew that the Englishman was Pierre Lacau's bête noir and that he set a bad example by working so hard. It became all the more necessary to get rid of him. Egyptologists began to make fun of the 'valley's madman' who removed tons of sand and rock in search of a tomb Davis had already discovered a long time ago.

Demosthenes put his case to three young ambitious members of the service who pocketed envelopes containing their 'travel expenses'.

'Gentlemen, I have the unpleasant duty to tell you that Howard Carter is corrupt. He has just made a secret agreement with the Americans, and makes them pay a small fortune for rare artefacts.'

'Have the artefacts been stolen?' asked the highest-ranking inspector.

'Of course.'

'Was Carnarvon the official owner?'

'He was indeed.'

'In that case, we cannot interfere.'

'This is a theft, a crime against Egypt's heritage!'

'The business only concerns Carnarvon and the buyers.'

'And this is not all,' insisted the Greek. 'Carter acts as an expert for collectors. He charges them huge amounts of money for his precious advice. Even the billionaire Calouste Gulbenkian, the wealthiest oil merchant in the region, has paid him a princely sum. Gentlemen, Carter is growing rich at the expense of Egypt!'

'Have you any proof?'

'Is my good faith not enough?'

'Anyway, Carter is not a civil servant. How he earns his living is his business. We need an obvious professional misdemeanour, an attack on a site, a systematic destruction of archaeological remains.'

Demosthenes ordered a hemp drink. He needed to drown his sorrows in an induced artificial paradise, far away from Luxor and Carter.

Carter summoned the *reis*, forty men and 120 boys. February would be decisive. He asked the large team to step up their efforts in a new location, east of the tomb of Siptah, a pharaoh of the end of the Nineteenth Dynasty. As the area had not been explored by Davis, there might still be a pleasant surprise. It was a time of intense activity. Under the management of Ahmed Girigar, the workmen worked energetically. A huge quantity of rubble was removed and tipped into a ravine close to the tomb of Tuthmosis III. Within a short time, thanks to his team's efforts, Carter reached the earliest level of the valley, where he hoped to discover Tutankhamun's tomb.

A cable warned him of Carnarvon's imminent arrival.

When the Earl entered the site, Carter noticed his worried look. He cast a discreet glance at the excavations.

266

'Fine work, Howard.'

'The team has been wonderful. They deserve a bonus.'

'They will get it. Any results?'

The archaeologist was on the verge of tears. 'Nothing. Absolutely nothing. Neither a tomb nor any artefacts.'

'I have important news for you. Tomorrow, on 21 February, Egypt will be recognized as a sovereign and independent state.'

'Britain is giving up.'

'Not completely. The real master of the country remains the British high commissioner and our army will continue to occupy the country. His Majesty's Government will defend Egypt against any outside attack, protect its interests, ensure the security of its means of communication and control the Sudan.'

'A sovereign state . . . this is a masquerade.'

'Not really. Egypt will enjoy more dignity and Britain will have to adopt a different attitude.'

Carnarvon did not mention the role he had played in the negotiations.

'Our results seem minor,' said Carter emotionally, 'but our knowledge of the valley has increased significantly. The plan which produced the Eighteenth Dynasty tombs has no more secrets for me and I am beginning to understand how Ramses' craftsmen worked. The last excavations were thrilling. Do you want me to go into detail?'

'I'll take your word for it, Howard,' answered the Earl wearily.

On 15 March 1922, Fuad I relinquished the title of sultan and proclaimed himself King of Egypt, with the British authorities' agreement. Carter and Carnarvon had dinner together in the modest dining room of the house, where the archaeologist offered a meal worthy of the Earl: stuffed vine leaves, spiced lamb meatballs, Red Sea fish, melon and Egyptian pastries.

Carnarvon did not beat about the bush.

'Is there still any hope to make some major discovery?'

'I am convinced there is.'

'Our results are not good. With the exception of commercial transactions which have nothing to do with the valley, we have only unearthed vases from Ramses' time.'

'Winlock has proved that Tutankhamun's tomb has still not been found.'

'I believe you, Howard. But couldn't it be some small tomb in line with the rule of an insignificant king, and which might have been plundered a long time ago?'

'It's not been plundered, that's for sure. Otherwise some artefacts would have been circulating among the antique dealers.'

'I'll grant you that. But even if it is untouched, it might not contain much. Does the quest for this chimera require new campaigns and months of relentless work?'

'As long as an inch of soil remains unexplored, we should persevere. You promised me I would be lucky, sir.'

'It would be wrong for me to deny it. But luck is an unfaithful mistress, and she may have left me.'

'We have been through the worst, and now we are close to success, I can feel it!'

'The concession is coming to an end.'

'Lacau wouldn't dare refuse to renew it.'

'You're mistaken. He hates you.'

'I hope his venom suffocates him! The long and apparently sterile years must be a prelude to a find. My team has now got into the way of things. It has perfect cohesion and we are moving towards the end of our quest.'

'Could it be in another site?'

'Let's not betray the valley!'

Carnarvon sensed that he would not alter Carter's determination. 'As you wish . . . So we'll devote one last season to the valley . . . Which area will you choose?'

Carter thought a long time. 'This may seem absurd, but I

want to dig under the foundations of the workers' houses, near the tomb of Ramses VI.'

'But you have already examined that area thoroughly.'

'I couldn't complete my investigations because of the tourists and officials. This time I shall forbid access to the tomb and I shall know whether the houses hide a dump from the original foundation work. That would give us the key to the enigma.'

On 9 May 1922, Carter celebrated his forty-ninth birthday on his own. He drank a bottle of champagne and wandered in the valley. So many memories sprang up along the way: the discovery of the tombs of the founder, Amenhotep I, and Queen Hatshepsut, hopes and failures, Raifa's love, Ahmed Girigar's faithfulness and the strange friendship of George Herbert, Earl of Carnarvon, who was both so close and so distant. He felt broken and exhausted as it seemed as if his future was no longer of interest.

Within less than a year, Carter would be forced to dismiss his workmen and close the site. Lacau and Egyptologists would triumph. The valley would be neglected and abandoned to the tourists. The chill thought of failure made him shudder.

57

Carnarvon remained prostrate in a deckchair overlooking the Highclere parkland, resplendent with summer colour.

The August heat enveloped the full tops of the cedars of Lebanon. Lady Carnarvon took tender care of her husband and consulted his doctors increasingly often. The Earl was no longer able to take Susie for walks. Sensing that her master was ill, the dog spent most of her time at his feet.

While Lord Carnarvon's son enjoyed the English aristocracy's traditional sports, Lady Evelyn constantly watched her father. Usually quite talkative with her, he now sank into long periods of silence. He did not even enjoy archaeological books any more. He had fallen asleep several times and the books had dropped on the lawn. Nothing could cure him of a lethargy which looked like slow death. Neither Lady Carnarvon's prayers nor Lady Evelyn's softness mitigated his suffering and he refused all visits.

His daughter brought him a cup of tea.

'Eve . . .'

'Yes, father?'

'Sit down beside me. I can see that you are annoyed, almost rebellious. I am giving you an example unworthy of a father.'

'Don't worry so much. You're going through a bad time.'

'At the age of fifty-six, I'm now just an impotent old man.'

'A sick man who could be much better if he agreed to share his worries.'

Carnarvon straightened up and looked at his daughter. 'You know me better than I know myself.'

'What are you afraid of? To fret like this, you must have a heavy burden weighing down on you!'

'Heavier than you can imagine.'

'Well, then do something! A man of your calibre cannot continue to shut himself up in remorse.'

'You're right.'

She kissed him on the forehead. 'Send a cable to Howard Carter,' he ordered. 'And summon him here, immediately.'

With some trepidation the son of an unknown animal painter entered the huge estate of his chief. Highclere impressed him by its size and splendour. But the dryness of the valley had made him lose his taste for perfectly mown lawns, green hills, beeches and oaks. However, as a man from the country in love with landscape Carter would have liked to own such an estate. The Earl's wealth stared him in the face and reduced him to his mean condition: a servant in the service of a lord.

For one moment, he thought of escaping. But he remembered that his true master, the one who ruled over his destiny, was a forgotten pharaoh whose hardly audible voice had travelled down centuries. Clutching a briefcase full of documents against his heart, Carter followed the servant, who took him to the library.

Suddenly a violent storm broke out and the lights went out. Carter remained motionless in the darkness, surrounded by the reassuring presence of books. Then, a candleholder in one hand, Lady Evelyn illuminated the darkness.

'Mr Carter! What a pleasure to see you . . . even though I can hardly make you out!'

She quickly lit candles which bathed the room in a soft light.

'Do you like Highclere?'

'How could anyone not be captivated?'

'The castle filled my childhood with delight. If you want, I shall unveil its secrets for you.'

'Forgive my impatience. How is your father? The wire . . .'

The young woman's face turned sad. 'I'll tell him that you are here.'

A few minutes later, Carnarvon appeared, his features drawn and his hands hidden under a car rug which covered his legs; he was sitting in a wheelchair pushed by his daughter.

'Good evening, Howard. I fainted this morning and I have difficulty walking. Evelyn insists that I take great care of my health.'

'If my visit is ill-timed . . .'

'I asked you to come. We have to discuss some serious matters. Can you leave us, Evelyn, and order some port?'

The young woman withdrew reluctantly.

'Anything new, Howard?'

'Nothing significant. I have prepared for the coming season and summoned my team as usual.'

The Earl tossed his head back. 'I am weary, very weary . . . and Egypt is no longer safe. The violence constantly increases. The natives will soon reject all foreigners and take power. I shall have to choose another destination for the winter.'

Carter remained silent, waiting for more, but nothing further came. So he spoke up. 'Lord Carnarvon does not speak like that. The man I have known would never shrink from danger. He would never have been afraid of a country he loves more than any other.'

Would the servant's impertinence arouse the lord's fury? Carter did not care.

'Please forgive me if I offended you, Howard. Lacau discouraged me. The new regulation he wants to implement is a disaster.'

'I'll take care of Lacau.'

'You underrate the power of bureaucracy. It can deprive us of everything.'

'Lacau is afraid of you and of England. If we bare our teeth, he will step back.'

'I am not so sure of that . . . What results can we show? Over five seasons, we have cleared over 200,000 tons of rubble and I have invested over £20,000 to dig holes in the sand and unearth a few vases. Let's be clear: we have failed.'

'Do you think I am incompetent?'

'On the contrary, you are the best archaeologist in your generation. If you haven't discovered anything in this damn valley, it is because there is nothing to find there. What shall I leave behind me? Mounds of loose stones and craters . . . Tomorrow people will laugh at the name of Carnarvon. I am rich, Howard, but the Great War has upset the world and changed the economic rules. In the past, I did not have to count. Now, like everyone else, I must look after my finances. My fortune is not inexhaustible. You have to be an English lord, my friend, to have so much patience and waste so much money removing rubble in clouds of dust.'

'Such caution surprises me. Are you not going to ask for a renewal of the concession?'

'I can't. My health and the well-being of my family prevent me doing so.'

'If my last season shows you that—'

'There is no last season, Howard.'

'That is impossible! You are stabbing me in the back.'

'That is not my intention.'

'Give me a last chance.'

'It would not change things.'

Carter opened his briefcase and extracted a map of the Valley of the Kings, which he unfolded on the large table.

'Look. I noted the exact location of all the finds in the valley, from the most insignificant figurine to the most important tomb. I have not shown the map to anyone. It leads me to believe that the only really unexplored area is near the tomb of Ramses VI. I have hardly touched the central part of the site. It is there and nowhere else that Tutankhamun's vault hides.'

'You've talked so much about it, Howard . . . The dream has turned into a nightmare.' Carnarvon shook his head.

Christian Jacq

'Give me your support at least.'

'With what aim?'

'I shall finance the excavations myself.'

'You, Howard?'

'I have earned some money, thanks to you. I shall spend it to the last penny and to the last hour I can pay the workmen. Even if I can only pay for one month of work, I shall demonstrate to you that I am right. The only thing I ask you is to stay as a sleeping partner so that Lacau does not put a spoke in my wheel.'

Carnarvon took off the car rug and stood up. 'I agree, but on one condition.'

'What?'

'I am the one who will finance our last season's work. No one else will do it.'

58

Fired by a fierce determination, Carter arrived in Luxor on 2 October 1922. He immediately summoned Ahmed Girigar and explained his plan to him: they were to resume intense work north-east of the tomb of Ramses VI.

The *reis* expressed some surprise. Should they both forbid access to visitors and dismantle the workers' houses from the time of Ramses? That was indeed what the archaeologist intended.

Ahmed Girigar was leaving when he heard what sounded like birdsong.

'Have you got a bird in your house?'

Carter threaded his way through boxes full of French wine, biscuits and preserves bought in Fortnum and Mason and came back with a cage, in which a canary frolicked.

The *reis* was filled with wonder. 'The golden bird! It will bring you good fortune.'

'I need to listen to its beautiful sound.'

'The golden bird speaks the language of heaven. It will guide us.'

Every workman in the team knew that this would be the last season under the direction of Howard Carter, an exacting but understanding employer who took an interest in the lot of his men and their families. Tomorrow they would once again have to accept the yoke of a cold and distant foreigner who would content himself with checking the site every now and then and boasting about his efforts to distinguished visitors.

Focusing on his task, Carter gave precise orders. As soon as access to the tomb of Ramses VI was forbidden, he asked that the mass of rubble still cluttering the area he wanted to explore be removed. On 1 November, he took photographs of the workers' houses. He checked his lists and gave orders to demolish them so as to be able to dig deeper. Ahmed Girigar signalled him that the foundations of these basic houses were still at least 3 feet above the primeval rock. The clearance would require three or four days.

A man was waiting for Carter in front of his isolated house. He hardly recognized him, he looked so old and worn out.

'You are Gamal, Raifa's brother!'

'My sister has died.'

'How did it happen?'

'It does not matter. She expressed a wish that you come to her funeral. I cannot deny her dying wish.'

Gamal turned on his heel and walked away. Carter followed him.

Raifa's corpse had been washed with warm water and wrapped in a white shroud, while mourners sang dirges. Her ankles had been bound and cotton put in her ears and nostrils. Sustained by the prayer for the dead, she was now beginning her final voyage: 'We belong to God and we must return to him.' Only men followed the coffin, which was covered with brightly coloured fabrics. At the cemetery a few lines from the Koran were recited: 'Two angels will come and question you. To the question: Who is your Lord? answer: Allah is my Lord. To the question: who is your Prophet? Answer: Mahomet is my Prophet.' Above the pit, a hole was dug to enable the living to talk to the dead woman.

Spadefuls of earth covered years of youth and happiness.

By the evening of 3 November, the workers' houses had been

dismantled. It was now possible to dig into the ground and venture into an unexplored area. Carter slept badly that night. He woke several times, haunted by Raifa's soft face. At dawn the canary sang its most beautiful song, almost as if it were contributing to the birth of a new sun.

As Howard Carter arrived on the site, he felt a sense of disquiet whose cause he soon understood: everything was quiet. Usually the workmen chatted, talked and sang as they handled their tools. That morning, everybody was silent. Carter walked towards the *reis*.

'Has there been an accident?'

Ahmed Girigar did not answer. He beckoned the water carrier to come near. 'Can you explain?'

The man was trembling. 'I was having fun digging in the sand with my stick over there . . . Suddenly it hit something hard. Intrigued, I knocked again. With my hands, I freed a block. I believe . . . I believe it is very old! I was afraid and I hid it in the sand.'

'Show me the place,' ordered Carter.

He knelt down and freed the block in his turn. 'It is a stair . . . maybe a staircase hewn in the rock.'

It was too early to get excited. The workers took turns all day to clear a staircase leading about 12 feet under the entrance to the tomb of Ramses VI. The shape of the stairs, their width and contours resembled those of Eighteenth Dynasty hypogea, the time of Tutankhamun. But the clearance brought no confirmation: there were no dumps from the original foundation work, no fifth-level foundations and no small artefacts bearing the name of the pharaoh.

The night of 4 November was brief. Lying on his bed, Carter forced himself to close his eyes and take some rest. He tried to dismiss assumptions and hopes from his mind so as to focus on reality: he had just brought to light the staircase to a tomb.

The work day started very early, in an atmosphere of excitement. The workmen did not sing or talk much. They were all aware that they were taking part in an extraordinary adventure and they all wanted to know more. There was no need for the *reis* to encourage them. A legend was already spreading: this was the tomb of the golden bird, whose soul had guided the hands of men.

As the stairs were cleared, Carter felt increasingly nervous. Thousands of times he felt like mingling with the workmen and hurrying them. Hours passed too slowly, each charged with its own anxieties. Was it an unfinished vault or a simple cavity abandoned without having ever been used? The valley had so often cheated him by drawing him into a trap! How could he forget that it had never delivered up any undesecrated tomb?

In the early afternoon, Carter walked down the stairs, with shaking legs. He might have been the first man to perform this insignificant movement in 3,000 years. On the site complete silence prevailed, as if a sacred fear had taken hold of the place.

Carter had stopped the clearing at the twelfth stair, for the upper part of a door had appeared and he wanted to examine it immediately. On the block, mortar bore the imprint of several seals.

'So it was true,' he murmured. 'I was right not to lose faith in the valley.'

He recognized Anubis above the nine enemies of Egypt in shackles, unable to do any harm. This was the seal of the royal necropolis he had been hoping to see for so many years! Now he only had to identify the name of the king to know the owner of the tomb.

The disappointment was terrible. Only the seals of the royal necropolis had been affixed, some of them vertically and others sideways, when the door had been closed for ever. This meant that the sepulchre belonged to a high dignitary, who had been considered worthy of resting with the kings. Tutankhamun, whom he had expected to meet for a moment, was receding into the distance.

Only the bricked up door remained. Did it prove that the vault had not been desecrated? Its narrowness certainly ruled out the idea of a royal tomb. But did it not hide the secret of a master builder of the glorious time when Egypt shone with thousand splendours? Why had the person buried there been so carefully hidden? It might even have been a simple cache for more or less precious objects.

Carter examined the upper part of the door, inch by inch. Where the mortar had peeled off, he could see wood. It was a lintel. Was it the door of a cache or did it open on a corridor sloping down into the ground? He enlarged a small crack between the wall and the lintel and made an opening large enough for him to get a glimpse of what was on the other side of the sealed door with an electric torch.

There was indeed a corridor, but it was full of stones and rubble! Not only had the builders hidden the tomb under some workers' houses, but they had also concealed its entrance with incredible precautions. Should they demolish the door immediately and empty the corridor? He refrained from such a stupid impulse. Carnarvon should be by his side. It would be a most spiteful betrayal not to give him that joy.

Carter walked up the twelve stairs and asked the *reis* to cover them with earth and have them watched over day and night.

'You seem upset . . . Do you want me to see you home?'

'No, Ahmed. I prefer to be alone.'

Night was falling. The moonlight spread a silver veil over the valley. With a feeling of exultation, the workmen scattered, convinced that a huge treasure was hiding behind the mysterious door. In spite of the *reis*'s instructions, nobody would be able to hold his tongue for long.

Carter climbed on his donkey. His nerves on edge, he felt like wandering in the valley all night long. An unbearable wait was beginning. When would Carnarvon be able to walk down the stairs? What miracle could Carter promise him? This was certainly no royal tomb, but undoubtedly a very ancient vault

279

dating back to the dynasty of Amenhotep and Tuthmosis. If the Earl came and saw a plundered and desecrated cache, would he not put an end to the campaign without delay?

No, that was a delusion. Were not the sealed door and the blocked corridor proofs that the mysterious sepulchre had remained undesecrated?

The donkey roamed in the moonlight, while Carter's feverish mind became lost in wild dreams alternating between hope and despair.

59

Carnarvon was returning from a long walk in the park of Highclere with Susie. Lady Evelyn ran towards him with dishevelled hair, brandishing a piece of paper.

'Hurry up, father! There is a telegram from Howard Carter!'

The Earl had never believed he could feel such intense emotion. He ran in his turn. His daughter fell into his arms.

'Read it to me.'

'I know it by heart: "At last a wonderful discovery in the Valley. Splendid tomb with intact seals. Covered it up. Awaiting your arrival. Congratulations."'

'Congratulations,' repeated Carnarvon, overwhelmed.

'When are we leaving?'

'As soon as possible, Eve. Carter is a wizard. We mustn't keep him.'

'I'm so happy!'

'So am I . . . I didn't expect such good fortune any more!'

'Could it be Tutankhamun?'

'Carter doesn't mention his name.'

'Caution . . .'

'Let's not wonder about a thousand possibilities. The answers are in Egypt.'

The dinner was gloomy. Lady Carnarvon had received the news as a blow. As far as she was concerned, she had turned the page on Egypt.

'You are not healthy enough for such a tiring journey.'

'Did you read Carter's telegram properly?'

'Your Carter is a dreamer. He tries to dazzle you to keep you financing him.'

'That is not his style.'

'I thought you were completely happy here at Highclere. You can dedicate yourself in complete peace to your favourite occupations, reading and hunting, see children who admire you grow up, to say nothing of my love.'

'I am aware of my good fortune, Almina, but Carter needs me.'

'Can't he manage alone?'

'It is an undesecrated tomb.'

'How many times have you said that that was impossible?'

'I was wrong and Carter was right.'

'I have a bad premonition. Please take it into consideration.'

'I am afraid my trunks are ready.'

On 6 November, Carter watched over the bank of steps disappearing under a protective layer of soil. Forty-eight hours after the beginning of the task, nothing could be seen any more. Big blocks from the workers' houses had been hauled in front of the concealed staircase. Carter wondered if he had dreamed it all. Only the permanent presence of armed wardens signalled the existence of remains worthy of interest.

On 7 November, Ahmed Girigar woke him up with a start.

'What is the matter?'

'A man is asking for you. He says it's important.'

Carter dressed hastily. The visitor was waiting outside, a notebook and a pencil in hand.

'I'm a journalist. I heard that you have just discovered a fabulous treasure. Give me exclusive coverage and I shall get you on the front page.'

'Who told you this?'

'It is all the people are talking about in Luxor.'

Carter returned to the *reis*. 'Ahmed, please see this man off the premises.'

'Wait! You must keep the press informed!'

'Don't resist.'

The *reis*'s size and look discouraged the journalist.

'The press will come back, Carter, and in strength, believe me!'

He had hardly disappeared when a member of the work team brought a canvas bag full of letters and messages. Everybody in Luxor seemed to know. The archaeologist was being congratulated. People offered to help in the excavations. He was being threatened and asked innumerable questions.

He slumped into an armchair. 'I feel lost, Ahmed. I'm being carried away by the hustle and bustle.'

'You are too lonely. You need help.'

'Carnarvon won't be here for some twenty days . . . If pressure increases, how can I resist? I am not used to struggling against such waves!'

'I know a strong man who will lend you a hand. Get in touch with him today!'

Arthur Callender, a former Egyptian Railways manager, was enjoying a peaceful retirement in Armant, some fifteen miles south of Luxor. A famous engineer, he had taken part in archaeological digs as an odd-job man and several times he had come across Howard Carter, a man whom he esteemed. When he received the call for help, he answered immediately.

Tall and robust, with broad shoulders and a heavy face, Callender made people think of an elephant. Badly dressed, a big eater, he never lost his temper and reassured those around him. He was not afraid of any technical task. Electricity held no secrets for him and he knew how to handle any tool. Building a house, transporting crates, assessing the amount and nature of materials needed on a site were to him like child's play.

He and Carter hugged each other.

'How can I help you, Howard?'

'You don't want to know why I called for you?'

'It doesn't matter. Service is service.'

'We have found a tomb, Arthur. An Eighteenth Dynasty tomb.'

'You deserve it.'

'It may be empty.'

'Luck smiles on men of worth eventually.'

'I must go to Luxor to welcome Carnarvon and his daughter, who have just sent a telegram. My workmen are honest, but they will be under pressure and . . .'

'I understand. I shall watch over the tomb like a lover. You can leave in peace, Howard.'

On one of the big stones marking the site of the discovery, Carter had painted the coat of arms. Everybody would know the owner's identity.

During his stay in Cairo, Carter bought electrical equipment and applied to the Antiquities Service for a lighting permit. Because of the installation in the tomb of Ramses VI Lacau would not be able to refuse an arrangement which would facilitate excavations.

In the valley, Callender kept watch with a vigilance which discouraged onlookers as well as potential plunderers. In addition, the head of the Abd el Rassul clan discouraged thieves by reminding them that Carter and he had agreed on a non-aggression pact.

But then Demosthenes came into the picture. Enraged at the prospect of seeing Carter triumph, he intervened with a *sheikh* on the east bank, who was famous for his xenophobia. A wizard and a creator of talismans, he enjoyed great fame. The humble people feared him.

Followed by a crowd of disciples, he appeared in front of the tomb. Arthur put aside the cucumber sandwich he was savouring and faced him without lowering his gaze. Panic-stricken, Carter's workmen stood aside. The *reis* admonished them not to flee.

'The place is cursed,' said the *sheikh*. 'The tomb contains evil spirits. The door sealed by ancient demons must not be opened by anyone! Otherwise profaners will be punished. Evil forces will flood the world and no wizard will be able to destroy them.'

'Do you intend to stay here?' asked Callender, his arms crossed over his chest.

'Of course not,' answered the *sheikh*, surprised.

'Good. This is an archaeological site where entry is forbidden to the public and I am obliged to ask you to leave without delay.'

'You're an insolent fellow! You'll perish like all the others!'

'I'd rather die with a peaceful heart than with a mouth full of hate!'

'Cursed be the tomb and cursed be all those who enter it!'

The noisy crowd moved away. Callender sat down again and bit into his sandwich with gusto.

He stayed alone in Carter's house, where he enjoyed brief rest periods between turns of duty. He trusted only Ahmed Girigar and people close to him who were not impressed by the *sheikh*'s fanaticism. But he appeared unexpectedly on the site by day or night to make sure that his instructions were respected.

His best friend was the canary. As soon as he entered, the bird greeted him cheerfully. The engineer never forgot to share titbits with it. That evening he knew that something unusual had happened. As he entered, the door creaked and the bird remained silent. Listening, he could hear the flutter of wings. A cobra was swallowing the canary.

Callender killed the snake, but its prey was already dead. He buried it below the house.

The following day, people murmured that the *sheikh*'s curse had taken its first victim. The pharaoh, whose soul had crept into the body of the cobra, had taken revenge on the golden bird which had revealed the location of his tomb.

60

Carter was on tenterhooks and cursed the slowness of ships. An undesecrated tomb was waiting for him in the valley while he was stamping his feet on the platform of Luxor railway station!

But Carnarvon's ill-suppressed joy and the smile of Lady Evelyn, enthusiastic at the prospect of living a fabulous adventure, erased the memory of the days he had wasted. However, after the Channel crossing, the railway journey through France, another crossing from Marseilles to Alexandria and another train journey from Alexandria to Cairo and from Cairo to Luxor, the Earl was not yet out of the wood. After he had been greeted by the Governor of the province, come especially to welcome him, he still had to take the ferry to the west bank of the Nile and ride on a donkey to the Valley of the Kings. Wearing a grey hat with a white border, a thick coat with two rows of buttons and a woollen scarf, he was tired and shivery, and just could not get warm. Radiant, his daughter wore a light beige outfit. A fur collar recalled the European cold and the very sober skirt, fastened on one side, the deportment necessary for a well-bred young woman. The sparkling eyes of Susie, who ran by the donkey's side, did not miss a scrap of the show.

The more they progressed, the more numerous the onlookers became. Delighted, Lady Evelyn accepted the flowers she was offered. Boys played drums, girls danced and shouted to welcome them.

'If it was not 23 November 1922 and my name was not Carnarvon, I would readily believe that I was repeating Christ's arrival in Jerusalem. Your small discovery seems to have caused a great fuss, dear Howard.'

Carter looked at the Earl's daughter. The pretty girl had become a playful, beautiful young woman with a deep and lively gaze.

'Tell us the truth,' she asked mischievously. 'What is the name of the king buried in the tomb?'

'I do not know.'

'Did you really stop in front of the door?'

Carter turned red. 'I swear to you, on my honour.'

'Don't be touchy,' she said with a laugh. 'You're really an exceptional man. In your place, I would not have had the strength of will.'

The donkeys increased their pace as they entered the valley. Warned by a telegram, Callender had begun to clear the steps. Lady Evelyn jumped down from her mount and was the first to enter the site.

'When shall we resume work?'

'As soon as you want,' answered Carter.

'Some rest would be welcome,' said Carnarvon. 'We must be prepared for some busy days.'

On the morning of 24 November, Carter contemplated the steps. Where did they lead to? He sat on a block and mechanically plunged his hand in the sand. The burning sensation made him cry with pain. He bent forward and saw the tiny black scorpion which had just bitten him. Remaining calm, he called Ahmed Girigar.

'The species is not lethal, but you must disinfect the injury immediately.'

The best healer in Gurnah brought medicinal herbs and ointment and bandaged his swollen wrist.

The pain and fever were bearable. No poison could prevent Carter from directing operations. He thought of Raifa, who had also known ancestral remedies to fight venom. He knew that for about a month he would have violent pain. Then each full moon would revive the burning sensation. But his life was in no danger and, with the necessary stamina, he would continue to work.

He rested until Carnarvon and his daughter arrived in mid-afternoon. Hiding his bandaged left wrist in the sleeve of his jacket, he checked his bow tie and helped Lady Evelyn down from her donkey. Although slightly dizzy, he managed to allay any suspicion.

'Shall we clear the door?' asked the young woman, impatiently.

'We should not waste any more time.'

Callender had finished. Sixteen steps were now visible. Carter invited Carnarvon and his daughter to go down.

'There are several seals!' she exclaimed.

'The seal of the necropolis,' indicated Carter.

Carnarvon had gone down on one knee. 'The lower ones are different.'

Intrigued, Carter moved nearer. The lower part of the door still bore fairly clear hieroglyphic inscriptions. A royal cartouche had been repeated several times. Carter thought his heart would stop beating. He stepped back.

'Are you unwell, Mr Carter?'

The archaeologist was unable to answer. He pointed to the cartouches. 'Here . . . on the door . . .'

Carnarvon took his arm. 'What can you read, Howard?'

'Tutankhamun.'

The ecstasy of the saints could not have been greater than the ineffable joy which seized his whole being and transported him into an indescribable state between heaven and earth. He had found Tutankhamun at last. The king was emerging from the depths of time. His eternal dwelling was coming back to life in the valley, and becoming its heart and centre.

Carnarvon still held his arm. 'Brandy?'

'No . . . I need all my senses. I want to see the door again.'

Carter was afraid he might have been mistaken and deciphered another name. But he was right, Tutankhamun had been buried in this strange place.

'This is fabulous, Howard,' judged Callender warmly.

'Congratulations, Mr Carter!' said Lady Evelyn enthusiastically. 'May I kiss you?'

She did not wait for the archaeologist's permission.

'That was the best sign of gratitude,' estimated the Earl. 'You will be a famous man, Howard.'

'The authorship of the discovery is yours.'

'I have no intention of denying my contribution, but it is your dream which has come true.'

'*Our* dream.'

Carnarvon pretended to think. 'You're not completely wrong.'

Carter bowed again over the seals.

'Could another monarch share the same tomb?'

'This is much more serious.' Carter had grown pale.

Carnarvon perceived his concern. 'What is the matter?'

'The tomb has been desecrated.'

61

'How can you be certain?'

'One of the seals of the necropolis has been fixed to a kind of crack. The door was reopened after it was first closed and then sealed again.'

The Earl did not lose hope. 'That happened before the time of Ramses because the workers' houses were built on top of the tomb.'

'That is true,' acknowledged Carter. 'The funerary material may have been preserved.'

A muted anxiety had overcome excavators. Had thieves entered the vault?

Ahmed Girigar warned Carter. From the rubble cluttering the lower part of the staircase, he had just extracted a scarab. The archaeologist could not believe his eyes: it bore the name of Tuthmosis III. Intrigued, he examined the tiniest pieces. He was soon helped by Lady Evelyn, who found several fragments bearing inscriptions. She showed them to Carter who became increasingly perplexed. Again he deciphered the name of Tutankhamun, but other cartouches revealed the presence of his predecessors, the heretical Akhenaton and Smenkhkara. Another piece mentioned Amenhotep III, Akhenaton's father.

'Five pharaohs,' murmured Carter.

'What is your conclusion?'

'This doesn't look too good.'

Callender accumulated fragments of pottery and wooden

boxes which had contained royal jewels and clothes, some of which belonged to Tutankhamun and others to Akhenaton. The sight discouraged Carter.

'Why are you so pessimistic, Carter?'

'I am afraid that the vault might be just a simple cache which was plundered a long time ago. The relics prove that the priests moved the mummies of the kings to shelter them in this cavity. When someone tried to steal them, they were moved elsewhere.'

'There is another possibility: forced to leave Tell el-Amarna and come back to Thebes, Tutankhamun concealed the treasures he had taken with him.'

Carter nodded, but he was thinking of the numerous desecrations of vaults which were described in some papyrus. He imagined the thieves' secret meetings, their advance in the darkness, the attack on the guards and their penetration into the tomb in search of gold. The criminals did not respect mummies. They tore away necklaces, jewels and amulets, took off masks and burnt bandages. They took away vases, pieces of furniture and statues and shared the loot. When they left, the sacred dwelling was abandoned to chaos and desolation. That was what Carter was afraid they would find on the other side of the sealed door.

'We'll open it tomorrow,' decided Carnarvon.

'Why the delay?' asked Lady Evelyn, impatiently.

'Because of the regulations of the Antiquities Service.'

Carter did not object. He was too overwhelmed with the disappointment which had followed the exhilaration.

Lacau had sent his worst inspector to the valley, the thin and rigid Rex Engelbach, whom nobody had ever heard laugh. On the morning of 25 November, he came to examine the site. The sight of the stairs did not arouse any emotion in him.

'Is there a door to a tomb at the bottom of the staircase?'

'Probably,' answered Lord Carnarvon.

'In that case, you should consider putting in an iron grille.'

Christian Jacq

'That has been arranged. In the meantime, we hope to enter the tomb.'

'Don't forget that an inspector of the service must be present when you open the tomb. Pierre Lacau is very exacting on this point. Any breach of the regulation will be severely punished.'

'And you,' put in Carter, irritated, 'don't forget that the one who found the tomb is allowed to enter it first.'

Rex Engelbach stood up proudly. 'That is what is specified in your excavation permit. But please note that I deplore that, as an amateur's haste can be very destructive.'

'I am no amateur and I have been working in the valley much longer than you.'

Fearing a fight, Carnarvon interposed himself.

'Well, stay. Mr Carter is going to proceed to the opening of the tomb.'

Indifferent to bureaucratic quarrels, Lady Evelyn was already standing by the door. Carnarvon took a photograph of her and several of the seals.

'As you can see,' said Carter to Engelbach, 'we are serious in our work. I drew all the details and our publications will be as precise as it will be complete.'

'Let's hope so.'

'I must show you something.'

Carnarvon and his daughter stepped back. Carter showed Engelbach the upper part of the door.

'Is there anything specific?'

'The coating of mortar fills a hole which was used by thieves.'

'That is mere assumption.'

'That is undeniable fact. Be careful to record in your statement that the tomb was desecrated in antiquity.'

Engelbach took notes. Carnarvon exchanged a knowing smile with Carter. With Lacau and his administration, the difference between an untouched tomb and a desecrated tomb might be very important.

'What is the exact nature of the tomb?'

'To find out, Mr Engelbach, we have to enter it.'

'Will it take long?'

'The door is not very wide.'

'Well, then let's go.'

The workmen removed the blocks of stone one by one. Carter made out the entrance to a sloping gallery, about 6 feet high and as wide as the staircase. To go any further they had to remove the mass of stones and earth blocking the way. There were interesting remains hidden in the debris: broken pieces of pottery, lids of jars, alabaster or painted vases. Carter lingered over skins which had contained the water for the lining of the door or for making mortar. None of the objects mentioned the name of Tutankhamun or his predecessors.

'They are traces of the theft,' said Carnarvon. 'The bandits forced their way through the blocks and left behind part of their plunder.'

Engelbach continued to take notes. By nightfall, about 9 yards of the corridor had been cleared.

'There is no second door in sight,' noted the inspector. 'That is bad luck, Carter, you have stumbled upon a cache that had been emptied and filled in again.'

On 26 November, Rex Engelbach did not come to the site, which he considered as of no interest. Feverish, Carter did not think of the pain in his hand. It cheered him up to be rid of the narrow-minded civil servant. Under his direction, the workmen burst with energy and cautiously emptied the corridor. After 3 feet more, they were able to expose the bottom of a second door, which was soon cleared.

This was the moment of truth. Would the entry to the tomb be the door to hell or heaven? Carter remembered that, a hundred years earlier, on 14 September, in a moment of enlightenment, Champollion had penetrated the secret of hieroglyphs. If he opened the first untouched royal tomb, he would join him in legend.

'Shall we break down the door?' asked Lady Evelyn.

'It may be dangerous. If the air has not been renewed for thirty-four centuries, how can we know that it is not poisonous?'

'I don't care about the risk. Such moments make you forget your fear.'

Carter looked questioningly at Carnarvon. The Earl did not express any opposition. His daughter was as stubborn as he was.

'There is a way of detecting the possibility of toxic fumes: we can use a candle. If it goes out, we will have to leave the tomb as soon as possible.'

A lump in his throat, Carter made a small opening in the upper left corner. Then he inserted an iron bar which Callender passed to him and which only met emptiness. There was nothing to block it on the other side. Then he brought the lit candle to the hole. The flame flickered for a moment but did not go out.

'Please hold it,' he said to the Earl, 'while I enlarge the hole.'

Trembling, Carter looked through. He had the feeling that he was entering the other world and stepping over a sacred threshold barring a fabulous country from humankind.

At first he saw nothing. The flame continued to flicker and to cast its light over only a short distance. Then his eyes became used to the darkness and shapes gradually detached themselves from the shadows.

Carnarvon became as impatient as his daughter. 'Can you see anything?'

'Yes, wondrous things!'

62

'Strange animals, statues, gold . . . everywhere the glow of gold!' Carnarvon looked in his turn, dumbfounded. When it was Lady Evelyn's turn, she remained as silent as the two men. As for Callender he was flabbergasted. The adventure was turning into a miracle.

Carter coarsely filled the hole again. The quartet left the tomb in silence. Callender fixed a wooden grille to the outside door and asked the *reis* to keep watch day and night. Ahmed Girigar asked no questions. The three men and Lady Evelyn mounted the donkeys and headed for the house without uttering a word. Susie accompanied them silently.

Callender poured four brandies. The spirit brought Carnarvon out of his silence.

'There are dozens, maybe hundreds of masterpieces . . . The valley is bountiful, Howard.'

'This is the most beautiful day in our lives, the day of a miracle . . . To think that Davis stopped digging less than 6 feet from the tomb! But I do not understand its plan. It doesn't look like any other sepulchre.'

'Are there several rooms?' enquired Lady Evelyn.

'I caught a glimpse of the start of a passage in the north wall. Probably a bricked up door.'

'There is neither a sarcophagus nor a mummy,' noted Callender.

'So this was indeed a cache,' concluded Carter.

'But the passage may lead to a burial chamber,' objected Carnarvon. 'If the blocked door is intact, Tutankhamun is still resting in his sarcophagus.'

'We must empty the antechamber and explore the whole vault . . . We'll still need a lot of patience before we meet the Pharaoh – if he exists.'

Lady Evelyn stood up fiercely. 'Let's go back to the tomb.'

'Do you mean that . . .?'

'Yes, I do. We must act this very night.'

'If the Antiquities Service hears about it, our excavation permit will be revoked.'

'The *reis* won't betray us,' said Callender. 'He is an extraordinary man. We should let him in on the secret.'

'We must write a message to Engelbach,' suggested Carnarvon. 'We can explain that the second door has been cleared and that we are expecting him tomorrow morning.'

'If we send it tonight, aren't we running the risk of him coming unexpectedly?' wondered the young woman.

'There is no risk; the service closes at 5 p.m. So Engelbach will only get the message tomorrow morning.'

'Well then, gentlemen, take your torches. I'll go first.'

Ahmed Girigar tied the donkeys to a pole and stood guard again in front of the wooden grille he had shut after the quartet. Susie would keep him company outside.

Carter hesitated to force the door of the chamber which priests had closed at the time of the splendour of Egypt. Wasn't his endeavour stamped with the seal of madness?

'We should enlarge the hole,' remarked Carnarvon.

'We should stop,' said Carter.

Lady Evelyn came up and took his hand. 'That is for you to decide, of course . . . but don't try to stop me.'

In the shadows, her smile made her look like an Egyptian goddess.

Carter enlarged the hole.

'I would like to go in first. If there is still any danger, I should face it.'

'Lady Evelyn . . .'

'I have decided, Mr Carter. The archaeologist must survive at all costs to write a scientific report.'

Carnarvon helped his daughter. Carter managed alone. Then he reached out his arm to the Earl, whom Callender carefully eased forward. Lady Evelyn lit the way with an electric torch.

'I'm stuck,' complained Callender, who was much stouter than his companions. Carter pulled him. The stone crumbled and his friend came through.

Packed together, their hearts pounding wildly, they pointed the lights at the treasure. The sheer quantity of artefacts was beyond even the most insane dream: golden funerary beds, black wooden royal statues, painted and inlaid chests, alabaster vases, chairs, sticks, pieces of a dismantled cart . . . Their eyes jumped from one masterpiece to the next.

A faint smell pervaded the air which they were the first people to breathe after 3,000 years.

Lady Evelyn shouted, 'There's a snake!'

As she took refuge in Carter's arms, Callender interposed himself.

'It is indeed a snake, but a gilded wooden one.'

Once the emotion was over, the archaeologist measured the room: it was 20 feet long by 12 feet wide and 7 feet high. In that small space was crammed the most fabulous treasure ever found in Egypt.

'What a mess!' remarked Carnarvon. 'Artefacts were piled up on top of each other . . . unless thieves were surprised as they were plundering the place.'

'It is a rather orderly disorder,' corrected Carter. 'Look at the ground.'

On the floor lay pieces of cloth and dried flowers which had not been trampled.

'Those who trod this sacred ground for the last time took the trouble not to destroy anything. Not only are we presented with a material treasure, but also with the soul of Egypt. Our nostrils are filled by the fragrance of eternity.'

Amazed, Carnarvon stood in front of the three resurrection beds: the one with a lion head symbolized vigilance, the one with a cow head the celestial mother and the last one with a hippopotamus head embodied the matrix of rebirth. The shadows of the heads appeared on the wall as if they were coming back to life.

Lady Evelyn did not dare open the dozens of precious wooden chests and egg-shaped boxes. A set depicting Tutankhamun on his cart triumphing over his routed enemies made her ecstatic. Carter lifted the lid of the chest painted in praise of the young king; inside lay sandals and clothes embroidered with coloured beads.

'He wore these robes and sandals,' she said, moved.

Carnarvon admired a throne whose back showed Tutankhamun and his young wife. Facing the King, the Queen reached her arm out to him to express her affection, in a gesture of unequalled tenderness and distinction.

'This is the most beautiful work of Egyptian art,' murmured Carter.

'You must be so happy,' said Lady Evelyn. She was so close to him that she almost touched him.

Moments of delight followed one after another. A number of unique artefacts attracted the archaeologist's eyes.

'Come and look here,' suggested Callender who, despite his stoutness, moved without bumping into anything. 'There is an opening in the south-west angle of the antechamber.'

'I'll go first if it's narrow.'

A torch in her hand, Lady Evelyn did so without delay. She immediately called Carter, who crawled into a small square room which had been dug in the rock like the antechamber. It was also full of magnificent artefacts, golden beds, gold seats and alabaster vases. Complete disorder prevailed, as if a storm had hit the place and upset the original order.

Carter felt overwhelmed. Studying the contents of the antechamber and the annexe would require years of survey and research. He would have to understand why the only intact tomb in the valley had been planned in this way. Was 'tomb' the right term? Was Tutankhamun himself missing?

Back in the antechamber, Carter went to the start of the passage he thought he had distinguished in the north wall. He had to brave the gaze of two black wooden statues depicting the king as the warden of his own grave. He begged them to forgive him for the intrusion and promised to respect the Pharaoh's soul and body if he managed to reach the sarcophagus. Carter was now convinced that he was in a royal tomb and not in a cache, however prodigious it might be. On the other he wondered about the unusual plan, which had nothing in common with all the graves that were known. Usually a longish corridor flanked by shrines on both sides ended in a burial chamber. Was the latter hidden behind one of the walls of the antechamber?

A mortar whose colour differed from that of the wall proved that there was a passage. Several necropolis seals had been fixed to it. So the priests had filled in the opening again after they had left the secret room.

'Do you want to go further, sir?' he asked Carnarvon.

'Of course,' answered Lady Evelyn.

With the help of Callender, Carter freed a few blocks. The beam of his torch lit up only a kind of narrow corridor, probably a gallery leading to another chamber. He therefore had to remove more blocks and clear the lower part of the passage to be able to sneak inside. Carnarvon, his daughter and Callender held their breath.

Suddenly Carter disappeared, as if he had fallen into an abyss.

'Where are you, Howard?'

The archaeologist's head appeared again.

'Everything is fine . . . The floor is about 3 feet lower than that of the antechamber. I was surprised by the gap.'

'What can you see?'

'Nothing for the moment . . . I must pick up my torch.'

The silence did not last long.

'My God! A gold wall!'

Feet first, Lady Evelyn slid into the opening. Together with Carter's, her torch lit up a huge shrine which almost entirely filled a room which was smaller than the antechamber but larger than the other room.

'The burial chamber . . . We've found it this time.'

It was now Carnarvon's turn to come down. Callender's size prevented him from following them. He and Carter decided not to free any other blocks, so that it would not take too long to fill in the hole again.

Fascinated, the Earl laid his hand on the gold of a huge catafalque whose door was shut by a lock. 'I'm sure he is resting inside. A pharaoh in his gold sarcophagus, for the first time!'

Carter slowly pulled the lock. A linen shroud sprinkled with gold rosettes covered the coffin.

'He is here,' he murmured in a muffled voice. 'He is here and I shall take good care of him.'

He closed the door to the shrine and pushed back the lock with shaking hands. 'It's impossible to go any further tonight, without risking damaging these marvels.'

Squatting, Lady Evelyn pointed her torch at a passage in the north-east corner of the burial chamber. 'There is another room here . . . this is incredible!'

Carter and Carnarvon crawled behind the young woman. An extraordinary golden reliquary caught their eyes. In its four angles, four gold goddesses spread their arms in a protective gesture. Their faces looked so perfect and their bodies so wonderful that they experienced a feeling of real devotion.

'We must leave,' said Carter. 'We must get back to the house before dawn.'

'This is the greatest discovery of all time,' murmured Carnarvon. 'There are enough objects to fill the upper part of the British Museum's Egypt gallery.'

Regretfully they left the new treasure chamber, where a magnificent statue of the jackal Anubis lay on the roof of a shrine. Along the walls, boxes, vases, lamps, baskets, models of boats and jewels formed an extraordinarily beautiful décor. Almost dazed, they walked back to the burial chamber and climbed up to the antechamber. Callender put the blocks back and Carter left the lid of a basket and reeds in front of the passage.

Ahmed Girigar asked no questions. Four shadows mounted the donkeys and, under the guidance of Susie, vanished silently into the fleeting night.

63

Carter was not able to sleep. He could hardly believe that he was not dreaming and that Tutankhamun's tomb really existed. To reassure himself, he looked at the map he had drawn hastily.

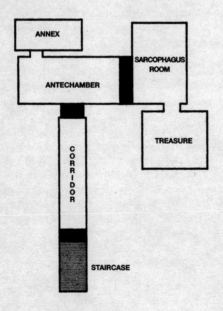

A series of four rooms of modest size comprised the only intact royal vault in the valley. Although it did not resemble any other, no essential element was missing. This was not a hastily arranged place, but a completed universe gathering all the ritual artefacts necessary for the king's survival. Thus Tutankhamun offered a perfect example to anyone who wanted to penetrate the secrets of Egyptian spirituality and resurrection.

At mid-morning, Carter woke Callender and asked him to prepare the electric installation which would enable them to bring light to Tutankhamun's tomb by linking it to the main generator in the valley. He himself would record the seals of the second door before it was demolished. With the help of his daughter, Carnarvon took photographs. They had not been able to sleep either. They all feared Rex Engelbach's arrival.

Around noon, one of his subordinates, Ibrahim Effendi, came to the entrance of the tomb. Carter greeted him.

'Mr Engelbach gave me your message. Other commitments kept him in town. I myself am rather busy, so if we could quickly . . .'

The man was rather hard and distant. Carter took him to the door of the antechamber and drew his attention to the traces left by thieves. He introduced the inspector to the Earl of Carnarvon and his daughter, who praised the competence of the service. Once civilities were over, Callender proceeded to dismantle the door.

On the threshold lay an alabaster dish. Carter picked it up and read the hieroglyphic inscription decorating its surround: 'May your ka [the creative power which survives after death] live! May you live millions of years, you who love Thebes, when you sit, your face turned to the north wind and your gaze contemplating beatitude.'

'That was the last offering,' suggested Lady Evelyn. 'His wife's when she left the tomb.'

The ground was covered with rubble, fragments of pottery and the remains of plants. Ibrahim Effendi walked cautiously and wandered about the accumulation of objects: one after another sticks, arms, baskets, pottery, sceptres, trumpets, chests and seats caught the eye. Carter, who was examining each wall with a powerful electric torch, indicated an open passage in the south-west angle of the antechamber. The inspector noted that there was an annex, even more cluttered than the main room. Carter drew his attention to the fact that a good number of chests and baskets had been opened and that the tomb should be considered as plundered.

'What strange thieves,' observed the inspector. 'They did not take much. Look at the golden rings wrapped in a shawl. It would have been so easy to steal them!'

'There is an obvious conclusion to be drawn,' declared Carnarvon. 'The bandits were surprised and stopped. Then the priests tidied everything up hastily.'

The inspector seemed satisfied with this explanation. Carter kept to himself another hypothesis which excluded theft: in order to preserve Tutankhamun's treasure, it had been transferred in haste to another sepulchre. Was the political situation troubled? Was magic involved? Had anyone wanted to preserve a message which they considered essential? A mixture of all these factors had probably been involved.

Ibrahim Effendi saw the lid of the basket and the reeds. He removed them and uncovered a damaged part of the partition wall.

'There is another room.'

'That's certain,' acknowledged Carnarvon. 'But it would be unwise to destroy the wall before we empty the antechamber.'

'How do you intend to carry on with the excavation?' the civil servant asked Carter.

'That is a huge task. We must draw plans, photograph everything, taking care that the magnesium flash does not cause a fire, and take the artefacts out without breaking them. It will probably be necessary to restore some of them before we can move them. My colleague Callender will take care of the erection of an iron grille which will protect the tomb from covetous hands. In addition, a guard will spend the night inside, in the corridor.'

'That is perfect. An inspector from the service will come and check the progress of your work every other day. Our director is very concerned about the law.'

The first wave of invaders flooded Luxor that very afternoon. People talked only about Carnarvon and Carter's fabulous discovery. Egyptologists rushed to the west bank, shamelessly asserting their right to examine the tomb that had been brought to light by the unusual archaeologist.

Firmly, Howard Carter refused to open the grille. The pack outside were to him howling dogs, whose barking he had heard throughout his career, and they did not frighten him.

'This is not Tutankhamun's tomb, but Horemheb's!' claimed a British scholar.

'That's wrong! You should get your facts straight. That tomb is indeed in the valley, but not in this area.'

'Isn't it just a cache for palace equipment?' suggested a French scientist.

'No.'

'It is said that Mesopotamian objects were identified,' stated a German. 'Therefore it could not be an Egyptian tomb.'

'It is the most magnificent pharaonic art, in the extremely pure style of the Eighteenth Dynasty.'

'Show us your masterpieces!'

'Lord Carnarvon has decided to proceed slowly. As we are faced with the most fabulous treasure ever discovered, we owe it complete respect.'

'You're not going to make us wait, are you?' protested the Frenchman.

'I'll let you wait several years, if necessary. Please excuse me, gentlemen. I enjoy your company, but Tutankhamun requires all my attention.'

That evening, the governor of the province had dinner with Lord Carnarvon and his daughter at the Winter Palace.

'Egypt is proud of you, sir. Your archaeologist, Howard Carter, is a very efficient man. Alas, he is a difficult character. His colleagues dislike his attitude.'

'He has disliked theirs for many years. People are jealous of success.'

'Certainly . . . But could the excavation not be hastened? People don't take so many precautions usually.'

'Belzoni smashed a tomb in ten days, sometimes ten hours, that's true . . . But Tutankhamun requires a lot of care.'

'I hope Carter doesn't intend to record all the artefacts one by one.'

'Of course he does,' answered Lady Evelyn. 'And no pressure will make him change his mind.'

'Science is waiting for a quick publication . . .'

'Science will have to yield to the demands of the excavations.'

'We should not repeat the unfortunate experience of tomb 55,' said Carnarvon, affably. 'It was devastated by specialists who cleared it at full speed.'

'Of course, of course . . . But a year's work would be very long for—'

'Tutankhamun will decide,' said Lady Evelyn with a charming smile.

Carnarvon judged that he had toyed enough with his guest's nerves. 'Don't worry, sir, we will organize an official opening so that you and other dignitaries may admire the treasure.'

'Ah . . . what a wonderful idea! Have you set a date?'

'Would 29 November suit you?'

'That would be excellent.'

The atmosphere became distinctly cordial. The Governor was given the assurance that he would be one of the first to see the as yet forbidden splendours. Carnarvon did not specify that invitations had already been sent and that he had forgotten to ask for the permission of the Antiquities Service.

The news spread like wildfire throughout Egypt. In the absence of precise information, journalists were forced to elaborate, giving free rein to their imagination, because Carnarvon refused all meetings with the press before the official opening, which was turning into a national event.

On 28 November the rumour spread that three planes had landed in the Valley of the Kings. Witnesses claimed to have seen Carter himself carry huge crates and fill the cargo holds. Loaded with Tutankhamun's treasure, the planes had flown off to an unknown destination and the perfidious archaeologist had disappeared.

'The valley is a prodigious place,' explained Carter drily to some twenty reporters who had come to check, 'but it cannot be used as a landing strip for it has too many holes and bumps!'

64

Lady Allenby represented the High Commissioner, who was held up in Cairo, and the governor of the province and the chief of the local police also figured among the high-ranking dignitaries who, on 29 November, crowded round the entrance of the tomb. Some noticed the absence of Pierre Lacau and a representative of the Ministry of Civil Engineering, the department in charge of archaeological matters. Lord Carnarvon behaved as if the vault belonged to him. Who could blame him at such a time?

Carter was nervous. He hated society and yet he would be obliged to act as guide to these talkative and undisciplined people, who only cared about the privilege of being the first to see the gold of the forgotten pharaoh. While he talked to them in the sloping corridor, Carnarvon took care of the press, whom he had reduced to the bare minimum: only Arthur Merton, of *The Times*, had been allowed to visit the tomb and write an article.

'My Egyptian colleagues are annoyed,' he acknowledged. 'As for Bradstreet, the *New York Times* correspondent, he is furious and threatens reprisals.'

'The Americans are susceptible. Do your work and don't worry about the rest.'

Delighted, Merton became the author of a world exclusive. *The Times* article, dedicated to the most sensational discovery of the century, quickly went round the world. Tutankhamun became a celebrity, to whom newspapers and magazines dedicated as many articles as to any living monarch. By 30 November, Reuters assessed the value of the treasure at several million pounds, touching the hopes and dreams of people everywhere.

Carnarvon was rather pleased with his strategy. By concentrating the information, he had achieved a masterstroke. Scattering it would have weakened its force. It was a relief for him to see journalists fighting each other and paying court to Merton. But he had no way of avoiding the opponent who, on the afternoon of 30 November, walked slowly towards the entrance of the tomb.

'What a magnificent discovery!' said Pierre Lacau.

'Carter deserves all the credit.'

'Yesterday's little ceremony went well, according to the people who were there.'

'Carter charmed our guests.'

'As the Director of the Antiquities Service, I would have liked to be present.'

'An unfortunate mistake in the invitation cards deprived us of that pleasure.'

'The mistake also involved the Ministry of Civil Engineering.'

'These things usually happen in series.'

'Did you intend to forbid me access to the tomb?'

The Earl became indignant. 'Of course not! Please allow me to guide you. Carter will be delighted to see you again.'

The two men did not shake hands. Carter had begun his survey and did not interrupt his work. Lacau showed no emotion at the sight of the unique works cluttering the antechambers. Carnarvon explained that the tomb had unfortunately been plundered and that the room communicated with two other rooms, one of which was inaccessible.

'When do you intend to make a hole in this wall?'

'Not before this coming February. I must go back to London and Carter wants to proceed with the utmost care.'

'This is all to the good. You are very lucky.'

'Didn't we deserve our good fortune?'

'These artefacts are exceptional. I hold you both responsible for their preservation.'

'I'm glad to hear you say that,' retorted Carter ironically.

With the back of his hand, Carter pushed aside the heap of telegrams and letters accumulating on his desk.

'They've all gone mad . . . I didn't know I had a hundred close relatives ready to come and help me and share the treasure with me!'

'The *Times* article, syndicated to all the press agencies, created a sensation,' recalled Carnarvon. 'Tutankhamun has become a great international star and you are his impresario.'

Lying on a deckchair, the Earl was drinking a beer. He was amused.

'I'm an archaeologist, and I want peace!'

'Calm down, Howard. Eventually the agitation will subside.'

'It's been going on for ten days and it keeps increasing! Hypocritical congratulations are one thing . . . but we are getting threats, curses, stupid pieces of advice and dubious jokes. Thousands of people ask me to send them some gold or sand, which they kindly say they will look after!'

'That's the price of fame, my dear Howard. You can demand anything of the richest man in the world.'

'Nobody will deprive Tutankhamun.'

'What a pharaoh! We don't know anything about him and yet he outshines today's crowned heads, international conferences, debates over war damages and even cricket matches. After so many centuries of silence, he is now pushed into the limelight.'

'Do you know that we are being accused of having woken up evil forces which were slumbering in the tomb? It is because of them, and therefore of us, that Belgian soldiers commit atrocities in the Congo!'

'You make the whole world dream, Howard. Don't worry about a few nightmares.'

'I cannot leave this place without being assailed by journalists. They want to know everything about Tutankhamun.'

'What do you tell them?'

'That he is dead and was buried in the Valley of the Kings.'

'They're probably not very amused by that.'

'I can't stand them any more! I am not a travelling acrobat, but a researcher who spent his life in the service of ancient Egypt, in the most remote and inhospitable areas, moving tons of sand, and learning patience, silence and solitude. I want to be rid of all these parasites.'

'Alas, Howard, this is only the start of the epidemic.'

In December 1922, crowds of journalists, scholars, merchants and particularly tourists streamed in Luxor. Tutankhamun's tomb was the place to be. People felt a need to see its entrance and try to get inside. In turmoil and dust, they wanted to argue with Carter, question him and hear the latest about his discovery.

From the first minutes of the day, tourists arrived in carriages or on donkeys and sat on the stone parapet Carter had ordered to be built around the tomb. People told each other that something exceptional was going to happen, such as the appearance of a gold statue or the mummy. Some people talked non-stop and others read while others took photographs of each other with the tomb in the background. When Carter walked out into the open, they shouted at him, becoming almost hysterical. More than once the archaeologist thought that the parapet would give way under their weight.

One morning a telegraph boy was allowed to cross the barricade of wardens and to enter the corridor where Carter was waiting for him.

'Is there a message for me?'

'Yes and no.'

'What do you mean?'

'I'm a tourist . . . The agency promised me that I would be able to visit the tomb. I found this uniform and here I am.'

Carter grabbed hold of the man by the collar of his jacket and flung him out of the tomb. He had hardly done so when a group of officials arrived. Carter had to check their letters of introduction, written by diplomats and the officials of the Museum of Cairo and make sure that they were not forgeries. For half an hour he showed them, as he had many others, the masterpieces in the antechamber.

As one of them left, he murmured to his wife's ear: 'After all, there wasn't much to see.' Furious, Carter shut the wooden grille, left the valley, went across the Nile and rushed to the office of the Antiquities Service, where Ibrahim Effendi was drinking coffee.

'Tutankhamun's tomb cannot be visited any more.'

The civil servant stood up, flabbergasted. 'Mr Carter! That is utterly impossible! It attracts thousands of tourists. The hoteliers and shopkeepers are delighted.'

'I intend to fill it in and disappear until the turmoil ends.'

'You will be accused of self-centredness and uncouthness.'

'Does a researcher who doesn't want to be disturbed merit such criticisms? Ten visits per day mean five hours of work wasted. Why does this privileged lot enjoy more rights than others, when they do not care about Tutankhamun, his tomb or even Egypt itself? They are only driven by curiosity and snobbishness. What really matters to them is that they are able to impress acquaintances by declaring that they have been able to get a pass.'

'Your profession compels you—'

'Let's talk about my profession! Archaeology is a billionaire's entertainment. This is what people say everywhere. How many "archaeologists" really use their hands on a site? They usually entrust the work to labourers or incompetents. For my part I must preserve Tutankhamun's treasure and that is what I shall do. I cannot let idiots damage the antechamber by overturning artefacts. In future I won't take any introductions into account; I am the only one who will give permission to visit.'

Carter banged the door. The civil servant considered that the researcher seemed to have an innate gift for making enemies.

65

On the evening of 2 December, Carter, Carnarvon and Lady Evelyn had dinner in a private room of the Winter Palace. In a low-necked turquoise dress, the young woman looked radiant. The Earl seemed in an excellent mood, but Carter appeared tired and worried.

'Howard, I have hilarious news. Budge, the curator of the British Museum's Egypt collection, has got in touch with me. He suddenly thinks that we are both great archaeologists.'

'He's after artefacts.'

'You don't seem to trust his motives.'

'The British Museum won't get anything.'

'That is my decision. You have become a bit vindictive.'

Lady Evelyn was concerned. 'You seem to be off colour, Mr Carter.'

'I'm very worried.'

'Why?'

'Studying the tomb and its contents is beyond my ability. Not only will it be a long and costly process to empty it, but I shall also need the help of experts.'

Carnarvon had been afraid he would hear those words. 'Long and costly,' he repeated.

'You're not going to give up, father, are you?'

'If we give the concession back to the service,' said Carter, 'you'll lose all your rights to the artefacts.'

'So what do you suggest?'

'We should form a team.'

'What a wonderful idea!' said Lady Evelyn.

'Of course,' said Carnarvon, 'you've already chosen your collaborators, haven't you?'

'My friend Winlock has been very helpful.'

'The Metropolitan Museum! Do you want their help?'

'It has been a faithful and devoted partner, hasn't it?'

'So what about the team?'

'It will be composed of Harry Burton, the best photographer in the world in the archaeological field, Arthur Mace, Petrie's nephew, and a specialist in the restoration and packing of artefacts, and two draughtsmen. Professor Breasted will take care of the inscriptions, with the help of Gardiner the grammarian. Callender will continue to assist me and Lucas, the chemist, will join us before long.'

Carnarvon lit a cigar. 'This is remarkable, Howard. Every day you have new surprises for me. I did not think that you were also a leader of men, able to gather the best team in our times. But I am wondering about one detail: how much will it cost me?'

Carter smiled. 'Nothing.'

In spite of long practice at maintaining his composure, Carnarvon swallowed some smoke and almost choked.

'I beg your pardon.'

'Lythgoe, one of the Metropolitan Museum's directors, is enthusiastic about our discovery. He has put his staff at our disposal, free.'

'Where is the snag?'

'He would like to meet you and negotiate . . . in another field.'

'I am relieved . . . I thought for a while that I had misjudged human nature. Where is he?'

'In London. He thinks that our meetings should not take place in Egypt.'

'He is right. Fill in the tomb, have it watched over and gather the members of your team as soon as possible. We shall leave for London on the 4th.'

315

'So early?' protested Lady Evelyn.

'We have no choice. Howard is a hard taskmaster. We shall come back as soon as possible.'

Carter understood that the sadness he read in Lady Evelyn's eyes concerned him.

'The photographer is an excellent idea,' continued Carnarvon.

'I know your taste for it, but—'

'I am not piqued; in spite of my talent all my snapshots went wrong! As for you, Howard, don't forget to paint. Tutankhamun is an inexhaustible source of work. People will fight over your paintings in the future. And you will become a billionaire.'

'I'll think about it.'

But Howard was wondering what *she* was thinking about the future.

On 4 December, the Earl and his daughter left Luxor for Cairo. Carter accompanied them. He had presented Carnarvon with a list of purchases. The staircase of the tomb had been filled in up to the first step. Egyptian soldiers, assisted by reliable men chosen by the *reis*, watched over the site. But tourists had eyes only for a colossus with a rifle who sat on a big block painted with Lord Carnarvon's coat of arms. Callender would shoot at anyone who tried to trespass on the forbidden territory. Neither the sun nor the tourists' gibes would distract him from his task. Thanks to his presence, Carter was able to leave without worries.

In Cairo, Carnarvon stayed at Shepherds, a luxury hotel built totally in the London tradition. Each winter, it welcomed the cream of British society. They enjoyed breakfast or tea in gardens separated by the grille from a clean, wide street. Elegant women happily displayed their dresses in front of the monumental entrance, embellished with palm trees.

Carter was thoughtful. During their trip, the Earl had mentioned two projects. The first was a series of books on the tomb, including a popular edition for the general public and an ambitious scientific publication. The second was an entertaining and attractive film. Carter protested that he was neither a writer nor a director, but the Earl advised him to work with specialists and to think of the benefits he would gain. If the tomb's discoverers were not able to take advantage of its commercial potential, then others would know how to exploit it.

'I have a boring meeting at the hotel, Howard. You might want to introduce my daughter to old Cairo. Otherwise there is only Susie and she may not be too good as a guide.'

'I would like to get on with my purchases without delay.'

Lady Evelyn intervened. 'Please take me with you! I have a mad desire to find out about the souks.'

'I am afraid the place is a bit . . .'

'You'll protect me.'

The British government envoy was as lugubrious as his predecessors. Of average height, his dull eyes and grey suit made him look as boring as the smog.

'We are very surprised, Lord Carnarvon.'

'I understand. You do not stumble upon a Tutankhamun every week-end.'

'I was not referring to your archaeological activities, whose technical peculiarities don't concern me, but to your inexplicable silence since your arrival in Egypt.'

'The reason is very simple.'

'Would you be kind enough to explain?'

'Tutankhamun.'

'I beg your pardon?'

'My activities also involve an inner adventure. Therefore I am less interested in politics. Dealing with a pharaoh's immortality make current human affairs seem insignificant.'

'You're wandering from the point, sir.'

'On the contrary, my dear friend, on the contrary.'

*

Carter needed an iron grille, chemical products, photography material, boxes of various sizes, thirty-two bales of calico, bandages, about a mile and a half of cotton wool and other items. He also intended to buy a car.

Khan el-Khalili, the largest oriental market, crammed its 10,000 shops into a network of tortuous dark streets where people sold gold, silver, precious stones, spices, fake and real antiquities, furniture, carpets, rifles, daggers and any other product of ancient or modern craftsmanship. Anything that was not on display in the shops might be obtained through interminable haggling.

Lady Evelyn appreciated Carter's skill. She admired perfume burners, became intoxicated with the essential oils of lotus and jasmine and bought two ostrich eggs for her own collection.

When he was certain that his orders would be delivered to Luxor as soon as possible, Carter took the young woman to the citadel, from which they contemplated the capital of Egypt. From that height the plague of the poor districts disappeared. Above a jumble of houses crammed on top of each other were rose minarets, domes and some Christian crosses. In the distance were the pyramids of Giza, Abusir and Saqqara.

'I don't want to go back to England. Could you convince my father . . .'

'You are the only person who has any real influence over him, Lady Evelyn.'

'I don't have the right to abandon him?'

'That would be betrayal.'

'But doesn't the most loving daughter have to leave her father some day?'

Carter did not dare answer. The glow of sunset mingled with the lights of the city and the yellow and red lanterns of the cafés.

'Don't ask me to interpret fate . . . Many years ago, I had to interrupt an excavation campaign a few yards from the staircase to Tutankhamun's tomb. Why did fate impose so many doubts, so many efforts and so much suffering on me? Maybe because you had to be twenty in the year of discovery.'

Howard Carter's tortured expression moved Lady Evelyn. He did not look like a seducer, he lacked charm and his manners were unpolished. But that evening he was just full of tenderness and yearning for an impossible happiness.

Neither of them broke the evening silence. In Cairo, the mother of the world, they hoped for a new dawn in their lives.

66

Sometimes the sacred responsibility of friendship was heavy. Carter was not at all happy with the mission Carnarvon had assigned him: he was to talk to the Director of the Antiquities Service and get him to give them certain guarantees.

On the previous day, a ship had taken the Earl and Lady Evelyn back to England. Her attitude and glances had made Carter begin to hope that she was not repelled by his feelings. But he had not had the courage to question her for fear of destroying his dream.

In answer to Lord Carnarvon's request, Pierre Lacau had agreed to receive Carter informally, far away from the official setting of his office. The appointment did not even figure in his diary. The two men met in the late afternoon in the sandy courtyard of the Bulaq Museum, where Mariette had arranged the first wing dedicated to pharaonic civilization.

That morning, Carter had received a telegram from the *reis*, Ahmed Girigar: 'I take the liberty to inform His Excellence that everything is fine and that his orders are being followed to the letter. Everybody here salutes your respectable person and all the members of Lord Carnarvon's family.' The short text had reassured him and moved him to tears. So much devotion gave him inexhaustible strength.

Cold and elegant, Lacau looked at him with superiority mingled with disdain. 'Are you in any trouble, Mr Carter?'

'No.'

'So why do you insist on so much mystery?'

'Lord Carnarvon is worried about the sharing of artefacts.'

'The sharing! Well we'll have to deal with that, indeed.'

'What do you intend to do?'

Carter knew that he was being too straightforward, even abrupt. Lacau's tone tried his patience.

'I shall follow the usual practice. As Lord Carnarvon is responsible for the expense of the long and costly work, he will receive some valuable artefacts.'

'Please let me remind you that the vault was plundered.'

'My inspectors took note of it. Yet the point is open to scientific discussion.'

Lacau did not spell out that all the contents of an undesecrated tomb had to come to the museum. Yet his half-smile betrayed his certainty that he had a major card to play.

'Could you notify us of your agreement in writing?'

'That is not necessary, Mr Carter. My word will be enough for Lord Carnarvon. He should be reassured that a certain number of masterpieces will enrich his collection.'

Ill at ease, Carter felt as though he was being watched like a prey.

'Has your team been formed?' asked Lacau, unctuously.

'I'm going back to Luxor to co-ordinate their efforts.'

'Take good care of Tutankhamun.'

Carter preferred a thousand hours of work in a stifling tomb to ten minutes of conversation with Lacau. Yet he would be able to cable Carnarvon that the negotiation had been successful.

On 16 December, Carter opened the tomb again and on the 17th, he had an iron grille fixed at the entrance of the ante-chamber. The supplies he had ordered in Cairo had arrived the previous day. Callender had checked everything thoroughly and expressed his satisfaction. Serious work could now begin.

On 18 December the team's first meeting took place. Carter distributed piles of underwear – because of the heat inside the tomb, it had to be changed frequently.

Christian Jacq

'Thanks for your collaboration, gentlemen. I suggest that I accustom you to the place.'

Breasted, the epigraphist, Burton, the photographer, Mace, the specialist in preservation and the Metropolitan Museum's two draughtsmen followed him as he walked slowly down the corridor. The grille was concealed by a white cloth.

'Is it a British ghost?' asked Burton.

In the antechamber, Callender switched on the light while Carter lifted the fabric and pushed the grille. Their gaze first rested on the two black wardens of the threshold and then on the golden throne. The majesty of the sight and its grandiose unreality suddenly transported the twentieth-century scientists back to the glorious time of a young pharaoh whose redis-covered soul shone with gold. With tears in their eyes they congratulated Carter and thanked him for offering them the most beautiful present in their lives. Breasted squeezed his hand so strongly that the Englishman had trouble freeing it.

'To my mind,' declared Burton in an attempt to overcome his emotion through irony, 'the Tutankhamun case is likely to go on for ever.'

Carnarvon did not know which way to turn. After a triumphal welcome on his arrival in England, on 22 December he was granted an audience with King George V in Buckingham Palace. Witty and playful, he had charmed the king even before enchanting a public greedy for details and anecdotes. On the occasion of a lecture attended by all London, in spite of his slight speech impediment, the Earl had been a great success when he had related the sixteen years of excavations, the doubts and the disappointed hopes which had preceded the extraordinary discovery. Numerous dignitaries – aristocrats, politicians, actors, bankers and even the famous jockey Denoghull – congratulated him.

On Christmas Eve, Carnarvon went to the Burlington Hotel, despite his fatigue. Albert Lythgoe, the official representative of the Metropolitan Museum, received him warmly.

'What a triumph, sir! Your visit is an honour.'

'It was on my agenda, my dear friend.'

'Would you like some champagne?'

'I would not refuse the most joyful of wines.'

The anxious Lythgoe knocked over a glass. He talked precipitately, praised Carter's merits and celebrated Carnarvon's courage.

'A hard task awaits us,' confessed the aristocrat. 'There are so many artefacts . . . I'm afraid one year won't be enough.'

'The Metropolitan Museum team will be at your disposal as long as you need it.'

'I'm grateful to you. A most delicate matter remains of course: the sharing of these masterpieces.'

'Do you think that my museum . . .'

'Egypt was concerned about justice. So am I. Your help is so precious that it deserves some reward.'

Lythgoe could have kissed the Earl, had such eccentric behaviour not been contrary to the proprieties. 'What is Lacau's position?'

'He recognizes my right to a share.'

'Beware of him,' advised Lythgoe. 'If he does not confirm his agreement in writing, he may change his mind.'

'How can we convince him?'

'You should proceed to the restoration of artefacts, for the Antiquities Service is unable to do that. The more artefacts you save, the more Lacau will give you.'

'I would now like to wish you a merry Christmas.'

In the cold London air, the Earl thought of the trick he was playing on the British Museum, which had been so disdainful of Carter. He did not really like Americans, but they were the only possible choice in the present circumstances. Feeling perky, he whistled a popular song as he climbed into the car which was to take him to Highclere, where he would celebrate Christmas with his family. Eve would be delighted to hear that the adventure was progressing.

67

On 25 December, Carter decided to start to remove some artefacts from the tomb. As if it sensed the impending move, the furniture gave out strange creaks.

'It's the ghost again,' quipped the photographer.

The joke did not amuse Callender. Carter asked his collaborators to move with the utmost care in the narrow central passage they had opened up in the antechamber. Any abrupt movement might cause a pile of artefacts to fall. They were all covered with a thin layer of pink dust, which the archaeologist had to remove with warm water.

Mace grasped a pair of sandals. Hardly had he touched them than he put them down again, as if he was holding a bomb. 'It is impossible to handle them without first reinforcing them. Otherwise they will crumble into dust.'

The American used paraffin wax, which he left to harden for two hours. The funerary bunches of flowers he sprayed with celluloid. Carter understood that each type of artefact would confront them with a specific problem. Moving any of them could damage the others and a lot of them would have to be restored in the confined space of the antechamber. Even Callender seemed overwhelmed for a while by such a colossal endeavour, coupled with the need for nimble fingers.

'Any carelessness on our part would be criminal,' declared Carter. 'We must show the treasure to the world and prove that we are equal to our good fortune.'

'Sometimes it is good to be a photographer,' remarked Burton.

'Don't use too violent a light.'

'Half-light would be enough, but I would suggest a better solution: two portable projectors. They will diffuse an even light, which is much better than the flash, and I shall use a long exposure.'

In the afternoon, Carter was faced with another problem because of the profusion of beads in the necklaces and armbands. The threads were rotten, but he refused to sacrifice even one bead. Therefore he asked that they be drawn with the utmost accuracy and, taking a needle, took good care to restring them according to the order intended by the craftsman.

The crowds kept increasing around the entrance of the tomb. Mace and Callender took out the artefacts one by one, greeted by loud applause. This was turning into a permanent performance and people jostled each other to attend.

As he was carrying a large necklace, which sparkled in the sun, Carter noticed a young Arab who had succeeded in elbowing his way to the front row. He seemed fascinated. The archaeologist called him and Callender allowed him to come nearer.

'Your face reminds me of someone . . . What is your name?'

'Hussein Abd el Rassul.'

So he was one of the sons of the head of the clan! The powerful man had respected his promise. Carter wanted to make a show of thanking him. He tied the necklace around Hussein's neck and Burton photographed him. On the white *galabieh* a scarab stood out, lifting the sun between its front legs.

'As soon as the photograph is processed, I'll give it to you.'

'I shall keep it all my life,' promised Hussein, 'and show it to all those who step across the threshold of my house.[7]'

---

[7] The promise was kept: Husayn Abd el Rassul, the owner of a rest-home close to the Ramesseum (in West Thebes), still displays the photograph.

325

*

Soldiers, members of the Antiquities Service and Ahmed Girigar's trustworthy men continued to mount guard day and night. Some newspapers mentioned the arrival of gangsters intent on seizing Tutankhamun's treasures. Contrary to Abd el Rassul's instructions, local bandits were said to be consenting to come to their assistance. Carter gave these threats due consideration and constantly worried about security. Four padlocked chains closed the wooden entrance grille and a ton and a half iron grille blocked the way to the antechamber. Only Carter could give permission for someone to touch an artefact.

'We can't go on like this,' complained Burton. 'We urgently need a laboratory and a storeroom.'

'Is the darkroom not enough?'

'Tomb 55 is close to Tutankhamun's sepulchre, but it is too small. Who allocates premises?'

'The Antiquities Service. I'll take care of that.'

Again he had to confront Rex Engelbach, who rejected the idea starchily. Once his windy discourse was over, Carter returned to the attack.

'If you do not grant us more spacious premises, we won't be able to go on working. You'll be responsible for our failure.'

Annoyed, Engelbach agreed to negotiate. 'Where do you want to go?'

'The tomb of Seti II would suit us. It is narrow, but deep. As few people visit it, we would only deprive a few specialists.'

'It is too far from Tutankhamun's vault. It would be better to build a warehouse nearby.'

'The tourists would attack it. I accept that we will have a rather long way to go, but we could block the way and bar it to intruders. It will be easy to ensure security. I have already ordered an iron grille.'

Engelbach hesitated. 'The cliffs surrounding the tomb protect it from the sun,' continued Carter, 'and keep it cool, even in the summer. In addition, the area in front of the entrance has been cleared. We could arrange an open-air photography studio as well as a joiner's workshop.'

Engelbach yielded.

Each artefact was laid on a padded stretcher and fixed with bandage. Once a day an impressive convoy left Tutankhamun's tomb for the vault of Seti II. Armed policemen carrying truncheons watched over the porters and held back the onlookers who were constantly taking photographs. Hotheads shouted and jostled journalists scribbling notes. Irritated, Carter complained that more film was used in that winter than in the whole history of photography. The merest suggestion of a gesture and the clicks started.

As soon as the precious load arrived, the team worked with precision and speed. Each work was numbered, measured, drawn and photographed and its inscriptions listed so as to provide it with the identity tag necessary for further studies. Then it was stored at the bottom of the vault before being packed ready for transfer to the Museum of Cairo.

As a convoy was about to leave, the sun disappeared. Carter raised his head. Thick black clouds veiled the sky. Callender almost panicked.

'A storm. If it ever breaks, the funerary beds will be done for! We won't have time to shelter them.'

A flash of lightning split the clouds and a few drops of rain fell. Within less than five minutes it would become torrential, turn the bottom of the valley into a river and flood the tomb. No grille would be able to block the way to such a cataclysm.

Carter closed his eyes. There was nothing he could do but pray: an invocation to Amon, the god of winds, came to his mind. A powerful blast almost knocked him over. After a short struggle, the clouds were blown away and the storm died down.

'We are protected, up there,' said Callender.

Carter's dream continued. Lying on his bed, he was rereading

Christian Jacq

Lady Evelyn's letter for the tenth time. It was a long letter written in round, tender writing. The young woman mentioned their night expedition to the tomb. She expressed her gratitude to the archaeologist and described their adventure in detail. Her New Year greetings hinted at a deep and sincere affection.

She was an aristocrat and he was of common birth . . . This was shocking and impossible! Had she dared talk about her feelings to Lord Carnarvon? Certainly not. Who would have triumphed: the friend or the owner of Highclere? Carter had to give up any hope of happiness, because he had been born in a poor family. He hadn't been to a famous school and only had the skimpy culture of an archaeologist trained on the field and hated by his peers.

He rebelled against the convention and injustice which condemned the world to something as artificial and cruel as the class system. This time, he would not give up.

68

Most of the Luxor antique dealers were gathered around Demosthenes. They had all become fierce enemies of Carter, whom they accused of having ruined a once prosperous trade. The discovery of Tutankhamun's treasures had made the situation even more serious. Not a single artefact had left the site, and amateurs only thought of the inaccessible marvels. It was necessary to do something.

'If only Carter would commit some professional misdemeanour . . .' said a Lebanese.

'Forget that idea,' recommended Demosthenes. 'He is too careful.'

'Did he really discover the tomb?' asked a Syrian. 'Let's destroy the legend!'

'Unfortunately it has now become true.'

'There are laws, even in this country! To whom does the treasure belong? It doesn't belong to Carter!'

'Don't forget Lord Carnarvon. He only wants to enrich his private collection and deceives the officials of the Antiquities Service, whom we could easily have bribed.'

'Carnarvon is out of reach,' stated the senior trafficker. 'So we have to destroy Carter.'

'You can rely on me,' said Demosthenes.

'You'll be a rich man if you succeed.'

Howard Carter was immersed in his work. He saw to it that the most modest artefacts were treated with the same care as major masterpieces. Without making a fuss, Burton adopted the same infernal pace of work and developed over fifty photographs a day. Mace restored, repaired and packed. Callender built boxes.

In the evenings, while his collaborators were resting, Carter sorted out his notes, updated his excavation diary, classified negatives and prepared the next day's work so as not to waste too much time. Too much had already been spent on unnecessary visits. Only the night brought him a calm that did not prevail in the valley.

At the crack of dawn tourists and the press gathered in the hope of seeing him with a masterpiece. As soon as a member of his team handled an artefact, advice burst forth. Believers in the occult sciences even sent messages saying that they should pour milk, wine and honey on the threshold of the tomb to mitigate the fury of evil spirits.

The ever-increasing free-for-all put Carter's nerves to the test.

In Luxor people were getting restless. The little town became the scene of fights between tourists disappointed not to have been able to enter the vault, and journalists who, after trips by horse or donkey, jostled each other to use the telegraph.

The daytime commotion was followed by a different one at night; in the reception rooms of the luxury hotels, people danced the waltz or the polka and spent the whole night discussing the tons of gold buried in the grave.

Carter refused all invitations to these parties where stupidity rivalled their emptiness. His only entertainment consisted in having dinner on his own at the Winter Palace once a week. That was where a now close-shaven Demosthenes, dressed in a dinner-jacket, approached him.

'Have you made your fortune?'

The Greek sat down. 'No, I haven't, but you have.'

'You're mistaken. Tutankhamun's treasure is not for sale.'

'Not yet. There are hundreds of artefacts . . . You won't be able to exhibit all of them in a museum. When Lord Carnarvon and the Antiquities Service have taken their share, there will still be a few leftovers.'

Carter was savouring a sauté of beef and rereading a notebook to the left of his plate.

'As for the leftovers,' declared Demosthenes, 'I intend to buy them. There will be huge profits. If you only knew my clients! You will get seventy per cent and I thirty . . . not including this small advance.'

The Greek pushed an envelope full of banknotes towards Carter. The archaeologist lifted his fork just above it. A drop of sauce fell and stained it.

'Be careful, Demosthenes. You are staining your belongings.'

He put it back into his pocket, furious.

'Everything can be bought, Carter! I'll pay the price.'

'You waste your time. Tutankhamun's treasure is worth more than all the money in the world, because it holds a secret. And the secret is not convertible into cash.'

'You have ruined me, Carter. You'll pay for that!'

His black frock coat, red trousers and hat gave Demosthenes enough courage to go to the *sheikh* who was presiding over the *zâr* that evening, a magical ceremony in which dangerous forces were summoned. The Greek gave his name to the guard at the door of a low, sordid-looking house. Doubled up, he entered the smoky atmosphere and sat near a woman clad in a black shawl. The *sheikh* chanted formulae and cut the throat of a sheep. He spread its blood on himself, turned round and summoned the spirits.

The woman threw back her shawl, seized a knife and traced long cuts in her forearms. Without feeling the slightest pain, she cut the tip off her left forefinger. Crazed, Demosthenes backed away to the door. The *sheikh*'s incantation held him to the spot.

'Spirits of darkness, leave your caves and kill the pillagers and profaners who dare trouble Tutankhamun's rest!'

The Greek staggered. Unable to breathe, he put his hand to his heart and collapsed.

Carter pricked up his ears. This time he was not mistaken; it really was the noise of an engine. In the distance a cloud of dust showed the car's progress. Lord Carnarvon had taken the wheel and was driving slowly. The road was not suitable for speed and he wanted to avoid too many bumps for Lady Evelyn who sat by his side. The car covered the distance between the ferry and the entrance to the valley in half an hour. The whole team had gathered to greet the travellers. Deeply moved, the Earl embraced Carter, who intercepted Lady Evelyn's tender furtive glance. Burton asked them to pose for a photograph. Susie put herself in the front row.

Impatient, Carnarvon walked hastily to the tomb of Seti II. 'I have been longing to see this place for such a long time . . . It is magnificent!'

The Earl admired the restored works, which shone more brightly than in the gloom of the vault. Mace showed him several ornate sticks and ritual garments embellished with hundreds of gold rosettes.

'What a wonderful job you've done. You deserve some reward.' Carnarvon uncorked the bottle of Dom Pérignon he had brought. Burton filled the glasses. They all felt proud and happy.

'I am so tired, Carter.' Carnarvon lay in a wicker chair. Susie was sleeping at his feet. During the improvised cocktail party, the Earl had joked and given new energy to the small brotherhood.

'But you seem in excellent shape.'

'Appearances are misleading.'

'The journey has exhausted him,' explained Lady Evelyn.

'The vision of such treasures makes me feel young again, though.'

A broad-brimmed hat on his head, Carnarvon contemplated

the sunset. The terrace of the house opened on to the heights of the valley. Silent and pink they merged with the red disc sinking into the other world.

'Tutankhamun is not dead, Howard. He crossed the underground world and reappears in his own time, not in ours. That is why he should not be thrown to the lions. Journalists from all over the world keep approaching me. Why not let's grant exclusive coverage to *The Times*?'

'That is an excellent idea. Its correspondent in Cairo, Arthur Merton, is a friend and he has a good knowledge of archaeology. He will give an accurate account of our adventure.'

'The contract will bring a large amount of money and cover part of the expenses. It will save us having to deal separately with other journalists.'

Lady Evelyn looked at a series of photographs. 'Mr Carter, are you convinced that this is indeed Tutankhamun's tomb? Could it be some cache? Ramses I only reigned for two years and he was granted a larger vault than Tutankhamun, who was on the throne for six years!'

'I constantly wonder what our discovery really is,' confessed Carter. 'It is much more than a tomb. The builder wanted the location to remain *the* mystery of the valley. As soon as the New Kingdom ended, under the reign of the last Ramses, all traces of him disappeared from the archives. Concealed under craftsmen's houses, the sepulchre became inaccessible to thieves. Why? Tutankhamun embodied the link between the solar cult and the knowledge of the secret god, Amon. He epitomized the spiritual teaching of Egypt which had to be preserved at all costs. The insignificant king was a great pharaoh.'

69

Pierre Lacau lost his legendary calm. He tore the copy of the *Morning Post* into pieces and threw them in the dustbin. He had been rather amused by the first attacks on Carnarvon and Carter. As journalists had heard of the exclusive contract with *The Times*, they had flown into a rage and accused the Earl and his archaeologist of prostituting science, and of a sordidly venal attitude. Did they have the right to consider Tutankhamun's tomb as their personal possession?

The *Morning Post*'s Cairo edition was now blaming the Director of the Antiquities Service! Journalists reproached Lacau for refusing to give any information to the press, as if he were Carnarvon's slave. Egyptian newspapers followed suit: why did the French civil servant not disown the British aristocrat? Why did he not open the tomb to all journalists and refuse to acknowledge *The Times*' supremacy?

Caught in this turmoil, Lacau was not ready for such an ordeal. Because of the damned discovery, he was assailed by thousands of famous and unknown tourists all resentfully demanding permission to visit the tomb. He went to Luxor to meet Carter, who received him on the site, where he was busy wrapping a necklace.

'The situation is becoming unbearable.'

'Only the work matters. Let envious people make a fuss if they want to.'

'You should be kinder to Egyptian journalists.'

'A contract is a contract: they should get in touch with *The Times*.'

'Your refusal to allow visitors into the tomb arouses great resentment.'

'I don't care. I have no time to waste on such trivialities.'

'When a dignitary comes with an official government pass, don't stand in his way!'

'I certainly will. Otherwise the tomb would be full of tourists and we would not be able to empty it any more.'

Lacau felt as though he was caught in a stranglehold. 'At least let's agree on a date: I only ask that a day be reserved for visitors authorized by the service, and for Egyptians and foreign journalists. That is the only way to check the press campaign against you and me.'

'That is impossible.'

'I will set the date at 26 January.'

Lacau waited in vain for Carter's written agreement. He sent Rex Engelbach who, confident of his administrative prerogatives, spoke authoritatively and vehemently.

'The Director chose a date for official visits. Does it suit you, Mr Carter?'

'No.'

'Your stubbornness is unacceptable.'

'I am not interested in society.'

'The Antiquities Service—'

'The Antiquities Service cannot insist on the presence of lay people.'

'Are you a priest in a sacred place?'

'You're beginning to understand.'

Engelbach lost his composure. 'Your damned reinforced door infuriates the whole world! You behave like a tyrant who jealously looks after treasures which don't even belong to him . . . If you go on, I'll have to resort to firearms.'

'Why not use dynamite? That would be quicker.'

'I'll think about it.' Mortified, Engelbach turned on his heels.

Christian Jacq

*

Carter asked Carnarvon to enter the antechamber of the tomb. As usual the two men moved slowly and lowered their voices. The Pharaoh was resting close to them.

They stopped near a box numbered 43.

'Is it this one?'

'Yes.'

'Are you sure that it contains papyrus?'

'I only lifted the lid once. The honour of checking it is yours.'

Carnarvon's hand shook. The discovery of ancient papyrus might reveal Tutankhamun's mysterious reign, enable them to decipher one of the most obscure periods of history and understand why the tomb was unique.

The Earl took out a scroll and started to open it with the utmost care.

'This is just linen, Howard . . . just a strip of cloth.'

Carter examined the rest of the box. 'They are indeed rolls of linen . . . Yet I am sure that papyrus were hidden in the vault. If they were not locked away in a box, then they were concealed inside a statue. I have heard of several similar cases in the valley[8]. But will we have the time and the means to open all the statues without damaging them?'

'Why are you so pessimistic, Howard?'

'We are being attacked on all sides.'

'Work in peace. I am on your side. And remember that luck is on my side.'

The team worked with growing enthusiasm. Every day brought its share of marvels, be it a throne on whose back appeared the spirit of eternity connecting the stems of millions of years, a ritual bed with a lion's head, where Tutankhamun had lain during the regeneration celebrations, or a cedarwood

[8] Carter's intuition was right: in 1990, radioscopic investigation stated that statues belonging to Tutankhamun's treasure contained papyrus.

chest inlaid with ivory, with a text stating that the eyes, mouth and ears of the King would open again in the other world where, in a refreshing breeze, he would savour delicate dishes.

Carnarvon was able to enjoy the exhilaration to the full. The pain of living had disappeared. Sometimes he even caught himself thanking Tutankhamun for having granted him a grace he had not expected any more. His daughter shared this miraculous happiness. Her father did not mention his aches and pains any more, forgot his ailments, frolicked like a young man from the tomb to the laboratory and from the laboratory to the tomb. As for her she adopted Carter's frenetic pace. Sitting by his side, she learnt how to decipher hieroglyphs and write brief descriptions of artefacts as she recorded them and assessed their state of preservation. Inseparable, Carter and Lady Evelyn brought a childlike joy to the site.

Carnarvon was resting by the entrance of the laboratory when he caught a glimpse of a stranger to the valley, Pierre Lacau's elegant and frail figure.

'I appeal to your sense of duty, sir.'

'Why not?'

'Believe me, this is a serious matter. I am threatened because of Carter's intransigence.'

'I am sorry about that. Howard is a scientist who lacks diplomacy. But nobody questions his vocation, skills and integrity.'

'No, nobody does . . . But Egyptian journalists must be allowed into the tomb. They are plotting an increasingly fierce campaign against us.'

'Don't be so sensitive to criticism, Mr Lacau. My contract with *The Times* forbids me to make such dispensations.'

'As you won't see reason, I am forced to use other methods. You will today receive a former demand from the Ministry of Civil Engineering, and the continuation of your archaeological digs will depend on your response.'

Lacau stuck to his word. The official letter was mildly

worded. The lawyer from the ministry recommended Carter
and Carnarvon to adopt a more conciliatory attitude so as
to preserve their interests and not engage in a fight which
would be detrimental to all researchers intent on exploring
Egypt. Threats hovered between the lines, but the letter
ended with a single suggestion: take account of general
concerns.

70

Carter was drinking his early morning coffee when the *reis* announced a visitor.

'What name did you say?'

'Arthur Weigall.'

Carter laid down his cup and walked out to the steps. He did not want the bandit inside the house. A former inspector in the Antiquities Service, Weigall had been suspected of theft and forced to resign. And he dared come back to Egypt! A tropical helmet on his head, elegantly dressed in a striped jacket and grey trousers, the visitor was a rather handsome man, but as cold as the collar of his shirt. His thin lips and sharp look betrayed an underlying aggression.

Aware of his host's short temper and prejudices against him, Arthur Weigall did not bother about politeness. 'This is an innocent visit and I want to help you. I want to talk to you as a sincere friend. I beg you to listen to me for at least a few moments.'

Weigall had an animated face. He seemed to display several characters.

'Be brief.'

'You are in danger, Howard, in great danger. Egypt is no longer a submissive colony. Your disdain for the local press has turned public opinion against you. You are accused of being a thief and people begin to hate you. Tutankhamun does not belong to you. Freedom fighters consider him as one of them, whom you are holding hostage.'

'You are deluded.'

'You are wrong. Come back down to earth. Declare to the Egyptian press that you understand its grievances and regret your behaviour.'

'I have only my own morals; I feel neither regret nor remorse.'

'Don't persist, Howard. You can no longer lord it over everyone. The world changed while you were with the Eighteenth Dynasty, with your beloved pharaoh. Don't rely too much on Carnarvon's protection. He is a weak and ill man. And . . .'

'And?'

'People talk about a curse affecting all those who profane tombs.'

'That is stupid.'

'Remember the terrible warning of Ursu: 'He who will desecrate my tomb in the necropolis will be hated by light. He will not be able to receive water on Osiris' altar. He will die of thirst in the other world and he will not be able to pass on his possessions to his children.'

'That doesn't bother me,' said Carter. 'Ursu lived at the time of Amenhotep II, and not under the rule of Tutankhamun. I am not desecrating a tomb. I am preserving it from destruction and plundering. Moreover, I have no children.'

'You are wrong not to give the warning proper thought. I really want you to understand—'

'Go away.'

'You will never enter the secret room, Carter, or the curse will fall on you!'

After a long, and sometimes animated, meeting Carnarvon obtained Carter's agreement. On 26 January, the date suggested by Lacau, all Egyptian and foreign journalists would be allowed to visit the antechamber and see the remarkable way in which Carter's team worked.

340

The concession did not mitigate the vengeful passion of Bradstreet, the *New York Times* and *Morning Post* correspondent. The exclusive contract with the London *Times* was to him unacceptable. Therefore he continued to organize a campaign against the team of explorers, calling them unscrupulous traders who held Tutankhamun hostage. Carter was depicted as a vain and self-conceited monster, who did not give out any useful information and kept everything for himself, while his boss, Carnarvon, was called a businessman who only cared for profit and was ready to sign any favourable contract. These two pillagers had turned out to be much more efficient than gangs of thieves in Gurnah. Why had the masterpieces stacked in the antechamber not yet been displayed? Why was the tomb not open to visitors? Because, like a miser clinging to a bag of gold, Carter slowed the process of emptying the tomb using a thousand irksome aspects of officialdom to prevent the Antiquities Service from fulfilling its task.

Lady Evelyn was helping Carter to deal with the ever-increasing pile of mail.

'Would you like to read the latest article of the awful Bradstreet?'

'No.'

'Good idea. Keep your energy for more important things. Shall we try to answer the hundreds of requests for autographs that came today?'

'I shall share the chore with Mace and Burton. Your father and I decided not to ignore those who encourage us and perceive the difficulty of our task.'

'Shall we send seeds from the tomb to the British seed merchant who would like to grow Egyptian wheat?'

'Not before we have studied them here.'

'Here is a request from a Parisian fashion designer who requires fabric samples to launch a Tutankhamun fashion.'

'You'll have to answer him, Lady Evelyn.'

341

'He will manage without us. Ah . . . this is the third letter from a jam manufacturer who requests mummified food.'

Carter seized his head in his hands. 'I can't cope any more! It's all too much . . .'

She stood up, came close to him and wiped his forehead with a handkerchief soaked with eau de Cologne. 'You must hold out, Carter. If you get out of your depth, vultures will swoop down on Tutankhamun, and your life's work will be wasted.'

'Without you . . .'

'Don't say any more.'

February was exceptionally hot. The sand-filled wind irritated the eyes and made any movement difficult. The members of the team had to change their underwear several times a day. Lady Evelyn had discarded her tourist outfits and adopted a more casual dress. She had arranged a minute private room at the back of the tomb of Seti II. She took good care not to bother the specialists who, struggling against time, were restoring and packing. Their work had to be completed before April, when the climate would prevent them from continuing the already exhausting task.

The removal of the big ritual beds had been successful and remained a moment of unequalled emotion in the memory of the onlookers crowding around the tomb and along the way to the laboratory. When the lion's head appeared at the top of the stairs, murmurs of admiration ran through the crowd. The animal looked alive, and its eyes, both serious and playful, appeared to probe into people's souls. As a symbol of the past and the future, the lion spanned the centuries between the closure of the tomb and its reopening. Witnesses followed the slow gestures of Callender, who oversaw the packing of the masterpieces in large boxes lined with cotton wool.

From 6 a.m. onlookers had taken the best positions. They were not disappointed. The golden throne, whose décor told of Tutankhamun's love for his young wife, appeared, as well as a bust of the King which looked so realistic that some people believed the sovereign himself was leaving his long sleep.

Even the most blasé people felt that something exceptional was happening. It did not matter whether they liked Egyptian art, Tutankhamun and the history of the pharaohs or not. A force, which had been contained and withheld in darkness, was now sweeping the world like a wave, a magical wave washing along in its wake an energy which could overwhelm minds and hearts.

Eventually, Carnarvon gave a press conference. In the Winter Palace's largest reception room, journalists jostled each other. In spite of the presence of stewards to maintain order and the obligation to present an invitation card at the entrance, there were many gatecrashers.

With a sound sense of drama, the Earl waited for the hubbub to subside before he started talking.

'Thanks to efforts worthy of the Egyptians, Mr Carter and his team have kept to the schedule we had imposed on ourselves to let the world discover Tutankhamun's prodigious treasures. I hope that the outcome will silence slandering tongues and envious people. The artefacts in the antechamber, many of which have been restored in our laboratory in the valley, will be transferred to the Museum of Cairo by early spring. Then the Antiquities Service will take charge of arranging an exhibition worthy of these unequalled works.'

Some giggles burst forth. The incompetence of most service employees was notorious. Carnarvon was setting the cat among Lacau's pigeons.

'Will the tomb be open to the public,' asked Bradstreet, caustically.

'Certainly not.'

'Why?'

'For the best of reasons: excavations have not been completed.'

A shiver of excitement ran through the attendance. The nibs

343

Christian Jacq

of fountain pens were ready to run on paper. Convinced that he would get no precise answer, Bradstreet gave the *coup de grâce*.

'When will you be making a hole in the wall of the concealed room?'

'You are well informed,' acknowledged the Earl with a half-smile.

'So, when?'

'We'll open the walled-in door on 17 February, in the presence of the Queen of Belgium.'

71

A living queen visiting a dead king, a popular sovereign and an adulated pharaoh: with such dazzling publicity, Lord Carnarvon silenced his detractors. By 15 February, Luxor had become the centre of the world. Every capital had its attention overtaken by the Upper Egyptian town from whence issued hundreds of telegrams and dispatches about the Valley of the Kings. Egyptian Railways increased the number of trains from Cairo by three. Hotels filled with lords, ladies, dukes, duchesses and even rajahs, who did not want to miss the miracle for which the world had waited so long: the discovery of the undesecrated tomb of an ancient pharaoh.

The road to the valley had changed: where there had once been sand, rocks and silence, there was now a moving line of spluttering cars between two rows of Egyptian Army soldiers in ceremonial dress, forming a guard of honour for distinguished visitors.

Carter was cursing. The influx of tourists, be they billionaires, the influential or the famous, disturbed his work and threatened the security of the artefacts. How many clumsy lords and cramped duchesses had he prevented from knocking over an alabaster vase or treading on beads? Only Lady Evelyn's presence gave him the strength to put on an act.

On 16 February, the Queen and her son, Prince Leopold, arrived in Luxor, just when the canary's sad death was made public. The newspapers took advantage of the tragedy. Some of them even added that the burial chamber was swarming with cobras which would attack profaners. Bradstreet wrote ironically that only emptiness, or at best a plundered sarcophagus, would be discovered in the famous room which had remained out of reach for so long.

On 17 February, at noon, the antechamber was cleared. Only the two statues of the black king framing the way to the burial chamber remained. Carter contemplated the bare room regretfully. A whole part of his life was disappearing. Maybe he should have contented himself with enshrining in his memory the first vision of these marvels and shut the tomb again.

At 2 p.m. the official ceremony began. Instead of the twenty people who had been expected, some forty invaded Tutankhamun's last dwelling. Lady Evelyn, Carnarvon and Carter tried to outdo their guests' classical elegance. The British high commissioner, Lord Allenby, and the highest Egyptian authorities had answered the Earl's invitation, as well as Lacau and Engelbach. The latter sowed doubt by recalling the sad adventure of Davis who, a few years before, had bothered the lord of the country to show him empty vases. The ailing Queen of Belgium had apologized for her absence.

Carter, Carnarvon and Lady Evelyn exchanged knowing glances with each other while cameramen and photographers filmed the brilliant assembly crowding the entrance to the tomb. Carter opened the iron grille. He advised men to take their jackets off so as to be able to bear the heat from the antechamber more easily.

'It's very dark,' complained a former Egyptian minister.

'Don't worry,' said Carnarvon. 'We won't be swallowed by the depths of the earth. We will enjoy a sort of concert. Carter will sing an unpublished song.'

Leaning his elbows on the parapet, Arthur Weigall looked glumly at the privileged who disappeared into the gallery.

'The Earl never stops joking,' said a journalist standing beside him.

'With such a state of mind I don't give him more than six weeks of life. The curse of the pharaohs . . .'

'You're joking, aren't you?'

Embarrassed, Weigall slipped away. Another journalist took his place. Like his colleagues, he was ready to spend the afternoon in the sun in the hope of being the first to get some information on the secret chamber. Rumours were already circulating. Reliable sources mentioned two mummies, which turned into eight a quarter of an hour later.

The archaeological team had set up chairs and a barrier between the onlookers and the walled-in door, in front of which had been built a small platform enabling Carter to work unhampered and without running the risk of damaging the black statues, which were protected by wooden boxes.

When Carter climbed on the platform, he felt a shiver of excitement running through the onlookers behind the barrier. Although his hand trembled, he hit the first blow on the wall, which was lit by projectors.

Once the wooden lintel indicating a door had been cleared, he removed the plaster and loose stones forming the upper layer of the filling and bored a small hole.

'Give me a torch,' he asked Callender.

He lit up the secret room. He was the only one who could see what was on the other side of the wall. The onlookers held their breath.

'I see a wall . . . a gold and faience wall!'

Callender held out a lever and helped him pull the largest stones free so as to enlarge the hole. Carter worked hurriedly and impatiently when he came across irregular blocks of varied size and weight. He insisted on removing each one of them and handed them to Callender, who passed them to a workman so as to take them out of the antechamber. Mace made sure that the partition wall did not collapse into the secret room, thus running the risk of damaging its treasures. Carter slipped a mattress into the hole and went through to the other side. Carnarvon followed him.

The onlookers waited for a statement, but Carnarvon had just trodden on some beads from a necklace. In spite of the crowd's increasingly obvious impatience, he picked them up one by one and refused to go on until he had done so. Lacau interposed himself as the third privileged explorer. Lost in ecstasy in front of the great chapel whose sides looked like a gold wall, Carter did not chase him away. The three men walked cautiously, because the soil was littered with symbols: magical oars enabling the royal boat to progress on the roads of the sky, naos containing ritual instruments used for the funeral, bunches of persea, wine jars, a silver trumpet, skins of Anubis rolled around a pole to depict death and rebirth.

Lacau was silent. The inscriptions and scenes of the huge shrine, which filled almost the whole room, formed an unusual series. How many years would be needed to study and interpret them? On the walls paintings depicted the opening of the mouth of the royal mummy once it had been dragged to the royal necropolis by 'friends of the King'. The weighing of the heart, compared with the guideweight, had been auspicious. Without doubt the spirit of Tutankhamun had entered eternity. Carter drew the latches, opened the large doors and disclosed a second shrine. On the door was a seal.

'It is intact,' said Lacau, 'and the veil turned yellow by time . . . has never been lifted by anyone since the king's burial!'

They remained silent for a long time. Who would dare break the seal?

Lacau's glance fell on the low door opening on to the last room of the tomb, the treasure room. Carter was the first to enter it. He noticed a clay brick, in which had been planted a reed torch. Lying on a shrine and wrapped in a linen cloth, Anubis was looking at the intruder. In front of the door, against the most distant wall, four gold goddesses reached out their arms to protect the chest containing canopic vases where the King's viscera had been preserved. They looked so natural and alive. Their faces expressed so much serenity that he hardly dared contemplate them.

Their eyes moved from boxes, models of ships, jewels, and equipment for scribes to a fan in ostrich feathers and statuettes . . . When Lacau left, dumbfounded, Lady Evelyn joined her father and the archaeologist. Carter deciphered hieroglyphs on various objects and identified the names of people close to the monarch and particularly, Maya, the Minister of Finance and supervisor of the royal necropolis. So he was the one who had ordered that the tomb be dug in this place and imposed the most absolute secrecy after he had led the funeral! Carter was Maya's faithful follower. Disturbed, he was about to leave the burial chamber when he noticed a lamp with a wick, whose clay base bore an inscription.

'What is written on it?' asked Lady Evelyn.

'It protects the tomb from desecration and keeps the secret chamber untouched.'

Neither Carter nor Carnarvon were able to utter a word when they came back to the antechamber. They just threw their arms up in the air. One after the other, the guests crossed the threshold of the holy of holies. Several of them left the fascinating world they had seen with difficulty. Their legs swayed; they were overwhelmed by so much beauty. The initial excitement was succeeded by seriousness when they realized that they had taken part in unfathomable mysteries.

Over three hours after the beginning of the strange ceremonial, sweaty, dusty and dishevelled, Carter and Carnarvon were the last to leave the tomb. The sun had set and the cold stung the skin. Carter put a shawl over Lady Evelyn's shoulders.

'The valley has changed,' she said. 'Look, it is illuminated by an unusual light! I have not seen anything like it before.'

'Never have I loved it so much . . . It offers us something that seemed impossible.'

72

Tutankhamun had become the supreme ruler of Luxor. He was present in all conversations and his name figured on a whole variety of goods in shops. Cooks invented 'Tutankhamun soups' or roasts *à la Tut*, while those who organized celebrations attracted crowds to 'Tutankhamun dances'.

Bradstreet, who had intended to write an ironic article on the diplomatic illness of the Queen of Belgium, was disappointed when he heard that she had quickly recovered and visited the west bank on 18 February. She probably preferred a visit on her own to the crowd of the official inauguration.

Callender had reserved a surprise for her. He had improved the electric installation and concealed bulbs, thus creating a soft and warm atmosphere, suitable to the discovery of the large shrine and the marvels of the treasure room. Moved, Jean Capart, the Egyptologist who accompanied the queen, clapped his hands.

'How can we preserve this moment in time? This is the most beautiful day in my life!'

He kissed Carter enthusiastically on both cheeks. 'You are a genius and a benefactor of humankind.'

Even though Carter did not aspire to such glorious titles, he was happy to receive a colleague's sincere affection. Tutankhamun really produced miracles.

A large-brimmed white hat on her head and her face hidden

behind a veil, the Queen wore a white dress. A stole of silver fox covered her shoulders. Her arrival had not gone unnoticed because her retinue was composed of no less than seven cars followed by a group of horse-drawn carriages and various vehicles drawn by donkeys.

The humble people of the west bank were happy to take part in the celebration and expressed their joy noisily. The head of the province had set the example by greeting the Queen with brassy music on the pier.

Her Majesty's flu had not been feigned. She was shivering with cold despite the heat. Yet she was fascinated by the visit of the tomb. She put numerous questions to Carter, who, delighted, opened boxes which had remained shut ever since Tutankhamun's death. One of them contained a gilded wooden snake which looked so alive that the visitors gave a start when they saw it.

The Queen never stopped praising Carnarvon and Carter at the press conference she gave that evening. Happy to be in Luxor and even happier for having seen masterpieces of such astounding beauty, she insisted that everybody owed the Earl and his archaeologist a debt of gratitude.

'Faintness?'

'Yes, Howard. This is the third visitor who has fainted as he leaves the tomb.'

'It's the heat.'

'The public rumour mentions a curse by the *sheikh*.'

'Do you believe it?'

'No,' answered Carnarvon. 'And it doesn't dissuade people from besieging the tomb. *The Times* is a precious ally. Its daily account of our work silences our adversaries.'

'Except Bradstreet and the *New York Times*! He claims that disagreements between the Egyptian government and us are on the increase.'

'The Ministry of Civil Engineering has just denied that and described Bradstreet's allegations as false. It has even

351

congratulated itself on the cordiality of its relationship with us. We also received a message from King Fuad: "I am particularly happy to express my warmest congratulations, at a time when your many years of work are crowned with success." Our enemies are now defeated, Howard. Even Lacau cannot lift a finger. You are untouchable now that you have become an international hero.'

Between 20 and 25 February, thousands of tourists stormed the west bank and rushed to the tomb of Tutankhamun. Even a sand storm did not discourage the onlookers. Luxor's night life was as busy as that of a great capital. Indifferent to the wonders of Egyptian archaeology but with a fondness for horse and camel races, a large number of Americans bet huge sums, drank a lot and gambled all night on cruise ships which plied the Nile.

Carter pushed aside two tipsy men and entered the reception room of the Winter Palace, where Carnarvon was having tea with a representative of the Metropolitan Museum. The Earl sensed an outburst.

'This cannot go on. Tourists are more insufferable than flies.'

'The Egyptian government asked us for permission to open the tomb to the public and—'

'We were wrong. These bands of hotheads are a danger to it.'

'Has anything happened?'

'A fat man got stuck between the wall and the shrine. The wall was damaged. Tomorrow, there will be more wear and tear. I'll accept no further responsibility if we do not close the tomb.'

As worried as Carter, Carnarvon arranged an urgent meeting with a representative of the ministry.

Desperate for solitude, the archaeologist was writing his diary when the door of the house opened softly.

'May I disturb you?'

Lady Evelyn's smile would have disarmed the fiercest conqueror. Carter put down his fountain pen. 'Please, come in.'

The sun was setting on the valley. The rock took on an ochre tinge and silence settled over the dwellings of eternity.

'My father is annoyed.'

'I am sorry about that. We do not really agree on the approach we should adopt with the authorities. Concessions will produce catastrophes.'

Lady Evelyn came close to Carter. She put her right hand on his shoulder. Paralysed he hardly dared breathe.

'You are a determined man, Carter.'

'I . . .'

'I like your character, Howard. It is both impossible and unique. You are convinced that the absolute can be experienced here below and that uprightness is the only acceptable behaviour.'

'I acknowledge that.'

She kissed him on the forehead. Carter clung to his desk, like a shipwrecked man to a raft.

'Am I uncompromising enough for you?'

'I would like to tell you . . .'

He stood up slowly, afraid that she might force him to remain seated. But she moved away, suddenly out of reach.

'I don't want to lose you, Evelyn.'

He took one step towards her. She did not step back.

'I do not know how . . .'

'Shut up, Howard. I do not want words.'

He took her in his arms. Lady Evelyn, Evelyn, Eve, a woman in love, happiness.

At six o'clock Carter had not yet risen. His eyes wide open, he was trying to fix in his memory each moment of the sublime night in which, for the first time in thirty-three years, he had not dreamed of the Valley of the Kings.

The door of the house opened with a crash.

353

Christian Jacq

'Are you here, Carter?'

The archaeologist raised himself on one side.

'Answer, Carter!'

'I am in my bedroom, sir.'

Carnarvon had a haggard face. He was muttering. 'Eve has told me everything.'

'She was right.'

'I forbid you to see her again.'

'Why?'

'You do not belong to the same world.'

'She is an aristocrat and I am of common birth!'

'Precisely.'

'If I ask for her hand, will you refuse?'

'I would be forced to do so.'

'What law would force you to do so?'

'Moral standards and customs.'

Carter stood up and dressed. 'You do not believe in them yourself. Your character as well as your life contradict such conformity.'

'I believe in them for my daughter and I shall fight her madness.'

'Is it madness to love me?'

'You should understand, Howard!'

'I don't. People say that the world has changed . . . Now a man of common birth can marry the daughter of an Earl.'

'You are mistaken. The Valley of the Kings is your sole love. That is the true reason for my refusal. I must protect you from yourself.'

'Please do not take decisions about my feelings.'

'Forget Evelyn.'

'Never. I did not encourage her, and I cannot turn her away.'

Carnarvon did not restrain his anger any more. 'Force yourself. She is twenty-two and you are fifty! This is monstrousness, Carter!'

The archaeologist straightened his bow tie. 'Don't demean yourself by talking with a monster. Leave here.'

354

'Do you know what this means?'

'The Earl dismisses the man of common birth. Our collaboration is over.'

73

Ragtime had invaded the Winter Palace ballroom and supplanted quieter dances. Young upper-class British and Americans devoted themselves to the new entertainment and formed romances.

In a nearby reception room, Carter was drinking.

Once again, he found himself alone, abandoned by everybody. His dream was within reach, yet everything had turned into a nightmare. Carnarvon would hire another archaeologist to open the chapels and discover the ultimate secret. What future could an unemployed archaeologist offer to the daughter of an Earl?

'Don't destroy yourself, Howard.'

Lord Carnarvon sat down in front of Carter. 'I apologize.'

'You . . .'

'You heard me. You are my only friend. It would be stupid to fall out with you. Whatever happens, whatever your feelings for me might be, my affection for you will never fail. I behaved like an idiot . . . Lies, irritation, the hubbub of glory . . . I'll grant you that these are only poor excuses.'

'They seem quite valid. It is wrong to drink on one's own. Would you like a glass of champagne?'

'Yes, with pleasure.'

After nine days of frantic visits, with the support of Carnarvon, Carter won his case. The Antiquities Service and the

Government agreed to shut the tomb, realizing that it was essential to its preservation. When the two men contemplated the empty antechamber, devoid of its contents, they experienced a deep feeling of discomfort.

'Walls a sad yellow colour, a bare floor, not even the outline of a décor . . . so much desolation! We are desecraters.'

'I don't believe that, Howard. Tutankhamun feels our respect.'

'Why would he forgive us for having upset his tomb?'

'Because we will let his message be known to the world. Ancient Egypt is only just beginning to reveal its secrets. Didn't you say that it was ruled by neither superstition nor idolatry, but that its real values were knowledge, loyalty to a universal rule and the sacredness of everyday life? Our civilization is miserable, Howard. Its gods are hypocrisy, corruption and mediocrity. A world war and millions of dead . . . this is the result of our famous progress. If we do not recover the Egyptians' faith, we are condemned to nothingness.'

Carter could not take his eyes off the two black statues which continued to watch over the entrance to the secret chamber. Their golden headgear and the light of their eyes purified the soul.

'Our era is devoted to cynical materialism. It destroys everything that is not in line with its meanness. Tutankhamun is a miracle, the most extraordinary of miracles, a lone gleam of hope.'

The large iron grille closed on the antechamber. Dozens of workmen, among whom were several children, poured hundreds of baskets of sand and fragments of stone in the corridor. The *reis* was walking to and fro along the human chain blocking access to the tomb. At nightfall, Callender lit the projectors. Work went on till dawn. At 5.30 a.m. on 26 February, Tutankhamun's dwelling of eternity had disappeared again.

'May he rest in peace,' murmured Carter.

'Nobody will be able to empty his vault,' said Carnarvon. 'What an incredible endeavour! Archaeologists usually unearth and we bury! This is probably the first time that excavators have willingly filled in the site on which they worked.'

'Sometimes I consider not disturbing his peace any more.'

'You owe it to me to persevere to the end, Howard. The King has been haunting your dreams ever since your adolescence. It would only be courtesy to meet him.'

Soldiers and wardens of the Antiquities Service settled around the parapet indicating the location of the tomb. Carter asked the *reis* to have it watched over by his own wardens. But who could imagine that the cavity full of rubble concealed the only intact vault in the Valley of the Kings?

Carnarvon shook Pierre Lacau's hand.

'The temperature in Cairo is less trying than in Luxor. Would you like a mint tea, sir?'

'Yes please.'

'I am honoured by your visit. The Egyptian court and the High Commissioner are completely with you. Everyone who matters in this country recognizes you as a national hero.'

'Fortunately I still have a few enemies. Otherwise I would rest on my laurels.'

'Freedom fighters? They're not serious.'

'You're quite mistaken, Mr Lacau. They won't give up. How do you plan to share the artefacts?'

The Director of the Antiquities Service had been afraid of the question. Carnarvon was taking advantage of his reputation to obtain illicit profit by circumventing the regulations.

Seething with rage, Lacau would witness the scattering of the most fabulous collection in all times.

'The sharing . . . we'll have to discuss that.'

'Are you against the idea?'

'Your question is rather embarrassing. Ancient customs

sometimes lack rigour . . . Don't you think that Tutankhamun's treasures could be gathered in the Museum of Cairo . . .'

'Suggest a list and we'll discuss it as you wish.'

Lacau looked at the Earl as he left. Without being aware of his gesture, he broke the pencil he was clutching in his right hand.

The sandy wind did not die down. Despite dust and heat, the team continued to work in the laboratory. The restoration of jewels, clothes, wood and pottery required patience and meticulousness. Carnarvon took an interest in the slightest detail and questioned the specialists on their techniques. Everybody noticed his growing nervousness, and the weariness that made his face look gaunt.

In the break that followed lunch, Carter made up his mind to question him. 'I haven't seen Lady Evelyn again.'

'You are free, Howard. And so is she.'

'Have you really forgiven me?'

'You have not done anything wrong.'

'You have seemed so far away in the last few days.'

'It is for a stupid reason. I have toothache. Two teeth have broken and one has fallen out . . . I am ageing and I long for Susie. Because of her health, she has to stay at Highclere. I miss her . . . She was used to watching over me and our treasures! And I am upset by an article in the Egyptian newspaper *Al Ahram*. What a lie! I am accused of wanting to take Tutankhamun out of his grave and transport his mummy secretly to England! I am weary of such slander . . . But I answered that, if the King was still resting in the sarcophagus concealed in the shrines, I would make arrangements to leave him there and not transfer him to the Museum of Cairo. I do not share the morbid passion of amateurs who like to see mummies displayed in glass cases. But the Egyptian journalists do not believe me! They think that Tutankhamun is their ancestor and that a British lord should not care about him.'

'Forget such foolish talk.'

'I cannot do that. Britain does not rule the world any more, Howard. It is no longer the guardian of peace and civilization. As for you and me, however much we have to protect this King who has become our brother, it will be a fabulous moment when we can contemplate his face.'

Carnarvon winced and felt his cheek. 'A mosquito . . . the sting hurts.'

There was a bead of blood on his skin. The Earl wiped it off with his monogrammed handkerchief.

'I must return to Cairo.'

'To see Lacau?'

'He is too quiet. I have the feeling that he is doing things behind the scenes so as to hinder our research and prevent me from developing my collection. We must make our final moves while there is still time. By the end of the month, the antiquities will be evenly shared. Can you imagine some of our treasures at Highclere?'

Thoughtful, Lord Carnarvon put his hat on and, leaning on his stick, left the laboratory. Like a fleeting shadow he disappeared in the whirl of white and ochre dust which covered the scars of the valley.

74

The ailing Lacau was not able to receive Lord Carnarvon. Lady Evelyn expected her father to be intensely annoyed, but the weary Earl went back to the Continental Hotel, where he spent the day sleeping.

The following morning, he seemed more cheerful. As his daughter kissed him, she noticed his swollen neck. He saw her fear.

'Ganglions . . . they are slightly painful. I have been exhausted by the valley over the last few weeks.'

The barber came in. Carnarvon remembered the earlier episode when a colleague had threatened to cut his throat. This time the razor glided smoothly over the lathered skin.

Carnarvon let out a shout of pain. The barber stepped back, distressed.

'Forgive me . . . I injured you!'

The Earl felt his cheek. Blood was oozing from the place where he had been stung by the mosquito.

'Go away!'

Contrite, the man scuttled away. The Earl completed the shave himself. As he stood up, he was seized by dizziness, clung to a chair and managed to reach his bed, where he collapsed.

Shortly before noon, Lady Evelyn found him fully stretched out and unable to move. Panic-stricken, she immediately called a doctor, who diagnosed congestion of the lungs and prescribed anti-infectious medicines. Despite the treatment, the fever rose to over 104°F.

'I think this is serious, Eve.'

'Don't worry, father. I'm staying with you.'

'You should send a cable to your mother and to your brother. They should come as soon as possible.'

'I'll take care of that.'

Lady Evelyn also wrote to Howard Carter. She did not conceal her concern and promised to send news every day.

Journalists assailed the young woman that evening. She was forced to reveal that her father was bedridden and that several weeks of rest would probably be necessary.

Specialists took turns at his bedside. Pessimistic, they diagnosed general infection and blood poisoning. One of them was persuaded that the sick man had absorbed a toxic substance, but his colleagues contradicted him.

A medical bulletin was published every day in the Egyptian press, which Carter read greedily for the first time in his life. Press releases emphasized the patient's excellent morale, his courage and lucidity. Of course the fever persisted, but the fight against illness was taking a turn for the better.

A thousand administrative tasks kept Carter in Luxor, where Engelbach and his henchmen insisted on checking the restoration work every other day. He was, however, ready to leave for Cairo the moment Lady Evelyn asked him to.

In the last week of March, the Earl asked his daughter to tell him about the research described by Carter in his letters. The team was progressing on the assumption that Carnarvon would assess their work.

'Are you happy, Eve?'

'As long as you're ill, the word "happiness" won't have any meaning.'

'Think more of yourself . . . An old man can't give you happiness.'

'You gave me everything. How could I forget our walks in the park at Highclere, our moonlight talks, the reading lessons in the library, the hunting parties where we took good care to miss the game? And Egypt, your Egypt! The other world on earth, a pharaoh resuscitated in the radiance of gold, eternity within reach . . . you revealed all this to me.'

'Well, you'll have to make do without me.'

'That idea is unworthy of Lord Carnarvon.'

'Will you marry Howard?'

'I refuse to answer that.'

'Why?'

'Go on living and you will know.'

In early April she brought her father a letter which had been signed both by Lacau and the Ministry of Civil Engineering. They agreed to change nothing in the legal regulations until the end of 1924. This meant that, as a backer, the Earl would be legally allowed to take a number of artefacts.

'Are you satisfied?'

'It is too late, Eve.'

'Of course not! You'll recover.'

'I have heard the call and I'm getting ready for it.'

'No . . .'

'I want to be buried at the top of the hill overlooking Highclere. It will soon be spring there . . . My only funeral music will be the song of larks. The ceremony should be simple and brief . . . those close to me, my old servants, the tenants on the estate, Susie . . . no politicians, no dignitaries.'

'What about Howard Carter?'

'I am not dying for him. He should not leave the valley until he has completed the restoration. Tutankhamun's treasure is more important than an old lord at the point of death.'

Lady Evelyn burst into tears. 'You have no right to leave!'

'Death is a dubious joke . . . but I am not its author.'

Carnarvon fell into a coma. Lady Evelyn did not dare tell Carter. To his sole friend, the Earl wanted to leave the image of a strong and serene man.

The Earl did not recognize his wife, nor his son, an officer in the British Indian Army, whose ship had been rerouted. His eyes were already contemplating another universe, where human figures turned into insubstantial ghosts.

On 5 April 1923, at 1.45, Lord Carnarvon breathed his last.

All the lights in Cairo went out at the time of his death, even though electricity was distributed by six independent power plants. For long minutes, technicians worked in vain to discover the origin of the breakdown. Everywhere people lit candles and paraffin or oil lamps.

At Highclere, Susie, the Earl's favourite dog, let out a long howl and died at the very moment when her master was taking the way of the other world, on which she would guide him unfailingly.

75

Past and present merged to follow Anubis, the ruler of death. Mystery remained ruler of the valley where the souls of kings continued to live.

How would Carter go on living without Carnarvon, his friend, his brother? Carnarvon had only survived the discovery of Tutankhamun's tomb by six months. He would never see the sarcophagus and mummy, supposing that they were intact.

The archaeologist constantly saw before his eyes the accursed death certificate, written in French, stating that George Herbert of London, Earl of Carnarvon, born on 22 June 1866, had died of pneumonia after a seven-day illness. He was aged fifty-seven.

Carnarvon had been an upright man, an adventurer who concealed his enthusiasm under a mask of elegance, a non-violent conqueror . . . Without him, the days would be grey and cold, even under a hot sun. Carter felt like closing the laboratory and leaving the valley and the tomb for ever to silence and dust. But Carnarvon would never have allowed such cowardice. Within less than a month, all the artefacts from the antechamber would have to be ready for a long journey. He had to forget sadness, tiredness and the acrid taste of loneliness.

'A new victim of the pharaohs' curse': several newspapers published the sensational front-page information as it quickly went around the world. Consulted, the medium Conan Doyle declared that Tutankhamun had probably taken revenge on his main desecrater. Even the serious press referred to a text in the tomb which prophesied the annihilation of all those who dared touch the treasure. It was recalled that the Egyptians were fearsome wizards who brought evil to those who desecrated tombs.

Famous doctors rose up against the nonsense. They stated that pathogenic germs might have caused a general infection in the Earl. The question arose: should the tomb be disinfected before people entered it again?

The death of several tourists spread more panic. Of course they had all been elderly and sick, but they had all visited the tomb. A dozen American politicians requested careful examination of mummies preserved in museums. Perhaps they were responsible for unexplained deaths, or even epidemics? In Great Britain, the owners of Egyptian antiquities sent them to the British Museum so as to be rid of the evil objects.

Carter agreed to appear before a pack of journalists. Questions burst forth.

'Are you in good health?'

'Excellent, even though I am deeply afflicted by the death of Lord Carnarvon.'

'What about your stomach pains?'

'They have remained unchanged over the last ten years.'

'Will you dare to go down into the tomb again?'

'Yes, as soon as possible.'

'You are accused of being a desecrater.'

'Nobody respects Tutankhamun's memory as much as I do. My dearest wish is to greet him and to ensure his mummy's absolute security, if it really exists, so that future centuries may revere it.'

'Is it true that there are Egyptian texts which forbid the entering of tombs?'

'They curse the desecrater who lacks respect and requests that love and care be felt for the human being in his dwelling of resurrection so that his name may last. You should never pass a vault without reading its inscriptions. Tutankhamun was waiting for us, gentlemen. It was our duty to keep the appointment.'

Carter was thinking of Evelyn's distress. She had witnessed her father's agony and experienced the death of the man she cherished, and who had opened all life's paths to her. He felt that if he tried to write her a comforting letter the words would be meaningless. Doomed, like himself, to solitude, where would she turn her love?

He was restoring a necklace when a high-ranking Egyptian civil servant came to the entrance of the laboratory with Engelbach. Callender barred the way and asked them to wait until the archaeologist had completed his task. Stringing beads precluded any kind of haste.

An hour later, the two men were exasperated. Carter came to meet them at last.

'I want to visit the tomb,' declared the Egyptian drily.

'Why?'

'I have a permit delivered by the service.'

'That is meaningless.'

'What does that mean?'

'It means that the tomb is closed until the next excavation campaign.'

'Who took that decision?'

'I did.'

'This is an Egyptian tomb. It does not belong to you!'

'I am responsible for its preservation.'

'I advise you to let me in, Mr Carter.'

'I advise you to beetle off.'

Engelbach added fuel to the flames. 'Howard Carter believes he stands above the law . . . It won't always be like that!'

'If the service employed less incompetent people, the pharaohs' legacy would be better preserved.'

Christian Jacq

'Let's go,' recommended Engelbach. 'We'll settle the matter with the authorities.'

'We'll have you fired!' promised the civil servant.

'There is no hope of that,' retorted Carter, smiling. 'I don't belong to any administration.'

The last spadeful of earth had finished covering the grave of George Herbert, fifth Earl of Carnarvon. From the top of Breacon Hill, he would look over his estate for ever. The cedars of Lebanon presented their tops to the spring sun.

In accordance with the Earl's wish, his funeral had been celebrated in the utmost simplicity. Only those close to him and sincere friends attended it, with the exception of Howard Carter, who had to pursue in Egypt the mission Carnarvon had wanted to complete. Susie was sleeping near the master she had never left, whether in life or death. Larks were singing, happy to be flying high in the sky. The concert was so sweet and charming that it mitigated the sadness of the farewell. Lady Evelyn thought of the bird with a human head Carter had shown her on the walls of tombs. Perhaps her father's soul had left his body to take part in the cosmic dance which would take it from his motherland to the Egypt of Tutankhamun.

At the time of his friend's funeral, Carter dropped a wreath of foliage and a twig of acacia by the entrance of Tutankhamun's tomb. A hawk crossed the blue sky of the Valley of the Kings, an area whose unchanging light erased the victories and failures of humankind.

Even though Carnarvon was resting at Highclere, his ancestral home, it was here in the valley that his roaming had come to an end and his dream come true. He deserved the crown given to true beings, those who are able to tread without weariness or betrayal along the way of their own metamorphosis.

Without Carnarvon, the journey would only be a series of ordeals. The future looked dark. The only light was the presence of a forgotten pharaoh whose magical power had given life to an everlasting friendship.

76

On 19 April 1923, King Fuad yielded to political demands by granting the country a constitution. He kept executive power for himself, while the Parliament retained the legislative power. Championing independence, the WAFD party organized a shopkeepers' strike and peace marches. With popular support, it obtained a clear majority in Parliament. It was determined to work against both the King and Great Britain. Fuad, who readily dismissed ministers when they dared question him, immediately thought of dissolving an arrogant and useless Parliament. But the WAFD and Prime Minister Zaghlul, were able to spread the ideal of Egyptian nationalism, even though their allies were bankers and landowners opposed to any social reform.

The tomb of Seti II, now turned into a laboratory, seemed to Carter's team to be safe from the surrounding agitation. However, a high-ranking policeman dressed in a splendid white uniform covered with medals, summoned the archaeologist to Gurnah's police station. Seated behind a huge desk, he was leafing through a bundle of reports.

'You are in an irregular situation, Mr Carter.'

'You surprise me.'

'There are obvious facts.'

'What facts?'

'The security of Egyptian workers is not assured on your site.'

'That is untrue.'

'I have proof!'

'Show me.'

The policeman took a sheet out of the bundle. 'Here they are: illnesses, accidents, attacks!'

Carter read the administrative report. 'All of them are fakes.'

'Do you dare question these official papers?'

'Without the slightest hesitation. *Reis* Ahmed Girigar will bear witness, as will all my workmen. I request an immediate settlement of these issues.'

'If you are sincere, that may not be necessary.'

'I insist on it.'

'I'll submit the matter to my superiors.'

The policeman stuck the files under his right arm, stood up and climbed into a horse-drawn carriage. As it moved away in a cloud of dust, Carter wiped his forehead with a handkerchief.

The temperature was 102° in the shade on 13 May 1923, as Carter and his team wrapped up the treasures of the ante-chamber in wool and fabrics. Once they had been well protected from possible shocks, they were divided into thirty-four boxes. A steamer chartered by the Antiquities Service was waiting alongside the quay.

'There are almost six miles of track between the laboratory and the Nile,' remarked Callender. 'How shall we manage the transportation?'

'I thought of porters,' answered Carter.

'That is impossible. It is too hot and too far.'

'What about trucks?'

'I would advise against them. The road is bad. It winds constantly and it is full of stones . . . We run the risk of a lot of the artefacts being broken.'

'Then there is only one solution: the railway.'

'It's going to be a lot of painstaking work.'

'We have no choice.'

At 5 a.m. the following day, Callender directed the laying of the first rails delivered by the service. But the straight and curved sections only amounted to a 90-foot length. When he requested the rest of the materials, the civil servants said that they had brought all the rails the administration had promised.

At eight the disaster came to Carter's attention. His fit of anger against the service did not really disturb its representatives: they had obeyed Lacau's orders and could not be reprimanded. Noticing that his friend was on the brink of giving up, Callender reacted. With the help of a few workers he loaded the boxes on the wagons and pushed them to the end of the railway track, then took the rails to pieces and set them up again in the front.

'Nothing is simpler,' he concluded. 'If we repeat the manoeuvre some hundred times, we will eventually reach the Nile.'

With self-sacrifice and courage which moved Carter, some fifty workers carried the operation through successfully. The *reis* Ahmed Girigar paced the effort with songs and often offered drinks to his men. Callender constantly watered the hot rails and watched over the boxes. On 17 May at noon, the convoy left the valley. Carter thought of the slow procession which had carried the masterpieces to the king's tomb 3,000 years before.

'We cannot go on today,' groaned Callender. 'The road is getting too difficult and the workers are exhausted.'

Carter rushed to the track, removed dozens of stones and attempted to move the rails alone.

'Don't be stubborn, Howard.'

'We can't stop here!'

'We have to. Let's have a rest.'

'What about security?'

'We can take care of it ourselves, with the help of the *reis*.'

The boxes were unloaded and stored near the bed of a wadi. Carter did not get a wink of sleep all night. In the early morning, the *reis* and his men drew renewed energy from their

371

exhausted bodies. They made it a point of honour to overcome
the obstacles. The infernal pace started again. On edge, Carter
feared accidents or injuries. In spite of his haste, he insisted
that the heavy rails be handled slowly.

Soldiers sent by the governor of the province kept onlookers
and intruders away, but none of them agreed to come to help.

At last they reached the Nile.

'The water is low,' said Callender. 'And the bank is very
steep. The most dangerous part remains.'

The rails were laid on a bumpy slope. They bent under the
weight of the wagons.

'Hold them back!' shouted Carter.

The fifty men slowed the descent of the first wagon. Tied
together the boxes seemed about to topple. With a pathetic
gesture, Carter tried to push them back.

'Move away,' ordered Callender. 'You might be run over!'

Carter refused. With a rattle of metallic moanings, the
wagons slid to the end of the railway track that reached the
water. Not one box fell. Carter, Callender, Ahmed Girigar and
the workers spontaneously let out a shout of triumph.

'My God, Howard, I did not believe we would do it!'

'Tutankhamun protects us.'

'You're turning into a mystic, aren't you?'

'One more effort. We have to get the boxes to the ship.'

The beautiful ship that had been promised turned out to be
an ordinary barge. Without making a fuss, up to their waists in
the water, the porters loaded the boxes on the ship, which was
then towed by a tugboat. Carter kissed the *reis* and congratulated the men with an enthusiasm none of them ever
forgot. Their families would mention the feat for years.

At the bow of the barge, Carter enjoyed the breeze.
Carnarvon would have been proud of him.

On 27 May, Pierre Lacau waited for Carter on a landing stage
about a mile from the Museum of Cairo. Worried, the Director
of the Antiquities Service forgot the usual civilities.

'Are the artefacts intact?'

'Despite your lack of co-operation, my team achieved the impossible.'

Lacau did not respond to the criticism. 'Let's open a box.'

Carter agreed. Lacau saw sticks and the legs of chairs wrapped in thick bandages appear.

'And now another one.'

The fragile caskets wrapped in thick layers of cloth had also not suffered from the journey.

'Are you satisfied, sir?'

Lacau mumbled vague thanks.

'Your restoration was rather slow, Carter. It will also take a lot of time to unwrap everything. But the public is impatient to see these works which, alas, we won't be able to exhibit for six months.'

'You are wrong.'

Lacau stood up. 'What do you mean?'

'All the artefacts have been registered and described. So your service won't have to do any of the scientific work. Moreover, Callender and I wrapped them so that they are in the best order. You will only have to follow the numbering of the boxes when removing objects. Last, our restoration was so meticulous that your laboratory won't have to do anything.'

'How soon do you think we might be able to exhibit them?'

Carter pretended to reflect. 'If your workers are competent . . . a week!'

'That is ridiculous!'

One week later, filled with wonder, visitors marvelled at the six showcases of the first exhibition of Tutankhamun's treasures. Thousands of curious people pushed to get into the museum. Nobody was disappointed. The resuscitated pharaoh deserved his reputation.

77

In May 1923, the temperature rose to over 106°F, but Howard Carter's ardour did not diminish. Indifferent to fatigue, he concentrated on a serious problem: how could he peel the gold shrines away like an onion so as to clear their core area, the royal sarcophagus? He discussed various procedures with his collaborators, who were also concerned about how many risks they could take.

A letter from Lady Evelyn interrupted his deliberations. The archaeologist was to go urgently to Highclere where the delicate topic of Lord Carnarvon's succession would be debated. The summons made him anxious. Had the Countess decided to put an end to the financing of the excavations?

He was assailed by British journalists as soon as he stepped off the ship. On board he had had to complete his entry in *Who's Who*, with 'painter' as his main occupation. He attempted to flee, but the pack completely encircled him. The only way out was to answer their questions.

'Have you been struck by Tutankhamun's curse?'

'He follows me with his blessings.'

'Are you afraid of the Pharaoh's ghost?'

'We are the best of friends.'

'Have you become a billionaire?'

'Not yet. My schedule is too busy.'

'Aren't your excavations a little hasty?'

'Pierre Lacau criticizes us for being too slow.'

'Are you not a pillager of tombs?'

'Tutankhamun is my spiritual brother. The discovery of his tomb enables me to bring his message back to light.'

'When will you open the sarcophagus?'

'In little more than a month, if I can work in peace.'

Carter meditated at the grave of his friend. The radiant summer of Highclere denied death. Majestic and peaceful, the great cedars of Lebanon touched the sky. 'He has not left the valley. Every day I can feel his presence at my side.'

'He won't abandon you,' promised Lady Evelyn. 'Come, Howard, my mother may be getting impatient.'

Soft and harsh at the same time, Lady Carnarvon did not show any animosity towards the archaeologist. Yet he feared that she might accuse him of being responsible for the death of her husband.

'Thanks to you, Mr Carter, my husband experienced true happiness on this earth. Tutankhamun was the paradise he had been seeking for so long. For that reason I shall help you.'

Carter held back his tears. Fortified by her support he could go on fighting. 'The most urgent thing will be to retain the concession under your own name.'

'Do you expect any difficulties?'

'Lacau will balk, but he will be forced to yield.'

'Do you think it would be useful to extend the exclusive contract with *The Times*?'

'Yes, at least for a year. Otherwise the press will invade the vault. We must also request complete independence, so as to be able to prevent the intrusion of tourists and Antiquities Service inspectors.'

'You will have to solve these problems, Mr Carter. You are now my archaeological adviser, and the only man who is entitled to pursue my husband's work.'

The summer passed slowly. Gardeners watered lawns at

nightfall. Wooded hills turned golden in the sun. The white marble belvedere looked out over the estate, whose master would now never leave. Carter had accepted Lady Carnarvon's invitation to stay. It was an unexpected gift to be able to spend the summer at Highclere near Lady Evelyn. On 5 August he received a most moving letter. Ahmed Girigar and his workers wished him excellent health, hoped to see him soon and informed him that nothing untoward had happened on the site. The *reis* had made sure that his instructions about security were respected to the letter. During a picnic on the edge of a beech wood, Carter read and reread the letter to Lady Evelyn.

'These are good people! The world is not only populated by the jealous and the ambitious!'

'Had you turned into a cynic, Howard?'

'I have become a little more realistic.'

'Don't be bitter.'

'I know that people want to prevent me from reaching the end of my adventure and that they will use the basest means to destroy me. Some will act openly, but others will do it behind my back. Even if their interests differ, they will know how to unite against me.'

'Are you thinking . . . of the curse?'

'There is no evil force in Egyptian tombs. On the contrary, they preserve elements of a most fabulous treasure: the secret of immortality. Up to now it has only been revealed to us in snatches.'

The young woman rested her head on Carter's shoulder. Filtering through the foliage, a ray of sun illuminated her hair.

'Do you have to run so many risks, Howard?'

'An intact vault has never been explored. If I managed to do so, death will be defeated.'

'An insane dream . . .'

'Tutankhamun is very close, Eve. He is no longer a dream. As for the curse, it is not spread by him, but by the troop of envious people preparing to attack me. And your father is no longer here to help me. Without him, I feel helpless.'

'Trust yourself. You are much stronger than you imagine.'

A flight of wild geese flew over the wood. United in its flight, the small group left for a new land known only to its leader.

'The summer will soon come to an end.'

'Have you talked to your mother?'

'The whole family is opposed to our marriage. If we get married, the financing of excavations will be stopped.'

'Is that her last word?'

'It is impossible to discuss anything. You are recognized as a friend and as the pursuer of my father's work, and nothing more.'

'Why does she let me stay at Highclere?'

'Because I demand it. I am ready to follow you, Howard.'

'That would be folly. The daughter of an earl cannot get involved in a misalliance with an adventurer. "Painter" and "archaeologist" are not prestigious enough titles.'

'Well then, let's not bother about marriage!'

She stood up, passionate, seized his hand and made him follow her inside the wood. A light breeze made the foliage shiver. When the sun set, the light of the ending day tinged with gold the white dress draped on a hawthorn bush.

78

Archaeological work, administrative tasks, relationships with the press, the issue of sharing artefacts, the organization of official visits, commercial transactions, attempts at corruption . . . all these were in store for Carter when he arrived in Cairo on 8 October 1923. The serene beauty of the Egyptian autumn made the most dilapidated houses look almost attractive. Carnarvon's absence made him nervous and worried. He felt unable to confront the multi-headed monsters on his own, but he had no choice. In London, the atmosphere had become oppressive after the sudden death of Carnarvon's brother in September. Added to other unexpected deaths, some regarded it as definite proof of a curse, whose author could only be Tutankhamun.

The ordeal started with the Antiquities Service, where the Earl had in the past been able to manipulate Lacau as it pleased him.

Contrary to Carter's fears, the director received him with distinct kindness. 'Has your team re-formed again?'

'We've been travelling together ever since Trieste.'

'What does Lady Carnarvon want?'

'She wants the concession to be renewed in her name.'

'That is a legitimate request. I hope that you have been confirmed as her expert?'

'That was indeed her decision.'

'That's good. Who could dispute your competence?'

378

'On that subject, I would like to settle the problem of visitors with you. The best solution would be to allow nobody in the tomb until the shrines have been dismantled.'

Pierre Lacau grimaced. 'That is extremely annoying. Look here.' He pointed to two huge piles of letters cluttering his desk.

'They are all official requests from Egyptian dignitaries. They keep accumulating. They think that the tomb belongs to their country and nobody should bar their way.'

'Yet that is impossible.'

'Lord Carnarvon was more subtle. You put me in an embarrassing situation. What should I say?'

'That I am the only person who is entitled to give permission to visit.'

Lacau took a few notes. 'Is *The Times*' exclusive coverage coming to an end?'

'Several newspapers made agreements with *The Times* during the summer. Therefore it must retain its privileged position. That is why I hired its correspondent, Arthur Merton, for my team.'

'Isn't that a little . . . thoughtless?'

'He is an excellent amateur archaeologist. He will be on the spot to report what is going on.'

'I am afraid the Egyptian newspapers might take offence.'

'They will continue to enjoy the significant privilege of free communiqués. They are the only ones who won't have to pay for official information.'

'Well, well . . . Your file will be ready by tomorrow.'

Carter was in a hurry to go back to his valley, to enjoy again its wild splendour and to overcome the last hurdle that still separated him from Tutankhamun. Cairo was too large and too noisy. He had never liked towns, where man becomes insignificant, a jumpy being separated from heaven and earth. The emptiness left by Carnarvon could not be filled. Without him Carter did not know if he could make Lacau yield.

He climbed to the citadel and meditated in front of the

desert, which was beginning to be eaten away by the ever-expanding capital. He loved this eternal landscape, this call for an eternal truth that no vile deed could ever soil! The tenderness of the nomads permeated the area despite the violence of the wind and the rigour of rocks. This was where he would take Eve once he had uncovered the secret of the reborn pharaoh.

Lacau's thin face seemed more closed when he saw him than on the previous day. His hands rested on a red file.

'I am very embarrassed, Carter.'

'Why?'

'I put your case, but some members of the service came up with arguments I cannot disregard. In my position, I must take into account the opinions of everyone concerned.'

'Could you be more specific?'

'Merton's recruitment is almost illegal. As for refusing visits and neglecting the local press, you risk triggering a most unfortunate press campaign against you.'

'Isn't it enough that they have free information?'

Lacau slowly opened the red file. 'You are accused of hating Egypt and of considering the tomb as your own private property.'

'How could I hate Egypt when I have been living here since I was eighteen? This is my real country, sir. I have offered it my soul.'

'I believe you, of course, though such a declaration seems excessive . . . But you are heavily criticized for your intransigence about visitors.'

'Those who criticize me are snobs who don't care a fig about the tomb! They only want to strut about at dinner parties and pretend that they have seen Tutankhamun! And you would ask me to slow my scientific work because a gang of nosey-parkers! Sign the concession and let's put an end to our discussion. I must get back to the valley as soon as possible.'

Lacau brushed the file with the tips of his fingers. 'We'll see, Carter, we'll see . . . I must consult the minister.'

Abdel Hamid Sulayman Pasha, the Minister of Civil Engineering, was a jovial fellow who liked banquets and long siestas. His smooth social ascent had been based on his kind and patient character. Fiercely opposed to conflict, he had a talent for diplomacy and usually solved differences by flattering his opponents. He considered the independence of Egypt as a dangerous dream which would lead his country to ruin. Yet he had to be careful not to offend nationalist susceptibilities and to pretend to approve of some of their theories.

Pierre Lacau bowed to the Minister.

'What is the delicate matter you wish to discuss with me?'

'The Carnarvon concession.'

'Has the problem not already been settled?'

'Alas, no, Minister! Howard Carter is a stubborn man who doesn't want to yield to any request we make.'

'Yet his competence is praised.'

'I don't contest that . . . But he should be less intransigent with the Egyptian press and agree to open the tomb to dignitaries.'

'Mr Carter is a British subject, isn't he?'

'Yes, that's right.'

'The British colony in Cairo is essential to the well-being of the country.'

'Of course, but . . .'

'Annoy Mr Carter and you irritate the High Commissioner and create a lot of diplomatic troubles.'

'The exclusive coverage enjoyed by *The Times* is an insult to Egypt.'

'Don't exaggerate! This is just a commercial arrangement, and nothing else. As for visitors, can't they wait a little longer? A dispute would serve no useful purpose.'

Greatly frustrated, Lacau vainly tried to convince the Minister of his views.

'What do you advise me to do?'

'Sign the concession and allow Carter to pursue his work. As far as I am concerned, the matter is now closed.'

79

On 18 October, the workmen began to remove the tons of rubble which had protected the tomb in Carter's absence. Under the leadership of *reis* Ahmed Girigar, they worked energetically to do as the archaeologist wished and clear the entrance within a week. Despite the heat, a chain of people carrying baskets worked in rhythm, paced by chants.

Moved, Carter again followed the sloping corridor and entered the sanctuary. He felt Carnarvon walking beside him and facing the doors of the great shrines which were presumed to hide the sarcophagus. Callender, who was with him, had to impart some bad news.

'We are not ready, Howard. The service has not delivered the lamps they promised and we do not have the necessary material to preserve the shrines.'

'But I sent the money, specified the dates and insisted on the importance of lamps!'

Carter's anger was all the more intense because the public lighting around the tomb worked to perfection. His protests to the local inspector only resulted in the writing of an additional note pointing out the problems. With God's will, the lamps would be installed before the end of the month.

As he left the inspector, Carter bumped into Bradstreet. Built like an athlete, the journalist had left his office in Cairo as soon as he heard that the excavations had been resumed. Powerful and aggressive, his forehead furrowed with throbbing veins, he intended to make short work of the archaeologist.

'Well, Carter! Anything new?'

'I cannot tell you.'

'I am very surprised! You are talking to the correspondent of the *New York Times*, the *Daily Mail* of London and the *Egyptian Mail*. My mission is to inform the whole world, and you won't escape like a thief.'

'Get in touch with *The Times*' official representative.'

'This situation cannot last any longer! All journalists must enjoy the same rights.'

'That was not Lord Carnarvon's wish.'

'He is dead.'

'Not for me.'

'I insist that you break your exclusive contract with *The Times*.'

'You are said to be good at polo.'

Bradstreet frowned. 'That's true, but I don't see . . .'

'I am an expert in fighting.'

The journalist's veins swelled. His red face made him look like a furious bull. 'I'll crush you, Carter! Your enemies are becoming increasingly more numerous, and this is the last straw they need to unite.'

'I won't go,' said Carter, furious.

Callender raised a face like a beaten dog's to his friend. Despite his broad shoulders and massive looks, he shared Carter's distress. 'We'd better agree,' he suggested regretfully.

'This is a trap! Lacau summons me in Cairo to unpack boxes and install objects . . . what a joke! He wants to keep me in the capital so as to prove that I am neglecting the excavations.'

'If you do not co-operate, he will isolate you even more. Being aware of a danger is halfway to overcoming it. You've never been afraid of confrontation, have you?'

Carter embraced Callender. 'I'll fight.'

*

Christian Jacq

The Minister of Civil Engineering and several high-ranking British and Egyptian civil servants were in Lacau's office. Tutankhamun's tomb was turning into a state matter. Carter was in the position of a defendant facing a court determined to demonstrate his wrongs.

'Where are the boxes we need to unpack?' asked the archaeologist with a smile.

Lacau turned to the Minister for approval and addressed Carter with an unctuousness tinged with authority.

'In agreement with the highest authorities, we ask you to allow the Government to publish a news bulletin about the ongoing work each evening.'

'I refuse. The right of publication must be reserved for my team and myself. It would be most prejudicial to our work to divulge unchecked news too hastily.'

Lacau consulted the minister.

'That is a legitimate request,' he admitted. 'Would you agree to invite a representative of the daily press to visit the tomb?'

'Of course.'

'The commercial exploitation of the site is rather embarrassing,' said Lacau

Carter became vehement. 'The exclusive agreement with *The Times* is intended to protect me from a pack of curious journalists. The money received enables us to finance work on the site. Our sole aim is to protect the fabulous treasures discovered by Carnarvon and myself. That is why I ask the Government's and the Antiquities Service's full and unfettered support. No harassment by the press, no visitors, no administrative worries: that is what I ask, convinced that all of you who are here today will side with the sacred rather than the profane.'

Days went by. Carter called the Minister several times but he was either away or in a meeting. At the end of an annoying week, the archaeologist made another attempt, which he was determined would be the last. This time he managed to talk to

384

the powerful man. The conversation was cordial but embarrassed. The Minister worried Carter by explaining that Lacau wanted to start the negotiations all over again, but reassured him by saying that difficulties would soon be settled. If he wanted to, he could go back to Luxor and resume his tasks.

The archaeologist did not need persuading.

Callender brought a thick letter with the seal of the Antiquities Service. Carter opened it nervously. He recognized Lacau's thin, quick handwriting. Point by point the director of the Service agreed to the archaeologist's conditions.

'Did we win?' asked Callender.

Carter was about to answer that the result was beyond his hopes, when his eyes fell on the last lines. 'Of course,' concluded Lacau, 'the measures you wish to be taken can only be transitory, and they are likely to be modified according to the outcome.'

Carter let the document fall to the stony ground of the valley. 'This is a complete failure.'

'What do you intend to do?'

'I intend to continue. Tutankhamun is now my sole master.'

The very next day the dispute became worse. Lacau sent a second, and far less friendly, letter in which he blamed Carter for encroaching on the Antiquities Service's preserve. It was the service's and not a private archaeologist's task to regulate visits to a site belonging to the state. The director specified his instructions: the shrines should be dismantled without damaging their décor and the sarcophagus they expected to find should be cleared. Carter and his team were to obey these orders without delay and to confine themselves strictly to archaeological matters.

The Egyptian press launched an attack on the Englishman whom they accused of behaving like a colonialist even though he was a guest in Egypt. Tutankhamun was a pharaoh and not King of Great Britain. The contract of exclusive coverage with *The Times* was an insult to the Nationalist Party and to the people. In his answer to the criticisms, Carter emphasized the difference between modern Egyptians, most of them descendants of the sixth-century Arab invaders and followers of Islam, and the ancient Egyptians, opposed to all dogmatism. Such tactlessness increased his unpopularity and aroused the hatred of many religious zealots. The members of the team managed to dissuade him from making public statements, even though he was telling the truth.

'What is this world,' he asked Callender, 'where only liars and schemers are heard? Even the sacred earth here does not transform these kinds of minds. Where must we go to breathe some pure air?'

'Deep down in Tutankhamun's tomb. In your tomb.'

80

How could they dismantle the shrines without damaging them? Carter was obsessed by the mission. In the sanctuary of the tomb, he felt free and indefatigable. None of his collaborators managed to follow the pace of his work. Preoccupied by the condition of the gilding and the fragility of the sculptures he conceived several plans before actually starting the delicate operation. He began by removing the two guardian figures at the sides of the funeral chamber door. Wrapped in bandages, the black kings were laid on stretchers. Only their eyes could be seen, as if they were the ultimate signs of life of two large, injured bodies.

After consulting the members of his team, Carter asked Callender to build a wooden scaffolding around the outer shrine. He wormed his way with great difficulty between the posts, banged himself against them, hurt his hands and had to adopt the most uncomfortable contortions. Despite the heat and the cramped positions, and his fear that a panel might move, bend and fall on the others, he progressed inch by inch. He kept at bay the horrific vision of things shattering into hundreds of pieces with irreparable breaks.

After ten days of effort, they were able to lift the heaviest section of the ceiling. Carter called a young boy to slip wooden rollers under a beam they were going to use as a sleigh. Even when the panel was leaned against the lined wall of the funeral chamber, the archaeologist and his assistants did not celebrate their victory. The most difficult tasks still remained.

Once the ceiling had been removed, Carter admired the linen veil covering the second shrine. He called Merton, the correspondent of *The Times*. The journalist was shaking. 'The Ark of the Covenant . . . This is it, there is no doubt about it!'

He left the tomb and came back an hour later with the Bible. He read passages from Exodus about the precious relic. His imagination was all fired up.

'This is the secret of Tutankhamun! He had been to Israel to steal the Ark. It must be the most precious object ever found in the valley. That is why the tomb has been so well concealed.'

Carter remained sceptical. He lifted the tulle, which had sunk under the weight of golden bronze rosettes. 'We will open the sealed door of the second shrine very soon,' he said in an undertone.

Lacau was studying the 'Carter file' with his usual meticulousness. A zealous civil servant, as attached to regulations as to a holy book, he found it increasingly difficult to cope with the anarchic behaviour of the adventurer, who refused to adjust to any administrative hierarchy. His demands were treated with disdain. How could he bring Carter to his knees? So far he had failed. Of course the journalist Bradstreet and his Egyptian colleagues were waging a guerrilla war which day by day weakened Carter's position and showed him as an odious, venal and contemptible man. But the archaeologist did not care about other people's opinions and pursued his work with the same obstinacy. Moreover, as soon as he worked in Tutankhamun's tomb, he regained strength. To bring him down, his enemies would have to touch his heart, and not be content with superficial injuries.

Lacau had just found his opponent's weak point. He only had to develop a cautious strategy, without any visible takeover by force. Proceeding gradually, he would wear down

Carter's nerves, focus his attack on his vocation and thus compel him to make a fatal mistake.

An indignant Carter gathered all the members of his team in his laboratory. 'This morning I received the most offensive request in the history of Egyptian archaeology. The director of the service wants me to give him the list of the members of my team, as if he did not know them, and as if I were not the only one in charge of my collaborators on the concession which was granted to me.'

Merton, the journalist from *The Times*, took the floor. 'I am the one whose presence is being questioned. Bradstreet has probably intervened in high places. He wants to demonstrate that a press correspondent is out of place in an archaeologists' team.'

'You are more competent than most inspectors in the service.'

'If you want me to, Howard, I shall resign.'

'You are a friend and an efficient collaborator. You'll stay.'

'Beware of Lacau. He is a Jesuit accustomed to the vilest strategies.'

'He has no rights to the tomb and he knows it. His war of attrition can only lead to disillusion. Don't forget that the Minister is on our side.'

Callender's surly face did not brighten. He did not dare reply that ministers did not last for ever, nor that it had been a long time since he had been able to believe in law and justice.

'Will you send him the list?' asked Merton.

'Carnarvon would not have done that, so I won't do it either. As Lacau announces that he intends to visit on 13 December, we'll discuss it then.'

Lacau visited the tomb and the laboratory in the sole presence of *reis* Ahmed Girigar. Annoyed, he climbed to Carter's house, where, wrapped in a blanket, the archaeologist was drinking a hot toddy.

389

'I am sorry not to have been able to receive you more ceremoniously, but a cold forced me to stay indoors.'

Impeccably turned out, with his hands crossed behind his back, Pierre Lacau spoke in a sugary voice which contrasted with the stiffness of his attitude. 'Your requests are unjustified, Mr Carter. Only the Government, and not you, may issue duly registered visitors' permits.'

'I am the one who digs, and the Government is not.'

'The State has a duty to control excavations.'

'It is *my* concession. I am the sole master here. You can try to prove otherwise.'

'You have no right to hire Merton. He is a journalist and not an archaeologist.'

'The choice of my collaborators is mine. The service is not entitled to do anything in that regard.'

'If he does not resign, you will face serious trouble.'

'He won't resign. Your orders are unwarranted, sir. You are wasting your time with your threats.'

'The Minister will judge.'

'He has already judged.'

'We'll see. Do you know what people are saying in Cairo?'

Carter took a hot gulp. 'Tell me. Rumour is one of your favourite topics.'

Lacau avoided looking at him. 'Some people think that Lord Carnarvon was a spy and a businessman, completely indifferent to science and archaeology, and that you have followed his steps. If that is true it may explain your strange behaviour.'

Carter stood up and threw away the blanket. 'You are vile. The Earl loved Egypt passionately. The exploration of the tomb had become his entire reason for living. As for me, my whole life has been devoted to Egypt.'

'I accept that . . . But such sentimental impulses do not justify your arrogance.'

'I want to work in peace.'

'Have you given any thought to the sharing of the artefacts?'

'The matter has already been settled.'

'I am not so sure. And another even more serious issue still remains unsettled.'

Carter was shivering with cold.

'The concession won't last for ever,' Lacau reminded him. 'I must check, but I think it will soon come to an end. Its renewal depends on the Antiquities Service, which is increasingly demanding about the quality of the excavators and their work programme. A scientist like you can only appreciate such rigour. Take good care of yourself, Carter. We'll talk the matter over again, as soon as you have recovered. I hope that it is not Tutankhamun who is making you ill.'

81

On 15 December, seething with rage, Carter entered the office of the Minister of Civil Engineering, intending to tell him a few home truths and put an end to his persecution. Sulayman Pasha did not look as jovial as usual. On his desk was a thick file bearing the label of the Antiquities Service.

'Are you satisfied with your research, Mr Carter?'

'The Director of the Antiquities Service questions my wishes.'

'He does his duty in the best possible way. The press campaign against you is all the more unpleasant because some journalists are now beginning to criticize my own stand openly. As a minister, I must remain above the conflict.'

Carter turned pale.

'The presence of Arthur Merton is inconvenient,' Sulayman Pasha went on. 'According to my information, he is not a scientist. It is a mistake to accredit a journalist from *The Times*.'

'I can guarantee his competence.'

'You can't rely on that argument. Nobody will believe you. You are a man of science and peace, Mr Carter. You must forbid access to the tomb to this Merton without delay and then everything will be back to order. He can visit it with the other press correspondents on a day of your choice.'

'Is that an ultimatum?'

'Don't use fancy words! It's just a compromise.'

'I would like to make some objections.'

'Let's not waste any more time with details. I have removed Merton's name from the list of members of your team.'

'Is that legal?'

The question annoyed the Minister, who became brusque. 'That is my wish, Mr Carter.'

'If I agree, no archaeological team will ever be able to work freely in Egypt.'

'Don't paint such a black picture.'

'I shall submit your proposal to my collaborators.'

'Don't go too far, Mr Carter.'

'Neither should you, Minister.'

Back in Luxor, Carter gathered all his collaborators in the vault of Seti II. He did not conceal the seriousness of the situation and repeated the Minister's words. As he had no wish to take a hasty decision which might hinder excavations, he consulted them one by one. Their opinions all agreed: the politician was going beyond his rights. Manipulated by the nationalists and by the Frenchman in charge of the Antiquities Service, he was engaging in an underhand war against Great Britain and the United States. Surrendering would mean giving up the archaeologists' independence.

Fortified by this unanimity, Carter wrote to the Minister. He refused to dismiss Merton, said that the Metropolitan Museum specialists would leave the valley if their chief was submitted to bureaucratic pressures and that *The Times* would not hesitate to publish the facts. Sure that Sulayman Pasha would yield to reason, he said that he regretted the factors which had put them in opposition to each other, but that it was impossible for him to accept the suggested restrictions.

The Minister answered with silence.

The interior of the tomb looked like an operating theatre. The wooden stretchers, beds of reeds, miles of bandage, packets of cotton wool and electric light were more reminiscent of the sterile surroundings of surgical operations than the magical atmosphere of a royal tomb. Outside, the wardens and soldiers sometimes had difficulty holding back tourists who had tickets allowing them to visit the most famous tomb in the world. They had bought them from donkey owners or dealers in fake antiques and expressed their anger vehemently.

Convinced that his troubles were receding, on 3 January 1924 Carter cut the rope and pushed the bolt closing the second funeral shrine. Callender and the other members of the team watched him while he opened the golden doors.

'I need more light,' he said.

Callender plugged in two large lamps. They lit the double door of a new shrine.

'One more!' exclaimed Burton, the photographer. 'When will these rooms come to an end?'

The third shrine also remained undesecrated. Breathlessly, Carter opened the doors and discovered a fourth shrine. A pair of hawks with their wings spread out guarded the entrance. The hieroglyphs contained Tutankhamun's words: 'I am eternity. I saw the past and I know the future.' Troubled, Carter refused to go further, despite his colleagues' insistence.

'This may be the last obstacle,' said Callender.

'Probably . . . But do we have the right . . .'

'Think of Carnarvon. Would you have deprived him of such a joy?'

Carter broke the seal. The last flaps revolved slowly. The beam of light did not illuminate golden doors any more, but the arm of the goddess Nephytys, 'the ruler of the temple' who watched over a magnificent quartzite sarcophagus. The sight of the tender woman from the other world in charge of keeping intruders away was both unforgettable and marvellous. Faced with the incarnation of a millennia-old belief time had not yet eroded, Carter and his assistants were seized by a respectful fear.

'An intact sarcophagus,' murmured Carter, choking. 'The only one in the Valley of the Kings.'

He felt Lord Carnarvon's presence beside him. From the

other side of death, the Earl was taking part in the triumph.

Carter religiously closed the doors of the fourth shrine.

The archaeologist reread the text of his cable to Pierre Lacau: 'My research has enabled me to discover that the fourth shrine contains a magnificent and undesecrated sarcophagus.'

Hardly had the message been sent than the extraordinary news spread throughout Egypt. Thousands of tourists and nosey-parkers rushed to the valley. Photographers and journalists assailed Carter as soon as he left the tomb. Despite his collaborators' protection, he met Bradstreet, who, overexcited, barred his way.

'Are you sure that the sarcophagus is closed?'

'Definitely sure.'

'Will you find something unique inside?'

'Something unbelievable.'

'Why don't you open it immediately?'

'I must first have the walls of the shrines photographed and an inventory of the ritual artefacts in them made. Any haste would be criminal.'

'It is said that deadly gas will spread as soon as you lift the lid of the sarcophagus.'

'I'm ready to run the risk.'

'Is the mummy covered with gold?'

'Probably.'

'When shall we know?'

'I don't know. The next stage consists in dismantling the two last shrines. Will you allow me to go back home?'

Carter gave the order to close the vault. After such exultation, he needed silence and solitude while the archaeological team was taking care of the restoration of artefacts. The distant song of a bird reminded him of his canary, the golden bird whose influence had favoured the most fabulous find. He looked at his huge map of the Valley of the Kings, where he had written all the previous discoveries. In his thin handwriting he indicated the location of Tutankhamun's tomb.

He was preparing to have dinner on his own when Ahmed Girigar told him of the arrival of an emissary from the Ministry of Civil Engineering. Despite his fatigue, he received the civil servant, who was dressed in the Western fashion.

The man refused to sit down. 'The Minister congratulates you, but he is most annoyed with the way you proceeded to the opening of the last shrine. A representative of the Antiquities Service should have been with you.'

'I summoned Mr Engelbach, but he was taken up by more important obligations. Please be reassured, the sarcophagus did not suffer from his absence.'

'Moreover, the Government accuses you of having let a correspondent of *The Times* enter the tomb at the time of the opening, which is contrary to the archaeologists' professional code of ethics.'

'The information is incorrect: only members of my team were present.'

'I'll make a note of your explanations and ask you to sign the report which will be given to the Minister.'

Carter read what the civil servant had written, saw that his answers had not been distorted and initialled the document.

'I am afraid there may be serious complications,' concluded the emissary.

'Relax, everything is in order.'

Bradstreet and Lacau continued their insidious work. The closer Carter got to the sarcophagus, the more virulent they became. But even if the Minister of Civil Engineering was slightly favourable to their point of view, their attacks on Carter were limited to pinpricks.

'Another visitor,' announced Ahmed Girigar.

'No! Later.'

'You'd better receive this guest. She comes from very far away.'

Intrigued, Carter agreed.

Luminous and airy, Lady Evelyn walked towards him, wearing a violet dress.

82

'When did you arrive?'

'Just now.'

'Are you staying in Luxor for long?'

'Don't you need an assistant? Rumour says you have discovered fabulous treasures.'

Carter took Lady Evelyn tenderly in his arms, as if he was afraid to disperse a mirage.

'Your mother . . .'

'She agreed that I should spend the winter in Egypt to keep an eye on your work, in memory of my father.'

'He is beside me, Eve. Nobody can replace him.'

'That is why I shall never be able to marry you, Howard. My family's opinion does not matter to me, but he did not give his consent.'

'What if he gave you a sign from the heavens?'

'I hope his soul hears you!'

'You're shivering.'

'I'm afraid I may have caught a cold.'

He covered her shoulders with a woollen shawl. The young woman's eyes rested on the large map of the valley.

'You have succeeded, Howard. How happy my father must be!'

'Let's not crow over our victory too soon. I have heard of instances of intact but empty sarcophagi.'

'Not this one . . . Tutankhamun is alive. I can feel it!'

'Alive! Do you mean . . .'

She gazed at him intently with all the love a woman can give in the moment of communion.

'How can a pharaoh die?'

Night was falling over the valley. Carter turned the light off and took the woollen shawl. In the distance, the Nile was carrying along the happiness of bygone days.

The time had now come to dismantle the shrines panel by panel. Indifferent to the heat and dust, Carter struggled against haste and sudden movement. To free the sarcophagus required great safety precautions so that not a single piece of such priceless works were damaged. As he went by, he noted that the Egyptian carpenters had assembled the panels in a strange way. Their order had been reversed in relation to the cardinal points and hieroglyphic indications. They had probably been forced to act hastily. The builder's imperative had been to conceal the tomb as soon as possible.

While Carter was working quietly, Luxor's hotels were full of tourists. As each room had been overbooked four or five times, fights were raging. Those who gave the largest *baksheesh* won. As for the others, they had to content themselves with guesthouses or, even worse, bed and breakfasts. Shopkeepers, pedlars and owners of barouches worshipped Tutankhamun who made their business flourish. The town's most important forger obtained a meeting with Carter and begged him to intervene in his favour. He manufactured fake Tutankhamun scarabs according to traditional methods which gave satisfaction to a number of collectors. But since the discovery of an intact tomb had been announced, dishonest competitors had been flooding the market with products of very poor quality. The archaeologist deplored the situation and with the utmost seriousness advised the trader to consult the Antiquities Service.

Carter was leaving the tomb after an exhausting day when Lady Evelyn brought him a local newspaper, to which Lacau had confided his intentions.

'This is just gossip again.'

'No, Howard. This is a threat. According to Lacau, the Government plans to stop your work and allow tourists to visit your sanctuary.'

'This is stupid. Are there any other statements?'

'He accuses you of creating trouble and constantly bothering the service and the Government. According to him, you question the State's sovereignty and the idea of public ownership.'

'In other words, he refuses to share the artefacts, as he agreed to do it with your father! This Lacau is a real snake . . . Yet he knows that I am not driven by a desire for wealth but by justice. He is trying to rob your family and deprive it of its rights. I won't let him do that.'

'Be careful, Howard.'

'I must first be firm.'

Carter gathered a group of famous Egyptologists: his old master Newberry, the British philologist Gardiner, his American colleague Breasted and Albert Lythgoe, the Metropolitan Museum representative. In the name of science, Carter and the four specialists wrote a letter which was very critical of Pierre Lacau and the Antiquities Service, whose attitude jeopardized the progress of excavations. It said that Tutankhamun's vault did not belong to Egypt, but to the whole world. Howard Carter and his team were fulfilling their mission with a fervour and a commitment nobody questioned. Why were they constantly bothered by requests for visits when the preservation of treasures should come first? The Egyptian government had not spent a penny. Lord Carnarvon had been responsible for all the investment. Behaving like a pernickety bureaucrat, Lacau was failing in his duty. He had to acknowledge his mistakes and assist Carter's efforts at last. Copies of the letter were sent to the British high commissioner as well as to several scientific institutions.

*

Christian Jacq

Carter raised his glass of champagne. Lady Evelyn and his collaborators did the same.

'Lacau did not even dare reply.'

'We should beware of him,' recommended Callender. 'He is probably plotting in the shadows.'

'It's too late.'

'A Jesuit,' remarked Burton, 'can always invent a strategy nobody expected.'

'I'm optimistic,' stated Carter. 'He won't bother us any more. The royal road to the sarcophagus is now open.'

Worried, Lady Evelyn contented herself with drinking her champagne. She did not want to spoil the archaeologist's good mood.

'I sense that you have reservations,' he murmured in her ear.

'Let's be happy tonight.'

'Tomorrow, I shall show you the most perfect sarcophagus.'

Carter was annoyed. He had just noticed the trace of a break in the lid of the sarcophagus. A repair had been made in antiquity. Plaster and paint were made to imitate the granite, so as to conceal the accident. At each corner, a goddess spread her arms and wings to protect the king's soul and give him life constantly.

Carter raised his hand to his throat.

'Howard, what is the matter?'

'Just a fleeting feeling of discomfort . . .'

'What is the matter?'

'There is a crack in the lid . . . it means that the sarcophagus may have been desecrated.'

The young woman looked at the fissure in the stone coffin.

'No, that is impossible. Don't be afraid.'

'Why are you so sure?'

'I can feel it, deep down. The damage was repaired by the hand of one of the Pharaoh's workmen.'

Carter touched the lid lightly. Lady Evelyn's words reassured him.

400

Callender hurried down the corridor and stopped, breathless, on the threshold of the funeral chamber.

'There has been a disaster. You must go to Cairo without delay.'

83

Carter anxiously stepped over the threshold of the office of the new Minister of Civil Engineering, Morcos Bay Hanna. Normally indifferent to political changes, the archaeologist understood at last that the coming to power of the nationalist Saad Zaghlul changed the attitude of Egyptian officials towards strangers.

The minister was a well-built man with a narrow forehead and a martial appearance.

He did not bother with the usual civilities. 'Are you British, Mr Carter?'

'Yes, Minister.'

'I don't like Englishmen. They put me in jail for four years because I asked for the independence of my country. The people here made me a hero. I intend to thank it for its trust by proving that I have retained my ideals. Do you have an ideal?'

'Tutankhamun's tomb.'

'I don't know anything about archaeology. I am bored by old stones. I am more interested in people. What about you?'

'I have been keeping company with pharaohs since my adolescence. Tutankhamun is a companion who justifies any sacrifice.'

Morcos Bay Hanna lit a cigar. 'You should uncross your legs. That is impolite behaviour when you face a superior.'

Angry, unable to control his nerves, Carter complied reluctantly. He would not yield more ground.

'Why did I ask you to come? Ah, yes! The Tutankhamun case . . . There are many conflicts with the administration, far too many. I'm displeased by the troubles. An archaeologist should keep silent and obey.'

'Provided he is allowed to work in peace and complete his exploration.'

The Minister was surprised that a foreigner should dare argue with him.

'Pierre Lacau,' he explained, 'has given me the gist of the file. According to him, your excavation permit gives you no right of ownership over the tomb, which is considered as undesecrated, and, least of all, over the treasures it contains.'

'The agreement made with Lord Carnarvon—'

A British lord has no right to impose his rule in Egypt! Settle the matter with the Antiquities Service and don't bother me any more.'

'Its behaviour is iniquitous.'

'And so is yours, Mr Carter! Didn't you sign an exclusive contract with *The Times*, disregarding the Egyptian press, which had a right to be the first to hear the news?'

'Lord Carnarvon thought, rightly, that the daily presence of dozens of journalists would hinder the progress of our work . . .'

'This is British hypocrisy! Let's talk about your work . . . I strongly recommend you to stick to the orders you receive, and not to leave Egypt.'

Outraged, Carter stood up. 'I do not understand.'

'It is very simple: as an employee of my ministry, you are to be a zealous civil servant.'

'I am in the service of the wife of the late Earl of Carnarvon, who is the owner of the concession.'

Morcos Bay Hanna pressed a bell. A door opened on his left and Pierre Lacau appeared, his arms loaded with files. He gave a slight bow to the Minister.

'Here are the various elements of our dispute.'

Carter felt trapped. He was preparing to leave the office

without further fuss when the Minister reacted unexpectedly.

'I'm bored by all the papers. The past is the past. When shall we arrange a ceremony for the opening of the sarcophagus? The day after tomorrow would suit me very well.'

'That is impossible,' retorted Carter.

'Why?'

'Because I know neither the number nor the quality of the coffins it contains. It may take several months to remove them from the stone grave.'

The Minister turned to Lacau. 'What do you think?'

Pierre Lacau could not lie. 'Howard Carter is right.'

Morcos Bay Hanna did not conceal his disappointment. 'Archaeology is disappointing. Let me know when you are ready.'

The Minister left his office, leaving Carter and Lacau face to face.

'I couldn't do anything different,' explained the director of the service.

'You should put your files on the desk,' suggested Carter. 'Their weight will exhaust you.'

On 12 February, at 3 p.m., Carter asked his guests to stand beside Tutankhamun's sarcophagus. After wondering a long time about the real intentions of the Minister and Lacau, he had followed Lady Evelyn's advice and hastened the pace of the work and invited a few people to attend an exceptional moment: the removal of the stone lid. Besides the members of the team, there was the under-secretary of the Ministry of Civil Engineering and Pierre Lacau, whose black suit gave a funerary touch to the ceremony.

Callender checked the solidity of the winches and ropes. He indicated to Carter with a glance that he was satisfied with the lifting arrangement. Then latter gave the order to begin. In a deep silence the huge slab rose.

Carter slipped his head under the lid which was suspended over him. The twelve stone quintals swayed for a moment, then stopped. Lady Evelyn was about to grasp the archaeologist's arm to tug it backwards, but he was already removing a shroud, rolling it extremely slowly. His hands shaking, and his forehead dripping with sweat, he had to do it several times. As he touched the last veil he let out a shout of wonder.

Serene and sublime, Tutankhamun's golden face looked at eternity. The features had been modelled on gold leaves, with aragonite and obsidian eyes, and lapis-lazuli eyebrows and eyelids. Crossed over his chest, his hands held the shepherd's magic crook and the peasant's flail, inlaid with blue faïence.

It was now Lady Evelyn's turn to slide under the lid of the sarcophagus. The beauty of the golden face went far beyond anything she had seen before. Tutankhamun was not dead. A resuscitated life dwelt in his stone eyes. The crown protected by the vulture goddess, the mother of the world, and the cobra goddess, symbolizing the vital power, placed the king in a divine universe from which humankind was excluded.

All the guests contemplated the Pharaoh. There was not a murmur to interrupt their thoughts and the sacred quality of the meeting with a memory come from beyond the grave, out of darkness. Callender wept. Despite being a Christian, Lacau experienced strange emotions. The perfection of the effigy seemed to have a celestial origin.

One by one, they left the tomb hesitantly. It was heart-rending to leave the young king. Howard Carter was the last to walk up the corridor leading back to the outside light. The vision of the royal being remained engraved in his mind.

'He is alive,' he murmured.

84

For a long time, Carter was unable to speak. Lacau and the under-secretary did not dare leave before the archaeologist had come back to his senses.

'That is magnificent,' acknowledge Lacau.

'It would be wise to allow a few visits,' recommended the under-secretary, 'and to give a press conference. This is such a miraculous event . . .'

'As you wish,' agreed Carter, in a state of shock.

'I think the wives of the members of the team should be allowed to see the Pharaoh before the journalists,' suggested Callender.

'That is obvious,' said Carter. 'They deserve the reward.'

'Of course,' admitted the under-secretary. 'But we need permission. That little problem will soon be solved. I'll call the Minister.'

'Wonderful,' repeated Lacau, lost in his dream.

Carter was suffocating. He walked down into the tomb again, under the pretext of checking the ropes. He actually wanted to be alone with Tutankhamun to question him about the secret of a gaze death had not extinguished.

The air was light and transparent. Carter's collaborators and their wives congratulated him. In the February morning, intense joy enlivened their conversation. Everybody was aware that they were taking part in an historical moment.

*

Reis Ahmed Girigar was the first to see the postman approaching on a donkey.

'An urgent letter for Mr Carter!' he announced in a loud voice.

Surprised, the archaeologist read a message signed by Pierre Lacau. He had received a cable from the Minister of Civil Engineering positively forbidding the wives of Carter's collaborators to visit the tomb. He was faced with the obligation to formulate his order most clearly. Although he deplored the unfortunate misunderstanding, he asked Carter to implement the Minister's decision without further discussion. No lady would be allowed to enter the tomb without a written permit.

Carter clenched his fists. 'I am sorry,' he said. 'The Minister refused to give your wives permission to see Tutankhamun.'

There were protests, but Callender and Burton advised them against forcing the issue.

Lacau's letter was official. Carter would be in breach of the law if they refused to take it into account.

'It would be cowardly to give in.' He wrote a brief and abrupt note in which he mentioned the intolerable humiliations to which his team and he were subjected. They therefore refused to complete their work and were closing the tomb.

Greatly irritated, Carter asked Merton to publish an accurate account of facts and to denounce Lacau's role in *The Times*. He strode towards the vault of Seti II, set up the iron grille with the help of Callender and padlocked it. Then he closed the grille protecting the entrance to the tomb of Tutankhamun, slipped the only set of keys into his pocket, climbed on a donkey and headed for the pier. Although he usually liked to breathe in the light wind during the trip across the Nile, he did not even pay attention to it this time. A barouche took him at full speed to the Winter Palace. He rushed into the hall and clipped the note to the notice board, which was passed by hundreds of tourists and dignitaries.

A few hours later the quarrel had become public. Carter's accusations and his extraordinary decision were soon the only topic of conversation among the Luxor smart set.

He pursued the fight on another front. He sent a cable to Prime Minister Zaghlul, begging him to intervene and condemn the unspeakable attitude of the Antiquities Service. To prove that he was within his rights, the archaeologist even considered starting proceedings against the Government.

'We'll win,' he promised Lady Evelyn.

'Most tourists oppose your stance.'

'I don't care.'

Zaghlul's answer was quick and very curt.

'This is unbelievable!' deplored Carter. 'Not only does Zaghlul not recognize the facts, but he also reminds me that the tomb is not mine and that I have no right to stop work.'

Worried, Lady Evelyn read the Prime Minister's letter. Despite the coldness of the tone, she discerned encouraging hints. 'He acknowledges the interest of your discoveries for the whole world.'

'That is just a polite phrase . . . He supports his minister and disowns me.'

'The fight is getting unequal, Howard.'

'Certainly not. The law is on my side.'

Pierre Lacau read the reports with satisfaction. Only *The Times* took Carter's side and accused the Egyptian government of having sent policemen to stop some ladies of quality from entering the tomb, by force. All the other newspapers criticized the archaeologist's reaction. He was considered to be a megalomaniac, an exhausted man on the edge, or a colonialist of the worst sort. The Minister of Civil Engineering, Morcos Bay Hanna, had spread his own version in Egyptian newspapers. They considered that, as a troublemaker and a striker, Carter should not direct the excavations any longer. He had violated the rules of the profession and compromised the rest of the research.

Lacau was jubilant. Naive and awkward, Carter had made a fatal mistake. The victim of patient tactics of harassment, he had not suspected the traps set in his path. The hotheaded adventurer was becoming a kind of bandit in the eyes of the public. It was now the Government's task to break him and assert its sovereignty.

Distressed, Carter was caught up in the tumult. Callender vainly tried to comfort him. Burton's jokes did not amuse him any more. Only Lady Evelyn's presence stimulated him.

'Politicians are the most despicable of men. Lies and treason are their code of behaviour.'

'Are you just discovering the world, Howard?'

They had retired to the house, over which Ahmed Girigar and his men kept watch.

Some tourists, furious at the closure of Tutankhamun's tomb, had tried to climb up the path so as to insult the archaeologist.

Carter was drinking more than usual.

'Why does all this happen to me? First your father's death, then the hostility . . .'

'Hold on, Howard. If you give up, Lacau will triumph and my father's memory will be held up to ridicule.'

She talked without aggression. Carter drew new strength from her softness.

'I'll fight, Eve. I'll fight to the end.'

He and his collaborators held a war council. Everybody came. They all agreed that the Minister of Civil Engineering and the Director of the Antiquities Service were going beyond their rights and following a policy of intimidation. Howard Carter had never yielded to threats in all his troubled life. His team's unconditional support cheered him. Fortified by the heartfelt unanimity, he decided to refuse any concession. The exploration of the tomb would now be under the sole responsibility of the archaeologist in charge of the site.

On 15 January, at dawn, he walked down the path to the

valley. In front of Tutankhamun's tomb soldiers mounted guard. He believed the usual security measures had been reinforced. A senior officer stepped forward.

'The area is forbidden,' he announced.

'I'm Howard Carter.'

'Do you have a written permit from the Ministry of Civil Engineering or the Antiquities Service?'

'I don't need any.'

'I have received positive instructions: the tombs of Tutankhamun and Seti II, registered as number 15 and used as a laboratory, are closed and nobody is allowed to enter them.'

'Are you making fun at me?'

'Don't make any rash move, Mr Carter. If you do, I shall resort to force.'

85

Like an injured animal, Carter hid himself in the innermost recess of the house. For two days he did not eat anything. Then Lady Evelyn succeeded in making him swallow tea and rice. The archaeologist read and reread the article of the *Saturday Review* in which the journalist expressed his concern about the solidity of the ropes keeping the lid of the sarcophagus open. If they broke, the damage would be irreparable.

'I must take care of that.'

'That is impossible, Howard. The soldiers won't allow you to go in.'

'Did the Minister receive my letter of protest?'

'Of course he did, but he won't answer.'

'What should I do, Eve? They are annihilating my life. They are destroying Tutankhamun!'

'Wait and pray. The ropes will hold, I swear it.'

He believed her. That look could not lie.

One week after the official closure, public opinion changed. The Government was criticized for putting the sarcophagus at risk by not appointing another archaeologist to complete the task. The ropes would eventually break and the fall of the lid would destroy the golden sarcophagus.

The Times emphasized the authorities' clumsiness. Their intransigence fell at a particularly ill-chosen moment.

411

Local journalists changed their minds. Was Carter perhaps a victim rather than a culprit? On Lady Evelyn's advice, he agreed to receive one of them. With his clean-shaven face, his well-trimmed moustache and perfectly balanced bow tie, the archaeologist attempted to put on a serene face.

'Do you acknowledge your mistakes, Mr Carter?'

'I haven't made any, except that of believing in justice.'

'Do you maintain your criticisms of the ministry?'

'The Minister lies in presenting me as an enemy of Egypt and its people. The country is mine too. I have only refused to open the tomb to any visitor until the coffins have been removed.'

'You call the Minister a liar?'

'That is the right term.'

'What are you asking for?'

'That the police be dispersed and the greatest archaeological adventure of all times be allowed to carry on. Only my team has the necessary competence to do so.'

Lacau folded the newspaper in which the interview with Carter was published. Invited to the Council of Ministers, the Director of the Antiquities Service had expounded the facts and given the main documents of the file to the whole government. The indictment against Carter was damning. The Minister of Civil Engineering approved it altogether and considered that, by insulting him, the Englishman was also insulting the nation. None of his colleagues took the archaeologist's side.

'Do you think that Howard Carter has broken his contract with Egypt and trampled his scientist's duty underfoot by closing the tomb without permission?' asked Zaghlul. The council unanimously voted 'yes'.

'Do you approve the action of Mr Lacau and his service?'

The same answer was given.

'Therefore,' concluded the Prime Minister, 'Howard Carter is no longer allowed to carry on with the excavation and to enter the tomb. In future, it will be the Government's duty to take charge of the Tutankhamun case.'

The official communiqué stunned Carter. His defeat seemed to be complete. Zaghlul had developed a demagogic argument. He had taken his decision so as to enable the people to visit a high point of human culture discovered in their homeland as soon as possible.

Callender and the other members of the team were shattered. A wonderful dream was crushed because of ambitious politicians and civil servants, indifferent to the efforts that had been made for so many years. Carter tried to keep up his group's morale.

'Britain won't abandon us.'

'Are you referring to the High Commissioner?' asked Burton.

'No,' answered Lady Evelyn. 'He did not like my father and he won't put his career at risk by rebelling openly against the Egyptian government.

'Is there any other solution?'

'Parliament! I cabled my mother to obtain the support of my father's political friends. Our government will make the Egyptian government yield.'

The young woman's enthusiasm was infectious. Carter recalled the exultant moments which had punctuated the epic and opened bottles of champagne. The whole night long, the team was united in renewed joy.

Dawn was coming. In front of the valley and its furrowed slopes, Eve and Carter still believed in the impossible. Huddled against each other to escape the early morning cold, they enjoyed the silent complicity of a couple able to triumph over a thousand demons and to overcome a thousand obstacles. But they knew that personal happiness did not await them at the end of their quest. Their hearts and souls would be shattered by their eventual separation. Before being engulfed in the abyss of solitude, they savoured the exultation of sharing their thoughts near the western summit.

'Is it love, Evelyn?'

'It is the most violent and painful kind of love.'

'When are you leaving?'

'Spring will come again. My mother is waiting for me at Highclere.'

'Is it so important . . . to maintain your rank?'

'It is both essential and stupid.'

'If only I could keep you . . . I am nothing now.'

'You have a destiny, Howard. Your path is laid out in the stars. It is like Tutankhamun's gold. I am just a stage along the way.'

'Do you doubt my sincerity?'

'Not in the least. But I am not your future.'

'Why?'

She smiled and kissed him. 'You are the most surprising of men, Howard, because you do not change. Neither I nor any other woman will make you depart from your path. I love you and admire you.'

The British parliament was dozing. No major issues disturbed its peace.

The Prime Minister Ramsay MacDonald was abruptly questioned about the Tutankhamun case.

'Is it true that Mr Carter holds the archaeological concession?'

'His contract is with the Earl of Carnarvon's widow who actually owns the concession.'

'In the dispute between Howard Carter and the Egyptian prime minister, what is our position?'

'His Majesty's Government granted no privileges to the archaeological team working on the site.'

The Prime Minister pretended not to hear the protests aroused by his statement. A protester insisted and asked him to explain his words.

'The Tutankhamun case does not come within our jurisdiction,' he said. 'It is a private matter. As for Mr Carter's behaviour, it is subject to Egyptian law and not to ours. I do not want to hear anything about the individual any more. I consider the matter closed.'

86

Reis Ahmed Girigar was completing his morning prayers a few yards from Tutankhamun's tomb when he saw a troop of soldiers and policemen arrive. It was headed by Pierre Lacau. Camels and horses progressed at a slow pace.

The *reis* walked to the start of the path to Tutankhamun's tomb. Flanked by a senior officer and a high-ranking civil servant from the Ministry of Civil Engineering, Lacau stopped 2 yards away from him.

'Let us through, my friend.'

'I was appointed foreman by Mr Carter. It is my duty to keep watch over the site.'

'It does not belong to him any more. The site is under the Government's direct control.'

'Mr Carter is my sole employer.'

'You are mistaken. You are now at the service of the Government.'

'Do you have a document to prove it?'

The civil servant began to get excited.

'Obey the orders of the Prime Minister immediately!'

'Show me an official document.'

At a sign from the senior officer, two soldiers pointed their rifles at the *reis*. The latter did not move an inch.

'I am indifferent to your threats,' he said in a steady voice. 'Shoot and you will become murderers.'

Lacau interposed himself. 'Don't lose your tempers . . . I do not want an incident. The *reis* is an intelligent and reasonable man. He must understand that it is folly to oppose the Government's orders. I am convinced that he won't force us to use violence.'

Lacau's icy tone impressed Ahmed Girigar. 'I must inform Mr Carter.'

'As you please.'

The *reis* moved away and ran to tell Carter. Taking advantage of the opportunity, Lacau led his commando towards the grille. A locksmith sawed the padlocks and policemen rushed into the tomb. The Director wanted to act quickly.

'Bring the lid down.'

The soldiers did as he said. Lacau was both triumphant and anxious. Pulleys creaked. The ropes became hot but they did not break. Gradually the huge slab moved. The Director followed its slow progress with his eyes. When it rested on the sarcophagus, he knew that he had become the sole master of the site. At the entrance to the tomb, soldiers prevented Howard Carter from following into the sloping corridor. At the sight of Lacau, he flew into a rage.

'How dare you act in this way?'

'It is my duty.'

'If you have damaged the sarcophagus, I will . . .'

'Don't worry about it any more, Mr Carter. Tutankhamun's treasures are under the State's protection.'

'This is illegal! The concession is in Lady Carnarvon's name.'

'That is wrong. It has been cancelled for the season. This is why your presence is illegal.'

'You are a monster.'

'I must add that the laboratory has also been requisitioned and you cannot use it any more.'

'I shall sue the Egyptian government immediately.'

'That is one more foolish mistake, my dear Carter. Egypt has behaved in a very worthy way, fully respecting the law and

417

ethical standards. Stop attacking me and let me suggest a compromise.'

'You disgust me. I demand an apology and the immediate reopening of the tomb.'

Lacau turned away and walked into the corridor. Carter tried to follow him, but he was intercepted by the soldiers. Mad with rage, he seized a stone and threw it at the heavens.

As a result of clever organization, the Egyptian press took the Government's side. It believed it was defending the greatness of the nation against a foreign adventurer, whose sole aim was to get rich at the expense of people, the only legitimate owners of Tutankhamun's tomb.

On 6 March 1924, a special train came from Cairo to Luxor carrying 170 guests invited by Prime Minister Zaghlul, who was at the climax of his popularity, to see the tomb.

Along the route, nationalist militants shouted slogans hostile to Great Britain and Howard Carter, who had taken refuge in his house. Although, indifferent to Egyptian antiquities, Zaghlul had not taken the trouble actually to be there, a huge crowd chanted his name as the train reached Luxor station.

None of the officials had the slightest wish to waste time in the Valley of the Kings, because of the heat, but the pilgrimage was compulsory. Lacau was overflowing with kindness when he welcomed the 170 guests in the little funeral chamber. The lid of the sarcophagus had been removed and leaned against a wall. A lamp illuminated the golden face of the king. The extraordinary sight touched even the most insensitive. The politicians congratulated Lacau.

With the support of Lady Carnarvon, Carter hired a lawyer, F.M. Maxwell, to initiate legal proceedings against the Egyptian government in a court in Cairo composed of local people and foreigners. Inherited from the Ottoman period, the court aroused the hatred of the nationalists who demanded that it be abolished. The Minister of Civil Engineering, Morcos Bay Hanna, constantly poured scorn on it.

Lady Evelyn encouraged Carter to fight: Maxwell enjoyed an excellent reputation and he knew Egyptian law to perfection. Of a sad, and even disenchanted character, the lawyer never smiled. The rigour of the law appeared to him as an essential condition to the survival of a society, be it Western or Middle Eastern. He was certain that the Tutankhamun case would be decided in favour of Carter, who was the victim of a clear abuse of power. Thanks to his relations and to the technical qualities of his file, the lawyer was able to have the case heard without delay.

The day before it began, Carter and Lady Evelyn felt optimistic. Maxwell did not commit himself thoughtlessly. He usually fought his own ground and gave his opponents only minimal chances.

'Lacau will yield and so will the Egyptian government. Though this is not what I care about. What I want is to take care of Tutankhamun again.'

'My father will help us. I feel him close to us.'

Callender interrupted the conversation. At the sight of his haggard face, Carter immediately knew that an unexpected difficulty had come up.

'Maxwell, your lawyer . . .'

'What about him?'

Paralysed, Callender found his words with difficulty. 'He is an intransigent man and a determined supporter of death penalty.'

'That has no bearing on the case.'

'On the contrary, he requested it a few years ago against a traitor Great Britain wanted to punish with the utmost severity. Fortunately the verdict was much milder.'

'"Fortunately" . . . why such relief?'

'Because the accused was none other than Morcos Bay Hanna, the present Minister of Civil Engineering and our main enemy.'

*

Maxwell's defence speech was most convincing. He presented Carter as a disinterested scientist whose sole aim was to preserve Tutankhamun's treasures. No court could accuse him of corruption, nor present him as a mere underling. The facts proved that he had run the excavations with commitment and rigour. The legal case presented no ambiguity. The Government was abusing its power in cancelling the original contract and preventing Carter from entering the tomb and resuming work.

The judge was dozing. For him the case was clear. Carter and Lady Evelyn shared his opinion. Despite his apprehensions, the archaeologist felt that the Minister of Civil Engineering had not succeeded in hindering the course of justice. At the end of the lawyer's technical speech, the judge asked a question which intrigued him.

'Why did Carter close the tomb before informing the court?'

Maxwell realized that he had not listened to his speech. Irritated, he repeated an essential argument.

'My client enjoyed the legal use of the site and his behaviour did not violate the law. As for the agents of the Government, they acted like bandits!'

The insult spread trouble in the courtroom. Ill at ease, the judge spoke up without hesitation. 'Don't you think that the term is exaggerated?'

'Bandits, thieves, pillagers: it is the truth. Civil servants, soldiers and policemen acted in an illegal way.'

The Egyptian press laid into Carter and his lawyer. They were accused of having insulted Egypt in the vilest way. The entire nation felt slandered by the two Englishmen, who supported a colonialism on the brink of extinction.

Morcos Bay Hanna's reaction was quick and abrupt. Not only would Carter be unable to practise his profession in Egypt, but the Minister of Civil Engineering would refuse any negotiations. The career of the discoverer of Tutankhamun had come to an end.

87

Morcos Bay Hanna was walking to and fro in his office in front of a photograph depicting him, with other Egyptians, dressed in the dreary outfit of prisoners.

'Here are the bandits who turned into ministers!'

Pierre Lacau was holding a file in his hand. He let the outburst subside.

'Am I a renegade, a bandit, a minister of the government whom the British would like to send back to jail? Is it your opinion?'

'Reason will prevail.'

'This Carter is a dangerous lunatic! Have you found a successor at last?'

Lacau opened the file.

'I got in touch with several American and British archaeologists, but all refused.'

'Don't you have some competent scientists in your own service?'

'This is too delicate a task.'

'What about your assistant, Engelbach?'

'He is more of an administrator.'

'And what about you?'

'My numerous tasks forbid me to spend several weeks in the tomb.'

'So whom can we appoint?'

Christian Jacq

'Nobody will agree to risk damaging the coffin. Only Carter could complete—'

'Never! He must either leave Egypt as soon as possible . . . or bow down before me and present his apologies.'

The unanimity of the press broke. One newspaper wondered what should be done: was it not better to play down the quarrels and take care of Tutankhamun? Did the intransigent stand of the Minister of Civil Engineering not endanger the most fabulous archaeological treasure ever discovered?

Carter took advantage of the split to request a meeting with the High Commissioner, Lord Allenby, an austere and icy character who had not supported the Egyptian government in the struggle against his fellow countrymen.

'Sit down, Mr Carter.'

'Thank you for receiving me. Your advice will be valuable.'

'I am not really skilled in archaeology.'

'The Tutankhamun case goes beyond that field.'

'Alas! You're right . . . we've been facing a kind of war ever since your unexpected strike.'

'I did not want that.'

'It would have been better to avoid it. You cause me many worries.'

Carter was shocked. 'Me? It would be more accurate to say the Minister of Civil Engineering!'

'We must respect his official position.'

'He is trying to rob Lady Carnarvon by refusing to give her some artefacts which, according to the custom, will refund her expenses.'

'That point of contention is none of my business.'

'It comes into the contract. The Antiquities Service has no right to break it.'

'Put an end to the dispute; that is the general interest of everyone.'

Carter stood up, stunned. 'Don't think about it! Tutankhamun is at stake.'

'You don't seem to understand: independence fever may overcome the country at any time. Your pharaoh is turning into a political stake. He should be left to the Egyptians.'

'It would be denying my vocation.'

'Your vocation does not fit in well with the political imperatives of the time.'

'I don't care.'

'You're wrong.'

'You must help me.'

'Go away.'

The High Commissioner grabbed an inkstand and threw it at Carter, who moved back just in time.

'Britain is betraying me.'

Lady Evelyn did not contradict him. They were walking along the bank of the Nile. It was a mild evening. Distraught, the archaeologist grasped the young woman's arm and told her about his meeting with the High Commissioner.

'Let's go back to Highclere,' she suggested.

'My presence at your side would be frowned on. I do not want to embarrass you at any cost. London rejects me, as Cairo does. It is better to move away from an outcast.'

'Don't exaggerate, Howard.'

'I am not exaggerating. I have lost your father and Tutankhamun. People want to chase me away from the valley and the land I love.'

She stood still. 'Have you lost me, too?'

'I'm afraid so.'

'I must go back to Highclere, but I shall come back.'

'Neither of us knows that for sure.'

The nationalists did not yield. Carter became their pet hate and was subjected to constant attacks. One of them was particularly harsh: the archaeologist was accused of having stolen papyrus about the Exodus in the tomb. It was claimed that they

Christian Jacq

contained the true details of the adventure and explained the actions of the Jews in leaving Egypt.

The British vice-consul summoned Carter. He shouted at him, 'I want the papyrus. Their mere existence is a threat to peace! Don't you know that we must take into account both Egyptian nationalism and the development of the Jewish colony in Palestine? None of the texts should be published.'

'There's no risk as the papyrus don't exist.'

'Weren't they hidden in the Ark of the Covenant, inside the tomb itself?'

'You pay too much attention to the most fanciful rumours.'

'Are you calling me an idiot, Mr Carter?'

'If you give the slightest credit to this nonsense, then yes.'

The vice-consul himself opened the door of his office.

'The High Commissioner warned me: you are insufferable. I can now add that you are no good to anybody.'

With his usual duck's gait, Winlock walked up the stairs to the room where Carter had taken refuge. In the poor district where he had once survived as best he could on his painting, he had memories of the most painful period of his life, smells of cooking, bawls of children and bleats of sheep.

The American collided with two women dressed in black. He apologized in Arabic and pushed the door.

Carter was painting. Under his brush appeared a lane.

'I have bad news, Howard.'

Usually lively and smiling, Winlock looked desperate. Carter continued to prepare his colours.

'The Egyptian and British authorities have agreed that you are definitely forbidden to enter Tutankhamun's tomb. The Metropolitan won't desert you. We will succeed in breaking this iniquitous decision. But there is one condition.'

Intrigued, Carter turned towards Winlock.

'You must leave. If you stay in Egypt, the Minister will take you to court and Britain will let it happen.'

'Leave . . .'

424

'You must distance yourself from what has happened. In the United States, nobody will bother you. On the contrary, you are awaited as a hero.'

Carter put down his brush and his palette. 'Is this exile really necessary?'

'Here you'll make mistake after mistake. Your enemies are too powerful. They hold all the cards.'

The archaeologist stood up, staggered like a drunkard and clutched the back of the chair. 'My life . . . my whole life is in this tomb.'

88

At the end of March 1924, Pierre Lacau headed a committee of Egyptian experts to take possession of Tutankhamun's tomb. The triumph of the Director of the Antiquities Service was complete. Carter had left Egypt, certain that he would never come back. The Minister of Civil Engineering couldn't stop praising Lacau, thanks to whom his country had won a major victory. As for the nationalists, they used Tutankhamun to champion their cause. The pharaoh had cursed the colonialist Carter, who was now forever prevented from desecrating his corpse.

Methodical and meticulous, Lacau set himself the mission of taking stock of all that had been found when excavations had stopped. In this field he was in his element. Classifying, numbering, writing cards and lists . . . he was seized by a form of enjoyment.

On the verge of tears, for the last time Ahmed Girigar tried to oppose what he considered as a violation. He was pushed aside without further ado and threatened with imprisonment if he continued to oppose the law. He silently followed Lacau and observed the new master of the place.

The Director did not forget anything. Not only did he record the artefacts belonging to Tutankhamun's treasure, but he also made an inventory of the photographic material, the chemical products, the contents of the laboratory, the archaeologists' furniture and even their food.

Winlock's arrival interrupted his feverish work. The American ran to the tomb of Seti II, where Lacau was opening each box before his henchmen emptied them.

'I make a solemn protest in the name of the members of Howard Carter's team and of the Metropolitan Museum.'

'Your protest is useless, my dear Winlock. We are implementing the law.'

'You're not doing it in the best possible way.'

'The way does not matter. Carter knew the valley perfectly. On one of his excavation diaries, I read "storeroom". Where is it?'

'I don't know, and out of solidarity with Carter, Callender, Mace, Burton and their colleagues will not help you.'

'*Reis* Ahmed is more knowledgeable than everyone else. Make him speak and I advise you to do it quickly.'

Winlock's short legs took him to Ahmed Girigar through the tombs. The *reis* had settled on top of a hillock in the full sunlight, just as if he wanted to be absorbed by it. Winlock convinced him to co-operate. Any form of resistance was becoming useless. As the *reis* knew that a workman would betray him sooner or later in exchange for a reasonable amount of money, he agreed.

A few minutes later, a locksmith forced the door of the tomb number 4, the sepulchre of King Ramses XI, where Carter had stored furniture and small boxes. According to the testimony of a warden, he came to eat a meal there from time to time. One of the Egyptian inspectors, a small man with a moustache, seemed very excited. Lacau made him calm down. An inventory should be made properly, without haste. Although the inspector wanted to begin with the back of the tomb, Lacau adopted his usual order. He marvelled at the discovery of a notebook: Carter had made a clear and precise register, as methodically as he would have done it himself. Duly numbered and labelled, each artefact was easy to spot thanks to the same number repeated both inside and outside the box containing it. In his heart the Director paid tribute to

Christian Jacq

his fallen colleague. He would have been worthy of working with him.

The Egyptian inspector with the jerky gestures started to open a pile of boxes with the name 'Fortnum and Mason'. He threw two of them, which were empty, to the floor. Lacau begged him once more to behave according to his position and to take care of something more important than insignificant empty packages.

'Here,' he said. 'Look at this box!'

Lacau saw the inscription 'red wine'. His subordinate must have been shocked by the presence of alcohol.

'We'll deal with that later.'

'No, no! You should open it immediately!'

Surprised, the Director gave in. Inside he saw several layers of cotton wool. Within the protective nest lay a magnificent wooden head, intensely lifelike.

'It does not figure on the register,' said the inspector. 'This is proof that Carter is a thief! We must cable the Prime Minister immediately and initiate legal proceedings.'

'There is no hurry. This is a strange discovery, but there must be some explanation.'

'Theft! Carter is a thief!'

The inspector brought out his colleagues who repeated the accusation to the point of hysteria. For the first time, Lacau regretted Carter's absence. He hated the man and his character, but he did not believe that he was guilty. He was obviously the victim of a set-up of which he, Pierre Lacau, a law-abiding civil servant with an irreproachable record, was becoming the unwitting instrument.

Carter received Winlock's cable in London, shortly before his departure for America. Written in a code, according to the system used by the Metropolitan to transmit confidential information, it did not conceal the seriousness of the situation. The wooden head had already been transferred to the Museum of Cairo. Prime Minister Zaghlul was jubilant. Carter had to

428

intervene without delay to give Lacau the information he needed before the situation worsened.

Disgusted, Carter felt like throwing the message into the waste paper basket and taking refuge in silence. Had he not already lost everything? Now his enemies wanted to destroy his reputation. A colonialist and a thief thrown to the lions of public opinion . . . how could any explanation justify his dismissal? No, he had to fight. As long as he breathed, and even if the task seemed impossible, he would try to reconquer the lost paradise.

He prayed to the immortal soul of Tutankhamun, and drew renewed strength from his veneration of the resuscitated pharaoh. Giving up would be a form of betrayal. Whether or not he succeeded, he would not despair any more. It would be sheer cowardice to abandon the king he had been dreaming of ever since his discovery of Egypt. Many people wondered about the meaning of their lives, but Howard Carter had found his answer to the question: it was to serve Tutankhamun, to serve Egypt and to serve humankind by offering it the power of divine light residing eternally in that gold figure.

He wrote his answer with calm. The wooden head was waiting in tomb number 4 to be recorded, numbered and registered on the official list the archaeologist had neither taken with him nor concealed. He said that, in the corridor, he and Callender had picked up fragments of the painted décor which had become detached from a head. The latter would require very careful restoration.

On Pierre Lacau's desk lay four documents, side by side. The first was an article by Bradstreet, one of Carter's fiercest adversaries, published in the *New York Times*. The journalist boasted about his contribution to the downfall of a conceited archaeologist, hostile to the freedom of the press. Whoever opposed it would meet the same fate.

The second was the official cancellation of the concession

Christian Jacq

granted to Lady Carnarvon and Howard Carter. It was a legal
document the court of Cairo could not question.

The third was Howard Carter's cable.

The fourth was the new concession written by Morcos Bay
Hanna. The Minister of Civil Engineering had not consulted
Pierre Lacau, and meant to control archaeological work in
Egypt in a dictatorial way without bothering about the advice
of the Director of the Antiquities Service.

Lacau had been a puppet in the hands of a politician. By
obtaining Carter's head, he had put his whole life at stake.

As soon as the steamer *Berengaria* reached New York on 21 April 1924, Howard Carter understood that the world had changed. Celebrated and adulated like a star, he was not able to enjoy a day of rest. Lectures, parties, dinners and interviews followed one another at a frantic pace. All America wanted to see and hear one of the heroes of modern times, the self-made man who had unravelled the greatest mystery of Egyptology.

In the reception room of the Waldorf Astoria, Carter received his first honorary title: honorary member of the Metropolitan Museum. The presentation was greeted by a thunder of applause. Some people thought that he could only be American. The rumour spread quickly, despite denials. A passionate and fascinating lecturer, Carter used Burton's magnificent photographs to maximum advantage. Without striving for dramatic effects, he bewitched the audience. The warmth of his voice, the quality of his information and the marvels he showed took his listeners to Egypt and to the Valley of the Kings, right into Tutankhamun's tomb. He knew how to convey his experience in the field and how to share the most exciting moments of the epic. Like an athlete, he gave his full energy to the task and was exhausted by the end of his lectures. New York, Philadelphia, New Haven, Baltimore, Worcester, Boston, Hartford, Pittsburgh, Chicago, Cincinnati, Detroit, Cleveland, Columbus, Buffalo, Toronto, Montreal, Ottawa – now an honorary doctor from Yale

University, he travelled the length and breadth of the New World.

But he missed the silence of the valley, the solitude of his house and the pleasant hours of meditation in front of the western summit! Now he was only leafing through the gossip pages of a sham life, deprived of everyday contact with his land and of the meeting he had so eagerly awaited with Tutankhamun. His only hope was that his American reputation might change the Egyptian authorities' attitude. His Carnegie Hall performance in front of over 3,000 people on 23 April marked the climax of his tour. Invited to the White House, he spoke about Tutankhamun to a small privileged circle in the presence of the President of the United States, Calvin Coolidge. To the lecturer's surprise, the latter knew his work very well. Carter began to dream that the most powerful man in the world would intervene in his favour.

He became disillusioned when he received the final text of the concession written by the Ministry of Civil Engineering. Carter was presented as a danger to science. By leaving the tomb, he had behaved in an iniquitous way which justified the Government's attitude. He was, however, surprised by the body of the text, which mentioned his possible return as Director of Excavations, under the strict control of the Antiquities Service. The contents, however, made it impossible. Once again, Morcos Bay Hanna behaved like a clever cheat, so that responsibility for failure fell on Carter only.

The Ministry formulated its demands drily: all artefacts would be owned by the State. Carter would not be able to hire any collaborators without the permission of the Government, which compelled the archaeologist to recruit five Egyptian trainees. Only the Government would issue visitor permits. Carter and Lady Carnarvon were to write scientific reports which would be examined by the Antiquities Service. Lastly, the Minister was expecting two letters of apology: one from Lady Carnarvon and the other from Carter, who would agree never to insult the Egyptian government again and to yield to its decisions.

'Well, Mr Lacau, how are things going?'

'Nowhere, sir.'

Morcos Bay Hanna hit the table with his fist. 'What does that mean?'

'Nobody wants to or can replace Howard Carter.'

'That is unbelievable!'

'It is none the less the truth.'

'What do you suggest?'

'We should call Carter back. He is the only one who is able to remove the coffin without breaking anything.'

'Have you looked at his notes?'

'I have read and reread them. They prove his universally acknowledged competence. He knows the traps of the tomb and moves through difficulties with a sound instinct.'

The minister considered Lacau with astonishment. 'Aren't you praising a man you hate?'

'Scientific objectivity compels me to do so. This is why I sent him your demands, in the hope that he might yield to them.'

'There is no chance of that!'

'We left out something essential: Carter loves Egypt more than himself. Tutankhamun's tomb is his reason for living.'

Carter was a brilliant lecturer, but after his performances he often withdrew into himself, taking refuge in his hotel room. The news from Cairo worried him. On 30 April, the Government had ordered that a large budget, some $20,000, be devoted to the completion of excavations on condition that Carter and his team were kept away. Yet no archaeologist approached the minister to obtain a position which was the answer to an Egyptologist's dreams.

The cause seemed definitely to be lost. Faithful to what he had promised to himself, Carter continued the struggle on another front: he wrote a detailed account of what had happened, with the intention of publishing it and denouncing the machiavellianism of Lacau and the Egyptian government. The document would demonstrate that he had been the victim of unscrupulous people who only cared for their own careers.

On the *Mauretania*, the liner which took him back to England in the summer of 1924, however, he gave up the idea of publishing his pamphlet. The scathing attack would only aggravate his enemies. He increasingly missed Egypt. The pain worsened with time. He was so exhausted that he did not enjoy the trip at all.

His return did not arouse any reaction in the British press. The American enthusiasm was followed by the indifference of London. Carter left very quickly for Highclere, where Lady Evelyn was the first to welcome him.

'I read the American newspapers. You had a great success there.'

'Superficial success would be more accurate.'

'Don't underestimate yourself, Howard. You've become a star.'

'It is useless if I cannot work in Egypt any more.'

'Your true love . . .'

Carter did not answer. He followed the young woman, who took him to the library where her mother was reading Shakespeare's poems. Lady Carnarvon seemed nervous.

'Egypt is becoming increasingly more intransigent. I've often been thinking about my husband and you. How can we respond to such an iniquitous government?'

'We must give in.'

'Give in? You?'

'I cannot act without you. Your agreement is necessary.'

Lady Carnarvon looked petrified.

'Would my father have agreed to that?' said Lady Evelyn indignantly.

'Would he not have sacrificed material interests to pursue his quest to the end?'

'Be specific,' demanded Lady Carnarvon.

'You will have to give up all the artefacts. None of them will leave Egypt.'

'We were guaranteed some compensation . . . My fortune is not inexhaustible. Please go on.'

'You and I must announce that we won't initiate any legal proceedings against the Government.'

'In other words, we give ourselves up, bound hand and foot.'

'That is true.'

'What will it give us?'

'The opportunity to resume work and remove the sarcophagus.'

'I need to think it over.'

The end of the summer was rainy and sad. In the course of their long walks on the estate, Carter and Lady Evelyn spoke very little. Initially their conversations turned to Lord Carnarvon, whose presence haunted every grove. Carter did not defend himself. Even though the woman he loved did not approve of his stand, he did not attempt to convince her. Had she not known from the first moment that he could not survive without Egypt?

On 13 September, Lady Carnarvon sent a letter to His Excellency Morcos Bay Hanna. She agreed with the terms of the new concession but reminded him that her late husband had been financing unfruitful excavations for over ten years in the hope that his efforts would be rewarded like those of any archaeologist. Did not scientific institutions themselves receive some valuable artefacts to thank them for their investment? Lady Carnarvon begged the Minister to think of a fair solution after close examination of the whole contents of Tutankhamun's tomb.

She told Carter what she had done in front of the castle's main fireplace after dinner. The great cedars of Lebanon bent under a strong wind. On Carnarvon's grave, a dead bird offered its corpse to the icy rain.

90

Lady Carnarvon's polite and moderate letter embarrassed Morcos Bay Hanna. On bad terms with Lacau, and hated by most of his colleagues because of his authoritarianism, the Minister of Civil Engineering was, now in his turn, the victim of a press campaign which began to displease the Prime Minister. Public opinion did not like the fact that Carter's successor had not yet been appointed. Lacau's underground manoeuvres had proved too efficient: no professional dared take the risk of bowing to the yoke of the Ministry and then damaging the infinitely precious sarcophagus. Neither the security nor the independence of a scientific team could be guaranteed.

Morcos Bay Hanna did not expect the aristocrat to react nor Carter to submit. He had hoped that the archaeologist would continue to attack him and discredit himself. Now he was in danger of losing face.

Carter was bored in London.

According to Lady Carnarvon, the Ministry's answer would not be long. She was wrong: there was no official letter allowing him to go back to the valley for two months. Each morning, Carter questioned the postman, who was apologetic that he was not bringing what he was waiting for so impatiently.

Politicians turned a deaf ear, despite several unofficial

interventions and protests in America, Europe and even Egypt. Carter continued to pay the price of his mistakes. The time had now come to forgive. The whole world wanted to know Tutankhamun's ultimate mystery. Only the British archae-ologist possessed the necessary skills to talk with the Pharaoh.

Morcos Bay Hanna remained silent.

The telephone rang at 7 p.m., startling Carter out of sleep. He recognized Lady Evelyn's voice.

'Have you read the newspaper?'

'Not yet.'

'Hurry up.'

'Is it so important?'

She had already hung up.

Carter dressed hastily and bought all the morning papers. Prime Minister Zaghlul had just resigned, taking the members of his cabinet with him. The fierce nationalist had had no choice. After the murder of Sir Lee Stack, the Governor of the Sudan, in a street in Cairo, Great Britain had not bothered to compromise. The Army had taken the country over and proclaimed martial law. Zaghlul could not accept the invasion, and the equally anglophobe Morcos Bay Hanna had followed him.

Carter kissed the article mentioning the name of the new Prime Minister: Ahmed Pasha Ziuar, one of his oldest Egyptian friends!

Winter seemed so mild in Cairo! In Egypt, on 15 December, Carter revived. Even the noisy capital appeared like an oasis of peace.

The country had changed. The people who had been so hostile to the British were now asking them to defend them against terrorists who killed innocent victims and spread fear in the large cities. Once praised to the skies, the WAFD party and the nationalists were now held up to public recrimination.

On his way to the Antiquities Service headquarters, Carter

came across Ahmed Pasha Ziuar. The two men embraced each other.

'How long have you been in Cairo, Howard?'

'Since this morning! You are the first person I've met, Minister.'

'This is Tutankhamun's blessing. Fortune is now favouring you. Zaghlul and his henchmen subjected you to the worst injustices. I am aware of that. Rely on me to help you. You will soon be back in *your* tomb.'

Carter thought he was dreaming. 'Ahmed . . . if only you knew . . .'

'Don't say anything, the greatest happiness is unspoken.'

Lord Allenby considered that the Tutankhamun case was turning out well. Of course the nationalists had not been annihilated, but they were no longer rash enough to discredit Carter. The prestige of Great Britain required that he resume excavations. In addition the economy of the Luxor area would benefit from the boosting of tourism in the Valley of the Kings. As soon as the archaeologist started work again, tourists would stream in.

Allenby got in touch with the new Egyptian prime minister, praised Carter's qualities and did not hesitate to criticize Lacau, whose bad faith was obvious. Ahmed Pasha Ziuar was suspicious. Despite being a friend of Great Britain, he was first of all an Egyptian. He had to restore a balance without tipping too much on either side. He asked his friend Howard Carter to write him a letter specifying his intentions.

Surprised and disappointed, the archaeologist did so. An awful thought crossed his mind: was the Prime Minister beginning to betray him? Now that he had reached a major position, why should he risk losing it because of a pharaoh who had been dead for centuries?

Ahmed Pasha Ziuar agreed to meet Carter at the Mohammed Ali Club, in a quiet atmosphere, away from inquisitive eavesdroppers.

'My letter confirms that my only interest is to restart work as soon as possible in Tutankhamun's tomb. The rest is forgotten.'

'Don't worry. Your case is shaping up well. A tiny problem remains: it would be good to give up your rights to the treasure for good. If Lady Carnarvon puts that in an official document, we may be able to progress more quickly. People should not have the impression that they were being deprived.'

'Doesn't Egyptian law grant the excavator a fair reward?'

'Of course, of course . . . But in the present circumstances, we should not stick to the letter of the law.'

'Lord Carnarvon was extremely generous.'

'Nobody denies it. But your fiercest enemy will not relent.'

'Pierre Lacau?'

'Yes. He is a strange character. He wants you back, but on his terms. Beware of him.'

The Prime Minister stood up.

'I must go . . . an important meeting. Before that, I have interesting news for you: nobody has touched your tomb. If you agree to give a little help to Lacau at the Museum, the administration will be grateful to you.'

Lacau and Carter did not shake hands: Lacau did not feel like it, and Carter did not because it was not the English custom.

'I must acknowledge that your help would be precious, my dear Carter.'

'In what field?'

'To unpack the contents of a few boxes with me.'

'Is it too difficult a task for members of the service?'

'Well . . . we had an accident.'

Carter became angry. 'What do you mean?'

Lacau hesitated. He swallowed his saliva and confessed: 'The linen veil covering the sarcophagus has been destroyed.'

'How could you let such a thing happen?'

'I am sorry. I have taken measures to make sure such an accident cannot happen again.'

'Measures! Show me the boxes.'

Furious, Carter noted that the officials of the service had mixed artefacts and that they had not succeeded in reassembling the ritual golden wooden carts correctly.

'Illiterate people would have worked better,' he grumbled.

'You promised that you would restrain your criticisms,' Lacau reminded him.

Carter held back. In the past, he would have written a report several pages long against Lacau, the service and the Government. Anyway his time was better spent in repairing mistakes and negligence.

On 13 January, his patience was rewarded. Starchy, Lacau presented him with a sealed envelope. Carter slipped it in the right pocket of his jacket and left the Museum as if he did not care about the Director's gesture. He compelled himself not to run, hid behind Mariette's statue and opened it.

It was for him a fabulous document: a permit to carry on excavations in Tutankhamun's tomb.

91

On 25 January 1925, Pierre Lacau handed the keys of Tutankhamun's tomb to Howard Carter. The two men gave each other a challenging look under the sun of the Valley of the Kings. Then Carter opened the padlock and removed the grille. The Director followed him as he walked down the corridor, across the antechamber and into the funeral chamber where, his eyes open, the Pharaoh slept in the golden silence.

Carter moved noiselessly and slowly recovered possession of his domain, which had remained unchanged. The magic of the place again took hold of his mind. He contemplated the frescoes of the funeral and bent over the pacified face, from which all trace of death had disappeared.

'This is your triumph, Carter. As for me I have also won. Now treasure hunters won't be allowed into Egypt any more. They won't plunder the riches of the ancients. History will only remember you, Carter. But I instituted a restrictive regulation of which I am proud.'

'I don't understand you.'

'I'm glad that you are here. This is really your place.'

'You were not a lot of help.'

Lacau turned away. 'Stay with Tutankhamun, he has been waiting for you.'

The team set to work again with unaltered passion. Faithful among the faithful, Callender's heavy body again moved enthusiastically. Burton, the photographer, and Lucas, the chemist, resumed their tasks. They all regretted the absence of Mace, whose poor health did not augur well. Nobody mentioned the all too notorious curse.

Before Carter started on the sarcophagus, he made an inventory. He spent most of his time in the laboratory, where he meticulously prepared the remaining work and set up his catalogue. There were no more mistakes. When the Government requested it, Carter opened the tomb and allowed visitors in. Although always on the watch, the press did not criticize him. The archaeological team pursued its task in a peaceful atmosphere. Rooted in eternity, the calm of the valley slowed gestures and moderated thoughts. Although still one of the great stars of the day, Tutankhamun was no longer a matter for scandal. Journalists acknowledged that hurry would be disastrous.

Lady Evelyn managed a meeting with Carter again in the summer of 1925. They walked along the Thames, through the streets of Cambridge and in Hyde Park. Like two adolescents, they spoke of the happiness they would never experience. She was twenty-five, and he was fifty-two.

'I don't care about your age. Doesn't the company of Tutankhamun turn you into a young man for ever?'

'I have received too many blows and I was too often betrayed. Soon I shall be an old man.'

'I shall age too!'

'I should not take you on such a dangerous path.'

'You are selfish, Mr Carter!'

'You're right. But only because I could not bear to see you sad in my company.'

'I am not a dream, Howard, but a real live woman.'

'The only real home for me has to be Tutankhamun's tomb.'

'How can I fight a pharaoh?'

'It is a power and a secret I don't know and can't explain. But this coming autumn, we will be face to face, and I still need your love, Eve. My real life begins then.'

*

Ahmed Girigar shifted the heavy wooden fence which shut off the entrance of the laboratory. Proudly he showed Carter that there had been no theft. Despite the unbearable heat of the summer, trustworthy men had mounted guard.

As soon as the archaeologist arrived, workmen cleared the entry to the tomb. They removed the mass of rubble which had been left in front of the staircase to prevent any attempt at plundering. Within two days, Tutankhamun's dwelling was accessible again after the oak partition wall barring the entrance to the corridor had been removed and the door of the antechamber opened.

Each time he entered the sloping corridor, Carter experienced such an intense emotion that he could barely continue. Invisible forces dwelt in the sanctuary. The shadows of Egyptian divinities and of the transfigured king retained all their power over him.

Carter remained alone in the presence of Tutankhamun for a long time. He prayed to his invisible soul to grant him the necessary time to give back to the world the wisdom of the immortal monarch.

When he walked out of the sepulchre, Callender was afraid.

'You seem upset . . . Do you want a pick-me-up?'

'Your friendship will be enough.'

'Are you satisfied with the condition of the tomb?'

'The insecticides worked. There has been no damage and I did not notice any trace of parasites, except a few silverfish.'

'Have you come to a decision?'

'Please connect the electricity to the central generator. Tomorrow, 10 October, we will open the golden coffin at 6.30 a.m.'

Powerful projectors illuminated the sarcophagus. Everybody asked the same question: did it contain one or several coffins? Carter was more inclined to favour several, but he was put out by one detail: the size of the coffin, covered with a golden leaf. It was colossal, some 7 feet.

443

He decided to use the original silver handles. They looked sturdy enough to support the weight of the lid, which had been fixed to the coffin by ten tongues of solid silver which fitted into holes. The first difficulty consisted in extracting the large silver pins with gold heads which fastened it. The delicate operation succeeded, except in one place: the head, where he had to saw the pin.

Callender set up a winch, composed of two blocks of three pulleys with automatic brakes. When the belts were in place, Carter gave the order to lift the lid infinitely slowly. Failure was not allowed.

In an atmosphere of profound reverence, the lid rose.

A second coffin appeared, wrapped in a linen shroud. On top of it lay garlands of olive and willow leaves, blue lotus petals and cornflowers. As a reminder that the king had been judged as fair by the court of the other world, a floral wreath adorned his brow.

Once the linen veil was removed, Carter contemplated a masterpiece of incredible beauty.

The second coffin was perfection itself. It represented the king as Osiris, covered with a gold leaf inlaid with molten glass the colour of lapis lazuli, turquoise and jasper. Soft and calm, the face looked both young and ageless.

Tutankhamun's wife herself must have left the flowers on the shroud as an ultimate testimony of her love. The splendour of the gold combined with the delicacy of the dried plants, whose colour had not altogether faded. Three thousand years had vanished.

Lucas examined the clues closely. 'Taking into account the flowering season of cornflowers and the stage of maturity of the mandrake and nightshade, it is my conclusion that Tutankhamun was buried between mid-March and the end of April, taking into account the seventy ritual days of mummification.'

The scientist's analysis interrupted their contemplation.

'This is worrying,' remarked Callender. 'There are traces of dampness here and there. Some inlays are in danger of coming off. The royal mummy may have been badly preserved.'

Carter was seized by anxiety. He noticed that the second coffin fitted so perfectly into the first one that he could not even insert his little finger between the two. How could he separate them without breaking them?

When Burton had completed his photographic work, Carter used the only possible method: the coffins had first to be removed from the sarcophagus. This turned out to be much more difficult than he had expected.

'It's a huge weight,' said Callender, covered with sweat.

'The coffins are heavy.'

'Not that heavy . . . The second one must contain a mass of jewels.'

The outer coffin was put back into the sarcophagus, while the second one remained suspended, supported by ten copper threads of great solidity. Burton photographed the different stages of the operation. When the gold Osiris rested on a wooden slab, Carter lifted the lid.

A third coffin appeared, wrapped in a red linen shroud. On the chest was a bunch of flowers. Only the face was uncovered.

'Impossible . . . this is impossible. It is made of solid gold!'

92

An incredible golden block of some 6 feet met the astonished eyes of Carter and his team. No similar work had ever been found in Egypt. For the first time an archaeologist had brought to light a masterpiece of the art and spirituality of the ancients, the golden sarcophagus sheltering the resurrection body of the Pharaoh. The wings of the goddesses Isis and Nephtys intertwined to protect him. The vulture Nekhbet, keeper of his sacred title, and the cobra Wadjet, source of his inner dynamism, also watched over the monarch.

Carter thought of the unimaginable treasures the valley must have held before pillagers came. Tutankhamun was the sole survivor and witness to a luminous time when the most fabulous riches of this world were offered to the other world, to open its gates and triumph over death.

The gold face was covered with a blackish layer. Lucas identified unguents. 'This is the cause of the dampness.'

As Carter lightly touched the wreath of flowers and blue faience, it disintegrated under his fingers. Alarmed, he stepped back.

'We must not touch anything! The works are more fragile than they seem.'

Callender reminded him, 'But we'll have to reach the mummy . . .'

'Let me think.'

*

The Tutankhamun Affair

Carter shut himself up in the house. Now he was afraid. Would he be going too far? Would he uncover a mystery which should be left alone? On the brink of meeting Tutankhamun, could he content himself with venerating the greatest marvel ever shaped by human hands?

He realized the vanity of his position. Neither his team nor the Government would allow him to stop halfway. Lord Carnarvon was no longer here to give him advice. Lady Evelyn had chosen to stay at Highclere. Alone with the Pharaoh he had been in search of for so many years, Carter felt both miserable and unworthy. What right did he have to disturb his rest? In his eyes, curiosity became a serious vice. No science could justify a breach of eternity.

The experience overwhelmed him. If he left, who would be in charge of excavations? Egypt and Britain would not bear further delay. The whole world was impatient. Defeated, Carter knew that he no longer had a choice.

After long discussions with his colleagues, he took a series of measures to remove the second sarcophagus from the third one. His priority was to save the inlays. Once he had dusted off the surface and washed it with warm water mixed with ammonia, a substance whose name derived from the Egyptian god Amon, Carter covered it with a layer of warm wax he applied with a brush. As the wax cooled, it would fix the inlays.

Another difficulty seemed almost insurmountable: solidified unguents glued the two coffins together. The black substance was partly soft, partly thick. Once heated, it emitted a pervasive resin fragrance. They managed to saw through eight golden pins which prevented the coffins from being detached from each other. But that was not enough. The mask and the mummy remained stuck. Only strong heat would work, several hours at 117°F. A higher temperature might destroy the gold-covered wood. Carter thought of protecting it with slabs of zinc and wet blankets. Placed under the coffins laid on trestles, paraffin lamps emitted a heat of some 90°F.

Christian Jacq

Three hours passed.

'They are moving!' shouted Callender.

Carter had not stopped dampening the blanket protecting the gold mask.

'We have succeeded!' exclaimed Burton, enthusiastically.

'Stop!' ordered Carter.

He noticed with horror that fragments of faience were becoming detached from the back of the head. After a long pause and the chemist's intervention, the second còffin rose out of its gangue. In the early morning of 28 October, the gold mask was cleared: 'Alive is thy face,' claimed a text engraved in the precious metal. 'Your right eye is the boat of the day and your left eye the boat of the night.' Along the sarcophagus, another inscription revealed that the fair Tutankhamun had become a light in the sky and a master of life for ever.

The gold mask was the purest face ever engraved in any material. Pharaoh was ageless. Carved out of time by the hand of a sculptor of genius, Tutankhamun had become a god with a lapis lazuli beard. The smile from the world beyond expressed total detachment. Joy transfigured the pacified features.

Callender completed his sums.

'This is incredible . . . the last sarcophagus alone must consist of over two thousand, two hundreds pounds of solid gold!'

'Even more incredible,' said Burton: 'the gilded wooden bed which supported the three coffins has not come apart! As regards the resistance of materials, we have found our masters.'

Carter called for silence. In a solemn voice, he declared: 'I dedicate the gold in the night of the tomb to the memory of my friend Lord Carnarvon, who died at the time of his triumph.'

The only pharaoh in the valley who had been buried in a gold coffin . . . Carter could not yet believe it. When a life thus swings into miracle, it loses its usual landmarks. Archaeologist,

448

Egyptologist, excavator, the words had no more meaning. He had been fated to serve a king who had died 3,000 years before and revived in the light of the gold. The world would never be the same. How many dozens of years would be necessary to publish, study and understand the treasure of Tutankhamun? Through the texts and objects accompanying him into eternity, the Pharaoh was transmitting the wisdom of ancient Egypt and the key to its mysteries. Carter had the privilege of experiencing them on the spot, of being united with the ineffable moment of discovery. Other people would pursue his work.

'Mr Lacau has arrived,' announced Ahmed Girigar.

Wearing a jacket and flannel trousers with faultless creases, Carter carefully arranged his white pocket handkerchief. As elegant as usual, the Director of the Antiquities Service held out a hand which the Englishman agreed to shake.

'This is wonderful, Howard. I have just left the tomb . . . It is fantastic! I must acknowledge that you are the greatest.'

'Tutankhamun, the forgotten kinglet, is the greatest pharaoh. Tomorrow, my name will be forgotten, but his will remain popular over centuries.'

'Maybe . . . But what about the mummy?'

Carter offered Lacau bread he had baked himself. The Frenchman refused it.

'What are your intentions?'

'The Museum of Cairo seems—'

'No, it would be a mistake. I have never begged you before. Today I beg you to let Tutankhamun rest in his sarcophagus. When we have examined the mummy, give instruction that it should come back here to the tomb and never leave it again.'

'Why?'

'The sanctuary is a centre of living energy.'

'Are you turning into a mystic, Howard?'

'No more than you are. You know the sacred texts better than I do. Invisible forces emanate from the solar resurrection body. They spiritualize the world and enlarge people's hearts.

449

Christian Jacq

Egypt chose this place to hide its most essential treasures. Let's not be destructive, let's respect its will.'

Carter looked his former enemy straight into his eyes. 'I beg you.'

93

Lacau and the Government had given their agreement. Tutankhamun would not leave his eternal dwelling, even if pieces of the treasure were exhibited in the Museum of Cairo. Carter was smoking a last cigarette before going to sleep when he heard the noise of hasty steps on the path.

Ahmed Girigar knocked at his door. 'Hurry! An attack!'

Carter dressed hastily and ran with the *reis* to where a large man with a narrow forehead and a nose streaked with scarlet veins lay, bound by his men. He was struggling and calling for the person who was responsible.

'I think you want me,' said Carter.

The large man became calm. 'Have you exhumed Tutankhamun's mummy?'

'In a way.'

'Then listen to the voice of God and the angels! It should be destroyed forthwith! Otherwise it will spread plague on the planet! I tried to go into the tomb and tear it to pieces, but these infidels prevented me from doing so. Release me!'

'I'm afraid this is impossible. I am on the infidels' side.'

The news stupefied the world: struck by the curse of Tutankhamun, Howard Carter had just died. He was rather astonished to hear about it and he had to organize a press conference to deny it. More sceptical than his colleagues, a journalist tugged at his moustache to make sure that he was real.

At the end of the meeting, a frightening figure wearing a black suit and a long violet coat on which shone silver brooches approached Carter. 'May I make you a proposition?'

'I'm all ears.'

'I am the representative of a religious organization numbering several thousands of people in Europe and in the United States. We really appreciated your work.'

'I'm flattered.'

'As it is now completed, we must now enter the picture.'

'How?'

'The mummy won't be of any use to you. So we are offering to buy it. Whatever price you ask, we will pay.'

'Tutankhamun has been priceless for a long time. Who could assess the value of the gold of the gods? I'm sorry, my friend: a dozen other sects have already offered large amounts of money which I refused.'

'I shall address the Government.'

'Do that. But you should now that it has also refused attractive offers from several foreign powers. Tutankhamun belongs only to eternity.'

At the beginning of 1926, 13,000 visitors came to the valley to admire the vault and the Pharaoh. Cameras filmed constantly, rotary presses worked at full speed and the new wireless cables were hot with traffic. Tutankhamun outshone all other celebrities on the front pages of the magazines.

Carter, however, did not appear. He had taken refuge in the laboratory to restore the inner coffins and the gold mask, which would soon be carried away to the Museum of Cairo. A letter from Lady Carnarvon told him that Lord Carnarvon's collection had just been sold to the Metropolitan Museum of New York, to the great displeasure of the British Museum which felt taken in. They accused Carter of having betrayed his homeland. His homeland; it was here, in the heart of the valley which so many curious onlookers crossed at a run, both enchanted and disorientated. It was a land of sand, stones and tombs, where the wind of the imperishable blew.

In November 1927, five years after the discovery of the staircase, Carter started to empty the annex. He only met Lady Evelyn at official parties, where, without cold-shouldering him, she only offered smiles. Heart-broken, he recognized that she was right. Why would a beautiful young woman with a title commit herself to an old greybeard like him, who looked increasingly more like a block of stone from the valley?

'Over four thousand objects are crammed in an area eight feet wide,' he remarked with concern. 'In addition, everything may crumble at the slightest breath. We should re-establish a balance, albeit precarious, before we remove the chests and boxes.'

Callender was smiling. 'Marvellous . . . we have enough work for two years!'

'What do you think the small room represents?' asked Burton.

'The last stage of resurrection,' thought Carter.

'Look: its door faces the east, where the morning light breaks.'

'It contains so many oddly assorted artefacts!'

'Our eyes do not know how to see. Read the text on top of the door. It tells us that the king spends his life shaping the symbols of the gods, so that they give him incense, offerings and libations every day. Through his constantly repeated actions in the invisible world, Tutankhamun triumphs over the forces of destruction. The annex provides proof that he continues to live here as well as in the world beyond. Look at these baskets full of dried fruit, grapes, nuts and mandrakes, and these jugs of wine. The soul needs food and dress: ritual robes, corselets and sandals.'

'Also sport,' added Callender. 'There are bows, arrows and boomerangs!'

'Everything expresses its power and vitality.'

Carter bent over a chess set. The king had probably won the game against an invisible opponent. He had to establish that he was a fair player, as only such could be Reborn. It was not unlike a little bird coming out of its nest, a sculpture of which Callender had picked up and was handling with tenderness.

In the south-east corner of the small room was a throne which represented the union of the King and the Queen in the other world and their love made immortal by rituals. The inscription mentioned both the names of Aton and that of Amon, whom scholars had wrongly described as enemies. Thus Carter gained the certainty that, refusing dogmatism, the Egyptian faith had not generated religious wars. It had only been guided by the love of eternity.

On 11 November 1927, at 9.45, Dr Douglas Derry, a professor of anatomy at the University of Cairo, performed the first cut in the bandages of Tutankhamun's mummy, under the careful supervision of Carter, dressed in his strictest three-piece suit, embellished with a ceremonial bow tie. He had asked great respect and conversations were conducted in low voices. Lacau, Burton, Lucas and Egyptian civil servants, dressed in the Western fashion, their heads covered with cone-shaped hats, attended the ceremony in the corridor of the tomb of Seti II.

Carter himself unwrapped the thirteen layers of bandages, with inscriptions, referring to the sail of the boat on which the spirit of the resuscitated Pharaoh sailed in the other world. The oxidation of the resins and an excessive use of unguents, holy oils and natron had burnt the cloth and attacked the bones of the mummy, which looked charred. As Carter moved it, he noticed that it was enclosed in a magic armour composed of 143 jewels divided into 101 pieces. Sometimes he had to detach the hardened silver layer which adhered to the members. A breastplate, a diadem, a gold dagger, the lower part of his headdress and armbands turned the corpse into a body of gold, precious stones and amulets. It was no longer a person, albeit a monarch, but a completed Osiris, guarantor for the survival of those initiated into his mysteries. A cushion under his neck intrigued the onlookers. There was no doubt that it was made of iron, a rare material in Egypt. The blade of the dagger with the rock crystal pommel and the golden sheath were made of the same metal. Carter reminded them that to the eyes of priests, iron was of celestial origin and enabled the king to cross the space separating him from paradise.

The human body which had fulfilled the Pharaoh's life needs was no more than a miserable corpse. Aged some twenty years, he measured about 5 feet 6. Parts of the corpse were dislocating. Gold cases protected his penis, fingers and toes.

When the dignitaries left, Carter stayed alone with Tutankhamun. He watched over him with the fervour of friendship and the veneration of a humble servant.

94

With a marten hair brush, Carter had removed the rotten bandages and cleared the peaceful face of a young man. It had a beautiful shape and a noble expression. Tutankhamun had been a king with a superb appearance. On his head, instead of hair, was a small skullcap of very thin linen, embellished with woven strips ornate with faience and gold beads. Carter also discerned the outline of four cobras, a symbol of life sliding through the worlds.

New Empire Egyptians knew how to mummify to perfection. As they inundated the corpse with unguents to the point of burning it, they acted in a determined, ritual and conscious way. The miserable corpse, so frail compared with the magnificence of the gold mask and the sarcophagus, had become the raw material of alchemy: a contemptible, charred body supported the transmutation into divine metal. On his breast, two gold straps proved that Tutankhamun was no longer considered a king, but a god. The mummification of the face, so different from that of other monarchs, referred to its threefold nature as a divinity, a priest in charge of the celebration of rites and a pharaoh illuminating the earth.

Tutankhamun, the forgotten kinglet, had escaped wars, murders and pillagers and taken refuge in the mind of a modern Westerner, who was now to ensure his ultimate protection.

*

In 1930, the nationalists came back to power, after the death of Carter had once more been proclaimed. His old enemy Zaghlul had died in 1927, and the WAFD party did not really bother about the archaeologist, who was now completing his prodigious mission in the Valley of the Kings. Of course, the new government, which claimed to represent the people, immediately passed a law forbidding anything discovered in the course of excavations to leave Egypt. But Lady Carnarvon had known for a long time that she would not get the smallest artefact from Tutankhamun's treasures. However, in autumn, the authorities gave Lord Carnarvon's widow £36,000 as compensation for all the campaigns financed by her husband.

When Arthur C. Mace, Deputy Curator of the Metropolitan, died of chronic pleurisy, the press made a thing of the Tutankhamun curse again. Twenty victims had already been identified, among whom were the Curator of the Louvre and several of Lord Carnarvon's relatives.

The agitation did not really disturb Carter, who was supervising the packing of the large gold shrines to send them to the Museum of Cairo, where they would be reassembled. The fever was subsiding. Famous all over the world, Tutankhamun had entered the collective memory of humankind. Now peaceful, the valley welcomed streams of tourists in the winter and slumbered during the hot season.

At the end of February 1932, duly restored, the last objects left the laboratory for the capital. In tears, Callender closed the tomb of Seti II. The next day it would be open to tourists again.

'It's over, Howard. Over . . .'

Carter patted his shoulder. 'You have to accept that.'

'Can't you discover another tomb?'

'Alas! Tutankhamun's vault was the last one. The great voice of the Valley of the Kings has now definitely faded.'

'What do you intend to do, Howard?'

'I don't know. Obtain an official position, open a new site . . .'

'They wouldn't dare refuse that to you. I'm going back to my village. I am obsessed by the gold face. I dream of it each night.'

'It is the most beautiful vision.'

The two men bade each other farewell. Carter had already said goodbye to the other members of his team. He walked down into the tomb, where only the limestone tank and the largest sarcophagus sheltering the mummy remained. This time, Lacau and the Government had kept their promise. Tutankhamun would rest for ever in his eternal dwelling.

The gold room taught the secret of eternity. 'Relive as a god', that was the aim of the invisible task performed in this modest grave, so cleverly concealed. The young king with the serene face embodied faith in immortality. The age of the corpse did not matter. He was 'a living symbol of mystery', as his name proclaimed. Tutankhamun had succeeded in mastering the mutations of light and incorporating them into the gold of his sarcophagus. His existence was definite proof that death could serve as a material for eternal life. Here in the four little rooms, the greatest civilization had enshrined its most essential message. How many generations of scholars would be necessary to decipher it?

Carter bowed before Tutankhamun, the ruler of eternity.

As he left the tomb, to which he had devoted most of his life, the day was fading. Deserted and silent, the valley was preparing for darkness. Carter embraced *reis* Ahmed Girigar who restrained his tears until the archaeologist had disappeared behind one of the stone hillocks overlooking the royal sepulchres.

Sitting on a rock eroded by winds, sun and storm rains, he contemplated the bare summit glowing in the sunset. Thanks to Tutankhamun this place of emptiness had been transformed into one of hope: everything would remain motionless and unchanging for, on this land of gods, nothing had ever begun with time nor would ever end with it.

An owl let out a cry sharp enough to turn the soul to ice.

But Carter experienced it as a serene call. No, the valley would not die. It would now speak in the voice of a young, transfigured king.

95

The Egyptian Minister and the new Director of the Antiquities Service raised their cups of coffee together, drank elegantly and put them down slowly on the table. Who would speak first? The Director did.

'The case of Howard Carter is not easy to deal with—'

'That is not my opinion,' retorted the Minister, irritated.

'Ah? Are you taking his fame into account?'

'Not at all.'

'Ah . . . you mean that . . .'

'I mean that Egypt won't give him any archaeological excavation work . . . Nor will you, I hope.'

The Director remained silent.

'Carter is a colonialist, with a backward and arrogant mind.'

'Aren't you afraid that international opinion . . .'

'It has other things to worry about. Carter has already been forgotten. Believe me, my dear friend: it would be a serious mistake to allow him to work on our soil again. His colleagues do not like him very much apparently.'

'Yes indeed, Minister. With the exception of the members of his team, Egyptologists consider him a dilettante and a lucky amateur. You cannot disregard the fact that he did not attend a school of any consequence.'

'So you see! The matter is closed. Never again will

Howard Carter dig in Egypt. He must content himself with whatever distinctions Great Britain grants him.'

The British Minister greeted the three Egyptologists who had been appointed to represent their profession, and sat at his desk.

'I am pleased to welcome you, gentlemen. Egyptology has become a first-class science.'

'That is not its function,' said a small stout man who spoke on behalf of his colleagues. 'It is a discipline and Howard Carter has damaged its reputation.'

'To what extent?'

'Even more than you imagine, Minister. Howard Carter is the shame of Egyptology. He is a self-made man, the son of a penniless animal painter, an insignificant country bumpkin who stole the glory from serious colleagues!'

The Minister looked embarrassed. 'Under such circumstances, it seems difficult to give him the official position he is asking for.'

'It would be an insult to Egyptology. All the authorities would strongly oppose it.'

'A decoration would placate him . . .'

The small, portly man stood up, followed by his two colleagues.

'That would be an insult to our country, Minister. What did Carter actually do? Nothing. He was just lucky. That is not enough to justify a distinction.'

'In my position I need to follow authoritative advice. Thank you, gentlemen.'

'That is strange,' thought the Minister. 'Howard Carter, the most famous archaeologist in the world, will not even receive an MBE, the lowest decoration, given to meritorious postmen and railway clerks. By avoiding archaeology's corridors of power, he committed the worst of crimes. He preferred Egypt to a career. It costs a lot to remain a mind nobody can buy.'

*

Tourists were crowding around the tomb of Tutankhamun. Nobody wanted to give up his vantage point. Gallantry was trampled underfoot. People braved heat and dust to contemplate the little tomb, now emptied of its treasures, except for the gold sarcophagus where the young king rested, and which aroused shouts of admiration, every day.

When the visitors became less numerous, a man of some sixty years, elegantly British in his dress, left his observatory and walked down a desert path to the world-famous tomb. When silence was restored in the valley, Howard Carter revived his epic. Sick and affected by a tiredness he could not get rid of any more, worn out by jealousy, meanness and treason, the archaeologist had only one friend, Pharaoh Tutankhamun, whose dwelling was wide open to so many talkative, inattentive or indelicate guests.

Since 1936, Europe had been shaken by a turmoil which, according to the most pessimistic, foreshadowed a new war. Carter remained unaffected by the possibility. Ever since the closure of the most exceptional site in the valley, he had left the world and now faced the prospect of his own death without fear. He was no longer interested in humankind. He hardly heard the greetings of wardens who bowed before him when he walked in the valley, like a shadow among shadows.

On a cold and rainy day, the burial of Howard Carter, who had died on 2 March 1939, went unnoticed. Britain likes unobtrusive deaths, which don't upset public order or arouse displays of vulgar taste.

He had died at the age of sixty-six, isolated and forgotten. Lady Evelyn Herbert Beauchamp, the only dignitary at the funeral, held back her tears. Howard would not have appreciated an outburst. Still as beautiful as ever, Eve watched the poor coffin sinking into the earth and thought of Tutankhamun's gold.

462

The soul of Howard Carter would not remain imprisoned in the icy cemetery. It had already flown back to its original homeland, the Valley of the Kings, to merge with the light.

Glossary

Baksheesh: tip.
Fellah: peasant.
Gaffir: man who is in charge of keeping peace in the village and protecting it against thieves.
Galabieh: traditional male garment in Egypt.
Khedive: title of the ruler of Egypt at one time.
Mucharabieh: small balcony closed by a grid.
Ostraca: pieces of limestone used as draughts by beginner scribes.
Reis: boss, chief, foreman.
Sheikh: title of reverence.